PHANTOM COVE

A Port Stirling Mystery BOOK 5

KAY JENNINGS

Phantom Cove/Kay Jennings—1st ed.

ISBN (Hardcover edition): 979-8-9855544-4-1
ISBN (Paperback edition): 979-8-9855544-3-4
ISBN (E-book edition): 979-8-9855544-2-7

Publisher's Note: Phantom Cove is a work of fiction. As of this publication date, the events and circumstances that occur within are a product of the author's imagination. While certain locales may draw on real life, they are used fictitiously to add authenticity to the story. The cast of characters are fictitious and are not based on real people, businesses, or organizations.

Cover design and Port Stirling Map: Claire Brown
Interior design: Steve Kuhn/Kuhn Design Group

Printed and bound in the USA
First printing 2022
Published by Paris Communications
Portland, Oregon, USA

www.kayjenningsauthor.com

OTHER BOOKS BY KAY JENNINGS:

Shallow Waters

Midnight Beach

Code: Tsunami

Dark Sand

While Dr. Nathalie Kumar has a role in this story, she is a fictional character. However, I have my own Dr. Nathalie who provided excellent care and advice with a health issue I suffered while writing this book. It's dedicated to her.

PHANTOM COVE

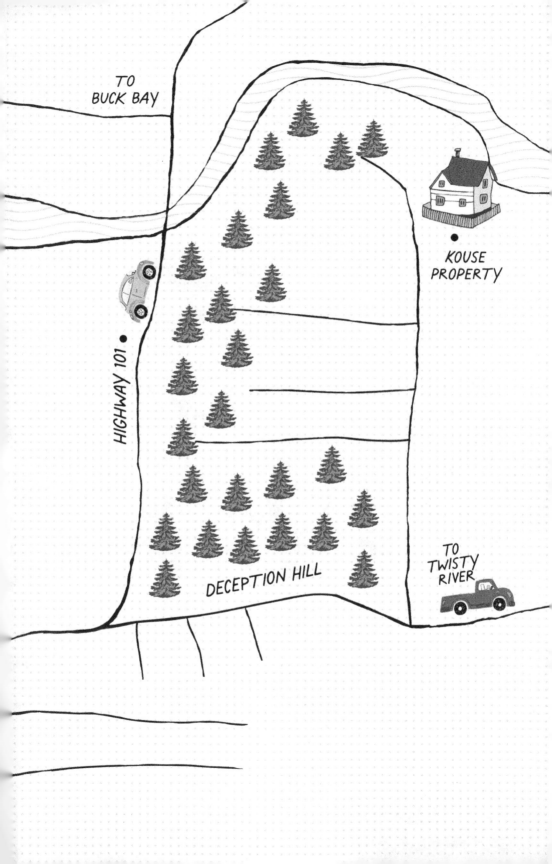

ONE

Zhang Chen drove his blend-in-with-the-crowd black Honda Civic through the old-town section of Port Stirling, Oregon. The damage from the September 2021 killer earthquake and tsunami was still visible now in late November 2022.

Word reached Chen in San Francisco that a prominent international geologist studying the effects of the tsunami had been murdered, and he decided that it might be a good time for him to sneak into town unobserved by police chief Matt Horning and his annoying team of local cops.

Chen didn't know whether to laugh or cry when he read the killer was taken out by Fern Byrne. Oh, yes, Chen remembered Ms. Byrne. That cop bitch and her police chief boss had almost single-handedly brought down his business operation in Chinook County. *Her and that disgusting pink tee shirt.* He shook his head now at the very thought of it, as he'd done a million times since the night his ship, the Anselmo, was raided sixteen months ago.

It really is a charming little town, he thought as he drove slowly down the main street looking for a parking spot near the newly refurbished wharf. His destination was the harbor. He wanted a look at the Coast Guard presence.

Chen steered the Honda into an angled parking spot on the one-way street. Even though the day was mostly overcast, he reached for his Oliver Sun Horn sunglasses in the passenger seat. He wanted to blend in with the other tourists strolling along the pier, but he loved his Italian shades. Besides, no one in this backwater village would know how much his Olivers cost anyway, and they made him look cool rather than the nerdy guy he really was.

He zipped up his black fleece vest, locked the Honda, and took off strolling toward the harbor with his hands in his pockets warding off the chilly breeze blowing off the Pacific Ocean. The sky and the ocean were the same steel color, and it was difficult to tell where one ended and the other began.

Chen was hardly inconspicuous. As a Chinese immigrant, he could have blended in with Oregon's growing Asian population. But there was something about him. Something different. He was tall, for starters, and very slim. Cheekbones so sharp they could cut paper. Flinty black intelligent eyes, and glossy raven hair expensively styled. And it was the way he carried himself, sort of an above-the-fray attitude — like nothing could touch him. He looked tidier than the rest of today's tourists, the sleeves of an ivory sweater sticking out from his vest, clean, perfect jeans, and spotlessly white Balenciaga sneakers that looked straight out of the box.

Try as he might, Zhang Chen did not blend in with the crowd. And people kept smiling at him and saying "hi", forcing him to be friendly in return. *Don't welcome me to your town*, he thought. *It's not smart on your part.*

Since the Anselmo fiasco, Chen had researched how the U.S. Coast Guard operated on the Oregon coast. Part of the Department of Homeland Security, he knew that the USCG station in Buck Bay was responsible for all of Chinook County, along with most of the southern and central coastal area and extending east to the I-5 corridor. The port of Port Stirling only had a seasonal search and rescue detachment stationed near the mouth of the Twisty River. Apparently, there was often heavy fog near the jetty and harbor, making the bar hard to cross for smaller boats, especially during the May-to-September timeframe, when the CG had a presence there.

But now, in mid-November, all was quiet near the Coast Guard's historic waterfront building, and there was no boat in sight, just as Chen expected. He read the notice on the old building's front door advising people to call 9-1-1 in an emergency.

No emergency here, he smiled inwardly. *I've got until the end of April to quietly go about my business.* And this time it would end in his favor, unlike the Anselmo. He'd hired fools for that job. Not surprising they'd gotten caught. And killed. This time he would do it right. He'd manage the operation himself and hire people he knew—people he trusted. Most importantly, Chen would keep a close watch on the local law enforcement scene.

· · ·

"Hi, Joe. I'm on my honeymoon," Fern said as she winked at her husband and moved from the lanai into the condo's kitchen to pour them another round of margaritas. Matt gave her his mega-watt smile and put his feet up on the outdoor ottoman. She could tell her handsome, hunky husband thought this was going to be a long phone call and was making himself comfy.

"I know," answered Joe.

"Which you personally approved," she said.

"I know," he repeated.

"But you're calling me."

"I know. How long are you going to be in Maui?"

"Why do you ask?" Fern was fond of Joe Phelps, her new boss at the U.S. State Department. She checked her watch. "And why are you calling me now? It's 7:45 p.m. here, which makes it the middle of the night in D.C."

"It's 1:45 a.m. to be precise, not the true middle of the night. And I'm headed home soon. So, again, how long are you staying in paradise?"

"We planned to stay another week or so," Fern said, setting down the pitcher of margaritas on the kitchen's old tile countertop. "But I'm getting the distinct feeling that might not be in the cards. Amirite?"

"No, I promised you this honeymoon, and you both deserve it. But I do have a slight change in plans. We need you to come directly for training when you leave Hawaii."

"Why the big hurry? I thought you didn't schedule it until early next month?" Joe officially hired Fern during the Stuarts' murder cases after completing an extensive background check on her, but she'd remained acting in her Port Stirling police department detective's capacity. Her new title was Public Affairs Liaison for the west coast, but her real role would be far, far under cover on the State Department's behalf. And for that, she was to go through intensive training.

"Earl called me a little while ago," Joe said.

"Why would the sheriff call you?" Fern asked, suddenly alert. Sheriff Earl Johnson, a Chinook County institution with over three decades on the job, was not the sort of law enforcement officer to pick up the phone and call the State Department.

"He said he has a job for you as soon as you get home," Joe said. "I believe it was Earl's way of telling me that he knows what you'll really be doing."

"Yeah, there's no fooling Earl," Fern admitted. "Even though I gave him the official version. The sheriff and I worked together at the county before I joined the PSPD. We bonded over our mutual dislike of working with D.A. Dalrymple."

"You guys are too hard on Dalrymple," Joe scolded. "He does his job."

"He's an ass," Fern said.

"You'll have to figure out how to handle your colleagues. You guys have been a tight-knit group, and you all seem to read each other well. And I'm including Ed Sonders and Patty Perkins in that assessment, as well as Earl."

"Yeah, but I can finesse it. Jay will be the hardest, especially since I'll be right down the hall from the police squad room. He'll be bird-dogging my every move. But don't worry about it, Joe. I've got some ideas on how to keep my business my business. Now, tell me why Earl called you."

"Two of the sheriff's deputies followed up on a 9-1-1 call in a rural area just outside Twisty River tonight. A grandmother called, said her son-in-law was drunk and waving a gun around threatening her daughter and two small kids."

"Yikes."

"Yes, a bad scene apparently. But the deputies were able to talk him down. He turned over the weapon, and they hauled him off to the county jail."

"Sooo, how does this concern me?" Fern asked, puzzled. "And you, for that matter?"

"It's the gun. Earl said it's a ghost gun. No commercial serial number."

"You mean it's untraceable?" Fern had heard of this relatively new phenomenon but hadn't come across one yet. "Parts bought online, and the gun assembled at home or somewhere?"

"Precisely. Or what we're seeing is some wise guys who enlist drug addicts to buy the parts for them. They get paid in their drug of choice. And the wise guys run a gun manufacturing enterprise. My counterpart at U.S. Alcohol, Tobacco, and Firearms is on the trail of several of these, and he's my next call."

Fern had moved from the condo's kitchen into the bathroom down the hall and closed the door behind her. "Has Earl seen any of these guns before tonight?"

"No, he told me this is a first for him and his deputies. But, of course, it begs the question: Where did this guy get this particular gun?"

"And do we have one of these manufacturing operations somewhere in Chinook County," Fern added.

"Again, precisely, Agent Byrne. Where there's smoke, there is usually some kind of fire."

"And you want me to follow the smoke?"

"Yes. But first, we need to give you some training," Joe said.

"I had a lot of training before I joined the department."

"You haven't had this training. Let me know when you're back on the mainland." Joe ended the call.

Fern came out of the bathroom and headed back to the lanai. Matt wasn't there. She stepped outside and looked at the garden below, thinking he may have gone down to the barbeque area. She called his name quietly so as not to disturb the guests in the condo below theirs.

She jumped and whirled around when he said, "In here," from behind her.

He was standing in the doorway to the bedroom. Black curly hair a smidge too long for a police chief, several inches taller than her—and she was 5'8"—nice shoulders, just the right width, light blue smart eyes, and...she could go on and on. Fern loved him to pieces.

"What are you doing in there?" she asked.

"Packing. We're leaving, right?"

She looked at him wistfully and said, "'Fraid so."

• • •

The newlyweds flew from Kahului Airport direct to San Francisco International. There they split ways, with Matt flying to Portland and then the puddle-jumper to Buck Bay. Fern caught a flight to Washington's Dulles Airport after doing some quick shopping for business clothes and a decent pair of shoes. All she had with her were swimsuits, shorts, and a couple of sundresses.

"Save your receipts," Matt told her as they stood at the intersection of their departure gates, and then kissed her goodbye.

"That's the best you can do? 'Save my receipts?'," she said.

He laughed. "I want this to feel matter-of-fact to you, not the big deal it really is." He placed a strand of her long, wavy, coppery-red hair behind one ear. Her richly hued hair and beautiful pale skin had initially reminded Matt of a young Julianne Moore, the actress, but after their time in Maui, Fern looked even younger and slimmer, more athletic. Not as glamorous as the movie star, but more gorgeous than ever, healthy, and fit.

Matt wrapped her up in a bear hug and squeezed hard.

"Will you miss me?" she asked her new-ish groom.

"Yes. Tonight will be the first night we've slept apart since our wedding, and that fact is not lost on me." He made a child-like pouting face that was so unlike him, it made Fern laugh out loud.

"Tough guy. Seriously, I do appreciate your willingness to cut our trip short. Joe said it could wait, but what he meant was 'it can't wait'."

"It's your new job, honey, and it's important they teach you their tricks before throwing you to the wolves. That's paramount to another swim and another margarita in Maui."

"God, what if I was married to an accountant who didn't understand?"

"I know I had my doubts about you taking on this role," Matt said, "but we're going to make this work. Pay attention to what they tell you. I'll get with Earl as soon as I get home and see what needs doing on my end." Fern had briefed Matt as they drove their rental car back to Kahului.

"You and the sheriff watch your backs until I get there, OK?"

"Yes, ma'am."

"Goodbye, Tex."

* * *

Fern called Joe as soon as she settled into seat 2A up front. Matt had suggested that she pay the difference between the economy seat that her new employer would demand and the first-class fare, so she might get some sleep enroute. It would never have occurred to her. *Wonder if I'll ever get used to being rich?* she thought.

Her call went straight to voicemail. *Don't tell me my new boss is actually asleep. That's a first.* "I'm on my way, Joe. Landing at Dulles at 6:39 a.m, United flight 2247. Where do I go?"

* * *

Matt arrived in Portland too late for the last flight to Buck Bay, so he grabbed a room at the airport Hyatt. He took a shower—still had sand between his toes, and his hair was salty from swimming in the bay adjacent to their condo—drank a beer from the minibar, and climbed alone into a cold, hard bed.

Crap. He turned out the light.

* * *

As excited as she was to begin this new chapter in her life, Fern still managed to sleep on the flight. The truth was she wasn't as excited as she was upset about Joe's info on a ghost gun in her community. *Why don't these crooks get a life? Get a real job for crying out loud and let the good people go about their lives.*

Much of her job with the Port Stirling police department had been about helping people, especially in the year following the earthquake and tsunami. Almost everyone in her town was impacted somehow by the disaster, either losing people they loved, losing a job, or having to rebuild their lives both physically and emotionally. People were hurting. Folks were regaining their equilibrium and getting back on their own feet, but she knew Port Stirling was still vulnerable.

She shivered. Crime, except for the horrific circumstances surrounding the Stuarts, had been reduced to a minimum since the tsunami. No shootings, no fights, very little domestic violence, just a few drug arrests and some car accidents. But now…guns that can't be traced. That. Can. Not. Be. Good.

TWO

Matt landed at the Buck Bay airport just before noon on Tuesday, a day that he and Fern had planned to go hiking on the rugged Mahana Ridge Trail in the hills above Kapalua. It was so much fun for the newlyweds to discover all the things they had in common — a love of hiking was on both lists. *Maybe we'll go back to Maui before spring. Yeah, probably not, unless this ghost gun discovery is a one-off.*

Matt had called Earl the minute he landed and explained what his call to Joe Phelps had put in motion. The sheriff had scheduled a meeting with Ed Sonders for 2:00 p.m. today in his Twisty River Courthouse office and was delighted to hear that Matt was back in town and could join them. Ed was a lieutenant in the Oregon State Police responsible for the southern coastal area of Oregon. He was also one of Matt's best friends since Matt had taken the chief of police job and moved to Port Stirling from Texas almost two years ago.

Matt told Earl that he would stop at his house and make a brief appearance at his office to let everyone know he was home, and then he'd head to Twisty River.

He and Fern had remembered at the last moment that she'd packed their car key in her backpack, never dreaming they wouldn't land in Oregon together. He fished the key out of his pocket and drove the big SUV onto Highway 101 heading south to home. The late November weather matched his mood — overcast, stormy, and depressing.

He missed his wife already, and he sure as hell missed eighty-one degrees and sunny as the windshield wipers fought the pounding rain. But it was time to go back to work. Over his breakfast this morning, Matt researched the latest news on ghost guns, and it was disturbing. The U.S. Department of Justice had recently reported that almost 25,000 firearms without serial numbers were recovered nationally in the past four years by law enforcement. These gun kits were quickly moving from phenomenon to a more common occurrence, and if one had been discovered in Chinook County there were doubtless others. *We need to get a handle on this right now.*

Pulling into his driveway, his beautiful new home looked stark and lonely with the heavy grey clouds hovering over it, the angry Pacific Ocean just beyond, and dimness inside. *Get a grip, man. She'll be home in a week.*

But it was even worse as he unlocked the front door. Her muddy gardening clogs with the bright flowers, where she'd left them in a corner of the front porch, looked forlorn and out of place now. Inside, the chill worked its way into Matt's bones, and he quickly reached the thermostat and pushed it upward. He'd installed a device that allowed him to adjust the thermostat from anywhere, but this was the first time he'd been out of town, and he forgot he now had the capability to come home to a warm house. *Won't make that mistake again.*

He moved with purpose, switching on lamps and overhead lights to bring some brightness into the house. It was just past noon, but the gloom on this short November day was oppressive. He could feel the heat clicking on, and the lights helped dispel his melancholy.

The view at the top of the stairs to his bedroom never failed to exhilarate him. He paused at the landing and looked north and west as far as the eye could see. Visibility wasn't that great today because of the low-hanging leaden clouds and the almost-horizontal rain lashing at his floor-to-ceiling window. But the power and majesty of the Pacific — different every day — was fully invested this afternoon. Waves pounded the shore 300 feet below his bluff, their mean white tops laced with a tan foam now as the water churned up the sandy beach beneath him. A giant spray erupted as a fierce wave hit the natural rock jetty that protected a little bay to the north.

And the welcome home committee (of one) was just visible about 100 yards out. Roger, his pet seal! Not really a pet, of course, but Roger did live here. Sometimes Matt wouldn't see him for days, and just when he started to worry that something had happened to the harbor seal, he appeared again. Today, Roger bobbed up and down in the enraged surf, looking directly at Matt with what could only be described as a smile on his face.

"It's you and me today, pardner," Matt said out loud. "She's in our nation's capital until next week."

Roger ducked under a big wave, and then popped right back up, his smile wider than ever. "We can handle some time on our own. It won't kill us," Roger said. Not really, of course.

But such was the seal's effect on Matt.

. . .

He pulled into the parking lot at city hall and made his way to the police department's squad room down a hallway on the ground floor. When Matt pushed open the door, he was greeted with simultaneous, startled shouts of "Chief!", followed by "What are you doing here?"

Jay, Walt, Rudy, and Sylvia were all present, and huddled over their respective computers. Seventy-something administrative assistant, Sylvia Hofstetter stood to greet her boss, and said, "Does this mean you're divorced already?"

Matt approached her desk and gave her a hug and a chuckle. "No, ma'am. Fern got called to D.C. to meet with her new boss, and Maui isn't any fun alone. And I missed you guys."

"You did not," said Jay, coming up to Matt for his man-hug. Jay Finley had the most tenure in the department, but at twenty-nine years old was also the youngest officer. He'd experienced his first homicide on Matt's first day in Port Stirling—the murder of Emily Bushnell—and the two cops had bonded for life in that terrifying beach tunnel.

"Actually, I did miss you guys," Matt responded. He clapped Jay on the back. "Fern, too."

"How is she?" Jay asked. He was taking Fern's job change the hardest. The two of them had been assigned to work together much of the time since Fern achieved detective status, and Jay was not happy about her going to work for the feds. It wasn't just the change from their daily partnership; Jay understood immediately that Fern's new title was a phony. He knew she'd be in harm's way on a regular basis, no matter how much she and Joe Phelps tried to spin her true role.

"My beautiful wife is happy," Matt answered. "She's married to a great guy, and is about to start an exciting, important new job."

Sylvia snorted. "I hope Fern realizes that. How long will she be in D.C.?"

"Not sure. Phelps said her training would only take a few days, so I'm anticipating that she'll be back in Port Stirling sometime next week. What are you guys working on?" Matt asked, addressing Walt and Rudy as well.

"Not much," Jay answered for the staff. "It's been pretty quiet. Buck Bay had an after-hours robbery at a pizza joint Sunday night, and Chief McCoy asked us to help them out. We were over there yesterday knocking on doors with their detectives. Rudy helped them corner the perp in a parking garage last night, so we've been back here this morning."

Rudy beamed from his desk.

"Nice work, dude," said his chief, smiling.

"Yeah, they gave us some pizza—it's in the fridge if you want some," Rudy said. "Nothing going on so far today, so I'm writing my report."

"I won't keep y'all," said Matt. "Just going to check on my office and grab my journal. I'm headed to Twisty River to meet with Sheriff Johnson and Ed Sonders."

"What's that about?" asked Jay, all senses awake.

"I don't know much yet," said Matt. "This is Earl's deal, and I'll find out more when I get there. I'll fill you in when I can." He headed off down the hall to his office, which was on the other side of the wall from Sylvia's space.

Jay followed him. "What are you doing for Thanksgiving on Thursday?"

Matt stared at him blankly. "Thanksgiving is this week? Really?"

Jay laughed. "I guess you were on your honeymoon."

"Honestly, it never occurred to Fern or me, we haven't discussed it at all."

"Well, it looks like your first one as a married couple is going to be a non-event."

"What are you doing?"

"I'll be with my mom and dad, and we're eating at noon, and then Ed and I are going fishing at our spot up the Twisty—wanna come with us? We didn't want to waste a whole day off."

"That's the best idea I've heard all day," Matt grinned. "What time?" The three amigos were regular fishing partners.

"Let's meet at the Deception Hill parking lot at 1:30 p.m. I'll tell mom I have to eat and run."

"Great. I'll bring the beer," Matt said. He always brought the beer.

• • •

"You're not very good at this wedding and honeymoon stuff, are you?" joked Ed, greeting Matt with a hearty backslap as he joined him and the sheriff in Earl's office.

"Can you believe it?" Matt said. He smiled and shook hands with Earl. The sheriff always liked a congenial handshake among cops. "You started this one," he said, pointing now at Earl.

"Yeah, sorry about that," said the sheriff. "I never expected Joe Phelps to drag Fern home from your island bliss. Figured the feds would want to know, though. It's a hot topic on the national level."

Matt looked Earl directly in the eye. "Joe thought you were trying to let him know that you know something about Fern's job."

The sheriff stared back at Chief Horning, also his friend. "That she's the State Department's Public Affairs girl, you mean?" His face was neutral, but he couldn't keep out the mischievous twinkle in his eyes or the slight wrinkling around them as he tried not to smile.

"First of all, Fern is a woman not a girl," Matt said. "And second, you will both be advised—either by me or by her—only on a need-to-know basis when she's working on something with local relevance to you." Matt looked from Earl to Ed and waited.

"Like we were *advised* two days after we found Clay Sherwin's head in the marsh reeds?" said Ed. Not smiling. "This is Fern we're talking about."

"You don't think I know that?" said Matt, his voice rising. "But we need to let her spread her wings and do her job. A crucial job that some of our country's best minds believe she is the right person for. We all want to protect her, I get that. And we will if it's required. But if she were here now, she would say—and louder than I'm speaking—your attitude is insulting to her."

Matt, somewhat steamed, hesitated, and the sheriff filled the gap. "Gentlemen, let's have a seat." He motioned to his round conference table, and the three cops each pulled out a chair and sat.

"We love her, too, Matt. That's all," said Earl quietly. The tough-talking, stout sheriff with the left-over Marine haircut, now well into his sixties, was finally learning in life how to say what he felt. It scared some people close to him, but not Matt.

"I know you do," he looked at Earl, "and I know you do, too, Ed. She's going to soar like an eagle in this job. You just have to trust her. And the less talk there is about her "real" job, the safer things will be for her." He gently slapped both palms on the conference table, looked at the sheriff, and said, "Tell us what you've got."

"What I've got is our worst nightmare," said Earl. He rolled his chair and reached over to his desk behind him and placed an evidence bag with a gun in it on the table. "This is a home-assembled pistol, my friends. It has no commercial serial number, and our lab believes the parts for this firearm came from a build-it-yourself gun kit."

"Were the parts acquired from a retailer? Online? Where?" asked Matt.

"Don't know," Earl said. "Our wife-beater—Ray Peng—'couldn't remember' where he bought the gun."

"Where is he now?" Ed asked. "I might be able to help him remember."

"His wife wouldn't press charges, so we had to let him go," Earl said. He frowned. "But since he couldn't produce a permit for the weapon, we confiscated it, and gave him a warning."

"Chinese guy?" asked Matt. "Peng?"

"Nope, he's American, born in Oakland, California, but his parents were both born in Shanghai," said Earl. "He's a seasonal worker, in Chinook County now to help with the cranberry harvest. His wife's family is from around here, and the Pengs live in Twisty River for three months or so every year."

"Did your guys get a good look around his home?" asked Ed. "Any other firearms?"

"Not really," said the sheriff. "He was raging drunk, and they were concerned with de-escalating the situation. They just wanted to get him out of the house and away from his wife and kids. Said they didn't notice anything odd — except for the drunk-guy-with-a-gun part."

"Seems like we should go take another look," Matt suggested.

Earl shook his head. "Nope. Sorry. Once we knew the story on the gun, I asked our ace district attorney to get me a warrant to go back and search. He refused; said we didn't have enough probable cause. It's not against the law to buy these kits. My hands are tied."

"That doesn't sound like our D.A," noted Matt. "He's usually all over anything that might catch the public's eye…like a homemade gun."

"Strictly by the book on this one," said Earl, shaking his head. "I tried real hard to get him on my side, but he wouldn't budge."

"Where's this Ray Peng live?" asked Matt.

Matt and Ed exchanged looks. "Yeah, where does he live?" Ed asked.

THREE

Public Affairs Liaison for the U.S. Department of State Fern Byrne was now on her fourth flight in the past twenty-four hours. She had been met by a young woman at Dulles Airport—obviously, not Joe Phelps. The woman looked very much like Fern, tall and slender, auburn hair, although she appeared to be a decade younger than Fern.

Upon approach, she (Fern never did get her name) grabbed Fern in a big hug, squealing with some kind of joy, and whispered in her ear, "I'm your sister. Act happy to see me."

Fern did as she was told, and the two locked arms and strode off down another concourse, appearing to chatter ferociously. At some point, sis gave Fern another airline ticket with a final destination of Brunswick Golden Isles Airport in Georgia, with a plane change in Atlanta. Brunswick, Georgia, was the headquarters of the Federal Law Enforcement Training Center. *Who knew?*

This time Fern was greeted by a young man in shorts and a tee holding up a sign that read "Fern Burn" in large block black letters. *Close enough,* she surmised.

She went up to him, reached out a hand to shake and said, "I'm Fern Byrne. Are you here to meet me?"

"Yes, ma'am, I am," the twenty-something with too-long, straight blond hair and too much nose said. "Got a couple of questions for ya."

"O.K. Shoot."

"Where are you from?"

"Oregon," she answered. "A small town on the Pacific Ocean coast. Where are you from?" A smirk.

"Doesn't matter," he replied brusquely. "What's your father's name?"

"Conor Byrne."

"How long have you been married?"

Fern looked at her watch. "Three weeks and six days."

"Let's go," he said, reaching down to take her suitcase. "Follow me."

"I need to see your ID first," Fern said.

He reached into a pocket and took out his wallet, opening it to a federal government badge. The photo matched, and Fern nodded.

He led her to a black Ram pickup truck with an American flag flying from the cab. Fern thought it looked like a typical southern mode of transportation. She climbed up into the passenger seat, grateful for her long legs. *How do shorter women get in these things?!?*

Blondie settled himself behind the wheel.

"Where, precisely, are we going?" she inquired.

"FLETC—the Federal Law Enforcement Training Center. It's about five miles up the road. You'll be staying there for a few days."

"Why all the secrecy in D.C.?"

"Mr. Phelps didn't want anyone to know that you've been sent here. The curriculum isn't generally required for Public Affairs staff."

"Ahh."

"Can I say something?" He took his eyes off the road briefly and looked at her.

"You're the man in charge."

"You are really pretty."

That was not what Fern thought he was going to say. She looked over at him, hesitated a beat, and said, "I know."

"You *know*?"

"Here's a news flash, blondie. Attractive women know we are pretty. We've been told it since we were little girls. Almost every day. You don't need to tell us. Truly."

"It's just that I was surprised to see you. You're not the usual State Department type."

"Maybe that's a good thing."

"Whatever. Welcome to Club Fed."

"Club Fed…clever." Fern looked out the window. "Are we there yet?"

• • •

Leaving the sheriff's office in the courthouse, Matt and Ed decided they would show up at Coastal Cove Cranberries, where Ray Peng told the Chinook County deputies he worked, and get a read on him first. Since it was the middle of the afternoon, he was likely at work.

They approached the small office in the front corner of the massive processing plant. A pleasant woman with a long, horse-like face said, "Can I help you, gentlemen?" She had big doe eyes, and a double chin. Her nondescript hair was pulled back in a long ponytail, which accentuated the horse look.

"Hi, I'm police chief Matt Horning from over in Port Stirling," Matt said, stepping forward into the claustrophobic space crammed with desks, file cabinets, and lots of paper. "This is Lieutenant Edward Sonders from the Oregon State Police."

"We've met, haven't we?" said Ed, reaching to shake the woman's hand.

She laughed. "Yes, Mr. Sonders. We worked the grill together at the Twisty River fundraiser last summer. Didn't recognize you for a minute in your uniform."

"That's it," said Ed. "I never forget a face. However, I have no idea what your name is."

She laughed again. "It's Penny. Penny Hawthorn. And you told me you wouldn't remember my name."

"I'm a man of my word," Ed deadpanned. "I do have other skills."

"He does," said Matt. "Which is why we're here. We'd like to talk to one of your employees for just a minute. Ray Peng."

Penny looked confused. "I don't recognize that name."

"It's pronounced 'pong' but spelled 'P-e-n-g'. Does that help?"

She turned and opened the top drawer in a file cabinet and pulled out the "P" file. The two cops stood quietly by while she rifled through it.

"Nope. We don't employ anyone by that name," she said, placing the file back in the cabinet. "Never have, to my memory."

"How many employees do you have working currently?" asked Matt.

"About 120, and I know all of them," she said. There was pride in her voice, and Matt didn't doubt that she did. "Who is this Peng guy?"

"He had a little run-in with the sheriff's office last weekend, and we wanted to follow-up with him. Told the sheriff he worked here. Do you operate other shifts? Is it possible he works a night shift when you're not here?"

"We run seven days a week but only one shift — 7:00 a.m. to 5:00 p.m. Besides, I'd have a file on him in here" — she patted the file cabinet — "if he was an employee. Sorry men, but it appears you've been snookered."

• • •

Back in the state patrol car, Ed said, "What's the home address?" Matt read from the note Earl had given him. "638 Trout Creek Road, Twisty River." Ed plugged it into his GPS, waited a few seconds, and then took off.

"With Fern out of town, what are you doing for Thanksgiving?" Ed asked.

Matt laughed. "I'm going fishing with you and Jay in the afternoon. He already invited me. Can't wait."

"Did he invite you to eat with him and his folks, too? If not, come upriver and eat with us. For some unknown reason, Milly bought a six-teen-pound turkey, and we can't possibly eat all that. Even though it's just the two of us, we like to do the whole shebang — stuffing, mashed pota-toes, cranberries, and lots of pie."

"That sounds so good. I'll be there…and thanks."

"Come up about ten and we'll watch your beloved Cowboys first."

"Deal."

Trout Creek Road snaked up a low hill east of the center of town. The higher they went, the narrower the road became. "There it is," Matt pointed to a mailbox with the numbers 638 hand-painted on the side hugging the shoulder of the road. A dirt road headed off into the brush. Matt casually looked at Ed's holster to make sure he was wearing his gun. After what had happened with Phineas Stuart's killer, Matt would always — 100 percent the rest of his career — make sure that his partner was armed.

"Charming," Ed said, as he parked the car in front of a filthy double-wide perched on cinder blocks in a clearing. There was one car parked off to the side of the home, and from their vantage point it looked like an older model Ford Mustang, souped up and tricked out. Bright yellow.

"A blind moved on one of the front windows," Matt said. "Someone's home. Let's go have a chat. I'll knock and step to the side of the porch. You stand behind me."

"Why don't I knock, and you stand behind me?" Ed countered.

"Because you're too damn big and intimidating."

"I thought we wanted to intimidate him." It sounded like a question.

"We don't know who's in there," Matt said. "What if it's the wife or a kid? Let's go."

They approached the porch and took the three stairs. In the far corner of the porch, the weak November sun was shining on a blue and white Chinese porcelain pot holding a jade plant that looked surprisingly healthy. The front door burst open before Matt could knock.

A man who looked younger than the thirty-two years Ray Peng's file said he was stepped onto the porch, pulling his door closed behind him. "What can I do for you guys?" he asked the cops.

"We're looking for Ray Peng," said Matt. "Is that you?"

"Yeah."

"We understand you had some problems with Chinook County law enforcement last weekend, and we've come to make sure everyone is OK now."

"It was just a misunderstanding," Peng said. He shoved his hands into his jean's pockets. His black hair was short and well-groomed, with mod-looking sideburns and a shock of hair that swept across his forehead. A coral V-neck tee shirt was topped by a thin leather necklace that held a round coin or emblem of some sort. He was short, about five feet six inches, and clean shaven.

"That's not what the sheriff told us," Matt said. "Let's go inside and talk for a minute." He didn't wait for Peng to object, and brushed past him, opening the door.

Compared to the outside of the trailer, the inside was the Ritz hotel. The furniture was new Ikea stuff and organized nicely over an antique-looking Chinese pictorial rug. Somehow, the effect was pleasing. Only an overflowing, disgusting ashtray on a coffee table spoiled the room. Oh, and the four guns laying casually on the Swedish sofa.

"We'd like to meet your wife, Mr. Peng," said Ed.

"She's not here." Peng moved in front of the sofa, but he wasn't big enough to hide the view of the firearms.

"Where is she?" Ed again.

"My mother-in-law took her and the kids to Portland for a few days."

"Giving you time to sober up and calm down?" Matt inquired.

"Something like that. Yeah," Peng said. "I didn't mean to scare her." He looked very young and remorseful.

"I'd be scared if I were her, too," said Matt. He moved to the sofa and picked up a rifle. "A lot of guns, Mr. Peng."

"I like to hunt," he replied, and looked down at his shoes.

"What do you hunt?" Matt asked. He carefully inspected the rifle he was holding. No serial number. It was loaded.

"Deer mostly."

"Do you have a job?" Ed, who had been hanging behind by the front door, asked the young man.

"Yeah. I work at Coastal Cove Cranberries. Processing."

"No, you don't," said Ed. "We checked. They've never heard of you. It's really not a good idea to lie to a state trooper." He stood with his hands on his hips, taking up even more space in the trailer.

Peng twitched. "Oh, I meant to say that I used to work there. I'm currently unemployed."

"OK, let me summarize," Matt said. "You drink too much, you assault your wife, your home is loaded with untraceable firearms, and you don't have a job. This isn't a good trajectory, son. What can we do to help you get on track?"

"I'm fine," Peng said. He attempted a smile. "I'll be getting a new job any day now, and I'm off booze. Promised my wife."

"Where and how did you acquire these guns?" Matt asked. Ed moved in closer.

"You know, here and there," Peng answered.

"Did you make any or all of them from a build-it-yourself kit?"

Peng hesitated. "No, I bought them from a guy."

"All of them from the same guy?"

"Yeah."

"I'd like his name, please," Matt said and waited. He placed the rifle back on the sofa, and he stared hard at Peng.

"I can't remember his name."

In an instant, Matt crossed to Peng, grabbed his right arm, and twisted it forcefully behind his back. Peng let out a yelp. "Ow! That hurts!"

"It's supposed to," Matt yelled. He pulled up Peng's arm even more violently. "Now do you remember the guy's name?"

"No!"

Another tug on his arm. "I can do this all afternoon," Matt yelled again close to Peng's ear. "Is that what you want?"

"He can," added Ed. "I've seen him. Better to tell us where you got these guns now before he really gets pissed off. He's from Texas, you know."

Peng looked pleadingly at Ed but kept quiet.

Matt gave his arm another twist, and said, "Don't look at Lieutenant Sonders. I'm the one you should pay attention to."

Peng screamed in pain and fell to his knees. "Ok, Ok, I'll tell you what I know! Let me go! Please."

Matt eased up and helped Peng back to his feet.

"You can't do this to me," Peng sputtered. "I'm an American citizen and I haven't done anything wrong." He glared at Matt.

"Start talking," Matt said. His demeanor was calmer, but his eyes were flashing.

"I made them myself," Peng said. "I bought the kits online."

"Did you go through a background check to purchase them?" Ed asked.

"Nope. Nobody asked."

Matt and Ed looked at each other. Simultaneous eye roll.

Matt picked up a pistol and waved it at Peng. "This one is plastic. How'd you do it?"

Peng held up a hand, palm facing Matt. "It's loaded, be careful."

Matt pointed the pistol directly at Peng. "Not so much fun when you're the target, huh?" Peng was starting to sweat. *Good.*

"I made that one with a 3D printer," Peng admitted. "All the parts are plastic."

"All the better to take through airport security or evade metal detectors," Matt said. His voice sounded like subterranean thunder.

"I won't do that," Peng said quickly. "I just wanted to see if I could do it."

"Was it hard?" Ed asked. "To build?"

"No, it was easy to make," Peng said. He rubbed his sore arm, and some color came back into his washed-out face.

"What are you planning to do with these?" Matt asked. He swept his arm over the sofa.

"Dunno. Maybe swap them or sell them."

"Like on a website or some kind of social media deal?" asked Matt.

"Yeah. Like that."

"Tell me," Matt said.

Peng hesitated. "Are you going to arrest me? If so, I want a lawyer." He raised his chin in Matt's direction.

"We can't arrest you. You've done nothing illegal," Matt told him. "But what we can do is try to close this fucking loophole in our gun-safety laws. And we can—and will—watch you like a hawk." Matt did the fingers pointing from his eyes to Peng's. "One bad move and you're toast, Ray. Got it?"

Peng nodded.

Back in his patrol car, Ed said with a smirk, "Who do you think you are, Rambo?"

FOUR

Fern settled into her room at the Federal Law Enforcement Training Center. It was eerily similar to her dorm room at Stanford, many years ago. Comfortable, but bare bones.

Blondie had pulled the car up at Building 1 outside the main gate. They were expecting Fern and had her housing assignment and Center identification badge ready. She was also given a packet containing information regarding the Center with specifics such as building number, location of classroom, starting time and maps. Approximately 1,600 acres, the Center was served by a bus transport system.

He dropped her off in front of the building that would be her home for a few days and gave her a sharp salute. He yelled "Good luck" out the truck window as he drove off.

She threw her bag on the floor of the tiny closet and put her laptop and the orientation packet on the desk in front of the window. The window looked out over the sprawling campus and the flat landscape with a few scraggly trees that looked hot and miserable. *Not exactly my magnificent Pacific Ocean view.*

A long twin bed hugged the wall on one side, with a TV mounted on the wall at the foot. The smallest refrigerator Fern had ever seen sat on a spindly table on the opposite side next to the closet. She opened it now, praying for a cold bottle of water.

One bottle of water, six Coca-Colas — *welcome to the south*, she thought. Dried out from the hours of flying, she guzzled the water, looking out her sad little window and feeling restless. *What the hell have I done?*

Fern unpacked, setting aside a clean pair of cropped cotton pants and a tee shirt. Although it was November, it was quite humid, and felt too sticky for her jeans. When everything was neatly stored in its place, she grabbed a bath towel and washcloth from the short stack on her bed, and wearing her room key bracelet, went to the women's shower room across the hall and a few doors down on the left.

Thankfully, it was empty on this late afternoon — everyone was likely still in class — and she had a lovely hot shower that removed all the airplane from her. Back in her room, she spread some luxurious Maui body cream over her parched skin. It smelled of coconut and plumeria, and Fern felt a wrenching pang, missing Matt and their honeymoon paradise so much it almost took her breath away.

Snap out of it. You're the one who wanted this, and this place is a brief interlude until you're back home with a cool new job. She pulled on the pants and tee, sat down at the desk with her orientation materials, and tried to locate the dining hall. Once she'd figured out where to go for dinner, she snatched her phone out of her bag and dialed her husband.

"Miss you already," she said when he answered saying, "Howdy, gorgeous."

"Can you talk for a minute?" she asked. She always asked him that question when she called him because she never knew where he was or who he was with.

"Yep. Just parted ways with big Ed and I'm pulling into the city hall parking lot. What's new in D.C?" Matt asked his bride of three weeks plus change.

"Haven't a clue. I'm in Brunswick, Georgia."

"Huh?"

"Club Fed. Cute, right?" She smiled into the phone. Now that she was talking to Matt, everything looked brighter than it had moments before.

"OK, I get it now. Joe sent you to the feds training center, right?"

"That would be correct. And it's so lovely here, just like Maui."

He roared into the phone. "Ha ha. No, it's not. I've been there, it's a hellhole. Sorry, honey."

"I'll handle it. It's only for a few days, and my curriculum actually looks interesting."

"What've they scheduled for you?"

"I have classes in behavioral sciences, counterterrorism, cyber, firearms, enforcement operations, investigative operations, and physical techniques."

"Wow, soup to nuts."

"Phelps told me it would be thorough. He wants me to be prepared for anything."

"Please pay special attention in firearms. I think that's why you're there."

"What do you mean?"

"I don't know how much you've talked to Joe yet, but the reason Earl called him was they confiscated a ghost gun in a domestic violence situation in Twisty River."

"Yes, I knew that," Fern said. "Do you know more?"

"I do. Ed and I paid a not-so-friendly call on the guy earlier today. He had four firearms lounging on his sofa. All four were made from gun kits he says he purchased online. Not registered, untraceable."

"Good grief. Are you alright?"

"I'm fine. Ray Peng's arm might hurt a bit tonight."

"Who is he?"

"In Texas, we would call him a punk. About thirty, Californian of Chinese descent, unemployed, lives in the boonies in a trailer. Lied about having a job, but he's not destitute — his place was fixed up nice and he's got a car and family."

"Do you believe him about how he got the guns?" Fern asked.

"Not entirely. No. He made it sound like a one-man operation, but both Ed and I suspect he didn't want to give us any names. I'm worried that there might be a gun manufacturing business somewhere around here, and that we've just discovered the tip of the iceberg. And maybe that's what Joe Phelps thinks too, and why he wants you trained and on the job sooner rather than later."

"Could be. He told me that the sheriff's phone call was a wake-up call for Chinook County. That maybe this new evolution of guns has found its way to southern Oregon."

"He's right, Fern. It has. And Ray Peng knows more than he's telling. I'm sure of it." He paused. "How long will you be in Georgia? It sucks here without you."

"My schedule runs through the end of the week, and the minute I can leave, I will. Depending on flight schedules, my guess is I'll be home Sunday or Monday at the latest."

"Do you have classes on Thanksgiving day?"

"Yep. Not how you view the federal government, huh? Once you're here, it's intense and there are no breaks. You be careful until I get home, OK? What are you going to do tonight?"

"I'm going to Whale Rock and let Vicky take care of me."

"Just for dinner, right?" She knew her husband was kidding her, but it didn't hurt to ask.

He laughed. "Yes, Mrs. Horning. Just for dinner. Do you remember that old Paul Newman line when people used to ask him if he was faithful to Joanne Woodward? He would say "Why would I go out for hamburger when I have steak at home?'"

She laughed on the other end of the line.

"But tonight, I don't have any hamburger or steak at home—nothing to eat. So, I'll see what the special is at Whale Rock."

"Give Vicky my best and tell her I said hands off," she joked. More seriously, "What are you going to tell people when they ask where I am?"

"The truth. You're with the government getting some training for your new job. You know, how to write a press release, how to be diplomatic—that kind of thing."

"Good answer. If only it was that easy."

Matt held his phone close to his mouth and said softly, "Show 'em how it's done, darlin'. You'll be home before you know it."

• • •

Ray Peng pressed the name at the top of his phone's Recents list, initiating a call.

"We've got a problem," Ray said.

"No, I'm fine," answered Zhang Chen. "Do you mean *you* have a problem?"

"Yeah. I have a problem." Ray was nervous, but he knew he had to make this call. He hesitated.

"Are you going to tell me about your problem?"

"I got arrested by the sheriff's office. My idiot mother-in-law called them when I was fighting with my wife."

"Are you in jail now?"

"No, Cindy wouldn't press charges — it was just a silly argument. They had to let me go."

"OK. Is there more?" Chen asked.

Ray gulped. "Yeah. They kept one of my guns, a pistol. Said I didn't have a permit for it."

Chen, enraged at this lack of discipline, kept his cool. "Did they ask you where you got it? If so, please tell me what you told them."

"The sheriff was no problem," Ray said, speaking fast. "I told him I bought it from some guy and couldn't remember his name. That was three nights ago, and nothing else happened, so I thought I was in the clear."

"So what, exactly, is your problem now?"

"The police chief of Port Stirling and an Oregon State cop were just here, at my house."

"Matt Horning and Ed Sonders paid you a visit?" Chen said through a clenched jaw. His free hand tightened into a fist and his knuckles turned white.

"You know them?"

"You might say that, although we've never met in person. What happened? Did you let them inside?"

"I wasn't going to. Went out to the porch when I saw the state cop's car. But Horning just walked in. Unfortunately, they saw my other guns."

"Ben dan!" Chen swore in Mandarin.

"I am not a fool!" argued Ray. "I couldn't stop them. I'm sorry, but there was nothing I could do."

"You could not call attention to yourself in the first place. Do you not recall me asking you to be invisible?" asked Chen, his voice toneless. "What happened when they saw the guns?"

"Horning threatened me. He hurt me, but I didn't tell them anything. I stuck to the legal argument—I made the guns myself. There's nothing the cops can do."

"That's where you are wrong. Horning will watch your every move, Ray. He killed my last head of operations—did you know that?" Chen didn't wait for Peng to answer. "He's relentless, will stop at nothing if he even sniffs what we're about. Believe me, he's checking on you right now. He'll go back even before you were born. By tomorrow, there is nothing that Chief Horning won't know about Ray Peng and his ancestors."

"I'm sorry."

Chen sighed wearily. "I suppose it was inevitable. It's a small area, and these local cops are better than they should be." He paused. "I'll be in touch soon; I need to think. Are your mother-in-law and wife under control?"

"Yeah, they've gone to Portland for a few days. Took my kids, too."

"Do you know where they're staying?"

"Of course," Ray said, offended by the implication that he couldn't control his own wife.

"Send both your wife and your mother-in-law flowers today. Tell them you're sorry and that it won't happen again. Wish them a pleasant stay. Be generous with the flowers, not cheap. Do you understand?"

"That's a good idea, boss."

"Yes. And then you stay quiet at home. Read a book and don't drink."

"Should I talk to a lawyer about Horning beating me up? He had no right."

"No!" Chen shouted into the phone. "Leave it alone. That would only get him more involved. Do as I say, and I'll phone you tomorrow with further instructions."

• • •

Zhang Chen was right about one thing; by Wednesday afternoon Matt did know everything knowable about Ray Peng. He was born in Oakland, CA, to Chinese immigrants from Shanghai. Father and mother owned a popular jewelry store in Oakland, and the family was solidly middle-class. Ray attended nearby Merritt Community College, where he studied liberal arts and sciences, and information technology.

There were no previous brushes with the law, and nothing stood out about him since his arrival in Oregon. He'd married Cindy Atkinson of Twisty River, Oregon, in 2015, and they have two sons, aged three and five. On Ray's Facebook page, it appeared to Matt that he and Cindy met at a Giants baseball game in San Francisco.

They owned a nice bungalow in Salem, Oregon, where the family lived most of the year. Ray bought the Twisty River trailer just last year. Matt couldn't tell who actually owned the land the trailer sat on, but it didn't look like Peng owned it. He'd asked Sylvia to track down who did, and she was on it.

Without a court order or subpoena it was impossible to see Ray's tax returns, but, again with the help of social media, it looked like most of his income was from work managing agricultural harvests, mostly in Oregon's Willamette Valley. He appeared to work the fields, migrating from town to town during the seasons for berries, pears, potatoes, and peppermint harvests. And, of course, cranberries brought them to Chinook County every late fall and winter.

Ray was photogenic, and he looked happy at both work and home in his numerous posts. The only thing that niggled at Matt was did he make enough money in the fields to support what looked like a better-than-average life for a young couple barely out of their twenties? And if he wasn't currently working for Coastal Cove Cranberries, why not? How was he earning a living?

He wanted a look at Peng's tax returns, but that was going to take some time and effort since he had no justification for a subpoena. Sylvia would snoop around for financial records, and they might get lucky, but otherwise Matt's hands were tied.

He had no concrete reason to be suspicious of Ray Peng, but all his instincts were on high alert. Something was fishy.

It was nice to be back in his office. The view wasn't much on this late November afternoon. A vigorous squall had blown in last night, and it packed a punch. It had been calm when he went into Whale Rock for dinner about 8:00 p.m., but when he'd come out an hour later, the wind was picking up steam again. Tenacious rain and gusts had flung themselves against his bedroom windows for most of the night.

The gale winds had stopped on Tuesday morning, leaving a gentle, but steady breeze behind, but the rain had been insistent all day along the coast. The sun had peeked out when he was in Twisty River, in the valley, but back in Port Stirling all he saw was the current downpour. He looked to the north out of his big office window at an unrelenting, restless Pacific Ocean.

Matt couldn't quite see the site of Phineas Stuart's discovery, the tsunami-uncovered lost Native American village — it was on the other side of a rock outcropping to the far north of his view. Del Kouse had agreed to manage the development of the important historical site and was working with a Native archaeologist and local and regional authorities. Because of the murders now associated with the location, Del was proceeding cautiously, and, as his friend Matt had known he would, carefully involving the right people. Matt was eager to catch up with Del and see how the new cultural center was coming along.

But first, he would call a staff meeting so he could share the ghost guns info and arrange for coverage during the coming Thanksgiving holiday.

He punched Sylvia's line.

"What, boss?"

"Is everyone here?"

"Almost. Jay and Rudy are at the gym. Said they'd be back by 1:30 p.m. Walt and I are here."

Matt looked at the clock on the wall opposite his desk. One twenty. "Good. Keep the guys corralled, and I'll come in for a quick meeting."

"Sounds good. I have one financial nugget of info on your new best friend, Ray Peng."

"I love you, Sylvia." Matt smiled at the thought of how his seventy-something assistant was far cleverer than any of them at online research. "Save it for the meeting and we'll talk about Mr. Peng."

* * *

"Here come the Port Stirling cop studs," Matt said as Jay and Rudy came through the squad room door.

Jay did a 'Hulk' pose and growled, causing Sylvia to say, "It's going to take more than one workout, sweetie."

Rudy laughed hard. He was the department gym rat, and a perfect physical specimen. Jay was known more for his love of Oregon beer and copious amounts of food. No one could understand how he stayed so slim. It was bound to catch up with the young cop at some point.

"He did his all-time best on the treadmill today," said Rudy, defending his colleague.

"Ten minutes?" said Sylvia.

"Twice that," said Jay defensively. He pointed at her. "Take that, you who sits at your desk all day."

"I walk on the beach every morning before I come to work," Sylvia said. "You should try it. It's that six-mile sandy thing before the water starts."

"Har har," said Jay.

"Anyone in the room want to talk about law enforcement issues?" asked Matt drily.

"Thank you, boss," said Jay, relieved to have the conversation off his physical fitness.

"I met with Sheriff Johnson and Ed Sonders yesterday, and I want to bring you guys up to speed," Matt started. He related the sheriff's department run-in with Ray Peng.

"A ghost gun," said Jay. He shook his head. "As if our job isn't already hard enough."

"It gets worse," said Matt. He explained his and Ed's visit to Peng yesterday afternoon.

Walt, the sergeant, did a massive eye roll and said, "Shit."

"My feelings exactly," said Matt. "One ghost gun is a fluke, four at one residence is a trend. We need to get on top of this before every household in Port Stirling has one."

"They are legal, you know," said Jay.

"I wish people would quit telling me that," frowned Matt. "Ed told me that the head of the state police has been yakking at the Oregon Attorney General, trying to get the state to close the loopholes that allow these gun kits to be bought online with no background check. That's the biggest problem. Any asswipe with some cash can buy one, no questions asked."

"Language, chief," said Sylvia.

He smiled at her. "Yes, ma'am. Sorry."

"It makes me mad, too, Matt," said Rudy. "It gives the bad guys an unfair advantage."

"It does, especially if they want to get up to no good, but even if they're just waving a gun at their wife for fun like Mr. Peng."

"Shall we keep an eye on him?" asked Jay. "Since he's the only person we know of so far who has these guns?"

"Oh, yeah. We're gonna watch him," said Matt. "Something about this guy doesn't add up."

"His finances don't add up real good either," said Sylvia.

"What've you got?"

"He and his wife bought a house in Salem in early 2019, about four years after they were married," she said.

"Yes, I saw it on his Facebook page," said Matt.

"Well, his parents, who live in California, provided a fairly significant down payment, and co-signed his mortgage. Down payment was $250,000 on a sale price of $450,000."

"That's not all that unusual for people his age," said Matt. "How'd you find that out, by the way?"

"A friend at Willamette Title in Salem," she said.

"Do you have friends everywhere in this state?" asked Jay.

"Yes," she said to Jay matter-of-factly. "And that's not what's unusual," she continued. "What is unusual is that he refinanced the mortgage last year in December. His parents are off as co-signers, and the house is now in the names Ray and Cindy Peng. This would indicate to me that it was either a gift, or he re-paid his parents the down payment they contributed."

"That sounds right," said Walt. "My grandfather gave me and Sharon the money to buy our first house, and then we paid him back once we'd saved up."

"Exactly," nodded Sylvia. "But here's the rub. You've had a good, steady job for years now, Walt, and Sharon, too, in the school district. Well-paying jobs and you live within your means. Ray Peng is employed in agriculture — and I believe that to be on a sporadic basis, I'm trying to find out — and Cindy is a stay-at-home mother with two small children."

"So how did he come up with the cash to pay back his parents?" asked Matt. "Is that what you're thinking?"

"That's exactly what I'm thinking," said Sylvia. "All they've got is Ray's salary, and it can't be much. I've just started looking, but it doesn't appear that there's much money in Cindy's family."

"A quarter of a million," Matt said. He scratched his chin.

"Maybe he had a rich uncle who died," said Jay.

"Or he won the lottery," added Rudy.

"Or," said Matt, stretching out the word, "he has another source of income. A side hustle." The room quieted as they all considered that.

"It would have to be lucrative," said Sylvia. "I don't know of any local jobs that pay $250,000 in a year. At least none that Peng would seem to be qualified for."

"Maybe he works remote with Silicon Valley entrepreneurs," Matt said. "Like Del Kouse. Del might make that much. Or he's on the payroll at Port Stirling Links and works for the owner in some capacity? But if that's the case, why wouldn't he have told Ed and me when we caught him in his lie about Coastal Cove?"

"He didn't tell you because it's under the table," said Sylvia. "Whatever "it" is."

Matt jerked his thumb in Sylvia's direction and said to the room, "She's right, you know. Spot on."

Matt made the Thanksgiving holiday staff assignments. They expected a quiet day.

FIVE

Things were quiet in the police department on Wednesday, and Matt was able to catch up on the paperwork that had stalled while he was in Maui. Port Stirling City Manager Bill Abbott had arranged for an all-employee party at 3:00 p.m. before he let everyone go home for the holiday weekend. Only the skeleton crew required to keep the small town running would be working.

It was still raining when Matt arrived home and it was well past sunset, as the daylight was short at this time of year. He'd stopped at Goodie's market and picked up some food to see him through the week. He was pretty sure that Ed and Milly would insist he come home with some turkey leftovers after fishing, but after tomorrow, he wanted to stick close to home for a couple of days and do some research. The chief had volunteered to be on call until Monday so the rest of his staff could have a break.

Dark, stormy, no running on the beach, no wife...what shall I do? He dropped his groceries in the kitchen and put away the perishables, jogged up to his bedroom and changed into workout gear. Then he headed to the small gym he'd built at the side of his garage.

This room had been an afterthought until he hit last winter, and realized that the days were short, and he couldn't always fit in a beach run after work. He'd gone to the town gym occasionally once it reopened after the earthquake, but there was always someone there who wanted to chat.

Women mostly, during the period he and Fern were split up. He didn't mind the flirting, but it defeated the purpose of trying to get a serious workout.

So, he asked his architect if he could add on the small room on the south side of the garage, and it had turned out nicely. It had one window that looked southwest to the Pacific and the stretch of mostly deserted beach to the south. He'd installed rubber floor tiles with a bright speckled print, bought a treadmill and a universal weight system, and hooked up a TV on one wall. A set of free weights completed the efficient space.

Before they'd left on their honeymoon, Fern had snapped a terrific photo of Roger, their resident harbor seal. Unbeknownst to Matt, she'd had it blown up and framed, and it now hung in the middle of the windowless back wall. Roger appeared to be smiling in the photo, and Matt laughed out loud when he saw it now. He figured his wife had hung it in this room so no one else would see it; she knew he was sensitive about people thinking he was crazy talking to his "pet" seal.

Sometimes he listened to music on one of the TV's streaming services, but tonight he tuned in to CNN to see what was going on in the world and jumped on the treadmill. It couldn't replace the joy of running on the beach in the fresh air, but he worked up a good sweat anyway. His last run had been on Maui Sunday afternoon, and he needed the release.

Watching the preparations for the Macy's Thanksgiving Parade on CNN made him a little homesick. The Horning family had always watched that corny, fun parade together. *I should give them a call in the morning.* He did thirty minutes at a good clip and then moved over to the free weights and started some bicep curls.

What was that?!? A bright light shone in the room's window for an instant and then it was gone. *Must have been from a boat moving from south to north. Odd, though.*

Matt looked out the window, but it was pitch black. He thought about going outside and looking around, but it was raining hard again, and he wanted to call Fern before it got too late on the east coast. He lifted for about fifteen minutes and then replaced the weights in their holder, gathered up his towel, and headed back into the house.

He looked out his bedroom windows before hitting the shower, and the rain had turned into a drizzle. There were some breaks in the cloud cover, and the new moon drifted in and out as the clouds chased across the Pacific. He could see a smallish ship about halfway between the beach and the horizon, but its lighting was, if anything, duller than the usual—no bright lights. *Huh,* he thought. He drew the charcoal velvet bedroom drapes tightly closed.

· · ·

"I can't believe we forgot tomorrow was Thanksgiving," Fern said. "Although you'd never know it in this place. There are no excused absences if you're supposed to be in class tomorrow."

"Well, we were enjoying our honeymoon on an island that felt un-Thanksgiving-y," Matt rationalized. "I'm surprised neither one of our mothers called us to see what our plans were."

"Both of our moms know better than to call us on our honeymoon," Fern laughed. "But we'd better give them a call to fill them in on the latest. I'll call mine next since it's still early out there, and I have another full day of classes tomorrow."

"I'll give my family a shout early tomorrow. Maybe we can get down to Texas in late December, and do a combined wedding reception, Thanksgiving dinner and Christmas. Take your folks with us."

"That sounds great," she agreed. "And then we'd be off the hook for family matters for a while."

"How is your training going? Learning anything?"

"The feds know what they're doing, Matt," she said. "I can't believe what I didn't know before this week started. Especially the counterterrorism stuff—there's so much that's new. Cyber, too. I can't wait to get home and share it all with you. And the firearms class yesterday was what you expected—a lot about ghost guns, along with some of the more standard training you've had us doing in Port Stirling."

"Are other parts of the country dealing with these ghost gun kits?" he asked.

"Oh my, yes. Talking to some of my classmates at dinner last night, it's a real problem in much of the country, especially L.A. and Miami. Compared to them, our little part of the world is uninitiated. But they all say, "get ready" because it will hit us soon."

"I think soon is now."

"Did anything more happen with this Ray Peng guy?" she asked.

"Nope, but we're watching him from a distance. He hasn't left his house since Ed and I were there," he said. "Unless he crawled through the woods behind his house and hailed an Uber in Twisty River. He didn't come out his driveway."

Fern laughed. "There are no Uber drivers in Twisty River."

"I beg to differ. Earl told me there is one young woman doing it. Has Uber and Lyft stickers on her car. Mostly takes old people to Safeway."

"Well, good for her, I guess. She should have been in my 'Confronting a Hostile' class this morning. Bring on the bad guys!"

Matt shuddered at the thought of his beloved wife confronting a real bad guy. It would inevitably happen. Had already happened, actually. But that didn't make it any easier to think about. "Let's don't get carried away, Mrs. Horning. When are you coming home?"

"I finish my last class Friday at five, and I'm going to try to get to Atlanta and overnight at the airport. There's a direct flight from Atlanta to Portland early Saturday morning, and I think I can get on it. I'll keep you posted. What are you doing tomorrow?"

"I've been invited to an early afternoon Thanksgiving dinner at Ed and Milly's, and then Ed and I are going fishing. Jay's meeting us on the river. And I'm on call until Monday. Thought I'd give the staff a nice break. Other than Mr. Ghost Gun there's nothing going on around here, and I think that will last through the holiday weekend."

"Yeah. Unless you get a small riot at the Black Friday sales."

Matt snorted. "Even if we do, it will be three people trying to get into the hardware store at once. I think I can handle that."

"I'm glad you're eating with the Sonders. Milly makes a killer marionberry pie, and I'll bet you get that along with pumpkin. If you get leftovers, bring a slice home for me, and stick it in the fridge, OK?"

"Yes, dear. I wish you were here, but we'll have plenty of holidays together."

"We will," Fern agreed. "I'm planning to live until 110, and I'm counting on you keeping up with me."

"Right beside you, darlin'. I love you so much," he said softly. "I'll see you soon."

. . .

Matt put a sticky note on the mirror above his bathroom sink that read 'call your mother', brushed his teeth, and got into bed to read for a while. He'd done his usual check of the house locks and double-checked that he had turned off the cooktop where he'd pan-fried a chunk of halibut for dinner.

It was still and quiet on this Thanksgiving eve, and even missing Fern, Matt was comfortable as he relaxed into his bed. The workout was just what he needed, and if Milton — Port Stirling's 9-1-1 operator — didn't call, and they didn't have another earthquake, he knew he would sleep in a little in the morning. He turned out his light a few minutes before 11:00 p.m. and was asleep immediately.

. . .

A bright light shone through the staircase landing window directly into Matt's eyes. Fern always closed the bedroom door, but he hadn't thought of that tonight.

What the hell is that? He looked at his nightstand clock. Two-thirty a.m. *It's the same light I saw earlier tonight in the gym.*

He got up and moved quickly to open his bedroom drapes, but the light was gone. With the patience that years of doing stakeouts had taught him, he stood still, stark naked in the dark, and waited. Four or five minutes went by. Then his patience was rewarded.

The bright light came again, and it was aimed at his house. This time it didn't shine on the staircase window; it jiggled around on the deck at the opposite end of the house from where he now stood. With the binoculars they kept on a bedroom windowsill, Matt followed the beam as best he could in the dark of night. It appeared to emanate from the small ship he'd seen previously. It might not be the same ship, it was hard to tell in the dark, but it did look about the same size, and was now a little closer to shore.

As quickly as the light came, it went off, and his deck was engulfed in the pitch-black night again. He remained at the window, not moving a muscle for another ten minutes or so, but finally returned to bed after closing his bedroom door.

Zhang Chen. Could he be at it again? Something about the size of the ship he'd just witnessed reminded him of the Anselmo. Although the local cops and the feds tried for over a year, they never found any evidence that could link him to the Anselmo operation. But it had happened on his property, and Matt remained convinced that he was the ringleader, operating afar from his home in California.

Matt had continued to watch Chen's property on occasion, but all had been mostly quiet since the raid had ended things. Chen still owned it, and there had been some remodeling going on, but no action otherwise. There was no reason to suspect Chen was using the property for anything other than a future vacation home.

And yet…ghost guns tied to a young man of Chinese descent originally from the Bay area. Zhang Chen was an entrepreneur from that same area. Was there a connection? Kind of a coincidence. *And everyone knows how I feel about coincidence. And even if it's not Chen up to something, why the light on my house? What's that about? I'll think about it tomorrow.*

Matt fluffed his pillow and turned it to the cool side, rolled over, and went back to sleep.

• • •

Sylvia got up from her home office desk and went into the kitchen to check on her pumpkin pie. After decades of cooking Thanksgiving dinner for her family, finally her son and daughter-in-law said it was their turn to cook. *You think?* she thought, *it's only been forty-two years.* She'd offered to bake a couple of pies because it was her favorite part of the feast, and she was worried they'd get store-bought. Which certainly would not do.

Her homey kitchen smelled like pumpkin pie, and was there a better smell in the world? She pulled on a sturdy kitchen mitt, opened her oven, and stuck a toothpick in the center of the pie. *Just another minute or two.*

She went over to the sliding door to the patio and checked out her back yard while she waited on the pie. It didn't look like much this time of year, but her grandson took care of it whenever he came home for the weekend from college, and it was tidy, just the way she liked it.

Sylvia debated whether or not to call Matt. It was 8:30 p.m. on Thanksgiving eve, and she knew he would be interested in the information she'd discovered in the past hour.

Zhang Chen owned the property on which Ray Peng's mobile home sat. She found Chinook County tax lot records online, and had quickly found Peng's address, which showed Zhang Chen LLC as the owner of the ten-acre plot.

Of course, she had remembered Chen from the Anselmo case. He'd been nearly impossible to reach on the phone, and his office had caused her heartburn on more than one occasion when her boss wanted to talk to him. She had even driven herself out to his property one Sunday morning after the dust had settled from the raid, curious about the site of so much violence and grief.

Yes, Matt would be very much interested in this new development, but she hated to bother him at home tonight. He would be on call all weekend; she should let him have one quiet night.

You're not his mother, she told herself and reached for her phone.

But something stopped her, and she pulled back. *If you worked in a big city police department, you wouldn't hesitate to call the chief and give him an important piece of the puzzle. But I don't work in a big city department; I work in Port Stirling, and we take care of each other.*

She put her phone down and pulled her perfectly cooked pie out to cool on the counter. Always professional to the hilt, Sylvia decided this one time that her information could keep until tomorrow after Matt and the boys had gone fishing.

It was a decision she would regret for the rest of her life.

SIX

Thanksgiving Day at Club Fed dawned just like every other day this week. The sun was shining, and Fern could tell the humidity would be high by the time she walked to her first class of the day, which was Behavioral Sciences.

She dawdled a little getting dressed because she knew this was a class she could probably teach. Unless an awful lot had changed since she'd studied this discipline in college and put to work as first the county's victims' advocate, and then later in her role as detective on the police force, Fern figured this class would be a waste of her time. But she had learned so much at every other class that maybe this one would be the same.

It was also good to bond with her classmates. She enjoyed the physical fitness tests and had fun with the three other women in her class. The men had given the females a good-natured ribbing that only succeeded in bringing out their competitive spirit. Fern had cheered loudly when one of the women, Jody Simpson, finished first overall. Fern had finished a respectable sixth out of thirty-two, and she thought that she and Jody would be friends forever. The chatter from the men died down when the results were announced.

They'd all gone to the "pub" afterwards to drink beer, and Fern knew that some of them would not feel great this morning. She didn't attempt to keep up with the real beer drinkers but went along and resisted ordering the glass of wine she really wanted. She wanted to fit in, and more than that, she understood that there might come a time in her new job when she might need help from some of these guys. Almost every cop here had more experience in law enforcement than she did and might be a resource down the road.

Fern had considered lying to her parents about where she really was when she'd called them last night, but she couldn't do it—it just didn't feel right. She swore them to secrecy and positioned her training in Georgia as an advanced course in representing the country. She knew her mother would look up this place online and become alarmed if she came across the curriculum, but it couldn't be helped. *I know I can handle this job, and the people I love will have to trust me…and keep their mouths shut.*

• • •

The day flew by for Fern. Classes included International Banking and Money Laundering, Active Shooter training, Forensics Technology, Seaport Security, and Covert Electronic Tracking. Her head was spinning by the time she got to the group turkey dinner at 7:00 p.m. One more day, and then she would head for home with all the course materials to study in depth.

Tonight, she ordered her glass of wine and sat at a round table with seven of her colleagues. They all enjoyed the holiday dinner with lots of laughing and sharing of Thanksgiving traditions in their different parts of the country. Nearing the end of the pleasant evening Fern tucked into a generous slice of pecan pie with real whipped cream.

Her cell phone vibrated in her pant pocket, and she pulled it out to look. *Jay. How odd.*

• • •

Once Matt went back to sleep after the shining light incident, he slept until 8:00 a.m. and woke feeling refreshed. He pulled the bedroom drapes wide open and looked out to a calm, vacant Pacific Ocean. On this still day, the light sifted through high clouds, turning the water glossy, like metal.

He could hear the seagulls calling out to sea. The rain and wind had moved on, and the morning showed promise for a clear day. *I'll take my fishing rain gear, just in case.* The only action on the beach was one couple with a friendly-looking cocker spaniel, and one lone jogger far to the south end of his view.

The post-it on his bathroom mirror reminded him to call his parents and he did so while he fixed a light breakfast. His mother was horrified that he was alone on Thanksgiving, but somewhat mollified when he told her he was going to Ed's. Beverly had a soft spot for Ed, and not just because he was her son's best man at the wedding. The two had taken a few spins around the dance floor, a smooth duo who earned some applause. Ed was a foot taller than Beverly, but somehow it worked.

On the work front, his day started quietly. Nothing from on-call, no news or action whatsoever. Matt pictured families all over Port Stirling gathering to celebrate the holiday. But he wasn't Pollyanna and knew there were lots of people in town with no family and few friends to celebrate with. Many of those folks would gravitate to the bars that were open today to watch football and drink with the other lonely souls in town. If there was any trouble today, one of these would be the likely spot.

The Port Stirling Community Holiday committee was sponsoring a free Thanksgiving dinner at the city park's community center, and Matt stopped by there to greet the volunteers and patrons on his way to Ed and Milly's. Last year's free meal had been canceled because of the earthquake devastation, and it was great to see it back on the calendar. He thanked the committee for pulling it together this year and shook hands with the early birds. Everyone was in a festive mood, and he knew the expected large crowd was in good hands. Matt's young officer Rudy and his older brother were in attendance, and Rudy told his boss that they would stay during the hours of the event to make sure everybody behaved.

Although the temperature was a brisk forty-nine degrees as he drove inland, the sun was making an appearance and would warm up the day. Matt enjoyed the drive, cracking his window to let in some fresh air. Ed and Milly lived about twenty minutes beyond the town of Twisty River and had a beautiful place directly on the river. Matt hadn't been there since he'd helped Ed with some property cleanup after the tsunami did a number on their riverfront patio and lawn.

Pulling into their drive now, Matt was not surprised in the least to see the place looking pristine — that was Ed and Milly. Max, the Sonders' yellow lab, raced out to greet Matt. Max had alerted his sleeping people when the earthquake hit, and pointed out the water beginning to seep under their bedroom door to the patio as the raging Twisty River reacted violently to the tsunami, and jumped its banks precipitously.

Matt reached down now and scratched Max's ears with both hands. "What a good boy you are!" Well-trained, Max didn't jump up on Matt, but escorted him to the front door with great dignity.

"You've passed the guest-arrival test, so you might as well come in," Ed said, opening the door.

"The place looks good as new," Matt told him.

Milly waved from where she was working at the kitchen sink. "Hi, Matt. Come on in here and get a drink."

"I'm trying to set an example for our neighbors," Ed said. They moved down the hallway into the kitchen and took a seat on barstools at the small island. A TV mounted on one wall was on with the sound muted. Dallas Cowboys and Detroit Lions. "Some of them can't seem to complete their post-earthquake cleanup even though it's been a frickin' year now." He shook his head disgustingly.

"Yeah, I noticed a couple of places looking shabbier than usual on the way in."

"Don't get him started, Matt," said Milly. "Some people are still struggling, but they'll eventually get there."

"She's more sympathetic than I am," Ed said, jerking his thumb in Milly's direction.

"I noticed," Matt said. He and Milly exchanged smiles.

Ed poured three glasses of an Oregon sparkling wine, handed one to his wife, and set one down in front of Matt.

"We always start with a glass of bubbly," Ed explained. "Gets the taste buds prepared. We picked up this one," he held the bottle up, "at a winery in the Willamette Valley a few years back, and it's our go-to choice."

"Works for me," said Matt, picking up his glass. "Nice of you two to invite me. My mother was upset that I was alone today until I told her where I was going. She sends her warm regards."

"Beverly needs to know that you will never be alone here," said Milly. "If we hadn't invited you first, scores of others would have when they figured out Fern was out of town. When do you expect her home?"

"I think she'll get here late Saturday…airlines willing. Her training ends tomorrow afternoon."

"She'll make it," Ed said. "There's a non-stop from D.C. to Portland at 7:00 a.m. Plenty of time to connect to Buck Bay."

Matt took a sip of his drink and looked down at the countertop.

Ed noticed. "What?"

"She's not exactly in D.C."

"I thought Joe Phelps was training her for her new job."

"She is being trained, that's true," waffled Matt.

"Where?" asked Ed. "Oh, wait a minute. I get it. Phelps sent her to FLETC, didn't he?" He lowered his voice.

Matt stole a glance at Milly, who was peeling potatoes, looking out her window at the river, and not paying attention to the guys. "Yeah, but you can't tell anyone, OK?" He couldn't lie to his best man.

"You know I won't. Actually, this is good news. They do a great job down there. It will keep her safe. Safer, anyway."

"She's learning a lot, Ed. Tells me that she'll be prepared for anything."

"That's what Clay Sherwin thought, too," Ed whispered.

"Don't go there, Ed," Matt said firmly. "That ship has sailed as far as my bride is concerned." He knew that Ed didn't have much use for Joe Phelps, and he, like Matt, would worry about Fern's new role no matter what. Jay, too, for that matter. As much as Fern had explained her Public Affairs role, the cops that knew her (and loved her) understood that she would really be on the front line of any major crime on the west coast that had the potential to involve any international bad actors. But Matt expected them to band together and be discreet — it was the only way to keep her safe.

They had a good dinner, very traditional, and watched some football. As predicted, Milly insisted on loading up Matt with leftovers, and packed a small cooler for him to take home. He was prepared to ask for a second piece of pie for Fern, but Milly packed four slices of her famous Marionberry pie while Ed and Matt were washing up. "Save some of the pie for Fern," Milly said. "She loves this one."

Matt laughed. "She begged me to bring some home if you baked this one." He took the cooler from her. "Thanks, Milly. What are you doing when Ed and I are fishing?"

Milly looked down at Max, who was curled up in his bed in the corner of the kitchen. "We're going for a walk, aren't we Max?" she said in that tone that all dogs recognize. He jumped up and ran to her, barking once.

. . .

Jay was already at their fishing spot, unloading his car when Matt and Ed drove up, each in their own vehicles. Loaded to the gills with food, all three waddled to their respective favorite places. The sun did its part, softening the afternoon air to a pleasant fifty-five degrees, which was the absolute best you could hope for on a late November day.

"Does life get any better than this?" Ed said. It wasn't a question, but Jay answered anyway, "No, it does not."

"This is pretty good," agreed Matt, leaning back on the riverbank, and raising his face to the sun.

They drank one beer each, caught up on issues of the day, and caught their limit early. Not expecting to catch so many fish, neither Jay nor Ed had brought a cooler; only Matt had brought one from home. It was decided that they would go to Matt's house, and he would wrap their fish in ice. In truth, they all wanted to watch the sunset over the Pacific…a relatively rare occurrence in November.

They made it to Matt's deck with about thirty minutes to spare before the sun dropped into the water.

"Let's grab beers and go watch the show first, and then divvy up our fish," said Matt. Ed and Jay were already in their favorite chairs, each facing the ocean. Chuckling to himself at his buddies' predictability, Matt fetched an IPA for Ed, and two Porters for Jay and him. He took the chair next to Jay with his back partially to the Pacific, but he could still look south down the beach, his favorite view anyway.

There were only two ships out to sea, and one, farthest out near the horizon, was moving at a good clip headed north and would soon be out of their sight.

The second ship, smaller and closer in, was the one Matt had seen yesterday. He stared at it briefly before sitting down.

"See that boat?" he said, pointing at it. "Have either of you seen it before?"

Jay got up and went to the railing to get a better look. "Nope," he said. "Doesn't look familiar to me."

"Me neither," said Ed. "But I haven't been hanging out down here that much lately. I've had more action in Buck Bay."

"Why do you ask?" said Jay.

"So, last night I'm working out in my gym in the house, and I see this bright light shining in the window that faces the ocean," Matt explained. "It was pitch dark outside and raining cats and dogs, and I really couldn't tell where it was coming from. But then, I'm awakened in the middle of the night by the same bright light. I stood at my bedroom window and tried to follow the source. The only thing I could see through a break in the cloud cover was a boat that looked like that one."

"Have you seen it before?" Jay asked.

"No, not that I recall. And I think I would have remembered because it's closer to shore than we usually see from the house. Except for the smaller fishing boats."

Ed was peering out to sea. "It is in closer than normal for a ship that size. Got any binocs?"

"Yep, in almost every room," Matt said, laughing. "Be right back." He retrieved the ones from the corner cabinet in the dining room, right inside the door to the deck.

"Here you go." He handed them to Ed.

"Hold my beer," said Ed. "Not really, I don't trust you to not drink it."

"Funny guy," Matt said. Jay snickered.

"Well, that's different," said Ed, looking through the binocs.

"What?" asked Matt.

Ed lowered the binocs. "Most of the ships that pass by here, in fact, most on the west coast, are Panamanian registered. This one's not. If I'm not mistaken, your ship is flying the national flag of the People's Republic of China."

"Let me see," said Matt. He stood and took the binocs from Ed. "You're right, dude. What's the smaller flag below the Chinese?"

"I believe it's the flag for the Hong Kong Ship Registry. It's an administrative region and is getting more popular with ship registrations. I think it's like the third or fourth most popular registry now. After Panama and Liberia, and one other that I can never remember."

"The Marshall Islands," said Jay.

Ed and Matt turned and looked at him.

"How do you know that?" asked Matt.

"I know things. I drink beer and I know things." Jay smirked. "I'm friendly with our Coast Guard, and they know shit like that."

Matt turned back to the railing. "Did you see any people on it?"

"Not a soul," replied Ed. "They may be anchored. Does it look like it's moving to you?"

"Now that you mention it, no," said Matt. "Happy hour onboard, do you suppose?"

"Maybe." Ed took out a notebook and pen and jotted down the ship's registration number.

"Zhang Chen is of Chinese descent. Ray Peng is of Chinese descent. A ship flying the China flag," said Matt. He stared out to sea.

"You know that the state police could never find any evidence whatsoever that Zhang Chen was behind the Anselmo operation," Ed said. "Neither could the feds. And everybody looked hard."

"Neither could the Port Stirling police department," said Jay. "But you think this ghost gun thing is related to Chen somehow?" he asked Matt.

"I think that ship is keeping an eye on my house," Matt said. "I think that bright light came from it last night, and now they're back in my 'hood. That's all I think." But his jaw was clenched.

"It does feel a bit like an all-Chinese week," said Ed.

"Which is unusual for around here," added Jay. "Perhaps it's time for a spin down the road to Chen's property. I was last by there in August, not since then."

"How did it look then?" asked Matt. "Did you tell me something about remodeling the house? I can't remember exactly what you said."

"Yeah. Looked like a fairly major renovation of the house, down to the studs and an add-on closer to the ocean. Barn was getting a new roof, too."

"But to my knowledge," said Matt, "nobody's reported seeing the man himself, right?"

"No, but I'm not sure I'd recognize him if I did see him. I've only seen the newspaper photos of him, and his college graduation pic."

"I'd know him," said Matt. "He's distinctive looking. It would be tough to…"

The shot made a crackling, popping noise.

Matt slumped and immediately crumpled to the deck.

SEVEN

M att!" screamed Jay. "Oh, my God. He's been hit!"

He and Ed were out of their chairs in a split-second. Blood was pooling around Matt's head, and he was unconscious…or worse.

"It's his neck!" Jay wailed. "He's been shot in the neck."

Ed tore off his own shirt and immediately wrapped it around Matt's neck, trying to staunch the bleeding. "Call an ambulance, Jay. Do it now!"

Hysterical, Jay tried to collect himself and punched a number on his phone. "We need an ambulance RIGHT NOW at 1626 Ocean Bend Road. It's my boss. He's been shot. Hurry! Please hurry!"

Ed continued to apply pressure to the wound. Matt hadn't moved or opened his eyes. "I need to stay in this position, Jay, until the ambulance arrives," he said calmly. "You have to do everything else, OK? Pick up the binoculars and quickly look at the ship. Do you see anyone?"

Jay lunged for the binocs, spun around, and tried to focus them on the ship, his hands shaking. "The ship is in closer now, and there is some movement on the top deck. Dammit! I'm shaking and my eyes are watering!"

"Try taking a deep breath and blink several times," Ed said.

Jay turned to look at Matt. "How is he?" He scrunched up his nose and blinked a couple of times in a valiant effort to stem his tears.

"He's got a pulse. He's alive. But it's weak. And he's losing blood. We need help. Tell me what's happening on the ship."

Jay picked up the binocs again. "I think it's moving," he said urgently. "Yes, it's moving north. Looks like it's picking up speed. What shall we do? Did the shot come from there?"

"Had to. There's nobody on the beach," Ed said. "Shit! Go grab some towels from the kitchen." He shifted his position slightly to apply more pressure to the gaping wound.

Jay did as he was told and then held Matt's head while Ed tossed his blood-soaked shirt aside and wrapped a clean towel around Matt's neck. Still no movement from Matt.

"I need you to do two things," Ed said. "Call the Coast Guard and tell them to intercept that boat. Tell them I approved that action and it's a priority. Their only priority. Got it?"

Jay nodded mutely.

"Then go to the front of the house and wait for the ambulance. They should be here soon. No, wait!" Panic was starting to creep into Ed's voice. "Go wait for the ambulance now and call the Coast Guard while you wait. You should walk out closer to the road and wave them in."

"Got it."

Ed looked around frantically. "Do you see anyone else anywhere? Neighbors, fishing boats? Anyone?"

Jay made a quick sweep from one end of the deck to the other. "There's nobody," he said. "Nobody on the beach. I can't see another person anywhere."

"You're sure?"

"Positive," Jay answered. He peered around the south end of the house. "Not even any cars on Ocean Bend. It's like we're the only people alive."

"Then they need to get that boat. Go, Jay! Call the CG and get us the paramedics. I can hold on here."

Jay allowed himself a quick look at Matt. "Keep him alive." Then he ran through the house, yanked open the front door, and sprinted up the Hornings' driveway with his cell phone in hand.

The narrow, two-lane road was quiet, not a car in sight. Jay had the Coast Guard on his speed dial, and the local commander answered in two rings.

"I don't have the cutter here," he explained when Jay told him what had happened. "Dammit! We need a ship in Port Stirling year-round. I've told them until I'm blue in the face."

"They're headed north," Jay said, "Buck Bay can send a ship out and intercept them."

"That's our only option," the commander agreed. "Can you see them from shore? How far out are they?"

"They're close in. I'd guess between one-half and three-quarters of a mile."

"And they'll likely head further out to sea if they're the shooter. I'll figure out a schematic diagram of their possible routing, and we'll cover it with all three of our boats."

"Thanks, man," said Jay, his voice wavering.

"The Pacific's a big place, but we'll find 'em. And I'll pray for Matt."

"He needs all the help he can get." Jay hung up before the commander could hear his sobs.

He heard the siren before he saw the ambulance. It came roaring around the far corner and thundered down the middle of the straight stretch in front of Matt's house, lights flashing. Jay had never been so happy to see a vehicle in his life. He waved his arms and jumped up and down, and then dived out of the way, as it screeched to a stop directly in front of Matt's door.

"This way!"

The two paramedics and one volunteer firefighter seized a stretcher and ran after Jay.

"Thank God," Ed said under his breath as he heard them approaching the deck.

The older of the paramedics slid in between Matt's body and Ed. "I've got him now, Ed." Gratefully, Ed rolled away, and went to his hands and knees, his whole body shaking violently.

Silently, Jay patted Ed on the back.

"What happened?" asked the paramedic.

"We don't know, Mike," said Jay. Ed was still on the deck, trying to get a grip on his emotions. "We heard a gunshot, and then Matt went down. We think it came from a ship that's been lurking closer to the beach than most, but we're not sure. It took off right after the shot."

"Suspicious," said Mike.

"Yeah, that's what we think. Also, there was no one else around. I mean no one. It was a loud pop sound—likely from a rifle. Is he going to be alright?"

"Depends. It's a GSW, for sure. As you can see, he's lost a lot of blood. You did a good job, Ed. He could have bled out without your quick action."

Unable to speak, Ed just nodded.

"I can't tell yet if there's an exit wound, or any damage to organs, spine, blood vessels, that sort of thing. We'll get him to the hospital, give him some blood on the way."

The other paramedic was talking to the ER at Buck Bay, explaining what they had and giving them an ETA.

Jay watched as Mike gave Matt a shot of something. "Do you know if Dr. Ryder is on duty?" Jay asked. "We want her if possible."

Mike nudged his colleague, "Ask them if Bernice is there. If so, tell her to stand by." To Jay he said, "It's Thanksgiving, she might not be at the hospital."

The other paramedic said, "She's off today."

Still on his hands and knees taking deep breaths, Ed said softly, "Call Bernice, Jay. Matt needs the best."

With Mike holding Matt's head securely in both of his hands to stabilize him, the other paramedic and the firefighter slid him onto the stretcher.

"Be careful!" Jay shouted. He hadn't meant to, it just slipped out.

Mike had heard it before. "We'll take good care of him. You do your job, Jay, find whoever did this to the chief."

After the medics had gone, Jay offered a hand and an unused towel to Ed, and the big cop got up slowly, wrapping the towel around his naked torso for warmth.

• • •

Bernice was at her home up on the hill overlooking Buck Bay. Curled up in front of their big-screen TV in black fleece sweats and her favorite fuzzy slippers, watching football, her belly full of turkey and mashed potatoes.

When her ever-present cell phone rang, her husband sitting next to her in his favorite leather chair, feet up on the matching ottoman, said, "Don't answer that."

They both laughed because they knew that was never going to happen.

"Dr. Ryder," she said into the phone.

"Bernice, it's Jay Finley."

"Hi, Jay." She sat up straighter on the mustard-colored sofa and looked out her window to Buck Bay and the majestic bridge spanning it, as if she might see a problem. "What's up?" Calls from a cop on a holiday were never good news.

Silence on Jay's end.

"Jay? Are you there? What's wrong?"

"Sorry," he choked out finally. "It's Matt. He's been shot."

"What?"

"Yeah, he's in an ambulance on the way to your hospital right now. Ed and I were with him when it happened. Are you at the hospital?"

"No, but I'll be there in ten minutes," she said, rising from the sofa and moving quickly to her bedroom. "How is he? What's his status?"

"We don't know. It's not good, Bernice. There was blood everywhere. It's horrible."

"Is he conscious?"

"Not when he left here. Mike gave him a shot of something, and they're on the way to the ER."

"OK, I'm on my way. I'll meet the ambulance and call you when I can. Is Fern in the ambulance with him?"

Jay made a long, low sound that was part moan and part howl. "Oh, no! I have to call her, Bernice. She's out of town. She doesn't know."

"How far out of town?"

"Washington, D.C."

"Oh, Lord. It has to be you, you're the closest to them. You need to do this. Calm down and try to be as rational as you can. Tell her we don't know anything about his condition yet, but that she needs to get here as quickly as she can. Tell her that I'm taking care of him, and that you and Ed will be with him in the hospital until she can get here. Can you do that, Jay?"

"Maybe I should tell her parents, and they can call her. Would it be better coming from them?"

"I don't think so," said Bernice. "She'll have questions, and it sounds like you and Ed are the only ones that can answer them."

"Yeah, you're right. I can do this," Jay said. He sucked in some air. "Hurry, Bernice."

She kicked off her slippers and pulled on boots. Grabbed a raincoat, her briefcase, car keys and said to her husband, "Matt Horning shot, on my way to the hospital, and I'll call you when I can." A quick wave and she was out the door, still wearing her sweats.

• • •

"Mission accomplished. I got him in the head. Clean."

"You're sure?"

"Yes. It is done."

"Excellent. Were there any witnesses?"

"Yes. The state cop and some other guy. I tried to get off a shot at the big cop, too, but he moved too quickly. I had to go."

"Horning's death will be enough of a warning to his friends. Are you back on land?"

"Yes. I took the Zodiac off the ship and landed at the cove we discussed. I'm driving now and will be at the Canadian border tomorrow. I plan to stop in Seattle, wait for dawn, and then cross. Where are you?"

"I'm with my family in Boise at my wife's parents' house. Celebrating Thanksgiving far from the Oregon coast." He paused. "I will make sure that Mr. Chen knows of your success. Your money will be wired to your account first thing tomorrow morning. Is that acceptable to you?"

"Yes. Thank you. It's been a pleasure doing business with you again, buddy."

"The pleasure is all mine. Horning has been a thorn in my side for too long."

• • •

While Jay was on the phone with Bernice, Ed stood at the deck's railing scanning the horizon with the binocs. But the vast Pacific Ocean was giving up no evidence. Ed's hands still shook slightly, yet he was beginning to regain control of his body. His grief went through every inch of him. Even so, here and there was a spark of rage.

Rage was what had propelled the usually stoic and upbeat Ed Sonders into law enforcement over thirty years ago when his younger sister had been raped at a rest stop on I-5. He joined the Oregon State Police right after college and insisted on being assigned to the I-5 corridor where he patrolled for five years, working out of Salem. Homesickness for the beauty and nature of southern Oregon brought him back, and there was hardly a person in the region that didn't know Big Ed.

"See anything?" Jay asked. He moved to the railing, and they stood side-by-side, staring out to sea, not making eye contact.

"Nope. Nothing but water and seagulls. Is Bernice going?"

"Yeah, she'll meet the ambulance and take control of Matt."

Ed nodded. "Good." He kept staring at the ocean, willing it to give up a clue. The sun was down, and the last bit of daylight was going quickly. A lone gull swooped beyond the bluff, disappeared, and then popped back up in front of the deck. The gloom of twilight was upon them. "What the hell just happened here, Jay?" he whispered.

Jay shivered. "I don't know. I wish I did know because now I have to call Fern."

EIGHT

In the end, Jay and Ed decided to call Fern together. Their reasoning was that if one of them lost it, the other could continue talking to her. They moved into her house, instinctively steering clear of the big windows facing the ocean.

"Hello, Jay," she answered. "Why are you calling me?"

Jay cleared his throat which was suddenly thick and seemed to be filled with a foreign substance. "Are you alone? Can you talk?"

"I'm just finishing dinner, and I'm here with several of my classmates. What's up?" A wave of something elusive and unpleasant in the air made her shudder.

"Can you move to a place that's private?"

"OK, now you're scaring me. What's wrong, Jay? What's this about?" She got up from the table and moved outside through some nearby French doors to a patio. *Ugh, still humid.*

"I have bad news," Jay said haltingly. "Matt's been shot. He's alive, but it's not good."

"That can't be true."

"I'm so sorry, Fern, but it is true. You need to come home right now."

"Jay. How bad is it?"

Jay started to cry and choke, and reached out the phone to Ed.

"Fern, it's Ed. I'm here with Jay. We were both with Matt when he got shot."

"Tell me the truth," she said. "Is he going to make it? Is my husband going to live?"

"He's in an ambulance on his way to Buck Bay, and is in good hands," Ed said calmly. "Bernice is there to meet them."

"You didn't answer my question."

"We don't know. He was unconscious and lost a lot of blood. I tried to stop the bleeding, but I was only partially able to do so. The paramedics said it depended on what the bullet struck, and they couldn't tell until they get him to the hospital."

"Where was he hit?"

"In the neck."

She wailed into Ed's ear, and it broke his heart. "We don't know who did this Fern, but we have a lead."

There was silence while she tried to pull herself together. "I'm going to put us on speaker, honey, so Jay and I can tell you together what happened and what we know. Is that alright with you?"

"Yes," she croaked.

The three friends talked together for another five minutes or so. Finally, Jay, reaching deep for his composure, said, "Is there someone there who can look after you until we can arrange transportation?"

"I have a fr..friend who will help me, I think," Fern managed to say. "A classmate."

"Good, that's good," said Jay. "We're going to get you some kind of corporate jet. You know, like Matt's dad rented for the wedding. I think that would be the fastest. Do you know the closest airport?"

"It's Brunswick. I'm in Georgia."

"You're at FLETC?" Jay said incredulously. "The cop camp?"

"Yeah. Middle of nowhere. No one's supposed to know."

"It's OK, I know who to call," Ed said. "You keep your phone charged and on you. You won't sleep but try to get some rest tonight. We'll get you here soon, I promise."

"Get the fastest plane you can. I don't care how much it costs. I'll text you my credit card number when I get back to my room."

"Don't worry about that now," Jay said. "We'll take care of everything. Get your friend and tell her what's happened. Ed and I are going to deal with this, and then we're going to the hospital. As soon as there is any news on Matt, we will call you back."

"Don't let him die, Jay," she sobbed. Her phone fell out of her hand, and she slowly slid down the patio wall holding her up, and sat, legs splayed out, staring at her phone on the patio tile.

. . .

Ed, working with the FLETC Director, arranged for a plane to pick up Fern at Jacksonville International Airport. The Director personally drove her the hour-long drive there and saw her safely onboard. She flew through the darkness, arriving at Buck Bay shortly after 5:00 a.m. on Friday.

Jay stayed in the waiting room outside surgery while Ed went to pick up Fern.

Bernice had spoken to Jay and Ed after she examined Matt.

"He's stable for now, but we need to do some tests to show us the damage and to see where the bullet is. Mike was correct; there is no exit wound, so the bullet is still inside him. He'll need surgery so I can find the damage and see where the bleeding is coming from."

"Is he awake?" Jay asked.

"Technically, yes, but we've got him drugged up so he doesn't move and doesn't feel the pain."

"Can we see him?" asked Ed.

"No, I'm afraid not," said Bernice. "We need to keep him absolutely still until we remove the bullet. I will keep you posted as I can. Where's Fern?"

"In the air," said Ed. "She'll land about five o'clock."

"I'm gonna want to know who did this," Bernice said sternly, and her eyes were steely. "But first I'm going to try to save my pal's life."

. . .

Fern arrived at the hospital just as Matt was being wheeled into the surgical recovery room.

She wasn't allowed in the room, but she could see him through a window in the door. He was still out. Some kind of tube was attached to his neck and mouth, and to a respirator machine. His skin was the color of the sheet over him.

"Ohh!" Fern whimpered, and turned into Jay for support, her shoulders violently shaking.

"He will make it," Jay said. He stuck out his chin and gave Fern a squeeze in an effort to make himself believe it.

"He WILL make it," said Ed on the other side of Fern. "Matt is young and he's the healthiest person I know. Plus, he's a lucky guy. He landed you for a wife, didn't he?" He was more reassuring than Jay.

Taking a couple of deep breaths to gain control, Fern squeaked out, "But it's a gunshot wound. Doesn't feel lucky to me." Her knees wobbled a bit, Jay felt it, and said, "Let's go sit down in the lounge while we wait for Bernice to come out, OK?" He looked over Fern's head and nodded at Ed. Together they helped her to a sofa in the cramped room outside the recovery room doors.

Ed had filled in Fern on what little they knew about what happened on the quick drive from the Buck Bay airport to the hospital. Now, as she sank into the well-used hospital sofa and gratefully accepted a cup of coffee one of the nurses brought to their group, she asked, "How on earth could Matt have been shot on our deck? The beach is 300 feet below, and there's nothing but water for thousands of miles."

Fern's question went out to the universe instead of directly to them, but Ed answered, his voice quiet and low, almost a whisper. "We think the shot came from a ship that was very close to shore. Matt told us he'd seen the same ship the night before."

"Until two days ago, I would've asked if that was even possible," Fern said haltingly. "But now I know it is. A long-range rifle with a telescopic sight can be accurate well over one-half mile and sometimes up to one mile. Was that ship in this range?"

"Yeah, it was," said Ed. "Matt had his back to it, but I watched it. From the time we sat down on your deck, it moved in closer. It's a little fuzzy to me now, but I would guess it was just over one-half mile out."

"Did you see anyone on it?" she asked.

"No, and we even looked through the binoculars before…" Ed couldn't continue. Fern took his big hands in hers and grabbed him tightly.

"I looked afterward, too," said Jay quickly, to help Ed. "We didn't see a soul. But there was also no one on the beach when I surveyed the scene. No cars on Ocean Bend either. It was the boat alright."

Struggling to recover his poise, Ed said, "We think it was a Hong Kong registry because of two flags it was flying—one was China's national flag." He paused and swallowed hard. "Matt was thinking about our recent Chinese connections."

"You mean that Ray Peng guy?" Fern asked.

"Him… and Zhang Chen," said Ed carefully. Fern would not have good memories of Chen's local property.

Fern's eyes widened. "Is he here?"

Ed said hurriedly, "We have no reason to think that. Nobody's seen him. Matt was just thinking out loud."

"Once we know Matt's going to be alright, you guys need to track that ship," Fern said. She had a blank, dazed look on her pale face, but her voice was steady.

"The Coast Guard is on it," Jay said. He and Ed exchanged glances, and Ed gestured with his head for Jay to keep going. "By the time their cutters got down to Port Stirling from Buck Bay last night, the ship gave them the slip."

"They got away?" Fern frowned, not wanting to believe it.

"The Pacific Ocean is a big place," Ed said, "but the CG knows where to look. We gave them the photo and our take on the ship's registration. They'll find her."

Fern looked down and started playing with a tortoise-shell button on her sweater. "Zhang Chen would love to see Matt dead. And probably me too, for that matter. But why now?" She raised her face and, almost in slow motion, looked from one to the other. "We have to know more about that ship."

• • •

Jay's phone buzzed. Sylvia.

He stepped out into the hallway and answered. "I can't really talk now, Sylvia," he said hurriedly in a whispered voice. "Matt's been shot and I'm at the hospital with Fern."

"Oh, my God," Sylvia said. "I've been trying to call his cell all day. Is he OK?"

"We don't know yet," Jay said. "I have to go. I'll call you later."

"But I have something to tell you," she pleaded. "It might be important."

"Not now, Sylvia. Later." Jay ended the call.

• • •

Jay saw Bernice first, coming down the hallway wearing a clean pair of scrubs. These were light blue, he noted, while earlier, before operating on Matt, she'd been wearing dark blue ones. Jay feared he knew the reason why she'd changed.

Jay searched Bernice's face for some sort of clue. He was known in the department as being one of the most observant cops — he rarely missed anything and often saw things no one else noticed. To his horror, he saw that Bernice was trying very hard not to cry.

Fern jumped up and ran to her. "Is he alive?"

The surgeon and good friend took Fern's hands in her own and looked into her eyes. "I did everything I could, but it's bad. He's barely alive, and I have to tell you the truth. Matt might not survive." Both women were openly crying.

Fern's face crumpled up, but she pulled away from Bernice, taking a step backward. "That's not possible," she said. Tears were still pouring down her streaked, red-blotched face, but her voice didn't waver. "You can keep him alive, Bernice, he's a fighter like you are. You can't give up." Her voice was rising. "I won't allow you to give up."

Bernice said, "I'm supposed to be giving you the pep talk."

"Then do it!" Fern shouted. "Tell me exactly what's wrong with him, and what we're going to do to fix him."

Jay guided everyone to the seating area. Thankfully, they were the only four people in the hateful room. "Let's sit and talk, please," he said.

Jay had never seen Bernice upset like this, and it scared him. She was always the tough, controlled type, and she and Matt had a special relationship. It had begun the day they met on the beach at the site of Emily Bushnell's murder. Once they'd been introduced to each other and surveyed the crime scene together, they'd each said—practically simultaneously—"OK, here's what we're going to do." That was Matt, and that was Bernice, and why they became fast friends. Take charge, and get it done.

But now the two women looked at Jay and nodded. Fern took her spot on the sofa and Bernice sat next to her. She reached out and held Fern's hand. Jay and Ed each sat in an armchair on either side of the sofa. Jay found himself staring at a black and white photo of the Port Stirling lighthouse that was clearly taken during the original construction. It was centered over Fern's head.

Bernice pulled out some tissue from the box on the coffee table, handed some to Fern, and dabbed at her own eyes. She blew her nose gently. "What exactly is wrong with him is that he sustained a gunshot wound to his neck. I was unable to retrieve the bullet because it's too close to his skull, and there is substantial damage to his neck. And the bullet hit an artery, and he's lost a lot of blood."

Fern moaned, and Ed gently patted her arm.

Bernice continued, "I'm going to transfer him to a higher-level trauma center in Portland. I know you believe I can fix him, Fern, but I can't. He needs more help than I can give him. He needs a neurosurgeon, and soon." She reached into one of the deep pockets in the scrubs bottom and pulled out some papers. "I need you to sign these, sweetie. It gives us permission to have LifeFlight transport him to OHSU—Oregon Health and Science University."

Fern calmly took the papers and a pen that Bernice held out to her. With the pen poised in her hand, she asked, "What happens to him then?"

"I've got our region's best neurosurgeon standing by," Bernice answered. "Her name is Dr. Nathalie Kumar, and I would trust her with my own life."

Fern stared first at Jay and then Ed. Turning back to Bernice she asked, "What are his chances if I agree to transfer him?"

"Matt's type of injury is fatal about sixty percent of the time. But there are a lot of variables, the most crucial of which is how fast we can get him to a trauma center."

"So, there's a forty percent chance he will be fine?" Fern asked. She clawed at the papers in her hand, knuckles turning white from her grip.

"It's just numbers," said Bernice. She was composed now, the physician counseling the patient's wife. "Every case is different. I do know that if Matt stays here under my care—as loving and dedicated as it would be—his odds go way down. And even if we successfully transfer him, your definition of "fine" is a long shot. I need you to hear me when I tell you he's in bad shape."

"Quit being so negative," Fern told her. "He will be fine. You'll see."

Bernice looked at Ed and Jay. All three knew that Fern was in shock.

Jay slipped off his chair and knelt in front of Fern. He put his hands on her thighs and pressed slightly. "You need to sign these papers, and let's make sure that Matt gets the treatment he needs. OK?"

"Jay's right," Bernice added, softer now, putting her arm around Fern's shoulders. "Let's get him going, and then I'll take you home."

Fern, freckles standing loud on her ashen face, looked at Ed. He gently nodded, she blinked, and she signed the papers.

NINE

Once LifeFlight had landed on the hospital's rooftop, and Matt was loaded through the large bi-fold side door and secured in the medical transport, Fern, Bernice, Ed, and Jay stood silently shoulder-to-shoulder and watched it take off, each with their own thoughts. Airborne, the helicopter glided smoothly to the west into the setting sun, and then turned north. What a long, awful day it had been.

Fern wanted to accompany her husband to OHSU, but Bernice convinced her that she would only be in the way and slow down the ICU-level clinical team on the transport. Jay called Fern's parents, and they were on the way to pick her up and settle her at their home, in her childhood bedroom. Jay and the Byrnes knew that she would insist on going to Portland to be with Matt tomorrow, but they would look out for her tonight.

There was also some concern regarding Fern's own life. No one knew why Matt had been targeted. Ed and Jay had their suspicions because of the registry of the ship, and Ed, especially, intended to pay another visit to Ray Peng. But what if their old nemesis Zhang Chen was involved? He had just as many reasons to hate Fern as he did Matt. She might not be safe at her home.

But in their planning for Fern, Jay and her parents forgot one thing—Fern.

Standing on the tarmac, the four friends seemed reluctant to move. It was as if they would have to acknowledge life without Matt. As long as they stood still, he would be alright.

"Now what?" Fern spoke first.

"Your parents are on their way to pick you up," Jay said. "I called them."

Fern looked tenderly at Jay. "Thank you, that was thoughtful."

"They'll take you back to their house, and we can figure out what to do tomorrow morning," said Jay.

"No," Fern said. "I'm going home. I need to be in my own house tonight."

Here we go, thought Jay. "It's not safe," he said, shaking his head violently from side to side.

"I don't ca…"

"Well, I care!" Jay interrupted her. "We all care." He swung out his arm to include Ed and Bernice. "We don't know why Matt was targeted. We don't know if your house has anything to do with it. We don't know if Zhang Chen is involved. We don't know shit at this point, and until we do, we need to keep you safe."

Fern stared at Jay, eyes wide. "I appreciate your concern. I truly do. My parents can stay with me, and you can station Rudy to keep watch tonight if you must. But I'm going home. I need to look at the crime scene and think this through. There's a reason why Matt was shot, and I need to figure it out."

Ed stepped between the two of them. "With all due respect, Fern, we *all* need to figure this out. But that's not going to happen tonight. You're exhausted, whether you know it or not. I'm definitely exhausted, and so are these two. We will regroup in the morning and call in our colleagues. It will be all-hands-on-deck and, *together*, we'll get our shooter."

Fern teared up and put her face in her hands. Ed quickly moved to hug her. "I'm sorry," she whispered. She brushed tears away. "I know the three of you saved Matt's life and I will always love you because of that fact. Of course, we'll all work together. I didn't mean we wouldn't. The last thing I want to do is cause you trouble. But I'm going home tonight. I'll wait out front for my parents."

She turned and strode to the hospital loading dock door. Her three friends scampered behind her.

. . .

Dr. Nathalie Kumar was waiting on the OHSU roof for the LifeFlight transport, hands on her hips while she watched the helicopter approach. She had an extensive online video meeting with Dr. Bernice Ryder earlier in the afternoon, immediately following Bernice's surgery on Matt. Dr. Kumar understood the prognosis was grim.

The copter came in smooth, touched down, shut off its blades. The side door slid open immediately, and the flight paramedic yelled to her.

"We're losing him!"

. . .

Conor Byrne pulled into his garage, and his wife, Mary, turned to the back seat and said to her daughter, "Stay here with your father. I'll grab some overnight things and be right back."

"OK, mom."

Mary dashed into her house.

"You're sure about this?" her father asked.

"Yes. I know you're worried about me, dad, but I need to do this," Fern said. "And you and mom don't really need to stay with me tonight. Jay is going to post a guard. I'll be fine. I just want to sleep in my own bed."

"No, you don't," said Conor angrily. "You want to see where Matt was shot. You want to solve the crime!"

"That's not true. I just want to feel close to him. Can't you understand that?"

"It's not safe. The person who did this could even be in your house. You don't know."

"Ed is sure the shooter was on a boat out in the ocean," she said weakly. "It took off."

"Right," said her father. "And we don't know where that ship or any of the people on it are right now, do we? This is foolhardy, Fern, and I wish you'd change your mind."

"Not gonna happen."

Mary came out of the kitchen door carrying a small overnight bag and got in the car.

"Did you get my medication?" Conor asked her.

She patted him on the arm. "Of course, dear. Let's go."

• • •

"There's a car here, and a man on your front porch," Conor said quietly. He parked the car in Fern's driveway behind the Port Stirling police squad car.

"That's Rudy from the police department," Fern said. "Jay asked him to guard us tonight. He's great."

Rudy approached their car, hand on the butt of his pistol. "How is he?" asked Rudy when he saw Fern. He opened the car door for her.

"On his way to OHSU," said Fern. "I won't know more until later tonight."

"Sylvia wanted me to tell you that we are all very upset," Rudy said. "She said if you need anything you should call her, no matter the time. She said to tell you she means it."

Fern smiled wanly. "I'm sure she does."

Conor stuck out his hand and Rudy shook it. "How long will you be here, Rudy?" Fern's father asked.

"All night, sir."

"Can you stay awake?"

"Yes, sir. I'm not good at a lot of things, but I'm good at staying awake," he said seriously. "When an all-nighter is called for, I'm always the guy."

"What are you supposed to be on the lookout for?" Fern asked. She needed to know his instructions.

"Well, it's pretty wide open," Rudy said, rubbing his chin. "In a nutshell, anything, or anyone suspicious. Jay told me that we don't know who did this to the chief, so we have to be ready for anything. Lt. Sonders told me to be especially observant if I see any Asian men. On the beach, and around your house."

"Asian?" said Fern's mom, alarmed. She knew about the Anselmo raid and the suspicions about Zhang Chen's possible role in it. Those were a couple of the worst days in Mary's life, and she shuddered now.

"It's a longshot, mom," said Fern, trying to soothe her. "Ed and Jay think they saw a Hong Kong registered ship out to sea when Matt got shot. It may or may not be connected."

"But it is our only lead," Rudy said. "Ed and Jay will be working it hard first thing tomorrow morning. But now we need to get you settled in the house, OK?" He looked around nervously. "I can't believe we'll have any trouble on the Friday night after Thanksgiving, but we're going to do this by the book, Fern."

In another situation, Fern would've saluted Rudy and given him a sarcastic "Yes, sir!", but tonight, mentally and physically exhausted, she simply nodded and went up the broad three steps to her front door. Conor and Mary Byrne covered their daughter's back. Just in case.

. . .

After Rudy gave Fern (and her parents, because Fern looked a little shell-shocked to him) instructions to lock the door behind her, to make sure that all the windows and other doors were firmly secured, and that all drapes and blinds were pulled shut, he took up his post and gave Jay a ring.

"She's here with her parents, and everything is fine," Rudy said. "They're inside and we're locked up tight."

"Thanks, man," said Jay. "Ed and I have written our initial witness reports, and he's taken off for home. I've got Matt's cell phone and I'm checking on who he called and who might have called him the past few days. Not expecting any big revelations, but you never know. Once I'm done with that, I'm going to come by. Don't shoot me."

Rudy laughed a hollow laugh through his hangdog face. "I promise," he said.

"Is the crime scene tape still up on the deck?"

"No, forensics was just finishing up when I got here about 2:00 p.m," Rudy said. "They got what they needed and took off."

"All they'll find are prints from me and Ed, and Matt's blood," Jay grumbled. "Did they say anything?"

"Nope. Not the most fun guys," Rudy said. "Oh, wait. There was one thing. Didn't you tell me there was only one shot?"

"Yeah. Just the one that hit Matt. Why?"

"Because they found a bullet embedded in the wall of the house behind the table you guys were sitting at."

"What?"

"Yeah," said Rudy. "So, if there's still a bullet inside the chief, that means the shooter took two shots."

"I swear I didn't hear a second shot."

"It might have happened fast, and you were probably scrambling to help the chief. And like, really upset."

"True," admitted Jay. "Wonder who the second shot was for—me or Ed?"

"Probably best to not dwell on that now," said Rudy.

"Right. The good news is we've got a clean bullet to examine."

"Yeah. Forensic guys were pretty pumped about it."

"I'm going to drive around on Ocean Bend Road first," Jay said. "Just to make sure that everyone is where they're supposed to be. Then I'll check in with you at the house. If the clear sky holds tonight and we get some help from the moon, I'll go down on the beach, too, and have a look around."

"What car will you be driving?"

"The other squad car," Jay said. "If they're watching, I want them to understand that we are paying attention. Especially while Fern is at the house. Do you need anything?"

"Nope. Got it," said Rudy. "Big thermos of coffee, and two turkey and cranberry sandwiches. I'm good for the duration. Oh, and I brought a rifle and plenty of ammo in addition to my holster gun. Ready for anything."

"Let's hope you won't need it. But we need to be prepared. This was a brazen act."

"What do you think is going on, Jay?"

"Just between us, I think Matt and Ed stumbled into something with the ghost guns, and someone's desperate to send us a warning. Beyond that, it's anybody's guess. I'm calling a meeting of the county major crime team tomorrow—we need some help…again," he added. There was a deep, real sadness in his voice.

. . .

Inside the house, Mary Byrne went from room to room, tightly pulling closed all the window coverings. Conor Byrne checked the locks on all the windows and doors. Fern dumped her luggage upstairs in her bedroom and tried not to look at the bed she shared with her beloved husband.

Jay had asked Fern's father if he would notify Matt's parents, and Conor decided that this would be a good time. He stepped into Matt's home office and quietly closed the door. To his relief, Larry Horning, Matt's father, answered the phone. Conor liked Beverly, Matt's mother, but he was somewhat intimidated by her, and much preferred to talk to Larry. Especially with this news that he was about to deliver.

"My new in-law," said Larry. "How goes it up on the left coast?"

"I have bad news, I'm afraid," started Conor. "The worst news."

"What's happened? Tell me."

"Matt's been shot. He's in the hospital and they've just operated on him."

"No! My son! Is he OK?"

Conor hesitated. He wasn't sure what to tell him. "For now, he's alive. But I won't pull any punches, Larry, it's bad. He got shot in the neck and lost a lot of blood. Ed Sonders and Jay Finley were with him at the time, and they saved his life."

"Who did this? Did they catch the sonofabitch?"

Conor could feel the rage coming through the line. "We don't know yet, but our guys will find out. For sure, they'll get 'em. Matt's surgeon here, Dr. Bernice Ryder, insisted we send him to the trauma center in Portland, and we just put him on the LifeFlight helicopter. They've got the best neurosurgeons around, and they'll take care of him tonight."

"Oh my God," said Larry. It was sinking in. "Where are you now? Is Fern with you?"

"Yes, Mary and I have been at the hospital with Fern, Ed, and Jay, and now we're back at the kids' house. We're going to get some rest, and then drive to Portland tomorrow morning. As you can imagine, Fern is a mess. How unfair is this?"

"Is he going to make it? Is my son going to live?"

"I don't know. I'm so sorry, but all I can tell you is that if it's humanly possible to save him, he's with the people that can do it. You have to hold onto that."

"Obviously, it's too late tonight to get a plane," said Larry. "We'll come tomorrow. Should we fly to Portland?"

"Yes, but wait until I call you tomorrow. Let us get up there and talk to the docs. I'll call you the minute we can learn his status." *If Matt makes it through the night,* Conor thought.

"OK, we'll wait to hear from you, but please call me the instant you know. And, Conor, please thank Ed and Jay for me, and tell them I said, "God bless them. I'll think of a way to repay them."

"If I know those two fine men — and I do — they won't want anything from you. They did what they could to save their friend's life. That's all." He paused. "We'll talk tomorrow."

· · ·

The three Byrnes met up in the kitchen, where Conor was scrambling some eggs. He'd found the liquor during his locking-up duty and poured three small glasses of whiskey for them. At the wedding brunch, Matt told his new father-in-law that he bought that brand just for him, knowing it was his favorite. Conor never figured he would be drinking it without Matt.

"This house is beautiful," her mother said, joining them at the kitchen island.

"And big," added her dad. "I found several rooms I'd never seen before."

Fern, with her elbows on the island, her face cupped in her hands, looking the very picture of grief, said, "It's nothing without him. Just a bunch of walls."

"Matt's going to be back here soon," said her father. "Drink some of this." He passed a glass of whiskey to Fern. "It will help take some of the edge off."

"Bernice said I had to be prepared for the worst."

"Well, yes," said Mary, "but we still have hope, and you need to cling to that."

"What if he doesn't make it?" cried Fern. "What in God's name will I do then? I love him so much." She put her head face down on her arms and wailed, shoulders shaking.

Both parents rushed to her side, mom stroking her hair, and dad rubbing her back. They stayed like that while the eggs burned.

• • •

The night wore on, and a stillness settled over Ocean Bend Road. Rudy made regular trips around the property, including stopping on the bluff below the Hornings' deck to survey the beach 300 feet below. He'd brought the department's night binoculars. They had built-in infrared lights that were great for seeing, but the nighttime range was barely enough to cover the beach closest to the house. Still, he would be able to detect any odd movement nearby.

The surf, at high tide now at 11:00 p.m, was the only sound interrupting the quietude. It pounded the beach and rocks below him, relentless. The moon, hovering over the Pacific, provided some light on the water as the clouds blocked it intermittently. Rudy only saw one ship way out on the horizon, moving steadily north to south. He watched it for a while, but it was too far out to really see anything. By the time he got back around to the front of the house, he saw Jay's car approaching the driveway.

"Buona sera," said Rudy in greeting his colleague. Rudy was of Italian descent, and proud of his heritage. It helped him with the ladies when he would throw in an Italian phrase or two. At least, that's what he thought.

"How's it going?" asked Jay.

"All quiet on the western front. You're the only person I've seen, and there's only been two or three cars go by on Ocean Bend, and that was after Whale Cove finished their dinner service just after nine."

"Why are the lights still on?" Jay turned his attention to the house behind Rudy.

"How the hell would I know? I'm out here, they're in there."

"Take it easy. It was just rhetorical," Jay said. "I'm going to walk around on the other side and see if it's worth going down to the beach. I won't be long."

"Be careful, dude," Rudy said.

Jay patted his gun and took off around the south end of the house. He stopped when he reached the southwestern corner, thinking he'd heard something. The waves below him were crashing onto the shore, making a racket, and the wind whispered through the shrubs at the base of the deck. Somewhere, a wind chime gently clanged. But still, there was something. *A whimper?*

Nah, I'm just jumpy, he said to himself. *To be expected with what you've been through.* Jay took a deep breath and exhaled. He took a step toward the bluff, and then paused again.

No, there was definitely a noise coming from the Hornings' deck, and he saw a shadowy movement. *What the hell?*

Noiselessly, he unholstered his gun, holding it out in front of his body with both hands. *Why, exactly, did you choose to be a cop? You could have been an accountant, you're good with numbers.* He moved toward the staircase that led from the deck down to the ground, about eight feet from where he was standing. Keeping his head down, he tiptoed warily up the five stairs, pausing to listen on each step.

Fern! What the hell is she doing out here?

Jay said her name quietly, so as not to scare her. "Fern, honey, what are you doing out here?"

She was on her hands and knees, scrubbing the deck. She didn't look up, but said, "Leave me alone, Jay."

He moved quickly to her, but she didn't acknowledge his presence or stop her violent scrubbing. "I've got to get Matt's blood off his deck before he comes home. I have to."

Jay dropped to his knees beside her. "Stop it, Fern. We can have someone do this; you don't have to." He grabbed her wrists firmly and saw that she had giant sponges in each hand.

She pulled her wrists free of his grasp, and maniacally threw the sponges over the deck's railing toward the bluff, screaming and staring at the blood stains she couldn't clean up. She collapsed in a sobbing heap, and Jay held her tightly, silently to him, gently rocking them both.

TEN

Saturday morning dawned foggy and cold. Fern and her parents set off to Portland at 8:00 a.m. They decided to drive because no one knew how long they'd be staying.

Matt's new doctor, Nathalie Kumar, had called Fern at 6:00 a.m. She explained that she had performed a second surgery on Matt almost immediately after LifeFlight got him to OHSU last night, and that he'd made it through the night. But she cautioned Fern that his vitals were showing signs of weakness, and that she should get there as quickly as possible.

Once Conor Byrne drove them safely through the thick, wet fog along the coast, he turned inland and headed for I-5, driving his Volvo SUV faster than he had any time in the two years he'd owned it.

• • •

Jay called the meeting of the Chinook County major crime team to order at 9:00 a.m. Saturday. Sylvia had helped Jay notify the key members, and when they were asked what was going on, both told them they'd find out when they arrived. In a conversation with Joe Phelps earlier that morning, he and Jay decided it would be in their best interests to keep the news of Matt's shooting to as few people as possible. Residents may have heard or seen Matt's ambulance on Thursday, but being Thanksgiving, most people would've been occupied at home.

"This is the worst possible news," Joe Phelps told Jay. "The director of FLETC called me after he put Fern on the plane out of Georgia. I'm so, so sorry, Jay. How are you holding up?"

"Not so hot," said Jay. "None of us are. Matt's our leader and we all love him. Can't believe this has happened."

"Did you see Fern yesterday?"

"Yeah, I was with her at the Buck Bay hospital, and then last night at her house. She's a wreck, but insisted I tell you she's coping well. So…she's coping well."

Phelps had to smile at that, even though he didn't feel much like smiling. "Yes, that sounds like Fern. What's the latest this morning?"

Jay filled him in on Matt's condition and told him about the team meeting.

"Please keep me posted," Phelps requested. "And don't hesitate to call me if I can do anything. I'm guessing you and your colleagues will develop a plan of action and see where it takes you today."

"Yeah. There's going to be some real pissed off people in that room, and we all want to find out who did this and why. Work will be a good way to let off some steam."

"True, Jay. It can help salve your wounds. Stick to the fundamentals and be methodical. Is Lt. Sonders with you?"

"He will be here. He went home last night to get some rest. Ed saved Matt's life. He stemmed the bleeding in his neck until the paramedics arrived. Practically a super-human effort…he wouldn't let him die."

"Ed Sonders is an excellent law enforcement officer, and you've got some other good help there, Jay. If you let everyone do their job and get going immediately, you'll do Matt proud."

"Thanks, Joe. I appreciate that."

"One other thing," said Phelps. "It would be a good idea to keep this news within your small team for now. It could buy you some time if the bad guys believe they've killed Matt."

"Understood. I hope it doesn't turn out to be the truth," said Jay morosely. "I'll keep you in the loop in Fern's absence."

. . .

All eyes around the conference table stared at Jay in anticipation. As he'd predicted, the crime team was steaming angry at his news. Most of them, as professionals, went through the gamut quickly: denial at the news, grief, followed by anger and rage.

To their credit, none of the cops around the table said, "Who on earth would want to kill Matt?" They knew that an effective chief of police always made enemies.

Sheriff Earl Johnson was visibly upset. The crusty sheriff saw his younger, handsome, dedicated self in Matt, and he now felt like someone tried to kill him, too. "This shameless, cowardly act will not stand," he said, red-faced as he slammed his hand on the table. "Not in my county." He turned to Ed, who was seated to Jay's right around the big, cumbersome mahogany table. "So relieved you and Jay were with him when he got hit. Thanks for everything you did."

Ed looked down at the table. "Training kicked in," he said in a low rumble.

"Yes," Patty Perkins chimed in, "I talked to Bernice, and she said Matt wouldn't have even made it to Buck Bay if you two hadn't taken quick action. We're all grateful." Twisty River's lead detective, like the sheriff, was fond of both Matt and Fern, and it was eating at her gut thinking what Fern must be going through.

Jeri Schrader, the county's assistant D.A, said, "Jay, do you have any forensic evidence to go on?"

"Yes, I'm coming to that," said Jay, looking up from his notes. "Where's Dalrymple?" David Dalrymple, the county's District Attorney, was a member of the crime team. "Not that we're not delighted to see you, Jeri," he added quickly.

"Out of town for the holiday," she answered. "I'm filling in for him; he'll be back on Monday. He wanted me to ask about evidence."

"Once a D.A. always a D.A.," said Patty. It came out snarky. She didn't like Dalrymple, and most around the table knew it.

"All we have," said Jay, "is a bullet that forensics dug out of the side of Matt's house. Apparently, there were two shots fired, although I didn't hear the second one."

"I heard it," said Ed. "It whizzed by my left ear. Either the shooter wanted another chance at Matt's head, or they were aiming for me." He sat calmly with his hands interlocked and resting on the table.

"Did they get the bullet in Matt?" asked Jeri.

"Dr. Ryder operated on him, but left the bullet in," said Jay, all color leaving his face. "She told me she couldn't risk it because of its location. I don't know yet what happened during the night at OHSU, but I'll find out once we're done here."

"Has forensics examined the bullet they have?" asked Patty.

"Underway now," Jay said. "We'll know something later today, I think. But I'm not expecting much help on that front. We do have one possible lead, however. Ed, please tell them about your thoughts on the ship we saw."

Ed explained about the flags they'd seen through the binocs.

Jay added, "And the ship started moving almost instantly after Matt went down. We're ninety percent positive the shot came from it. Unfortunately, the Coast Guard coming out of Buck Bay was unable to intercept it, even though they responded quickly to our pleas for help."

Earl slammed the table again. "How in the hell did the Coast Guard let that boat slip through their fingers?"

"After sleeping on it—or trying to sleep—here's my theory," said Jay. "It was obviously a planned hit, and, also obviously, the shooter had help. They probably knew we would react fast, and they wouldn't have a lot of time to make their getaway. So, they took the ship north until it was out of our sight range, headed further west out to sea, and then took a sharp left turn south. Probably cranked it up as fast as they could go south, while the Coast Guard searched north and west because that's where we told them they were headed."

"They're probably in Mexican waters by now then," said Patty. "Damnation."

"I called my guy at the CG at 3:00 a.m. when I got this idea," Jay said. "He said they would work with California and see if they could get lucky with an aerial search as well as by sea." He paused. "There's something else. Before Matt was…shot, we'd talked about the other Chinese connection this week. Ed?"

"Yeah," started Ed. "He and I had gone to pay a visit to Ray Peng." He quickly glanced at Earl who put his hands over his ears. This brought some much-needed chuckling around the table, as everyone knew the sheriff had asked for a search warrant for Peng's residence and been denied.

"Your sheriff knew nothing about this visit," Ed deadpanned.

"No warrant, right?" asked Jeri, just getting in on the joke. She pulled some of her long, wavy brown hair behind one ear, as if she was afraid she might miss hearing something. Other than her luxurious hair, she had a sensible manner about her.

"It was a friendly visit…for the most part," answered Ed. "Matt and I checked in with him after we learned about his arrest by Earl's team. We wanted to gain more understanding about his ghost gun. Call it secondary education if you will. Anyhow, Mr. Peng had several other ghost guns laying out in plain sight, and it got a little heated between him and Matt when he wouldn't tell us where or how he got them."

"How heated?" asked Patty.

Ed looked down at his hands and thought for a minute. "Heated," he finally said. "As in Mr. Peng probably didn't feel that great after we left."

"You tortured him?" asked Buck Bay chief of police Dan McCoy who had been quiet until now. His eyebrows lifted, causing his forehead to wrinkle.

"Torture is a strong word, Dan." Ed said. He looked hard at the police chief to make sure McCoy got his point. "Matt just twisted his arm behind his back a little. And it eventually worked — Peng told us he'd bought gun kits online and built them himself. Said he used a 3-D printer, and it was easy."

"You shouldn't have entered his house, and you sure as hell shouldn't have touched him," McCoy said, undaunted.

Jeri looked down at her legal pad and remained silent.

"Have you been able to check Peng's credit card records yet to determine if he was telling you the truth?" asked the sheriff.

"No, but we plan to," Ed said. "Matt was going to come back to your office, Jeri, with this new information, and get permission to do so. It's important that we know exactly where these guns came from, and who Ray Peng really is. Now more than ever."

"Agreed," said Jeri, nodding. She scribbled a note on her yellow pad.

"Was Matt thinking there might be a local source for the guns?" asked Earl. "It crossed my mind when we arrested him."

"Neither one of us knew anything more than I've shared with you," said Ed, "but, yeah, I think there's a good chance that Peng realized that Matt wasn't going to drop this. He's stupid, but he's not stupid, if you get my drift. If there is something going on with ghost guns locally, my bet is that Ray Peng is in on it."

"The feds never did tie Zhang Chen to the Anselmo operation, did they?" asked Patty. She shifted in her chair.

"Matt said that, too," said Jay, "when we saw the Chinese flag flying on that ship."

"Great minds," said Patty. "Has Chen visited his property lately? Do we know?"

"He was apparently up here last summer managing some remodeling of his house," said the sheriff. "One of my deputies saw him, but said he wasn't here long, and he only saw him the one time. What are you thinking, Patricia?"

"If that guy was the mastermind of the Anselmo gig—and lots of us still think he was—he has balls of steel," Patty said. "That's the kind of person it would take to arrange a kill on a cop."

"Like I said to Matt on Thanksgiving," said Ed, "it was a Chinese-themed week. We need to know where Mr. Chen is these days."

"And whether he owns a rather substantial ship flying the national flag of China," added Jay.

"I can find that out," said Sylvia. She had been sitting quietly in the corner taking notes of the meeting. She volunteered to do that because, as she told Jay firmly, "Chief will want to read them when he's back."

• • •

Dr. Nathalie Kumar came to the family chapel at OHSU. She had been advised that her patient Matt Horning's family had arrived from Port Stirling. It was just after 1:00 p.m. Saturday.

Fern rose to greet her with fear in her eyes. Her usually glossy and gorgeous copper hair was a stringy mess, and she had a coffee stain front and center on her teal blue sweater. Fern's mother, a trim, Judy Dench lookalike with spiky close-cropped silver hair, held onto her daughter as she moved toward the surgeon.

Dr. Kumar clasped Fern's hands in her own and got close to her face, looking her directly in the eyes. "Your husband is one tough cookie," she whispered to Fern.

"He's alive?" Fern croaked. Her tears welled up until she could barely see the doctor standing in front of her.

"Yes," the doctor nodded. "But he's in ICU, and the next twenty-four hours are critical. His condition is unstable. I did the best I could. We removed the bullet which was dangerously close to his brain. A matter of millimeters and he would have died instantaneously."

Fern shivered violently and both Byrne parents moaned in the background.

"It's possible for him to recover from a gunshot wound of this nature, but there are several factors at play. We need to watch him carefully for the next few hours. I'm so, so sorry."

"Can I see him?" asked Fern. "Please. Please let me."

"Follow me," she said, taking Fern's hand in hers.

Dr. Nathalie Kumar sang "Amazing Grace" in a hauntingly beautiful, hushed tone as they walked down the hallway side-by-side.

ELEVEN

Detective Patty Perkins was still dealing with the aftermath of the Anselmo raid that occurred on Zhang Chen's oceanfront property just south of Port Stirling about eighteen months ago. Starting with the first girls they unloaded from the ship, Patty had volunteered to ensure their safety.

In all, one hundred seventy-three girls and young women originally from China and Costa Rica needed her attention and had gotten it. These victims weren't to remain nameless unfortunates to Patty; she knew each one of them by name and face, and they were all important to her. Whether it was reuniting them with their families, making sure they got the medical attention they needed, or, in most cases, finding those who wanted to stay, a place to live in Chinook County, Patty made sure each got what they needed. Some were placed with foster families, some were adopted throughout the state, and some she helped establish their own places and find jobs so they could support themselves for the first time in their young lives.

Their big earthquake last year had added to their problems and brought a whole new bag of responsibilities for the long-time Twisty River detective. And through it all, Patty had thought about the person who masterminded the Anselmo operation every single day of her life. She, along with all the other law enforcement officers involved in the raid, speculated about the big boss. The only person who could identify the architect of these crimes was killed in the raid, and they had only circumstantial evidence, not nearly enough to charge someone with Chen's immense wealth and connections. But in her heart, Patty was certain Zhang Chen was their guy.

She was too logical and had too much detective experience to ignore the circumstantial evidence: Chen's property was ground zero for the operation, the girls were mostly Chinese, and Chen was a first-generation Chinese immigrant. She also thought it was telling that Chen had never married. He wasn't gay either, and there was some evidence that he'd had trouble with women. Even though they couldn't prove it, he was the guy, alright. *And if you're up to no good in my county again,* she thought, *I'm going to nail you this time. If Matt dies, I'll take you out myself.*

Patty told Jay and the others in the crime team meeting that she wanted to pay a visit to Chen's property. Jay insisted, and all the other cops agreed, that during their investigation of Matt's shooting, they would only travel in pairs. Who knows what might have happened if both Ed and Jay hadn't been with Matt on Thursday?

"I'll go with you, Patty," said the sheriff. "I think Chen's playing at something again, too. That work for you, Jay?"

"Yeah, and I'll assign Rudy to go along, too," Jay said as nonchalantly as he could manage.

Patty stared hard at Jay. "You think we're too old to handle it ourselves? That we have to have a young buck cop hold our hand?"

Jay's face turned crimson. "No. No, that's not what I thought," he lied. "Look at this way, Patty. If Zhang Chen was the brains behind the Anselmo, and if he is in any way involved with shooting Matt, he's a dangerous guy. Who knows what might be going on at his house or property?"

"He's right," said Ed. "If Chen is responsible for this cold-blooded, brutal attack on the chief, not to mention the kidnapping he likely ordered during the Anselmo, it means he will not let anything get in his way. Or any cop, whether we be young, old, or zombie. Take the hunky kid with you."

Patty's mouth turned slightly upward. Ed could always make her smile, and she knew he was probably right. And maybe, just maybe, at sixty-three she was getting too old for this. *Nah, bring it on.*

"OK, Rudy can come," she said. Turning to Earl, "That alright with you, geezer sheriff?"

"Takes one to know one," Earl gruffed.

Surreptitiously, Jay wiped a bead of sweat off his upper lip.

"Besides Matt's shooting, the most troubling thing of this week to me is the stash of ghost guns that you and Matt found at Peng's residence, Ed," said Jeri. "We're hearing from other D.A.'s around the state, particularly in Portland and Klamath Falls, of all places, that they're running into them too, in the commission of all sorts of crimes — burglary, DV, drug busts and so on. Mr. Dalrymple thought we were going to be spared this particular unpleasant fact, but it looks like he was wrong." Her mouth downturned in a frown, exposing some deep creases.

"It's alarming alright," agreed Ed. "And both Matt and I thought Peng was lying about the source of his. As soon as your office can arrange for a warrant, I'm going to immerse myself in his credit card statements and phone records. Matt thought he bought those guns somewhere around here, and I owe it to him to find out if that's true, and, if so, where that particular retail business might be."

Sylvia raised her hand. Jay looked at her and said, "What?" Then he clapped his hand over his mouth. "Oh, no! I forgot to call you back yesterday. I'm sorry."

Sylvia smoothed her navy wool boot skirt and sat up straight. "It's alright, Jay. You were in an emergency with other priorities. Totally understandable." She looked at Ed. "I have a piece of information that might be useful to you. After you and he had been to visit Ray Peng," she began, "Matt asked me to check into him and see what I could find out online about his employment history, his background, and so forth."

"Oh?" said Ed.

"Yes. I have a report for any of you who want to read it, but there's one important fact I should share." Sylvia paused. "I should have shared it with the chief on Thanksgiving morning, but I decided it could wait. That was a mistake on my part." Her lower lip quivered slightly and her eyes watered, but she remained in control.

"What fact?" Jay asked. "What is it, Sylvia?"

"Ray Peng bought the mobile home he and his family are currently living in in Twisty River. He paid cash for it about eight months ago, about the same time as he refinanced his house in Salem, paying back his parents for a hefty down payment. But the land the trailer sits on — a ten-acre parcel — is owned by Zhang Chen's holding company, Chen Enterprises LLC."

They all stared at each other, and then focused on Sylvia.

"You're sure about this?" asked the sheriff.

"Yes, I looked up the address on county records, and traced back Chen Enterprises to an address in Palo Alto. It's the same address where Zhang Chen's office is. He owns the building."

"Well, I'll be a son-of-a-gun," said Ed. "So, there is a connection. Matt was right."

"That could also explain what his real job is," said Jay.

"Mr. Peng works for Zhang Chen," said Patty. "God only knows doing what on his behalf. Killing smart cops, perhaps?"

Ed shook his head. "I can't really see Ray Peng having the set on him to be a hitman. He's jumpy and has too much nervous energy. But that doesn't mean he doesn't do other jobs for the entrepreneurial Mr. Chen."

"Nice work, Sylvia," Jay said. He stared at the photo of big beach sea stacks with the sun setting behind them on the wall opposite for a minute. "If Ed and I are right about the shot coming from that ship, the gun is no doubt at the bottom of the ocean by now. Would you recognize the ghost rifles you and Matt saw at Peng's place if you saw them again, Ed? Could you be able to tell if one of them is missing?"

"Yes," Ed answered. "I took a photo of his couch arsenal while he and Matt were…talking."

"We need to question both of these guys, see what they say about their relationship," Jay said. "This is really good info, Sylvia. And it wouldn't have saved Matt from getting shot on Thursday. That decision had to be made by Thanksgiving morning at the latest and was probably made Wednesday. Don't beat yourself up."

Sylvia nodded at Jay, but there was no hint of a smile on her sad face, and she was unable to say anything.

• • •

"If this is a dumb question, I'm sorry," said Jeri, "but will you be able to tell what kind of gun was used by examining the bullet forensics found in Matt's wall?"

"Only on CSI Las Vegas," said Jay to chuckles around the table. "In real life, without the actual gun all we can tell is if it was fired from a rifle or a handgun and what caliber it is."

"And even being sure about the kind of gun can be iffy," added the sheriff. "You can't tell the model of gun, for sure. IF we can find the gun that shot Matt, and IF we can test it, and IF the test bullet matches the bullet we've got, we'll have some circumstantial evidence at best. And those are all big ifs. Because it's likely the bullet became deformed when it hit Matt's wall."

"In other words, we can't rely on that," Ed told Jeri. "Because we don't have any real evidence, we have to start with what we know and do some digging. That's why you're so important. We need permission to look at the people for whom we have probable cause in this deal. For me, that starts with Ray Peng."

"And for me it starts with Zhang Chen," said Patty. "Can we count on you?"

"Yes, ma'am," said Jeri. She pushed back her chair and collected her yellow pad and briefcase. "I'll be in touch."

After Jeri left the conference room, Patty said, "I don't feel that we need a warrant to look around Chen's property this afternoon. Obviously, we can't enter any structures — house, barn, etc. — but we can check if there is anyone there or not."

"Is it gated these days?" the sheriff asked.

"Not when I was last there," Jay said. "That was in August, I think. There are gates at both the official entrance off 101, and at that northern entrance that was used by the fishermen to get to the fishing hole, but they haven't been locked since the Anselmo raid, to my knowledge. Probably because of the remodeling, so Chen's crews could come and go."

"OK," said Earl. "We'll round up young Rudy and take off now." He looked over at Patty, who nodded in agreement. "What will the rest of you do this afternoon? Where will people be, so we can check in?"

Jay said, "While we wait on Jeri and the warrants, Ed, can you take me to see Ray Peng's place? Just to get a visual? I'd like to stay out of sight, though. If they think Matt's dead and we're frozen with grief, they might get sloppy."

"We can do that," Ed said. "Park and hide the car in the woods near his mobile home and walk in close enough to check the action without being seen. I'm in."

"Once we do that, Earl, we'll come back here and start researching that ship. See what we can find out about it, and, if we get lucky, who owns it," said Jay. "And I'll be in communication with our Coast Guard command. Call me on my cell if you turn up anything, OK?" Jay paused and swallowed loudly. "And thanks, you guys, for not making me feel like I'm in over my head. It means a lot."

"We've got your back, Jay," said Patty. "We're a team. We all fail or succeed together." She wiped a stray tear from her chin. "And I'm planning on succeeding big-time on this one."

Jay cleared his throat. "Thanks." He sniffed and turned to his left. "Dan, can you check with the airport and rental car companies in your town? See if you think there's anything there suspicious and worth following up?"

"Yeah, and we'll put some boots on the ground and see if there's any scuttlebutt on strangers in town," he said.

"Twisty River and Port Stirling PD's will do the same," Jay said. "For today, every cop is on a need-to-know basis. Just say Matt was shot and we're on the hunt for the shooter."

"My people will ask if he's dead," said Patty. "I may regret it, but I'm going to say 'yes'. I'd rather have the shooter think he got him. It might be the truth—as of right now, we don't know."

A heartbreaking silence around the table ended the meeting.

· · ·

At the same time the Chinook County major crime team meeting was ending, the shooter was sitting down to dim sum in Vancouver, B.C. He'd always liked this city's Asian restaurants, particularly those around Pender Street in Chinatown, where he was now enjoying a charming café. He'd been thinking about Char Siu Bao, the steamed buns stuffed with barbe-cued pork—his favorite dish—for the past two hours of his drive.

At the international border, his car had been singled out for a thorough search. *They can't be looking for me. They don't know who I am. It's just bad luck.* The border guards had been disappointed; nothing suspicious was found in his car, and his fake American passport would show up clean as a whistle when checked in their system. *Purpose of my visit? Why, that would be tourism, of course.*

He showed them his Vancouver Canucks vs. Los Angeles Kings hockey ticket on the Ticketmaster app on his phone. With a hearty "Go Canucks!", he was sent on his way.

He would play the tourist in B.C. for several days, surrounded by friendly, unsuspecting Canadians, and would then quietly make his way home to Los Angeles once the hubbub in Oregon died down. He called it "Getting away with Murder 101." And he'd become quite good at it over the years.

• • •

Fern gently placed her hand on top of Matt's. He didn't stir. Her full-of-life husband, who just days before, had been surfing in Maui, lay motion-less, hooked up to all sorts of tubes and wires.

This is not possible. It's not. He's too big of a spirit and heart to be snuffed out like this. His flame burns too bright. You can't kill my husband. It's not possible.

The only sounds in the darkened room were the occasional beeps and whirs of the bedside machines. Fern had no idea what the machines did, and she didn't care. Matt wouldn't need them for long. She bent down and kissed his hand. She was afraid to kiss his face. She might jiggle some-thing that she shouldn't. And, anyway, his face frightened her…so white.

She kissed his hand and talked to him, getting as close to his ear as she dared. She talked and talked, telling him all the things she thought he would want to hear. What she learned at her training, what they'd had for Thanksgiving dinner at the camp, how Jay and Ed had saved his life, how his favorite houseplant, the Christmas cactus, had bloomed just yesterday for him as if it somehow knew, how her parents were taking care of her until he woke up. And, especially, how they would catch the bastards that did this.

Oh, yes, they would catch them.

TWELVE

Detective Patty Perkins, Sheriff Earl Johnson, and Officer Rudy Tomaselli turned off Highway 101 about six miles south of Port Stirling and made their way down the one-lane road that led to Zhang Chen's property. They drove Patty's private vehicle, hoping to be less conspicuous than the squad cars would be. All three cops had visited the property since the night of the fateful raid, each with their own personal reason for doing so.

Patty had returned with two of the young women who wanted to see — now that the threat to them was past — the place of their freedom. They were two of the older girls, sixteen and seventeen, and both thought they would never know independence again. Patty had walked them down to the beach and recounted what happened that night. The three females laughed and played together on the beach on a bright, sunlit day. Patty knew they were trespassing through Chen's property to reach the ocean, but the place was vacant, and she honestly didn't care.

Sheriff Earl had been a regular visitor. Like Patty, he'd been convinced that Zhang Chen's hands were dirty on the Anselmo operation, and he would never give up trying to find the evidence to prove it. He'd made regular swings through the property, sometimes alone and sometimes with a deputy. It had been a tough night for all the law enforcement officers involved, but the sheriff had been solid, both in his strategy and pursuit during the live action. He was proud of his department and their role, but he wanted to be the guy that solved the big question—who was the mastermind? Earl wanted it to be Chen because he'd hated the guy since he took possession of the real estate and closed off Earl's favorite fishing hole to public access. Matt had solved that particular issue on behalf of Earl and his fellow local fishermen, but it was the principle of the matter that rankled the sheriff.

Rudy and the other officers in the Port Stirling PD had also made occasional excursions to the Chen acreage. Rudy and Jay thought they got lucky last August and would finally be able to meet the owner when they arrived to several vehicles in the driveway that was normally empty. But it turned out to be a construction manager overseeing the remodel and extension of the house at the center of the estate, and some of his crew.

The project manager happened to be of Asian descent, but Jay recognized instantly that he looked nothing like the photos of Zhang Chen he'd seen. Sure enough, the manager they encountered had lived in Buck Bay all of his life and had never actually met the owner of the house; all their communication was online and on the phone. All of the crew were local, too, and included one of Jay's former high school classmates, who confirmed to Jay that they'd never met the property's owner either.

Because of the current circumstances, the three cops were apprehensive as they approached the house today. Rudy remembered how terrified he'd been that summer night, really the first time he'd ever been scared of anything in his young life as a cop. But Matt and all of his colleagues had made it through that night; what if Matt didn't survive this?

Patty and Earl, the old hands, were extra cautious. They understood that if Chen was involved in Matt's shooting it meant that he would stop at nothing to achieve his goals—whatever weirdness he might be up to. And the two experienced, wily cops might not be able to thwart him this time.

There were no vehicles in the circular drive that curved around in front of the building, but far to the right, Earl could see an open garage door with a black Honda parked just inside. And Patty noted that there was smoke coming out of a chimney near the center of the house.

"There's someone here, gentlemen," Patty said as she switched off the ignition. "Let's get out of the car and see what happens, shall we?" She pulled the key out and stuck it in the pocket of her jacket.

"Unsnap your holsters and be ready for anything," the sheriff instructed. "Remember what happened that night—a bunch of them ran out the back door, so stay alert."

"Keep everything in front of you, Rudy," Patty instructed. "I'll go first because I'm not big and handsome like the two of you. Less threatening. Cover me." She bounded out of the car before either one of them could stop her.

As Patty approached the front door, the open garage door began to close automatically. She couldn't see anyone, and the deep red door was clearly being operated with a remote.

Just as Patty reached for the doorbell, the also-red front door opened slowly. A Chinese woman a few years older than Patty, maybe seventy, said "Yes, may I help you?" She smiled a genuine smile that lit up her friendly face.

Taken aback, Patty recovered, returned the woman's smile, and said, "We're looking for Zhang Chen. Is he here?"

"Of course, he's my son," the woman said in polished, perfect English, and smiled even brighter. She was petite, shorter than Patty and much slimmer. Her hair, in a stylish chin-length bob, was silver, and she was wearing beautiful jade earrings that hung just below the length of her hair. Dressed in neat jeans and an oatmeal-colored turtleneck that looked expensive, she looked more like a tourist who might frequent the northern Oregon chic coastal villages rather than the remote southern coast. Her sleeveless fleece vest was smartly zipped to top off her look.

Patty felt large and sloppy next to her.

The woman held out her hand and said, "I'm Biyu Chen. And who are you please?"

Regaining her composure, Patty held out her badge for her to see and said, "I'm Detective Patricia Perkins with the Twisty River police department." She turned and waved her arm at Earl and Rudy. "These are my police colleagues, and we wanted to introduce ourselves to your son."

Biyu smiled again and opened the door wide. "Please come in. It's a pleasure to welcome you, and I will find my son for you."

Patty felt that she had no option but to enter the home. Earl and Rudy quickly joined her. They all stood in the large entryway while Biyu punched a button on her phone and said, "Zhang, there are some people here to see you. We're at the front." She nodded, hung up, smiled yet again and said, "He will be right here. He's just in the kitchen. We were about to have pie left over from Thanksgiving." She rubbed her non-existent stomach and laughed.

"We're sorry to bother you, ma'am," said Earl at Patty's side. "We weren't sure if there was anyone here or not."

"Oh, yes, we've been here since earlier this month. It's so wonderful walking on the beach and snuggling up to the fire, we decided to stay another week. Did you all have a nice holiday?"

Patty answered her question. "For a while we did, but then we had to go to work."

Biyu frowned and shook her head. "No one should have to work on holidays. It's for relaxation and being with family."

A tall, elegant man came down the hallway. The three cops, who had all seen numerous photos of Zhang Chen, were still not prepared for his actual, charismatic presence. He stood by his mother, who he towered over, put his arm around her shoulder in a loving gesture, and said, "Who are our guests, mother?"

Biyu started to introduce them, but Patty intervened. "I'm Detective Patricia Perkins," she said and once again held up her badge, holding it closer to his face than she needed to. This is Sheriff Earl Johnson, and Officer Rudy Tomaselli. Thank you for allowing us in your beautiful home while you're enjoying the holiday weekend."

"Certainly," he smiled, but it wasn't anywhere near as genuine as his mother's. "What can we do for you, Detective?" He stood erect with his arms at the side of his black cashmere turtleneck. His jeans were neat like his mother's, and he was wearing shockingly white sneakers. Patty thought she had never seen such beautiful facial structure on a human being. *A little too sharp for my tastes, but beautiful, nonetheless.*

"We've been wanting to meet you for some time," Patty said. "You weren't at home the last time the three of us were here."

"Ah, yes, that would have been the unpleasantness with those criminals who unlawfully took over my house and property for their illegal business," he said coolly. His mother shook her head and made a tsk tsk sound.

"That's correct," Sheriff Earl said, taking a step forward. "We've always wondered how they got away with that without your knowledge. You know, as the owner of this place."

"My son was never here," Biyu said.

"It's OK, mom," Zhang said, patting her on the back. "It's a valid question. I would ask it, too, if I were the police. But mother is correct, I bought this property sight unseen, and didn't pay attention to it until recently. Those awful men were squatters who took advantage of my inattention, and I feel badly about it."

"I believe you've talked to Chief Horning of the Port Stirling police department," Earl said. "He told me that you told him you were planning to sell the property after that night. Why didn't you?"

"That's true," Zhang said. "I resented the chief's insinuation that I had something to do with those events, and I felt unwelcome. But then, my investment manager who bought this place on my behalf urged me to at least come and look at it. I did, and what can I say, I fell in love with your amazing part of the world. I couldn't sell once I'd seen it, and instead decided to renovate it and turn it into a place worthy of its stunning location. How do you like it?" He turned and faced the living area behind him.

"Nice," said Earl neutrally. "I remember the way this house used to look, and this is a big improvement. Must have cost you a lot."

Chen laughed. "Compared to California construction costs, not so much. Oregon is a bargain."

"Do you know a man named Ray Peng?" Patty asked abruptly.

A subtle cloud came over Chen's face, but he quickly recovered. "Yes, he is a tenant on some other property I own in the area. I've never actually met him. Why?"

"Just curious," said Patty.

"Mr. Peng has come across our radar recently," added Earl. "We're looking for links to other people who might know him."

"And because he has a Chinese name and I have a Chinese name you figured we were best friends?" snapped Chen. "Really, sheriff, you should know better than that. Racial profiling? We're all Americans, aren't we?" He glowered at Earl.

"We don't assume anything, Mr. Chen," said Earl. "We were looking into Peng's background because we arrested him recently and discovered that you own the land his home is on. That's all."

"It's what we like to call a lead in our business," Patty said. It came out snippy.

"I'm sure they are just doing their job, Zhang," said his mother. She smiled at Patty again.

Zhang was not smiling. "If there's nothing else, I think you should leave now," he said.

"We just have one more question," Patty said. "Where were you on Thanksgiving Day between 3:00 — 6:00 p.m?"

"Why do you want to know that?" Zhang asked.

"Because Matt Horning, the chief of police of Port Stirling, was shot and killed then," Patty lied. Her voice was strong and unwavering. "Where were you, please?" She added the 'please' because his mother seemed so sweet.

"I was here enjoying Thanksgiving dinner with my mother and father," Zhang said coldly. "I haven't left my property for several days except to walk on the beach."

"It's true," said Biyu hurriedly. "We've all been here at the house. I'm sorry for your loss," she added.

"Did you walk on the beach on Thursday afternoon?" asked Earl.

"No, I don't believe I did," said Zhang. "I was watching a football game."

"Which game?" asked Rudy, speaking for the first time.

"Giants and Lions."

"You have a good memory," said Earl. "I've already forgotten which games were on."

Chen stared at Earl for a moment. "I think it's time for you to leave, sheriff. I don't need to be harassed while my family is visiting."

"Where is your father, by the way?" asked Earl.

"My husband is fishing in the little river between here and the beach," said Biyu.

"Yes, I know the spot," said Earl. He scowled. "We won't bother you any further, ma'am. Please enjoy your stay in Oregon."

Zhang Chen closed the door firmly without saying another word, and the three cops headed back to Patty's car. Each took a look over their shoulder toward the barn and the surrounding trees, remembering that terrifying night.

"Pure evil," muttered Patty under her breath.

THIRTEEN

Ed and Jay drove to Twisty River immediately following the end of the crime team meeting. Ed recalled the way to Ray Peng's house, and he pulled his car off at a wide space in the gravel road about one-quarter mile before the clearing in the trees where his mobile home sat. The two cops headed off into the woods and approached the home from the north until they found a good place to hide where they could observe the front of the trailer without being seen.

The same car that had been there on Wednesday when Matt and Ed visited was still there and parked in exactly the same spot. A light shone in the window to the left of the front porch, but they could see no activity inside. The mild breeze that had been blowing most of Saturday was threatening to agitate into something harsher. Ed looked up to make sure there were no loose branches in the trees overhead. *State trooper killed by tree limb in windstorm is a headline I don't need*, he thought.

"Pretty quiet," Jay whispered. "I thought Peng has kids?"

"Two, but they are in Portland with their mother and grandmother," Ed whispered back.

"They left him home alone on Thanksgiving? Harsh."

"Perhaps to teach him a lesson that beating the shit out of his wife is not such a good idea. It looks like he's here. That's his car."

"If I'd just shot a police chief, I would hotfoot it outta here," Jay said.

"He's a cool guy. Playing it cool would fit his style."

"Tell me about the layout of his humble abode."

"The room you can see through the picture window is the main living area. The kitchen is behind it and faces south over the ravine behind the trailer. There are two hallways leading off in both directions. That's all I could see when we were inside. If you look through the window, the guns were on a sofa just out of your view on the left end of the room. Hope he locks them away before mom and the kiddies come home."

"Yeah," said Jay. "Do we know when they're coming back?"

"Nope. He told Matt they were gone 'for the holiday', but that could mean all weekend, too. They're in Portland at some fancy…"

Just then, the front door of the trailer opened, and Ray stepped outside onto the porch, cradling his phone against his ear. He listened, and then his face broke into a wide grin, and he pumped his fist in the air.

"Good news, it would appear," Ed whispered. They watched as Peng took a seat on a chaise at one end of his porch and chatted animatedly for a few minutes.

Jay shifted his position and became increasingly restless as Ed silently watched and listened. Stakeout was one of Ed's best events. It reminded him of fishing, without the fish, of course.

"You want to go in, don't you?" Ed said in a quiet voice. "Ask him what's making him so happy?"

"Yeah, I do."

"We don't have a warrant."

"I'm well aware of that fact," Jay said. "He doesn't have to talk to us if he doesn't want to." Somewhat belligerent.

"Jesus, you're just like Matt. It's so obvious who trained you. Let's go," said Ed. They made their way back to Ed's car. "Do you want me to turn on the siren?"

"Funny," said Jay. "You're a funny guy."

Ed checked his gun, started the engine, and quickly drove into the clearing. "I'll go first, he knows me. You cover."

"Gotcha."

Ray Peng stood up when he saw the car and hung up his phone.

"Mr. Peng," said Ed. "It's nice to see you again. This is Detective Jay Finley from the Port Stirling police department."

"I work for Chief Horning," Jay said. He moved briskly toward the porch. "You know, that guy you shot." He glared at Peng, daring him to make a move.

"What are you talking about?" Peng responded. "What is this?"

"Thursday afternoon is what I'm talking about," Jay said. Ed hung back and let Jay get this off his chest. "My boss — and my friend — Matt Horning was shot at his own home. I think there's a chance you might have been on a ship just offshore with a rifle when that happened. Am I correct?"

"Man, you guys are crazy."

"You don't like Matt Horning, do you?" said Jay. "He roughed you up a little. Hurt your feelings, right?"

Peng glanced at Ed. "You need to call this guy off, Lieutenant Sonders. He's nuts."

Ed could see that Peng was rattled. *Probably fears for his other arm.* "He doesn't report to me, Ray."

"I mean it. You need to leave me alone! I let Horning's harassment slide, but I swear I'll report it if you lay a hand on me again."

"Why don't you ask us how Chief Horning is?" Jay asked. "I told you he was shot. Don't you care if he's dead or alive?"

Peng's eyes darted back to Ed. "I just assumed he was killed. Wasn't he?"

Ed said, "We don't know. Where were you Thursday afternoon?"

"I was here."

"Was anyone with you?" Ed again.

"Yeah, a buddy. We were watching football and having a couple of beers."

"Wife and the kids still in Portland?"

"Yeah. They're coming home tomorrow. So, did Horning die?"

Ed ignored the question. "I need the name of your buddy and how to reach him. We're verifying alibis for the time the chief was shot."

"I don't know anything about a shooting," Peng pleaded with Ed. "I swear it. I was home. I've been home all week."

"What do you do here all by your lonesome?" Ed asked. "Besides build guns, that is?"

"I read," Peng stuttered. "I'm a reader. And I like to watch football. Where is Horning? In a hospital or something?"

"We ask questions," Jay said. Loudly. His face was red, and he looked enraged. "Not you, punk. And it would go better for you if you didn't say my boss's name again."

Ray Peng shrunk back toward his front door. "I'm done here, guys. Get a warrant or get off my property."

"You mean Zhang Chen's property, don't you?" asked Jay.

Peng's eyes widened, but he turned and went into his house without saying another word. Slammed the door.

· · ·

"Fun guy," said Jay, back in the car.

"You certainly rattled his cage," said Ed. "Interesting approach."

Jay looked over at him. "What does that mean?"

"It means that I might not have handled it precisely in that manner. However, it appeared to work. Mr. Peng doesn't know if Matt is dead or alive, but he did know that he's been shot."

"How could you tell that?"

"Because he didn't ask for details of the shooting you accused him of. Therefore, he already knew the details. He assumed Matt's dead, but now he's wondering. My guess is he wants to tell someone that Matt might not be dead after all."

"He's probably back on his phone now," Jay said.

"Which means we need an around-the-clock guard on Matt's hospital room, and we needed it an hour ago. Call the Portland chief while I drive and tell him what needs to happen. This is an emergency. I'm going to call my boss, too, and see if we have someone nearby."

"Damn. We should have thought of that this morning," Jay lamented. "I figured with Fern and her parents there, he'd be safe, but you're right, Fern's in no shape to protect him." He took a deep breath. "I blew it, didn't I? Losing my cool."

"Not necessarily," Ed said. "I've been rethinking this, and if they think

Matt is still alive, they might get agitated and sloppy. But we do need extra protection at the hospital."

Jay pressed a button on his phone and said, "Portland Chief Dale Mulrooney".

Jay jiggled one leg while he waited to be connected. "Shit. Shit. Shit," he said.

. . .

"He might not be dead," Ray Peng said into his phone.

"He's dead," said Zhang Chen. "That bitch cop told me."

"Well, the two cops who were with him just paid me a visit and indicated that he might still be alive."

"What did they say?"

"Just that he'd been shot. They wouldn't answer my question if he was killed."

"They're just being coy. Trying to scare you into doing something stupid."

"Shouldn't we check, though? Maybe call your guy and have him find out?"

Zhang Chen thought for a minute. "Why would Detective Perkins tell me he was dead if he wasn't? She is a tricky one, however."

"Maybe she's trying to scare *you* into doing something stupid," Peng offered. "Not that you would, of course," he hurriedly added.

"We do need to know for sure," Chen conceded. "I will continue to lie low and will see if my contact can get the truth for us." He paused. "Detective Perkins and her husband often eat dinner at The Grill in your town on Sunday night. Take your wife and kids there tomorrow and act normal. They do know that there is a connection between us — they discovered that I own your land. So, you need to act normal, as if there is nothing going on. Clear?"

"I understand. How do you know about the Perkins?"

"I know everything I need to know about the local cops."

. . .

When Fern and her parents came back from dinner Saturday night, a heavily armed and beefy Portland Police Bureau officer met them when they got off the elevator on Matt's ICU floor. He checked their IDs.

"What's this about?" asked Fern nervously. She looked at the officer's badge, and added, "Tim?"

Tim was a young guy, probably about twenty-seven. He looked like a cop—hefty upper body, clean-shaven, short, cropped brown hair. "We're just making sure that no one who shouldn't be here approaches your husband's room, ma'am. Now that we know you, you're free to come and go."

"Has there been a specific threat?" Fern asked. Worried.

"No, not that I know of. Our captain had a request from the Port Stirling PD. I'm sure it's just out of an abundance of caution. Please don't worry, and we'll try to stay out of your hair."

Tim pointed down the hallway, where a female officer, also heavily armed, was stationed outside Matt's room. "That's Gabriela. She'll make sure nobody gets into his room. Come with me and I'll introduce you to her."

"No, that's OK," said Fern hurriedly. "You stay here at your post. We'll tell her who we are."

Tim nodded and waved down the hall. Gabriela waved back. Fern walked down the hallway to greet her, instructing her parents to go in the waiting room, which was about halfway between the elevator and Matt's room.

She stuck out her hand at Gabriela and said, "I'm Fern Byrne, Matt's wife." She pointed at his door. "Thank you so much for coming to help us."

"It's no problem. I'm so sorry about your husband." She looked awfully young to Fern. Deep, warm brown eyes, dark hair pulled back in an elaborate bun. Looked a little on the chunky side, but that could've been because of all the gear she was wearing.

"Have you pulled this kind of duty before, Gabriela?" Fern asked her.

"Yes, ma'am. I guarded an important witness in a recent murder trial. I'm good at this," she assured her. "You can call me Gabby." She smiled a confident smile.

"Oh, I wasn't questioning your skills, Gabby." She looked at her directly. "Somebody tried to kill Matt. Once they find out he's hanging on, they may try again. Just want to make sure that you're fully aware of our situation. Also, I was a detective in the PSPD, and whoever our shooter is, there's a chance they may not like me either." She attempted a small smile.

"I know all about you, Fern." She returned her direct look. "I read about you in the Phineas Stuart case. Well done."

"Thanks, I guess. Not my favorite day to recall." Fern, remembering that violent, awful moment in her life, looked down at the floor.

"You did what had to be done. Just like I'll do whatever has to be done if we have any trouble here."

"Thanks, Gabby," Fern croaked, tears threatening again. "I'm going to spend some time with him before I take my parents to the hotel." She nodded at Matt's door.

"I've got your back, Fern." She turned away from her and looked straight ahead with those alert brown eyes. On duty.

FOURTEEN

Sylvia had worked at the Port Stirling police department since way before Matt Horning arrived. In fact, she began her job as an admin assistant shortly after the previous police chief had been hired. He retired after thirty years on the job, but Sylvia was showing no signs of slowing down.

Here she was now, at 7:00 a.m. on Sunday, at her desk, eyes glued to her computer screen. She had risen at 5:30 a.m. and immediately texted Fern:

"Is he still alive?"

She didn't know if Fern would be awake yet, but, of course, she was. She got a reply at 5:38 a.m.

"Yes. I'm at the hospital. Saw him for a few minutes. He's struggling but breathing. Tube."

"Thank God. Kiss him for me."

"Will do. Have u caught shooter yet?"

"Not yet. U take care of chief. We'll catch bad guy."

"Will call you later."

"OK. Headed to office soon. Love you."

"Love you too. Find him, Sylvia."

Sylvia had made coffee and brought it to her desk to wash down the slice of leftover pumpkin pie she was calling breakfast. She looked up the phone number for the Buck Bay Coast Guard commander, but it was still too early to call him. *That damnable ship is the key*, she thought. Ed and Jay had briefed them yesterday on the ship they saw just off the coast in front of Matt's house, and Sylvia had enough to go on to start researching.

She started on the Hong Kong Ship Registry website, and, just like Ed told her, ships registered via them would be flying the national flag of China as well as the HKSR flag. *So, how do I find out who owned this particular ship? Could I possibly get a list of every registered owner and see if anything suspicious jumps out at me? Anyone local or anyone we know? I need to talk to the CG here first before I dive into the can of worms that dealing with the Chinese might be.*

While she waited for a decent hour to phone him, she looked for any assumed business names associated with Ray Peng. There were none, at least, none that she could find. The HK Ship Registry website told her that ship ownership requirements were broad, extending not to just citizens of Hong Kong, but to any company registered as a non-Hong Kong company on Hong Kong's registration, or to a body corporate incorporated in Hong Kong. So, essentially, any company or LLC only had to register in Hong Kong to be eligible under the ship ownership requirements.

She went back into the deep research files she'd kept on Zhang Chen during the Anselmo operation. The billionaire entrepreneur had an extensive portfolio of companies and limited partnerships, and Sylvia knew nine of them. She made a list of the ones she'd verified that Chen had at least a partial ownership or board of directors' role, and created a separate Word doc.

The most substantial business was his headquarters company in Palo Alto, Redfire, valued at $1.6 billion. Next was what appeared to be a real estate holding company, Zhang Chen Properties, for the various commercial and residential holdings Chen owned around the world. That one was valued at $1.1 billion, give or take a few million.

Those two were obvious, so Sylvia started digging into the other seven companies. After a couple of hours, she was forced to admit that there was nothing remotely related to shipping, unless he was trickier than she was. She had worked around all manner of crooks and criminals for decades, and while she might not know all the ways to break the law and get away with it, she knew most of them. *Chen's out of my league, though. I have no idea what you can do internationally with that kind of wealth.*

At 9:20 a.m. she reached for her phone to call Captain Bob Adams, the head of the Buck Bay Coast Guard station. Sylvia figured that normally Adams wouldn't answer his office phone on a Sunday morning, but she knew he'd be taking seriously the issue of that ship slipping out of their grasp.

But her phone rang just as she touched it.

"Sylvia here," she barked into it.

"Hello, Sylvia, this is Joe Phelps. Am I bothering you?"

Sylvia automatically sat up straighter in her chair. An increasingly rare bird in Oregon, she still had respect for the federal government. "No, sir. In fact, you could be just the man I need to talk to. What can I do for you first?"

"I didn't sleep very well," Joe said quietly. "I'm so worried about Matt, and I wondered if you know anything new this morning? I didn't want to bother Fern."

"She and I traded texts at about 5:30 this morning. You weren't the only one having trouble sleeping. We're all just beside ourselves with concern. But Fern told me he made it through his second night at OHSU."

"Oh, that's great. What's his condition?"

"Fern said he's struggling but breathing. They've got him on some sort of tube, and he hasn't regained consciousness yet. His doctor says his condition is still critical."

"Dammit," swore Joe. "I'd hoped he might have woken up late yesterday after the surgery."

"His surgeon told Fern that the forty-eight hours after the surgery—which happened Friday night into early Saturday morning—were the most critical. So, I think that if he makes it through today, he'll have a better chance."

"From your mouth to God's ears, Sylvia. I thought you and Fern were close, so you will be my best contact for tracking Matt's progress."

"We're all close, Joe," she said. Quiet tears rolled down her face. "We're a small team and this is a devastating blow. It's bad, and we might lose him — you need to understand that."

"I do. But I also know how tough your boss is, one of the toughest I've come across and I've been chasing bad actors for a long, long time. And he's young and fit, real healthy guy. People recover from gunshot wounds, and Matt won't go down without a fight."

"I'm praying that's true. And I will keep you posted as I hear more from Portland." She cleared her throat, dabbed at her eyes with a nearby tissue, and said, "Now, let's figure out how we're going to find the shooter. I need your help."

"I'm all yours."

"How can we get a list of all the registered owners of ships from the Hong Kong Ship Registry without starting World War 3 with China?"

"Is that where the ship that Jay and Ed saw is registered?"

"We think so, but they aren't positive. We're going by the flags the ship was flying. Ed got the registration number, but they didn't see any name on it."

"Are they sure it was the People's Republic of China flag?"

"Ed says yes. And our local Coast Guard says they see that flag and the Hong Kong Registry flag more these days than in the past. It's still mainly Panamanian ships around these parts, but a Hong Kong ship is not all that unusual. Can you help me?"

"Yes, I can contact that company in my official capacity and explain that we're looking for one of their registered ships. I wish we had more to go on. This won't be fun."

"It will be more fun than Matt's having right now," she replied with an edge in her voice.

• • •

The county crime team met at noon on Sunday, and Sylvia brought in lunch for them. She knew they would work harder and smarter if they were fed.

There were two new cafes in the old part of town near the wharf that had been built after the tsunami cleanup was complete. Sylvia, along with the city manager's admin, Mary Lou — one of her best friends — felt it was their civic duty as city employees to support the new local businesses whenever they had the chance.

Today she chose the Wave Schmave café because she loved the owner — a New York transplant with a great sense of humor. Sheldon Weinstein never thought he'd leave New York and his second-generation delicatessen, but the pandemic had changed his entire outlook on life. He was now sixty years old, and when he lost his wife in the first bad Covid surge, he wanted a fresh start. Wanted a place with fewer people and better air. He'd been fascinated by the region's history-making earthquake and tsunami and knew there would be plenty of opportunity for new businesses. He was among the first to apply for a building permit, and the residents of Port Stirling had paid back his faith in them. They came in droves.

"How's my girlfriend today?" Sheldon said. He burst through the door of the police squad room bearing sacks of goodies for Sylvia.

"I'm at work on a Sunday. How do you think I am?"

"I always work Sundays, one of my busiest days."

"Who's minding the store?" she asked. "I was expecting Linda to deliver my order."

"We traded jobs because I wanted to see you." He grinned at her.

"You just know a good customer when you see one, and you want to keep me happy, you old fool."

"Guilty as charged. But you look a little glum today. Everything hunky dory?" He set the lunch sacks on the table in the middle of the room.

They didn't want the news about Matt to get out, so she covered as best she could. "I'm fine. Always a bit of a letdown once Thanksgiving is over with."

"I hate that holiday," Sheldon said. "Bad for business. Everybody wants a turkey san, no pastrami. But you, you have my most beautiful pastrami today on my best rye bread."

"And coleslaw? You brought coleslaw?"

"You know it, babe. I brought a lot of it because Sheriff Earl is coming, right? He eats my coleslaw by the gallon."

That got a chuckle from Sylvia. "That does not surprise me."

"Can I set up lunch for your meeting? Where do you want these?"

"That would be nice, Sheldon. The conference room is directly below where we're standing now. Stairs are on your left outside our door. Just set them on the credenza, and I'll take it from there. Thanks."

She turned back to her computer screen, but Sheldon remained standing, not moving.

"Is there something else?" she asked pleasantly.

"Uh, yeah," he stuttered and hesitated. "I was wondering if you might like to have dinner with me tomorrow night. Not at my deli," he quickly added. "Some place nice. Like Whale Cove or Port Stirling Links."

Sylvia stared at him. "A date? You're asking me out on a date?" She was incredulous.

"Well, not exactly a date. Just two friends having dinner," he explained. He ran his hand over his mostly bald head.

"That's a date in my book," she smiled. "I would love to…"

"…But," he said.

"But I'm not sure how my Monday is going to unfold. We're in the middle of something kinda big here, and my presence is needed, I'm afraid. Truly Sheldon, I would love to have dinner with you, but I can't commit to it until I see how today goes."

"Fair enough, but don't forget I asked."

She stared at him. "I'm too old for you, you know. But I'm thrilled you asked, and we will go soon, I promise."

"You're older than me in years," he conceded, "but you're younger in spirit and probably health. I figure it balances out."

Sylvia laughed. "You are a piece of work, Sheldon Weinstein."

• • •

A few minutes before the crime team's noon meeting, Sylvia entered the room and a voice from the far end of the table said, "Hello, Sylvia." Expecting to be the first one there, she jumped and gasped at the voice.

"Why, hello, Mr. Dalrymple," she said, recovering her poise. "I didn't expect you here today. Jeri said she would attend in your place."

"I cut my holiday a little short," he said in a clipped voice. "Sounds like we've got a real mess on our hands. I thought I should be here."

Sheldon had left the lunches on the credenza to her left, and she fussed with them, lining up everything to her satisfaction. "Yes, it's awful," she said quietly, almost inaudible. She didn't trust herself talking.

"I'm sorry about Matt. You must be taking his death hard."

Sylvia paused, with her back turned toward the D.A. *He doesn't know Matt's still alive,* she thought. *Best to keep my mouth shut.* Silently, she nodded and kept about her business.

Jay came in, followed by Patty, Ed, Earl, and Dan McCoy, each one in turn taking their usual seat, human nature being what it is.

"Thought you were gone?" said the sheriff to David Dalrymple.

"I missed you too much, Earl. Had to come home," smiled the D.A. The sheriff didn't smile back.

"Jeri filled in for you yesterday," said Jay.

"Yes, she called me to let me know what's going on," Dalrymple said. "We talked again last night, and I decided I should be here."

"There's lunch for everyone," Sylvia interrupted. "Please help yourselves." She took up her seat in the corner with pad and pen at the ready.

"Thanks, Sylvia," said Jay. "Been over at the Coast Guard station all morning and I'm starved."

"You hungry? What a surprise that is." She smiled.

"You are a queen, Sylvia," said Earl vigorously as he unpacked his sack. "Sheldon's coleslaw!"

"He told me you'd be thrilled."

"OK, people. Let's get started," said Jay. He was uncomfortable in this role, so he just tried to act like Matt would act. "The good news first: Matt made it through the night."

Ed slapped the table with his hand, Patty yelled, "Thank the good Lord!", and Earl teared up, his nose turning beet red.

"Yeah," grinned Jay. "Fern and Sylvia exchanged texts early this morning. He's still in critical condition and the next couple of days are important, but he's holding on so far."

"I don't understand," said Dalrymple. He looked confused. "I thought Matt was killed."

"He should be dead," said Jay. "Gunshot wound to the neck, missed his brain by centimeters, lost a whole lot of blood. Two surgeries. Bernice operated on Thanksgiving night and then made the decision to LifeFlight him."

"Gosh, that's great news," said the D.A. "Jeri indicated he was dead. I'm sorry I misunderstood."

"Honest mistake, David," said Jay.

"Where is Matt now? Where did LifeFlight take him?" asked Dalrymple.

"OHSU in Portland," said Jay. "Bernice felt she couldn't do anything further to keep him alive, and she sent him to the area's top neurosurgeon. Dr. Nathalie Kumar operated on him Friday night, and he's in intensive care now."

"Is Fern with him?"

"Yes. And her parents. They drove up yesterday morning."

"This is such a relief, Jay," said Patty. She turned to Sylvia. "Will you stay in touch with Fern?"

"Yes," answered Sylvia. "She will call me later, she promised. She said to tell you all to find the shooter."

There was a brief silence and then Jay said with conviction, "Yeah, let's do that." He recapped his and Ed's visit to Ray Peng to the team, and Ed added that he'd tracked down Peng's buddy—his alibi for Thursday afternoon during the shooting.

"Of course, his buddy confirmed that he and Ray were watching football at Peng's place, just like he told us," Ed said. "I checked him out and he doesn't have any kind of record. Plus, he seemed sincere. A straightforward kind of guy."

"He could just be a smooth liar," Patty said. "They're out there, you know."

"People lie to us cops?" Ed said wryly. "You've just burst my bubble, Patricia. Seriously, I think he was telling the truth. I also can't see Ray Peng as a sharpshooter."

"I have to agree with Ed," said Jay. "He seems too jittery. And he's averse to violence. He got all agitated when I got after him."

"Not more torture of potential suspects, I hope," Dalrymple said, frowning at Jay. "Jeri told me."

"Ray Peng was not tortured by Matt Horning," Ed said. He pulled himself up to his full height, which was considerable. "I was the only witness to their confrontation, and Matt behaved within the scope of interrogation."

"And I didn't touch him," Jay said. He looked directly at the D.A. "So drop it. Please," he added.

"It's my turn," Patty said to break the silence and the staring. "Earl, Rudy, and I had a conversation with the man himself—Zhang Chen."

"No!" exclaimed Jay. "He's here? In Port Stirling?"

"At his ranch, with his parents. Been here for at least a week, according to his mother," reported Patty. "Who, by the way, is an absolutely charming woman."

"She is nice, isn't she?" said Earl. "He's scary, however."

"How so?" asked Ed.

"Well, first of all, he's about a foot taller than me," said Earl. "And he's got these bones in his face that you could cut cheese with."

"And eyes that look right through you," Patty added. "Like laser beams or something. Eerie. I kept expecting to go up in smoke any second."

"Are you telling me that you drove right up to Chen's house and knocked on his door?" asked Dalrymple. He leaned forward onto the table and grabbed the edges of it. "Without a warrant? Are you nuts, Patty?"

"No, I don't think so," she replied coyly. "We were just doing a property check for a vacant owner. I couldn't have been more surprised when Biyu—that's his mother—opened the door and invited us to come in."

"Please tell me that you did not enter Chen's home," said Dalrymple, bordering on enraged.

"She insisted," Patty said. She shrugged her shoulders. "What was I to do?"

"How did he react?" Dalrymple asked.

Patty and Earl exchanged glances. "Well, it started out OK," said Earl. Patty nodded. "But he got a little ticked off towards the end. We asked him a couple of questions that he didn't much like."

"What kind of questions?" asked the D.A.

"Like where he was on Thanksgiving late afternoon," Patty said. "You know, does he have an alibi during the time Matt was shot. Cop questions."

"I specifically told you, Earl, that you didn't have enough probable cause for a Ray Peng warrant," Dalrymple seethed. "You have even less to justify approaching Zhang Chen's property. You people need to back off before you get all of us sued."

"Excuse me, David," said Jay. "Ray Peng…"

"No, you excuse me!" Dalrymple railed. "You can't go after two Chinese guys just because they're Chinese."

Jay slapped the table. Smack! It was so out of character for the young, easy-going cop that all eyes turned to him, widening. "I was talking," he said loudly, and looked hard at Dalrymple. "You need to shut up and listen for a minute."

Dalrymple leaned back, clasped his hands on his stomach, and rocked his chair. "Go ahead, Detective Finley," he said. It was very unfriendly sounding.

"Somebody shot my boss," Jay said grimly. "The shot came from a ship flying a China flag. Ray Peng has a cache of ghost guns — Matt and Ed saw them. Peng says he made them himself, but Matt didn't believe him. There was a major — major — criminal operation on Zhang Chen's property almost immediately after he bought it last year. Chen owns the land that Peng's house sits on. So, there's a connection there. The only lead we have is that ship. And when we put two and two together, we get a Chinese ship and two first-generation Chinese men who know each other. One of whom we know beats his wife and acquires shadowy guns, and the other one who we suspect may have been the head honcho for one of the worst crimes ever on the west coast. That's what we've got, David, and that's why we asked Jeri to get us search warrants. Has she done that?"

"Now I talk?" Dalrymple said snidely.

"Answer the fucking question, David," said Ed. Also, out of character for Ed to swear. Getting tense in the room.

"She has not. I forbid it," the D.A. said. "I'm upset about Matt, too, and I understand your hunches, but it's not enough probable cause legally to go on. I'll be crucified if I allow a bunch of ticked off police to harass two men just because of their Chinese descent. I'm sorry, but my answer is still no."

FIFTEEN

Sunday late afternoon, just before she was about to take her parents back to the hotel, Fern, with her hand covering Matt's, felt him twitch. She'd been resting in the chair — her chair — next to his bed, and at first, she thought she was dreaming. *No, he definitely moved.*

She leaned in close to his ear and whispered, "Matt. Can you hear me, Matt? It's Fern, honey. Please open your eyes if you can hear me."

She waited.

After about thirty seconds, Matt slowly opened his eyes until they were a tiny slit and blinked twice.

"Welcome back, my love," Fern said, crying, kissing his hand, and touching his arm.

His hand twitched again like he was trying to lift it. She covered it with her hand again and said, "Don't try to move, Matt. You're hurt and you have important machines hooked up to you. Just be still and listen to me, OK? I'm going to stand up and reach beside your head to the call button for the nurse. Everything is alright. You're doing great. Please don't move until the nurse can check on you."

She pressed the button, and the nurse came through the door in about twenty seconds. Gabriela, the cop, came in right behind her, and she spoke first.

"Everything OK in here?" she asked Fern. The nurse moved to Matt's bedside and checked the monitor.

"It's wonderful," gushed Fern. "His fingers twitched, and he opened his eyes."

"His vital signs are good," said the nurse. She smiled at Fern. "I'll call Dr. Kumar—she'll want to see him. He's not ready to go jogging yet, but this is a good sign. Keep him still and I'll be right back. You, out," she said to Gabby.

Fern took up her position in her chair and held tightly onto Matt's hand. Even another darn earthquake would not make her let go.

• • •

Dr. Nathalie Kumar came by at the start of her evening rounds and examined Matt. She reported to Fern and her parents, who waited in the lounge at the doctor's request.

"It's all good news," Dr. Kumar said. "The swelling in his neck and head is reduced. Slightly, but enough for me to tell. He's got some feeling in all of his extremities, and he can respond to an occasional command. He's groggy, of course, and I've given him further sedation. I want him to sleep through the night without any movement so he will continue the healing process."

"Is he going to be OK?" Fern asked and looked into her eyes. "I know you'll tell me the truth."

"I can't take him off the 'critical' designation just yet, but I like Matt's chances much better tonight than I did last night at this time. You should go to your hotel with your parents tonight and get some sleep. He will not wake up until 6:00 or 7:00 a.m. There's nothing here for you to do, and you don't need another night in that uncomfortable chair."

Fern smiled. "It's not so bad."

Dr. Kumar clasped Fern's hands and said, "Go to the hotel. Get some rest. Let us take care of him for a few hours."

Conor Byrne squeezed his daughter's shoulders. "Listen to the doc, Fern. Let's go." Mary Byrne crept into Matt's room and grabbed Fern's coat,

closing his door soundlessly behind her. She smiled at Gabby on her way
out and said, "You'll keep a close watch on the best son-in-law ever, right?"

. . .

As the Chinook County major crime team filed out of Port Stirling's city
hall conference room, Jay shook hands with everyone at the door. Everyone, that is, except the district attorney, David Dalrymple. Him, he nodded at and tried to turn his back on. Dalrymple reached out, put his hand
on Jay's arm and said, "I'm sorry, Jay. I know this is hard for you."

"Yeah, it's hard." He knew he should say something nice, more political
to show the D.A. they were still on the same team, but he didn't feel like
it. Dalrymple waited a split second and then left the room.

Ed lingered behind the others. "I don't know about you, Detective Finley, but I could use a beer. Haven't had one since…"

"Me neither," said Jay. He knew Ed was about to say Thanksgiving Day.
"Sounds good. Either I drink a beer, or I break something."

"Then let's go see Vicky," said Ed. He patted Jay on the back.

. . .

After a quick chat with his buddy, the shooter checked the score of last
night's Canucks vs Kings hockey game, packed his bag and backpack carefully, retrieved his rental car from the hotel parking lot, and headed south
to the U.S. border.

. . .

Although it was only 4:00 p.m, and a Sunday no less, the Whale Cove bar
was packed. Vicky greeted the two cops by saying, "the table in the corner
is just leaving. Let me wipe it down and then it's yours."

Efficiently, she picked up the former customers' drinks, cleaned the
table, and slapped down two coasters. "Have a seat, gentlemen. Where's
your third amigo?"

Jay and Ed traded glances for the third time in the last hour or so. "Who would that be?" Ed stalled.

"You know," Vicky said, "the cute, curly black hair one." Vicky liked Fern a lot and was happy to see she and Matt patch things up and get married, but a piece of her thought, dang, that's a good man getting away. "I suppose his wife won't let him out of the house." She laughed at the thought of the tough police chief taking orders from his new bride.

"He's had an accident and he's in the hospital," Jay muttered.

"What? What happened?"

"He's going to be OK, and we need to keep this quiet for now," Ed said. "But you're a good friend and need to know."

"Damn straight Matt and I are buddies. I was his first friend in Port Stirling," she said, and there was pride in her voice. "He tells me that all the time." She paused. "But you two aren't going to tell me what happened, are you?" She stood with her hands on her hips.

"We would if we could, Vicky," said Jay. "You know that. But the fewer people that know where he is and why, it's better for him. Can you trust me this one time?"

"I trust you all the time, honey," she said and patted the young cop on top of his head. "I'll go fetch your beers." She headed behind the bar, her brown pageboy and animal-print long cardigan moving with her.

"What in the bloody hell are we going to do now?" Jay asked. "We've got a horse's ass for a D.A."

"Agree in full," Ed said. "And he's not going to change his mind. His movie-star jaw was set. I've seen him like this before. He gets all prissy and wants to look like the most moral guy in the room."

"He's afraid he's going to lose the election next year. That's what I think."

"That too. And he might. People in this county are smarter than Dalrymple thinks they are. It's Earl and cops like you, Patty, and Matt they trust to keep them safe, not the politician. And the word is that Jeri might run against him."

"Dangerous on her part," Jay said. "He'd can her in a minute if she does."

"That would make him look bad. Petty and bad. But she might not care if she knows she has some support."

"This county is ready for a female D.A, don't you think?"

"I do. And Jeri was a rock in the aftermath of the earthquake, while he swanned around doing virtually nothing to help people. Folks are going to remember that."

"Man, I hope so. I'd love to get rid of him."

Vicky placed their beers in front of them and said, "Keep me posted on Tex."

"We will," said Jay. "And thanks Vicky. I feel better already." He took a sip of his beer, a Deschutes Black Butte Porter, one of his faves. *Vicky knows everything*, he thought.

"Seriously," he continued, "what are we going to do if we can't access Ray Peng's records or search Chen's house or anything, really? What direction do we go then?"

"It's tough," Ed said. "We can do some discreet tailing of the two of them, although I suspect that Chen is way too smart to get his hands dirty or do anything stupid. I would like to put a bug on his phone, but without the D.A.'s assistance, we don't dare. All we've got for sure is that ship."

"Sylvia told me that she and Joe Phelps talked this morning, and he's going to contact the Hong Kong Ship Registry and see where we stand on that front. She said that Joe wants us to give him the best description of the ship we can. Let's talk about that now and then I'll call Joe later."

"One more thing first. On my way home I'll stop in Twisty River and talk to Earl. Peng and Chen know all of us by now, but they don't know all of the sheriff's deputies, except the two that arrested Peng for DV. Maybe the sheriff can spare a couple of his guys to stake them out."

"Does that put Earl at risk? With Dalrymple, I mean?" asked Jay. "I don't want to get him in trouble."

"He doesn't need to know, does he?"

"What if they get caught?" Jay scrunched his face into a frown. "Peng's just the kind of crybaby who would run to the authorities and report them if he thought someone was following him."

Ed shook his head. "Don't think so. If Peng is involved—and I believe that his collection of ghost guns is proof that he's involved in something—he's not going to want any more encounters with us. Chen's the worry. He knows his rights, and he's savvy. Earl would have to put his best men on him and tell them exactly what they could and couldn't do."

"I don't know," said Jay. "It's risky."

"Letting these two finish the job on Matt is risky." Ed looked him in the eye. "Getting our hands slapped by the D.A? I could give a rip. How about Earl and I handle this? You're a young detective with a bright future, and Earl and I are pretty much untouchable."

Jay took a sip of his beer. "OK, but I'm in charge. It's my boss that got shot, and it's my town. I know that means I will have to make the hard calls as we investigate, and I want to do that, Ed. Understood?"

Ed nodded. "I'll be like the counselor to the president."

Jay laughed. "Yeah, that's what you are." He hesitated. "Talk to Earl. If he agrees with you, give it the green light." Another hesitation. "It occurs to me that Ray Peng doesn't know Patty, right? Put her in civilian clothes and civilian car, and she'd be pretty invisible on a tail, don't you think?"

"Good idea, Mr. President. And if Earl's got an older deputy, that would make one great team."

"Patty's perfect for this, and she's at her best when she's really ticked off. Like she is now."

"Agreed. Poor Ray Peng."

"Now, about that ship," Jay said. "How would you describe it for Joe?" He took out his top bound spiral notebook and wrote "Ship" on a blank page.

"Smallish freighter. Mostly black, but with a red band around the bottom. The color might be important," Ed said, "because I haven't seen many painted like that, and I thought it was distinctive."

"Same here. I don't remember seeing any cargo on board, do you?"

"No, if they were carrying anything, it was below deck. I also didn't see a ship name, at least not on the side of it that was facing us."

"I kinda remember seeing something on the back as it took off north," Jay said. He rubbed the stubble on his chin. "It might have been a name, but I was so upset, I can't recall for sure."

"Do you remember if it was lots of letters or a few?"

Jay thought. "I think it was two rows. A top row with bigger letters, maybe four or five, and below it more letters but smaller. Like six or seven, but because they were smaller, the two rows were the same length. And they were in a different color, maybe yellow or white—it stood out on the black."

"This is good, Jay. The wheelhouse was in the rear, right?"

"Yeah, and it was mostly white, I think. It was maybe two stories high."

"That sounds right to me. It definitely rose up over the deck."

"I remember some windows both on the side by us and at the rear."

"Maybe the windows went all around—360 degrees?" asked Ed.

"Couldn't tell you," Jay said. "But I don't think the top was round, more squared off."

"Do you remember seeing a small boat attached anywhere? Like a dinghy or a tender?"

"I don't think so," Jay thought. "Maybe there was an orange or reddish thing on the back of the wheelhouse down low, close to the deck. I'm not sure."

"Jot that down," Ed said. He wiggled his finger toward Jay's notebook. "You want to tell Joe every hit you got off that ship, no matter how small the detail might be."

"I should've paid better attention."

"Your best friend was bleeding all over his deck, Jay. It's understandable. I'm surprised you remember as much as you do."

Jay's face flushed and his lip quivered, barely, but noticeable. "I don't think I'll ever get over this," he said, looking up at Ed. "Will you?"

"No. Don't think so," Ed answered, his voice a whisper. "If he makes it, maybe someday. But even then, I'm never gonna forget that scene."

SIXTEEN

In the mystic hours of early Monday morning, about 3:00 a.m., the shooter entered the ground floor elevator at OHSU hospital and punched the third-floor button. He was alone, and the lobby was deserted.

Between the second and third floors, he pulled on a black ski mask that covered his face entirely except for his eyes. Taking the FNX-45 Tactical handgun out of the small backpack slung over his shoulder, he tightened the silencer onto it. He pulled on tight-fitting gloves stashed in his pocket, took a stance, and held the gun in front of his body with both hands. He waited for the elevator door to open.

Tim was there, waiting to check IDs of anyone coming onto the third floor. The door opened, and Tim stepped forward saying, "May I check your…"

The gun made a sound like a pen dropped on a desk from an inch above it. Tim took the bullet in the center of his forehead, and he was dead before he hit the floor.

Behind Tim at the nurse's station, one nurse stood from her post. The shooter put a bullet through her heart, figuring that only the cops would be wearing bullet-proof vests. He was right.

The second nurse cowered behind the counter and under the desk. The shooter reached over the counter and shot her, too.

The carnage took all of five seconds. Gabriela watched it unfold from twenty feet away, down the hallway in front of Matt's door. She jabbed at the emergency button on her belt and grabbed her pistol, as she simultaneously rotated to Matt's bed.

Suddenly, Gabriela felt as if she'd been hit in the chest by a sledgehammer. Her vest absorbed the impact, but the shot knocked her down and she was having trouble breathing. *Oh, shit, I'm going to die.* She was momentarily stunned and couldn't move.

The shooter stepped over Gabriela's leg that was sprawled across the doorway to Matt's room. She saw him enter the room, moving noiselessly and with caution.

You're not dead. Do something!

Still, she couldn't seem to force herself to move. She watched the shooter approach Matt's bed. He pulled the tubes out of Matt's nose and mouth, and leaned over him, gun still in front of his body.

From somewhere within her, Gabby summoned an ounce of strength, raised up on her left elbow, and held her right arm as high and as steady as she could manage. She pulled the trigger. No suppressor on her weapon, and the gunshot was deafening in the enclosed space. Her elbow collapsed and she fell back to the floor.

The shooter grabbed the railing of Matt's bed, and looked down at his leg, which was bleeding heavily. He pulled the sheet from the bed, made a running leap on his good leg over Gabriela, and was out the stairwell door in four seconds.

Gabriela passed out, but not before she heard the sound of an alarm coming from Matt's unplugged life-support devices.

. . .

The shooter limped down the two flights of stairs, holding the railing and putting all his weight on his good leg. It wasn't until he exited through a door on the ground floor and found himself in a dark, treed area that he stopped running. He tore off part of the sheet, wrapped it around his wound, fashioning a tourniquet of sorts.

There was another building in front of him across a small grassy area.

He darted across the grass, and then ducked around the side of the building, hugging the wall as he moved away from the door he'd come out. He rounded the next corner and bingo; he was in the forest that he knew would lead to the miles of parks and more forests that surrounded the hilltop hospital. He would find a hiding place until dawn, and then figure out what to do.

. . .

The hospital security that had been summoned by Gabriela's belt button found a horrific scene on the third floor. Three dead, Gabriela passed out, and Matt in his blood-soaked bed, appearing lifeless. ER physicians had also come running from the ground floor, when one of them heard what sounded like a gunshot above them.

One of them tended to Gabriela, who came to almost immediately. "Ow," she said when the doc took off her shirt and Kevlar body armor. She would later discover that even with the ballistic vest, she had sustained two broken ribs. She could expect major-league bruising and a healing period, but she would be fine. At least, physically.

"In here!" yelled one of the ER doctors at Matt's bedside. He was normally calm which is what made him good at his job, but this scene had him a little panicked. He knew immediately what had happened—Matt's life-support had been removed, and that meant he wouldn't survive long. They had to work fast. "Help me now! In here!"

. . .

The shooter stopped to rest under a couple of huge ferns that provided a roof of sorts. He unwrapped the sheet over his wound, took a small flashlight out of his backpack and surveyed the damage. It was deeper than a flesh wound but had missed the bone. It would need medical attention at some point, but, for now, he re-wrapped it, tightly tying up a clean part of the sheet. He swallowed three Advil from his backpack, enough to deaden some of the pain but still allow him to function.

He rested for about ten minutes, but then he knew it was time to move to Plan B of his getaway. It was only a question of time before the cops would be out with their damned dogs. He knew what he had to do next was going to hurt like hell considering his leg, but there was no choice. It was the only way to freedom.

. . .

Fern was woken by the ringtone on her phone. She flailed for it, coming out of a deep sleep. The time on her hotel room's nightstand clock read 5:08 a.m.

"Hello," she mumbled.

"Mrs. Horning, it's Nathalie Kumar at OHSU."

Fern froze. "Oh, no," she cried into the phone.

"No, no," Dr. Kumar said hurriedly. "He's OK. He's alive. But there's been an incident, and we need you to come up here as soon as you can."

"What kind of incident?" asked Fern, now fully awake.

"There was an attempt on your husband's life, but the ER physicians got to him in time, and he's stable. He is, in fact, asking for you."

"He's talking?"

"Sporadically, and it's an effort for him. But he has said your name twice now. It's clear he wants to see you."

"What happened?" She pulled the blanket up under her chin, suddenly chilled.

"I don't know all the details, but there was a shooting on the third floor. It would be best if you could come soon and talk to the police. Do you want me to call your parents and wake them?"

"Oh my God. No, I'll wake them," Fern said decisively. "We're sharing a two-bedroom suite, and they're just across the living area from me. We'll be there as soon as we can get dressed and in the car."

"Good. I'll tell the police you're on your way. Please be careful leaving your hotel." She hesitated. "The gunman got away."

Fern's body shook intensely. "Dr. Kumar?"

"Yes?"

"Thank you. You're a rock star in my book."

Fern felt the warm smile coming from the other end of her phone.

• • •

The night was heavy with cloud cover and a soft drizzle of rain. Without the moon and stars, and with still two hours until sunrise, it was pitch dark as Fern and her parents drove up the hill to the hospital.

Conor deposited his wife and daughter in front of the entrance, and then drove to the car park. Fern and Mary were met by several Portland police officers, along with four hospital security guards who formed a protective circle around the two women.

Fern explained who she was to the lead officer, and she and her mother were taken to a small room off the hospital lobby. The officer explained what they knew about what had happened, based on Gabriela's account. Obvious that they were mother and daughter, both women gasped and brought their hand to their mouth.

"Are Tim and the two nurses dead?" asked Fern. The officer had tried to be sensitive telling his story, but the result was that he was somewhat vague.

"I'm afraid so. They never had a chance against the shooter."

"So, it was a professional," Fern said.

"It has all the markings of a pro, yes," answered the cop. "If the second officer had not been wearing a vest, we never would have known what happened. No one saw him on the way in or out."

"Is she alright?" Mary asked. She'd grown fond of Gabriela in the short period.

"She's tough and she'll be fine."

"Was Gabriela able to describe the shooter at all?" asked Fern.

"Somewhat. He — and she's certain it was a male — was wearing a ski mask and a hat, so all we know are general things, like approximate height and weight."

"And what are those?"

The officer looked at Fern. "Don't you want to go up now and see your husband first?"

"I want to catch whoever just made a second attempt to kill him," Fern said, steel in her voice. "Please tell me what you can about his description."

The officer cleared his throat and shuffled his feet. "Male, age unknown, although he moved more like a middle-aged man than either younger or older. About five foot nine inches, slender build. Gabby didn't see his eyes before he shot her."

"Hair color?"

"She couldn't tell for sure, but said she got a hint of light hair, for some reason."

"What was he wearing?"

"Jeans—blue—dark sweater and black jacket. Black ski mask topped with a dark green Ducks beanie with a yellow O. She doesn't remember his shoes."

"Gloves?"

"Yes, black."

"Was he completely covered with clothing? Any tattoos or anything else identifying?" asked Fern.

"Covered. No skin showing, only his eyes."

"Where did Gabriela hit him?"

"Left leg, upper thigh, she thinks. She blacked out after she shot him. Didn't see him leave, so we don't know how bad he is. Limping probably."

"Did he say anything?"

"Not a word. Let his weapon do all the talking." The cop shook his head. "Awful scene."

"Did you bring in dogs?"

"Yes, ma'am. About an hour ago."

Fern looked at her watch. "So about 4:30?"

"Correct."

"He had over an hour's head start then?"

"I'm afraid so. The dogs were asleep, too. He picked a good time."

"Maybe," said Fern in an icy tone, "but he picked the wrong man."

SEVENTEEN

Fern took Matt's hand in hers and leaned in gently. "I'm here, honey. Everything is going to be OK."

He squeezed her hand, weakly but she could feel the pressure. Slowly, his eyes opened.

"Fern," he murmured, and then closed his eyes again as if talking were too much effort.

"I'm here. Don't try to talk if it hurts."

He laid there for about thirty seconds, and then his eyes opened again. "Get him," he rasped.

She moved even closer to his ear. "Oh, I will get him. Did you see him, Matt? Squeeze my hand once if you did."

He squeezed.

"Will you be able to identify him?"

Another pause and then, "No," he croaked.

"OK, I'm going to ask you some questions. If the answer is yes, squeeze my hand, if no, don't squeeze," Fern said. "Ready?"

Squeeze.

"Was it a male for sure?"

Immediate squeeze.

"Was he Chinese?"

Nothing.

"I'm going to ask you that question again, honey. Was he Chinese or Asian?"

Still nothing.

"Was he a white male?"

Immediate squeeze.

"Did you see his eyes?"

Squeeze.

"Were they brown?"

Nothing.

"Were they blue?"

Squeeze.

"OK, a white male with blue eyes. Is that right?"

Squeeze.

"Did you see his hair? Even a wisp or any stubble around his mouth?"

Squeeze.

"Was it brown?"

Nothing.

"Was it blonde?"

Squeeze.

"You're doing great. Just a couple more and then you have to rest," Fern said. "I need your best guess regarding his age. Think of how he moved and acted. Was he over twenty years old?"

Squeeze.

"Over thirty?"

Squeeze.

"Over forty?"

Squeeze.

"Over fifty?"

Nothing.

"So probably in his forties?"

Squeeze.

"OK, I'm going to call Jay and give him this info, and I'll also alert Joe. Since I'm in Portland with you, I'll work with the police department here, too."

"No," he said softly. "Go. Port Stirling."

"You want me to go home? Why?"

Matt closed his eyes again for a moment and then appeared to gather himself. "Peng," he said.

"Ray Peng?"

He squeezed her hand.

"You think Ray Peng is involved with your shooting?"

Another squeeze.

"Chen," he said, and collapsed back into his pillow.

"Zhang Chen, too?"

Nothing, and his eyes closed.

"I can't leave you," Fern cried. "I can't."

But she was talking to herself. Matt was out again.

. . .

About 4:00 a.m. and after his brief rest in the woods to care for his leg, the shooter made his careful way toward the upper tram terminal. Because of OHSU's awkward location on top of Marquam Hill, and because over 20,000 people a day visit it, the tram was built to ease congestion on the only two roads leading to it. Connecting to the South Waterfront area of Portland, the tram is one of the few commuter trams in the U.S.

He stayed in the trees between the hospital and Terwilliger Blvd, avoiding Campus Drive. It was rough terrain, and he had to use his flashlight in the ink black night. He would stop every few steps to listen for dogs, but nothing yet.

He knew the cops would find his rental car, but there was nothing he could do about that. By now, the roads off this hill would be blocked. The tram was his only hope of getting down into the city and disappearing. But he couldn't just buy a ticket and waltz on when it started operating at 5:30 a.m. Desperate times called for desperate measures.

Time to let out my inner James Bond.

. . .

Fern kissed her husband tenderly on his forehead and crept out of his room. Dr. Kumar was talking with Fern's parents in the visitor lounge.

"Change of plans," Fern said brusquely to her father. "We're going home."

"What?" said Conor.

"Matt wants me to go home and find who did this to him. So that's what I'm going to do. Is this wise, Dr. Kumar? I'll do whatever you think is best."

"I think your husband is a smart man," Dr. Kumar said. "We believe he is past the critical stage, and that he will recover."

Fern and her parents cried and hugged.

"The fact that he could breathe on his own during the minutes that he was disconnected from the machine is a very good sign. He's still struggling as you could probably see for yourself, and we'll keep his support going for a few more hours. But I'm going to move him from Level 3 ICU down to Level 2 later today. He'll still need close, frequent monitoring and will have a nurse nearby. He'll probably need some supplemental oxygen. But mainly, we need to keep him quiet, let him rest, and his body will do the rest."

"Thank you thank you thank you," said Fern, and gave her a hug, too. "Best news ever!"

"You should go home, at least for a few days," said the doctor. "He's not going anywhere for at least two weeks, and there's no reason for you to be here all that time. Go do what you need to do, and then come back. I will call you with regular updates."

"Alright," said Fern. Decision made.

"And Fern?" said Dr. Kumar. "I would like you to find whoever came in here, our sanctuary, and did this horrible thing. For my nurses, and for the policeman who gave their lives to this monster. I don't know your exact role in all this, but find him, please, and bring him to justice."

"She will," said Conor Byrne, and his wife nodded in agreement. Angry. Grateful. Exhausted.

. . .

Still in the dead of night, the shooter made it to the tram terminal. There was nobody around, as he suspected. There were only two roads off this hill, and he knew the cops would be allotting their manpower to them.

Now for the fun part.

Painstakingly and painfully, he climbed to the top of the roof housing the vehicle itself. He pulled himself up supports and utilized the walkway. Once on the roof of the terminal, he carefully lowered himself over the edge on the open end, and then dropped the ten feet or so onto the tram roof. He swore under his breath at the pain when his bad leg hit. Crawling along the roof, he reached the rear of the car. In the design, the rear was a foot or so lower, and he could wedge up against the higher part, and wrap himself around the arm that connected the car to the wires. If he could hold onto the arm when it started moving, he thought he could ride it to the lower terminal. *Almost to the lower terminal, that is*, he thought.

Nothing to do now but wait.

. . .

Fern knew she needed to call her boss, Joe Phelps, but she kept putting it off until she thought she could make it through the conversation without crying. With Dr. Kumar's latest report, now was the time. She felt stronger now that she and her parents were in the car headed down I-5 to Port Stirling, and she knew that Matt would be taken care of.

The Portland police were regrouping, and hospital security had beefed up considerably. When Fern left OHSU early Monday afternoon after a quick visit to Matt's room, they were installing metal detectors at the main entrances. *Too bad they didn't do that earlier*, she thought. *Hospitals are under-protected.* She was tempted to hire a private security guard as well, but the Portland police bureau chief assured her in a phone call this morning that his department was boiling at the shootings of Tim and Gabriela, and they would not be surprised again. There would be a hefty contingent of PPB officers all over OHSU. She had to trust that the cops would get the job done this time. She was one of them, after all.

"Dad, I'm about ready for a pit stop," Fern said now from the back seat.

"Next time we see a rest stop, could you pull in?" They were just north of Eugene.

"Great minds think alike," said Mary. "I need one, too. Too much coffee this morning."

"Can you ladies make it to Gettings Creek rest area? It's only about six miles, I recall. It'll be faster than pulling off in Eugene."

Conor pulled into a parking spot, and Fern wandered over to the grassy, treed picnic area and dialed Joe's number. It was a chilly, overcast day, and the rest area was nearly deserted on this Monday following Thanksgiving weekend. Only a few long-haul trucks were parked opposite the car parking area. She zipped up her down jacket and turned the collar up around her neck.

"Joe, it's Fern."

"If you're calling me, it's either really bad news or really good."

"It's good. Matt's going to be alright. His doctor says she's moving him out of ICU, and down one care level. He'll be in the hospital for another two weeks or so, but she expects him to fully heal."

Joe let out a long "Whew."

"Yeah, what a nightmare. And there's more," she said.

"Now what?"

"There was a second attempt on his life at 3:00 this morning." She recounted what happened.

"Holy crap. What in the hell is going on?"

Fern could hear the exasperation in his voice. "That's what I'm about to find out. We're headed home for a few days while Matt mends. He wanted me to go. He believes Ray Peng and Zhang Chen are involved, and he wants me to get them."

"I think it's tied to this ghost gun issue, and I agree with Matt that Peng is at the heart of it. If he was so nervous about Matt after he and Ed discovered the guns at his place to try to kill him twice, he's got to be protecting something big. And no one I've talked to seems to think Peng has mastermind leadership skills, so he's likely working with someone."

"Matt repeated "Chen" more than once to me. He's convinced, but I don't know why. Except that we all believe he had a role in the Anselmo case."

"Agreed," said Joe. "Can't decide if I'm being racist or pragmatic to think there's a Chinese connection between Peng and Chen. But I'm leaning toward pragmatic because of the real estate link between them."

"I'll be having a chat soon with both of them. OK with you?"

"In what capacity?" Joe asked. "Officially, it's not part of your job. You're the Public Affairs liaison for the west coast, remember?"

I knew he'd say that, Fern thought. "What would you have me do then?"

"Look, I understand how you feel. You want to rip these guys a new one, but you're undercover for a reason. It gives you more latitude. Marching in with your green eyes blazing is not the right move here. I'd like to see you shadow Chen for a while first. You know he's in Port Stirling currently, right?"

"Yes, Sylvia told me yesterday afternoon after Patty and the sheriff had reported at their meeting. That's an interesting fact, don't you think?"

"I do. At Sylvia's request, I'm contacting the Hong Kong Ship Registry. If we learn that Zhang Chen owns a ship registered with China, life will get even more interesting." He paused. "I'm sure his property has bad memories for you, but I really think the best use of your time right now is to snoop around there. But, by God, Fern, you'll need to be super careful. Did you get any training at FLETC on covert surveillance?"

"Yeah, it was great," Fern replied. "Wow, that seems like a lifetime ago, and it was only a few days ago."

"It should go without saying that we're good with you taking time to recover from these horrifying few days. You know that?"

"I know it and I appreciate it, Joe. But the difference between yesterday and today for me is night and day. Yesterday I thought he was going to die, today I'm confident I will get my husband back. I want him to be proud of me when that day comes soon."

"OK, you know what to do. If there's a ghost gun operation in Port Stirling and Zhang Chen is involved, I want to be the first to know. If we can't take him out for international drug smuggling and human trafficking, maybe we can get him for murder."

"You will be."

"Watch your back, Fern. I mean it. That shooter is still out there somewhere."

EIGHTEEN

Jay welcomed Fern home with an enthusiastic bear hug. "I'm so happy to see you. And, just, you know, so happy." He was beaming.

"I'm happy, too. What a relief, huh?" Fern grinned back at him. "Your boss will be back and barking orders at you in no time. Betcha can't wait."

"I can't," Jay said. "And before you start barking orders at me, I have something to tell you. I'm moving in." They were standing in the foyer of Fern's home. Her parents had dropped her off, and Jay came to greet them.

"Moving in where?"

"Here," he said firmly. "Just for a few days or until the Portland police catch your gunman."

"Don't you need to be invited to come and live with me?" Fern said, a sly smile forming.

Jay shook his head. "Not this time. If that madman makes his way to Port Stirling again, and I let something bad happen to the boss's wife, he will have my head on a platter. I'll be in your downstairs guest room tonight. Will you be here later to let me in? About 6:00 p.m? Don't make this harder than it is, Fern — my mind's made up."

She knew it was pointless to argue with him. And it wasn't a bad idea — backup.

"At least let me see if the sheets are clean and you have fresh towels."

"Not necessary. You're talking to the guy who spent last night on the floor of Matt's office in city hall."

"You didn't really," Fern said.

"Yep. Trying to figure out what he would do if he were me."

"This is all more than you bargained for, isn't it?" Fern said. *He looks so young*, she thought. *My heart breaks for him.*

"It's tough," Jay said. "One minute I'm fishing with my best friend, and the next he's bleeding all over the place and dying. And then I'm trying to knock some sense into our D.A, who, in case you hadn't noticed, is a total horse's ass."

"I noticed. What's Dalrymple done now?"

"It's more what he hasn't done," Jay told her. "He won't approve warrants for us to search Ray Peng and Zhang Chen. Won't let us go into their homes for a physical search and won't allow access to their phone or financial records. Says it's racist and he'd be hung out to dry if we failed to find anything concrete. Says we don't like Chen because we couldn't prove he was in on the Anselmo operation. I won't give up, but we're kinda at a dead end."

Fern stared at him, her face taking on a rosy glow with the addition of the two red circles on her cheeks. Jay knew her well enough to know those two red cheeks meant trouble for someone.

"When's your next team meeting?"

Jay looked at his watch. "In about forty minutes — 4:00 p.m. We're meeting each day so everybody stays in the loop. Gotta run." He opened the front door and then turned back to her. "Towels would be good — I could use a shower."

. . .

The 5:30 a.m. — first tram of the day — had started to move. *Here we go*, he thought. He hung on to the arm above the car with every ounce of energy he could muster. Just beyond the terminal barn, it made a sudden dip that almost tossed him off. *That's probably the worst. Just hang on and don't look down for a while.*

Even though the first light moment before dawn was still almost an hour away, he'd watched the frantic activity from his lofty perch — the roadblocks, the car-by-car searches on Sam Jackson Park Road, SW Gibbs, Campus Drive, and Terwilliger, along with the on-foot searches through the woods surrounding OHSU. Their efforts had turned up nothing. He had vanished into thin air, like a phantom.

Indeed, he had. But now it was time to reconnect with the ground. The tram was approaching the lower terminal at South Waterfront. Just before it entered the terminal barn, he let go of the arm and slid off the side of the car, landing hard on the pavement about fifteen feet below.

As he dropped past the car's windows, it looked to him as if the tram was empty. *Finally, a lucky break.* Gingerly, he rose from the ground in serious pain. There appeared to be no one around at all. *Guess no one goes to work early on Monday morning anymore.* He hurriedly pulled off the black ski mask, stuffed it in his pack, and limped away from the lower terminal, walking as fast north on Moody Avenue as he could without drawing attention, and as fast as his bloody leg would allow. In a few minutes he was on the Tilikum Crossing Bridge and would soon be absorbed into the city's Central Eastside district on the other side of the Willamette River.

He ducked into an all-night café on Grand Avenue that he remembered from his musician days, and cleaned up in their bathroom, locking the door once alone inside. After he tended to his wound, he pulled out a white tee, grey jacket, new black jeans, and a Blazers cap from his backpack, and replaced them with his bloody jeans, black jacket, sweater, and Oregon beanie. There were some small splatters of blood on his shoes, but he couldn't do much about that other than dabbing at them with cold water, as they were his only pair. He would ditch the clothes later today as he made his way further east from the tram.

But first, how about some breakfast? All that energy expended had made him ferociously hungry.

• • •

The Monday meeting of the Chinook County major crime team was called to order at 4:05 p.m. by PSPD Detective Jay Finley, filling in for Chief Matt Horning. Present were Sheriff Earl Johnson, Detective Patty Perkins, OSP Lieutenant Ed Sonders, district attorney David Dalrymple, Buck Bay Chief of Police Dan McCoy, PSPD's Sylvia Hofstetter, and joining them for the first time this week Dr. Bernice Ryder, Chinook County Medical Examiner.

"I know we — thankfully — don't have a body," Bernice said pulling out a chair around the big table, "but I decided to come today anyway. I want to know what you excellent cops are doing to find whoever shot up my patient." She looked sharp and professional in a short red jacket, crisp white blouse, and a black pleated skirt. Only dangly out-of-place earrings that looked like common road rocks gave away her inner Frances McDormand.

"It's good to see you, Bernice," said Jay, turning to his right to greet her. "And you picked the right meeting to join us," he smiled broadly. "I have good news about your patient."

"I know," she grinned. "I talked to Dr. Kumar at OHSU earlier today. Wasn't sure if you knew yet."

"You wanna share it with the rest of us?" said the sheriff. Gruffly.

Between them, Jay and Bernice reran the conversations with Dr. Kumar and Fern. Matt had been moved out of ICU and his condition was improving. Jay also filled in the team on the events of last night in Portland. All were properly horrified, and being cops, had lots of questions.

"The shooter got away?" repeated Ed, incredulous. "In Portland, with all the manpower and resources in that department? Are you kidding me?"

"And that hospital sits on top of a hill without a lot of roads in and out," added Bernice. "Why didn't they just set up immediate roadblocks?"

"They did," Jay said. "Fern told me that the hospital security was slow to respond, but the Portland police got there fast and took over. They have no idea how he got off that hill, but they're convinced he did."

"Do we know for sure it's a male?" asked Dalrymple.

"Yes," said Jay. "Matt was able to confirm some details about him with Fern before she headed home. All we know is the shooter was a white male, blue eyes, maybe in his forties, and maybe blond. Probably limping after a shot to his left leg."

"So, not Chinese?" Ed asked.

"Doesn't sound like it," said Jay. "But nobody except a drugged Matt really saw him. The cop guarding his door who got off the shot was wounded herself and passed out. Apparently, she remembers what he was wearing, but didn't get a good look because of the ski mask in the split second before she was shot. I've got a call in to talk with her as soon as she comes out of sedation. She's going to be fine."

"Did he say anything?" asked the D.A. "To Matt or to the police officer?"

"Not that we know," Jay said.

"Anyone could walk into my hospital at any time," said Bernice, "especially at three a.m. and do exactly the same thing as this guy. We need to do more to protect hospitals, we're just too vulnerable."

"I've been saying that for years," grumbled the sheriff. "There never seems to be enough cash in the budget. Maybe that will change when this story gets out."

"What's bugging me," said Patty, "is why it's so dang important to kill Matt. What's he seen or what does he know? Why go to all this danger and risk to eliminate him? What's at stake?"

"Yeah, that's got me going too," said Ed. "But it's clear he's in somebody's way. And I think there's a good chance that they were trying to take out Jay and me, too, in the initial hit on Matt."

"Like they wanted to cut out the heart of local law enforcement," mused the sheriff. "Something's up. It reeks of high stakes." He drummed his fingers on the table. "Where do we go from here?"

"We're trying to track the ship, and Joe's contacted…"

The door to the War Room opened behind Jay after three quick knocks, delivered with some force. He spun around to see Fern walk in.

"Fern!" the cry went up from around the table.

She smiled shyly and said, "Alright if I join you? I know I'm not officially on the team anymore."

Ed jumped up and pulled out the empty chair next to him. "You're always on this team, lady. Have a seat."

Fern sat and said, "Thanks, Ed. I don't want to interrupt, but I do want to thank some people. First, Ed and Jay. Matt wouldn't be alive without your quick thinking and action. If he'd been alone on our deck…well, let's not go there. And Bernice, your quick action and your skills got him through that dreadful first night. And if you hadn't insisted on transferring him to OHSU, he probably wouldn't have made it. Thank you, all. You gave me back my life, and I owe you."

"You don't owe us a thing," Ed said. Murmurs of agreement broke out around the table. "We're so glad you're home, even if it's just for a couple of days. You can help us figure out what to do next to catch whoever is using your husband for target practice."

Fern tensed and they could see it. A change in her demeanor.

"My boss, Joe Phelps, and I believe whatever is going on might be tied to the ghost guns discovery. Matt thinks it, too. We need to start with Ray Peng and Zhang Chen—those were Matt's specific instructions to me. David, we need access to those two, especially to Peng since that's where Matt and Ed saw the guns."

"She's right," Earl said to the D.A, staring hard at him across the table. "This began almost the day we arrested Peng for beating up his wife. You may be nervous about him, but I'm telling you he's the key."

Dalrymple shifted in his chair. "Look, I trust you guys. I know you think he's somehow involved here, but you don't have enough to go on. We're not going to harass him any further unless you bring me more evidence."

In an instant Fern was out of her chair and leaning over the table toward the D.A. in a menacing fashion. She pounded a fist on the table right in front of him and said, "Listen, you sonofabitch," she growled, "someone has tried to kill my husband, not once but twice, and you WILL NOT stand in our way. We're going to do whatever it takes to catch whoever is guilty, and your roadblock days are at an end! Do you understand me?" She leaned even closer to him, more than halfway across the big table, glaring. Her auburn hair pulled loose from behind her ears and was swinging wildly in front of her face.

Dalrymple paled and pushed his body away from the table with outstretched arms. Away from this bullying harridan. He composed himself. "I know you're upset, Fern. We all are. We hate that this has happened to you and Matt. But it doesn't change the facts of this case. We can't…"

Fern pounded her fist again, still standing. "The facts of this case are that we only have three leads. Number one," she held up a finger, "the ship flying the Chinese flag that may or may not be owned by local landowner Zhang Chen. Remember him?" she yelled at Dalrymple. "He's probably the guy who had me kidnapped. Number two" — another finger — "Matt and Ed were witness to Ray Peng's ghost guns collection, and Number three" — she pounded on the table again instead of holding up a third finger — "Zhang Chen is conveniently in Port Stirling, and coincidentally owns the property beneath Ray Peng's house. They're involved, David, and you need to get with the program before there's a successful third attempt on Matt's life. Or on Ed or Jay. Actually, I'm probably next."

"Over my dead body," said Ed, next to her. He pulled on her arm, urging her to take her seat. To Dalrymple he said, "We're going to do our jobs, David, whether you help us or not. It would be easier if you did your job and helped us. Perhaps my boss, you know, the head of the Oregon State Police and close confidant of the governor, might help you see the light. Huh?"

"And my REAL bosses," said Sheriff Earl, who technically reported to the district attorney, "the great people of the county of Chinook, aren't going to like it one little bit if word gets out that our own D.A. impeded the investigation of the near-killing of one of our local heroes."

Dalrymple shot his cuffs, sat up straight in his chair and said, "I can see that you're all united in an effort to ignore the Constitution of the United States of America. I will think about it overnight and see what I can do to help you." He took a much-needed sip from the water glass in front of him.

Jay, paralyzed by the near violence in his own conference room, cleared his throat and said, "Sylvia, can you tell us what you've found out about the ship that Ed and I saw off the coast at Matt's house?"

She did.

NINETEEN

Matt woke up. It was dark except for the machinery next to his bed that blinked their annoying blinks all night long. He looked around and could tell that he was in a different room. *Does this mean I might actually live?*

His memory of last night was dim, but it was there. *Someone tried to kill me. Again. What is going on? Where's Fern? Oh, that's right, I sent her home. She'll find out who did this, and they'll be lucky if there's not a fireplace poker nearby.* He laughed, but it hurt his head and especially his neck.

That guy. That guy. Hired killer. A pro. I could tell by the way he moved. He was working. On a job. To eliminate me. Why? Because I saw Ray Peng's ghost guns. Only thing that makes sense. Chinese connection? Ship close to my house? Past case? Jack Bushnell? Octavio's friends? Dianne Carmichael? Hates my guts.

Too much effort to think. Matt closed his eyes and went back to sleep.

* * *

"I'm not embarrassed," Fern said. She was belligerent. She and Jay were in a booth at Whale Cove. Neither felt like cooking dinner on this wet, cold, miserable Monday night.

"You shouldn't be," Jay said. "He got what was coming to him. But it did kinda nuke my meeting."

"I'm sorry about that," she said. The remorse was real. "I want you to have a chance to do your job. It's what Matt would want. It's just that Dal-rymple is being so unreasonable."

"He's always in our way and slows us down, but this," Jay said, shaking his head. "This reluctance to let us look at Peng and Chen leaves us in nowheresville. The ship is our only lead. Otherwise, we'll pound the pavement and see if there's any scuttlebutt. Do you think it's worth talking to some of the principals in any of our past cases that Matt was involved in?"

"Absolutely. At least find out where people were when he was shot, like Patty and Earl did with Zhang Chen, and you did with Ray Peng." Fern took a big gulp of the Chardonnay that Vicky sat down in front of her. "Mmm, this is good," she said, looking up at her friend.

"I wondered if you'd notice the difference," Vicky smiled. "With the holidays coming and tourists arriving, we decided we needed to up our wine game. The Chamber of Commerce tells us that Port Stirling is booked solid for over three weeks, starting the weekend before Christmas, and extending into the week following New Year's. And they told us to expect it to continue because of the new Native American lost city exhibit — it's really a draw."

"That's good news," Jay said. "An economic jolt in the arm."

"How's Tex doing?" she asked Fern. "I figure if you're here, he must still be in the hospital but doing OK. Right?" Vicky looked worried.

Fern glanced at Jay, not knowing how much Vicky knew. Jay said, "He's doing better, but we still can't talk about it."

"Does anyone else know about Matt?" Fern asked her.

"No, I don't believe so," Vicky said. "Folks have been doing the Thanksgiving thing — nobody's paying any attention to you cops. But you'll have to say something soon now that people are back at work today. If he's not in the office, word will spread. You know how it is around here."

"Oh, we know," said Fern. She smiled a tight smile. "Vicky's right, Jay. You're going to have to put out a release probably tomorrow."

"I have no idea what to say," Jay said.

"Something like "Chief of Police Matt Horning has been injured and will be taking some time off while he heals." You don't need to go into a lot of detail," Fern advised.

"She's right," said Vicky. "It's nobody's business what happened to him, including mine, and I'm guessing you have your reasons for keeping it quiet." She wiped her hands on the front of her apron. "I need to get back to work."

Fern reached out and grabbed her hand. "It is your business. You're his friend. And I will tell you all the details as soon as it's safe to do so. Matt would want you to be in the loop."

"Thanks, honey. Means a lot." Both women were teary.

Vicky retreated, and with a remote, turned down the volume on the Monday Night Football game playing on the TV set over the bar.

Jay said, "Back to work. Let's make a list of everyone we can think of who might have it in for Matt. Tomorrow morning I'll organize it, and we'll get our people out talking to them. At a minimum, we can start a chart of where people were on Thursday afternoon and start checking alibis."

"I'd put the remaining Bushnell family members on the list," Fern said, thinking. "We pretty much ruined their life in Port Stirling, and the parents, at least, probably aren't fond of Matt's role."

"Are you kidding me?" Jay said. His eyebrows shot up. "I don't see it that way at all. Yeah, we got to the truth, but surely, they'll thank us for that in the long run."

"A divorce, resignation for the mayor, and almost forced to move the family out of town?" Fern said. "Human nature would almost require they blame someone other than themselves. Matt's the perfect scapegoat. Is Jack Bushnell still in the state hospital?"

"As far as I know," Jay said.

"Let's make sure," Fern said. She twitched in her chair. "I know he was sick, but that kid scared the living daylights out of me."

"You'd think they would let us know if he were released," Jay said, now nervous himself. "I'll check tomorrow. Who else?"

"Well, the Anselmo raid had to put a target on Matt's back. I'll call and talk to one of the guys we captured—I spoke to him with Matt that night. He's in the state pen in Salem, and he'll remember me. I'll see if he's heard any buzz."

"What about the Carmichaels? They were totally pissed off at what Matt and Earl did to their family's reputation."

Fern shook her head. "Angry enough to risk ruining what's left of it by killing the town hero? Can't see it."

"I'll ask Patty to interview Dianne and Nick anyway. If only to cross them off my list. What about our favorite geologists? A couple of them are still in town."

"Don't remind me," she shuddered. "They're certainly worth talking to because they're a bunch of gossips. I'm not doing them, though."

"They're all afraid of you anyway," Jay laughed.

"True." She took a sip of wine and then said, "What about Texas? Do you think we should look into any old grievances when he was in Plano?"

"Oh my god," Jay said suddenly. "I forgot all about Larry and Beverly! Have you talked to them? Do they know what's happened?"

Fern patted his hand. "Relax. My dad's been in constant communication with them. I talked to Beverly on my way here this morning to give her the good news. They're going to come out now. They'll stay with him until I go back later this week."

"Whew, what a relief. I can't believe I forgot that. I'm no good at this."

"Stop that right now," Fern said sternly. "You are good at this, and you're doing what needs to be done. All while you're traumatized yourself. This is hard stuff, Jay. You're functioning at a high level, especially considering that you and Ed might have been targets, too."

"I try to not think about that."

"Good. Keep doing that."

Vicky put a plate of Dungeness crab cakes in the middle of their table — they would share them. Fern got a beautifully prepared Pacific Ling Cod with broccoli grown in the Twisty River Valley. Jay, renowned for his appetite, only ordered a bowl of clam chowder and a side of garlic bread. He hadn't had his usual appetite since Thursday night.

• • •

The shooter had wandered around Portland's east side all day, never stopping for long in any one place. Knowing he couldn't risk seeking medical attention for his leg yet, he bought some supplies from a big pharmacy inside a supermarket, and then locked himself inside a Multnomah County Library branch restroom and tended to the wound. Libraries were always good for these kinds of days when he needed to be just an anonymous guy.

It hurt like hell, but he knew it wasn't life-threatening and could wait until he could talk to his contact and arrange for a private doctor. But he needed to let twenty-four hours — at a minimum — go by before he attempted to get out of Portland.

Somewhere along his way, he found huge dumpsters behind a strip mall, and disposed of his bloody clothes, ski mask and gloves.

When it started getting dark, he found a cheap hotel out on Powell Blvd, and checked in without incident. The desk clerk was a pleasant woman in her fifties with an old-fashioned perm and a wrinkled upper lip from too much smoking, and she couldn't care less about a man walking in off the street as long as his credit card worked.

And — lucky day! — the room wasn't bad. He double locked the door, closed the heavy drapes, and turned on the TV. The news wouldn't be on for another hour or so, but he was eager to learn what the cops were saying. In the meantime, he filled up the tub in the bathroom's combination tub/shower, fearing what the shower's needles would feel like on his leg. Gently, he slipped into the hot sudsy water and cleaned himself thoroughly. He soaked until he felt himself getting drowsy — no surprise — and got out quickly. *It wouldn't do to drown in a bathtub after everything I've been through.* He knew he would sleep like a baby tonight.

The local news was a relief and a disappointment, if those two feelings were simultaneously possible. The cops clearly had no lead on him and warned the public that a gunman was on the loose after shooting four people at OHSU and killing three early this morning. No description other than a white male about five feet ten inches — he was five feet nine — and he was to be considered "armed and dangerous." *You bet your sweet ass.*

That was essentially the entire report. Nothing about a motive, why the hospital, the intended victim, or whether he was dead or alive. *Playing their cards close to the vest, huh?* He would have to talk to his contact about next steps. He took three pain killers, slipped between the slightly worn, but clean sheets, and changed the channel to Monday Night Football. He was asleep before the end of the first quarter.

• • •

The night passed quietly, both in Portland and in Port Stirling. The last day of November dawned in both locations just like the second-to-the-last day had — cold, grey, damp with hovering clouds.

Fern awoke in her own bedroom and listened to the ocean's waves breaking on the shore below the house. She'd cracked open one of her windows just a little last night before going to bed for this reason — she wanted, needed, to feel at home. The tide was high now, but it would be low tide later this morning when she planned to go to work. She needed the low tide for the first part.

She showered, washing her four-day-old dirty hair, and luxuriating in their big walk-in shower with the window looking out to sea. Which she avoided standing directly in front of this morning, just in case. Knowing Matt was on the mend was a huge part of why she looked better today, and she'd finally had a good night's sleep. *But it also felt so great to get clean, really clean. If someone wanted to torture me, the best way to get me to talk would be to not let me get clean. Best to not think about torture considering what I'm going to do today.*

She dressed in a black turtleneck and black jeans, eschewing shoes for now. She would find her black, beat-up sneakers in the garage before she left home. She called them her "nasty beach" shoes.

Heading downstairs to the kitchen to make coffee, Fern wondered if it would feel uncomfortable having Jay staying in the house when Matt wasn't here. But then he came into the kitchen, all sleepy-eyed, hair sticking straight up, and said, "I like this house better than my rental. Can I live here permanently?"

She laughed, and immediately relaxed. "No."

"Kill-joy."

"It's a pretty nice house, huh? I still pinch myself that I actually live here.

Growing up in Port Stirling, I never dreamed I could live in a house like this right on the ocean."

"I had that dream, too. Do you suppose all kids around here think the same thing? They all want to live on the beach?"

"Yeah, probably. The beach is such a fun place, no matter your age. Coffee?" She held up an empty cup.

"Oh, yeah." Jay took a barstool seat at the island.

"Why don't you buy a house?" Fern asked him. "You make a good salary. You can afford it now."

"Been thinking about it," he said. "Not sure I want to be tied down."

"You going somewhere?"

He smiled. "Nope. Not that I know of. It's just that the last couple of years have taught me that you can't predict what life will throw at you. I'd like to be able to pivot quickly if the situation called for it and owning a home might mess that up."

"Not in this real estate market," Fern said. "If you bought the right starter house and fixed it up just a little, you could sell it in a week if you needed to. I would help you find the right one, and your mom is a genius at decorating."

"It would be nice to do what I wanted to a place," he allowed. "But what if I lose my job and have to go to a new town?"

Fern looked at him. "You of all people are not going to lose your job. Your boss thinks you walk on water, and you've stepped up time and again in times of crisis. Where on earth is this coming from?"

"What if Matt had died? And I got a new boss?" He hesitated. "Or people think that Ed and I didn't protect him?"

"Oh, for crying out loud," she said, exasperated. "Is that what this is about? This lack of confidence, which I might point out, is highly unusual for you? I'm only going to say this once, Jay: You and Ed saved Matt's life. No ifs, ands, or buts. He would have bled out if the two of you had not acted, using all of your training. Once everyone in town learns what happened, you will be a hero. So, get over that right now."

"You think my job is safe?" He didn't look convinced, but maybe hopeful.

She filled up his coffee cup. "I think that Matt would have to appoint you co-chief if you asked." She smirked.

That got a chuckle of out him. "And he'd have to let me live in his house," he said, getting in on the joke.

"No, you're going to buy your own, and I'm going to help you find it."

"Deal."

"I'm going to make us a quick breakfast, and then I need to get rolling," she said.

"What are you doing today?" he asked.

"Can't say," she replied. "Top secret, so you don't know where I am, understand? I'll fill you in tonight if I learn anything related to your case. But it's just you, me, and Joe Phelps. Got it?"

"You know I hate this, but, yeah, I got it." He looked resigned. "Please…"

"Be careful," she interrupted. "Don't say it, Jay. We're past that."

"Yes, ma'am."

• • •

Unlike the uplifting sound of the ocean's crashing waves, the shooter woke up to the sound of trash cans being emptied onto a truck. It sounded like they were in his room. *What a racket. Guess I'm awake.* He'd been asleep for ten hours, and except for his throbbing leg, felt somewhat like his old self.

He reached for his phone, now fully charged, and called his contact. "He's not dead," he said on picking up.

"Not sure," the shooter answered. "I pulled out all his plugs and he wasn't breathing too good, but a cop shot me before I could get a shot off at him, and I had to make a run for it."

"You're not listening. I'm telling you that he's not dead. Hold on, I need to move to another room — my mother's here."

"For sure, not dead?" the shooter asked, hearing shuffling noises.

A pause and then, "For sure not dead."

"What do you want me to do?"

"Get out of Portland however you can. It's over for now. All the local police are in overdrive trying to find us, including the damn sheriff that helped ruin the Anselmo operation. He's like a mean bulldog. I can't risk them finding you and tying you to us. I need to rethink our options, but for now, we're on hold."

"I'm sorry I failed," the shooter said. "He was well-protected."

"I'm sure you did your best," he said coolly. "Horning will be out of commission for quite a while, however, so that will help us. Let me know when you resurface, and I will forward one-half of your fee. That will acknowledge your risk and keep you on the west coast until we need you again."

"Thank you. That's generous. I'll be in touch."

TWENTY

Fern left her car in a small beach overlook parking lot about five miles south of Port Stirling and made her way down the sandy wood steps to the wide beach. The morning was raw, and the wind was picking up. She zipped up her black parka, and pulled her black hat on, shoving her ponytail up into it so none of her red hair was showing.

Armed with high-powered binoculars and a couple of other tools that the best minds in the spy business had picked out for her before she left Club Fed in Georgia, she took off striding south down the beach. She set her pedometer at zero because she wanted to know when she'd walked 1.2 miles on the long-deserted beach. That mileage would put her right at the northern edge of Zhang Chen's property where the little river came in.

The closer she got, the jumpier she became. *It's OK to be a little nervous. This place was terrifying to you last year. But you survived that, and it's a new year,* she reassured herself. She hadn't been back on this beach since the tsunami, and she wasn't sure if the terrain would be as she remembered or not. As she approached where she thought the river started, she could see that it was now a little wider than before. But it didn't look any deeper; if anything, it was shallower than the night of the raid. She would still get plenty wet fording it to get closer to Chen's barn and the house, but she was relieved that the water would only be about knee-deep compared to its previous hip-high level.

She stopped and crouched behind a huge tree stump moored in the wet sand. She noticed her favorite green anemones circling the shallow waters around the stump. *So pretty.* Taking out the binocs, she pointed them at Chen's barn, the top half of which was easily visible from her location. She remembered her pink tee-shirt, tattered and filthy, flying from the top of it, and shivered remembering how close she'd come to dying that perilous night. *Again, new day, new situation. Move on.*

The barn appeared to have a recently restored roof, which jived with the renovation report she'd heard. *Maybe Zhang Chen is innocent. Just an investor who fell in love with the Oregon coast. Maybe they all had it wrong.* Since Fern was relatively new to the crime world, she knew she didn't have all the answers, but when seasoned vets like her boss Joe Phelps, the sheriff, Patty, and, especially, her husband all believed that Chen had to have been involved with the operation being conducted on his property, she fell in with them.

But now, in her new job, she had to think for herself. *What if he wasn't really the head honcho on the Anselmo operation? Where did that leave them now with this ghost guns deal, and the attempt on Matt's life?*

The big sliding door facing her was partially open, which likely meant that someone was home. She needed to get closer to really see if there was any action around the barn. There was a hefty stand of sand dunes with some tall grasses growing out of them just on the other side of the little river, and a bunker on one of the higher ones would make an excellent viewing spot. The grasses swayed in the wind, brushing against each other rudely, and changing colors as they did so.

She was pretty sure she'd be able to see the house from the top of the dune, as well as a direct look into the barn. But that meant crossing the river out in the open. It was risky, but if she wanted to see what, if anything, was going on, it was a risk she'd have to take.

It had begun to drizzle, and visibility up and down the beach was shortened as the mist swirled in and out. She would move quickly.

She turned off the ringer on her phone and stashed it in a zippered pocket. Checking that her handgun was loaded and ready, she took off at a sprint toward the little river. The water was chilly, but even in late

November, the shallower streams in Oregon never got icy cold. *Keep moving. Soon you'll be in front of your fireplace talking to your gorgeous husband on the phone, enjoying a nice glass of Roku with lemon on ice.* She hadn't abandoned her favorite Beefeater gin for martinis but had discovered the Japanese gin made for a tasty small cocktail on occasion. Fern always believed that it was important to have something to look forward to in life, even the small things, and she held this thought as the water crept higher on her legs.

What was that noise? She looked around quickly. Her only company was a lone seagull, mutely dipping in and out of the wind. It circled her and felt like some sort of omen. *Relax, it's just the water going around those bigger rocks ahead of you.* She kept slogging forward. *Almost there.* The water was just over her knees now, but she could tell from the clearer water ahead that this was the deep point in the river.

Made it! Once on the other side, she ran silently toward the dunes immediately in front of her, about fifty yards away. She clambered up the tallest one, sliding back down once, but regaining her footing quickly. This time she grabbed hold of some grasses and pulled herself close to the top. Scooping out a seat, she rested the binocs on a pile of grass and brought the top of her head in line with the peak of the ridge. She had a flashback of Buck Bay police chief Dan McCoy and his officers lined up on these dunes watching the action on this beach the night of the raid.

But today there was no action. She didn't see a single person near the barn, and there didn't appear to be any vehicles of interest inside it, at least, not in the part she could see through the open sliding door. There was a car in the circular driveway in front of the house, looked like a black Honda from here. *Wow. He did remodel; the house is much bigger than it was. Guess Mr. Chen has decided to spend more time in Oregon.*

Fern settled in, preparing to watch for a while. She took a granola bar out of her pocket and had a snack while she waited, careful to secure the wrapper back in her pocket. One hour went by and then two. Nothing, nobody in sight, no cars coming or going. She could see smoke coming from the house's fireplace. Someone was definitely at home, but clearly not eager to come out on this wet, yucky day.

By four o'clock, the light was dimming, and she knew with this cloud cover and light rain, it would be dark soon. Plus, her right hamstring was cramping. *Time to admit defeat, at least for today.* She slid down the dune, covering her tracks as best she could before she hit the firmer sand. This time, she went down the north side of the dunes, moving away from the house.

As she rounded the final bend and headed to the river, something caught her eye in the twilight. Something orange. Wadded up in a clump of grass. She checked her position in relation to the barn — no one could see her from the house — and kept close to the big sand dune while she investigated.

With her gloved hand, she gently pulled the folded thing up out of the grass and sand. As she tugged, it began to uncrumple. A small inflatable rubber boat. *Like you would use to make it to shore from a larger ship,* she thought. *Now what? I have two choices. I could return it to its original position and leave it here. Or I could take it with me and turn it over to the lab, and risk being arrested for theft. Not to mention possibly contaminating the chain of evidence.*

Her desperation to find out who shot Matt won out. Fern folded up the raft as small as she could make it, squeezing all the air out of it, stuffed as much of it as she could under her parka and held it close to her body. She took off running for the little river and didn't stop until she reached her car. Sopping wet, cold, and absolutely elated.

. . .

Once safely in her car, doors locked, Fern called Jay.

"Hi ya," he answered. "What's up?"

"I read your report about the description of the ship you and Ed saw off the coast of our house," she said.

"Yeah?"

"You mentioned you might have seen something orange or reddish on the ship by the wheelhouse. Do you remember that?"

"Yeah, I think so. I couldn't swear to what it was, but I saw a flash of something that color, maybe hanging from the side."

"Something like maybe a rubber boat, like a dinghy?"

"Could have been," Jay answered. "Yeah, that feels right. Why?"

"For your ears only, I may have just found what you saw. Can you meet me at my house soon?"

"Wow. Sure, on my way. Where are you now?"

Fern hesitated. "I'd rather not say on the phone."

"No prob. I'm on my way."

She hit "end call", and immediately clicked on "Dr. Bernice Ryder".

"Bernice, hi, it's Fern. Can you talk for a minute?"

"Hi, Fern. How's he doing this afternoon?"

"I haven't checked for a few hours — OHSU is my next call," Fern told her. "I was anxious to talk to you."

"What's going on?" Bernice asked, on alert.

"I might be bringing something to your lab tonight, and I want to know if anyone will be there working. I need to have Jay take a look first."

"Does it have to do with Matt's shooting?"

"Maybe. I think it might," Fern said. "It could be really important."

"Then I'll meet you there. Craig is there until 7:00 p.m."

"This is top secret, Bernice. Jay and you are the only people that can know what I have."

"Gotcha. If you call me back and tell me you're coming, I'll let Craig go home early."

"That's perfect," Fern said, breathing a sigh of relief. "I'll call you back within the hour."

Fern sat in her car for a moment collecting her thoughts. There was no one else parked at the overlook. *Why would they be? I can barely see the ocean.* Through the gloomy drizzle, a bank of fog was beginning to form on the horizon. It, along with the encroaching darkness, approached her windshield.

She started the engine and placed her stolen goods on the seat beside her. On the side that was now face up, there appeared to be something written. It was in Chinese.

. . .

Fern and Jay approached her driveway simultaneously on Ocean Bend

Road, her from the south, and him from the north. Fern opened the garage with her remote, and indicated for him to park inside, too. She flipped a switch on the side wall so the garage lights would remain on.

"You're all wet," Jay observed.

"Outside in Port Stirling in November wading a river…yeah, I'm wet," she whooped.

"But yet, you appear to be happy," he said sarcastically. "What the heck have you been up to?"

She reached into her VW, carefully extracted the goods, and unfolded it on the floor of her garage. "What do you think?" She waved at her treasure, and then stood with her arms crossed in front of her body trying to warm up while Jay moved around it.

He looked at the item, bending closer, knowing not to touch it with his bare hands. He took his time. "I think this is an inflatable rubber boat, and," he pointed at the lettering on one side, "it has Chinese writing on this side of it. Am I allowed to ask where you found this, Miss State Department?"

"Until Bernice runs forensics on it, you and I are the only two people who will know where this came from. Understood?"

"You're scaring me, Fern."

"Good. Because I'm scared, too. I found it on Zhang Chen's property. It was sorta hidden at the base of the big sand dune up near his barn."

Jay shook his head slowly from side to side. "You can't be on his property."

"I know."

"You went searching without a warrant, and you took this boat off his land? What are you, nuts? Dalrymple will have your ass for this, you know that, don't you?"

"He won't find out. I'm going to take this to Bernice tonight, she's going to do her thing with forensics, and then I'm going to put it back where I found it."

"You are nuts," Jay stated. "Did you surveil the house, too?"

"Stop calling me crazy. My orders were to 'have a look', and that's what I did. I sat out there in the rain for several hours and didn't see anyone or anything suspicious at all. This is my potential reward. Look here," she pointed at a dirty, smudged spot. "There is at least one fingerprint around this spot."

"How do you know that?"

She looked a little embarrassed. "I've got this kit thingy now."

"Kit thingy? Like a latent fingerprint kit?"

"A little more advanced version. I can't really say more, Jay. But I'm fairly confident that Bernice will be able to pull a set of prints, and who knows what else off this boat."

Jay took another look at the dinghy. "It could be from the ship. The color is the same color in my mind from Thursday. So, you're thinking that after the ship took off out to sea and then possibly turned south to make its getaway, that the shooter used this boat to get to Chen's property?"

"That's precisely what I'm thinking," Fern said. "He headed straight to Chen's cove, stashed the boat in the dunes behind some grasses, and took off."

"While all of us were searching the ocean for the ship," Jay said. He winced.

TWENTY-ONE

By Wednesday morning Bernice had indeed pulled prints off the inflatable boat. She also found some hairs, and a minute fragment of skin on one of the oarlocks.

Jay (officially), but really Fern (unofficially) immediately called a meeting of the major crime team while Bernice put together her report. Fern wanted buy-in from the team on next steps, which involved running their forensics evidence through state and national databases to see if they could come up with a match.

Jay believed that Matt's shooter was a pro, and that it was likely he or she had a record of some kind, and they had a good chance of coming up with a name. Fern was convinced that whoever was behind this was confident that the rubber boat would never be found. And, in all likelihood, if they'd gone in the legitimate route with a search warrant of the property, the chances of the cops going down to the open beach were probably slim. She had been lucky to see it…skill to know where to go, but luck in deciding to go out another route.

The big challenge for Fern and Jay was to dodge the inevitable question of where the dinghy was found and by whom. Late last night, over hot chocolate in front of the fireplace in their sweats while they waited for Bernice to call, the two cops decided that while it was unfortunate and went against every grain in both their bodies, they would have to lie to the team.

Together they decided that they would tell the truth about Fern finding it but be as wishy-washy as they could pull off about the actual location. The story would be that she had gone for a run on the beach and noticed the orange boat in a cove south of her home. She thought it was suspicious and had the potential to be relevant to the case, and so, brought in Jay and Bernice without delay.

Most of the story was true. There was no reason for the committee to know that Fern had been on a stakeout for the government. Ed and Patty would likely suspect that's what Fern had been doing, but she trusted them to not say anything in front of the other team members. Sylvia would positively know that Fern had gone to Chen's, but that prospect would so terrify her that she would button up completely. Fern was fairly certain that Sylvia would keep her cool, understanding what was at stake. This was one of those times that Joe Phelps had warned her about: she'd have to pull off a little deceit in order to protect herself and the evidence until they knew what they had to work with.

Jay opened the lunchtime meeting while the team was still munching on their tuna salad sandwiches. He explained that Fern had discovered an item that may or may not have relevance to their investigation of Matt's shooting. He also said that Dr. Ryder had joined them today to detail some forensic items.

"Fern, will you tell the group what you've found?" Jay asked. He nodded at her to proceed.

Fern told her story as they'd rehearsed, deliberately vague about the exact location of the boat. She made eye contact with Ed once, and his upturned mouth told her he knew what she'd done, and that it was OK with him. It was, in the end, Chief Dan McCoy of the Buck Bay police department who asked the question, "Where exactly did you find it, Fern?"

"There's a cove south of where I live on Ocean Bend Road," she answered. "I'm not even sure it has a name." She shrugged her shoulders as if to indicate that was all she knew about the location.

"Did you mark the location, or will you be able to find it again?" asked Dalrymple.

Fern hesitated. "I marked it with a stick," she lied to the D.A. "But it was low tide, and I'm not sure if it will survive high tide. I'm confident I can find the spot again, however. I run on that beach all the time. Bernice, what can you tell us?" Fern quickly turned toward her, and the message was "My part of the program is over."

To Fern's huge relief, Bernice quickly rose from her chair and approached the whiteboard. She started drawing a boat, and said to the team, "I've got a written report for each of you, but I thought it would be easy to show you what we have."

Sylvia passed around Dr. Ryder's forensics report.

"Looking at the first page of my report, you can see the item in question is a small, one- or two-person inflatable rubber boat. It's orange in color with black markings on one side and on the bottom. We got two nice sets of fingerprints off each of the oarlocks." She turned to her drawing and circled the two pegs that would hold the oars.

"Did you recover the oars, Fern?" asked Chief McCoy.

"No. There was nothing else at the site. The boat was deflated and kind of folded up. That was it," Fern answered.

"While it would have been nice, obviously, to find an oar as well," continued Bernice, "the prints we got — probably as the rower inserted the oars into the pegs — are solid."

She turned back to the board and drew two small circles, both toward the rear one-third of the boat. "If you flip past the fingerprints section, the next page describes the other evidence we found. These circles represent the location of two hairs, on the inside floor of the boat. They are identical and are from the same person. Both hairs are short, fine in size not thick, just under two inches in length, and blonde in color. My opinion is that they came from a Caucasian male."

"Meaning White, not African American, Asian, Hispanic or Native?" clarified Jay.

"Correct," said Bernice. "A White male, with short blonde hair. Could be female, but I don't think so — there's only about a five percent chance that the test shows the wrong gender." She turned back to her drawing. "Next in your report, you will read about a tiny piece of skin." She drew a small circle under the oarlock on the right side of the boat. "We found it here, and my educated guess is that the rower nicked something, probably the peg, and scraped this tiny piece of skin off the hand."

"Is it enough to catch some DNA, Bernice?" Patty asked her friend, speaking for the first time.

"Yep," said Bernice briskly. "If whoever was in this boat is on the registry, we'll get him."

"This is great work," Fern said. Her skin had high color, a flushed appearance. She looked like she was about to jump up and down in her chair.

"Wait, there's more," smiled Bernice. "Go to the next page in your report." She waited while the team turned their gazes downward at the paper in front of them.

"I've analyzed the black markings on the side and bottom of the boat. Anyone here speak Chinese?" She waited and looked around the table. "Thought not," Bernice smiled. "I attempted to translate the markings I found here," she drew a rectangle on the side of the boat. "I'm having it confirmed now with a translator at the University of Oregon, but I believe it says, "Property of Pearl Dragon."

There was a moment of silence around the table as everyone thought about what that could mean.

"That sounds like a good name for an ocean-going ship registered in Hong Kong," Ed said, breaking the quiet.

"Mic drop, Bernice," grinned Jay at the head of the table.

• • •

By Wednesday afternoon, several things had happened. Bernice's contact in the foreign languages department at the U of O had confirmed that the markings on the boat were Mandarin Chinese and read "Property of Pearl Dragon".

Ed, working with Bernice had sent her forensic evidence to the Oregon State Police HQ in Salem, where they would run everything through the computers. Because they both knew how long it could take the state lab for a review of DNA and, especially, latent prints, Ed phoned his boss and explained their situation. Cops didn't like it when other cops got shot, and the OSP would move this evidence to the top of their pending requests list. The fact that Matt had been targeted not once, but twice, helped Ed make his case.

Fern updated Joe Phelps in Washington, D.C, and they agreed on two actions he would take. First, he sent Dr. Ryder's evidence to his contact at the DEA Office of Forensic Sciences. Phelps had worked with the manager of their primary crime lab for almost twenty years, and she knew when she got a review request from Joe that it meant possible international ramifications. She was on it.

He also called the ambassador to China in Beijing. When he was patched through on the secure line, Phelps said, "How's the guy with the most stressful job in the world?"

The ambassador laughed and said, "Stressed out, Joe. Are you about to add to my anxiety?"

"I might. I need your help."

"What can I do for you?"

"We have a police chief on the west coast who was gunned down, we think, by a marksman on a ship just offshore from his beachfront home."

"Good God."

"Yes. He'll survive, but there was a brazen second attempt on him at the hospital. Two nurses and one cop killed, and a second cop wounded. The gunman is serious. The connection to you is that we believe the ship was of Hong Kong registry, and it was flying the Chinese flag."

"I was afraid you were going to say that. What do you need?"

"There's about a seventy-to-one chance that the name of the ship is "Pearl Dragon," and I'd like one of your folks to see what they can find out about it. Is it registered with HKSR, and if so, who owns it?"

"As you might expect, they can be quite secretive about who owns what, especially in Hong Kong. We'll try."

"I know you know how to pull the levers, Martin," Phelps said. "Please give this your best shot. We like this guy and our new agent on the west coast. It's important we keep them both safe."

"I understand. Does your new guy know what happened to Clay Sherwin?"

"She. And yes, she does."

. . .

Fern called OHSU immediately after the team meeting and spoke to the nursing supervisor on Matt's second floor. Her report was a good one.

"He's breathing entirely on his own and is able to talk in brief spurts. Motion in all extremities. Mainly he's experiencing fatigue and weakness, which we expect, and he still has a headache. But this morning he asked for a cup of coffee, and he's reported that his headache is better, more of a dull throb now than sharp pains."

"He likes his coffee," Fern told her. "Please give him two cups every morning. Would it be possible for me to talk to him?"

"Let me see if he's awake. I'll call you back, OK?"

"Yes, thank you so much. I miss him."

"I know you do, honey," sympathized the nurse. "Give him a couple more days and then come back. He'll be a new man by then, I promise."

"I don't want a new man. I want my original man."

The nurse chuckled. "Can't say I blame you, he's a sweetheart. I'll call you back as soon as I can." She ended the call.

Five minutes later Fern's phone vibrated, and she started to cry when she saw Matt's name pop up. She took a deep breath and said, "Hello, Mr. Horning."

"Hello, Mrs. Horning," he said. His voice sounded like sandpaper.

"I'm going to do most of the talking so you can save your throat."

"Else is new?"

"Very funny," said Fern. *That's my man!* "You got a B+ from the nursing supervisor. She says you're doing better today."

"Bored."

"Bored is good," Fern said. "But it doesn't mean we're springing you quite yet. I'll be up to see you soon, and we'll talk to your doctor then about next steps."

"Home."

"Not yet," she said firmly. "You've still got a bumpy road ahead, and we're going to do what the doctors tell us. They've been right so far, and they've earned my respect. Not to mention my lifelong gratitude. They saved you, Matt. Not once, but twice."

"I know."

"Therefore, they are in charge, and you and I will do as they say. But it sounds like you're close, maybe two or three days."

"Good news."

"Now, I have some news from this end," Fern said excitedly. "We found an inflatable dinghy that might have come from the ship you saw on Thursday before you were shot. Ed and Jay remembered some details that are coming in handy as we investigate. There's some evidence that indicates Chinese involvement at some level—we don't know who or how or why yet, but we've got a couple of leads."

"Zhang Chen?" His voice was a raspy whisper, and Fern could tell it was an effort for him to communicate. "Hooray," he said.

"We don't know yet, but I found the raft on his property."

"You?" Agitated.

"It's OK," she soothed. "I'm just doing my job. I'm safe, and I have protection. Jay is staying at the house. My personal bodyguard."

"My bed?"

Fern laughed. "No, sweetie, Jay's not sleeping in your bed. He's downstairs in the guest room by the front door. He does like our house, though."

Matt tried to laugh, but it hurt.

"Don't say anything more," she instructed. "I just wanted you to relax and know that we're trying to find out who did this to you. Everyone loves you, and we're all working together. We want you to concentrate on healing. I love you, Matt, and I'll be there soon."

"Love…"

TWENTY-TWO

Sheriff Earl Johnson, Detective Patty Perkins, and District Attorney David Dalrymple, all based in Twisty River, had ridden together to the meeting in Port Stirling.

On the way home they discussed the case. Earl said, "I find it odd that if Matt's shooter is a pro, as I suspect, he would leave his fingerprints on that getaway raft."

"It is careless," agreed Patty. "Maybe he was really in a hurry when he landed on shore. Threatened by someone or something."

"Or he or she never expected the raft to be found," said Dalrymple.

"Well, you leave a raft on a public beach, you have to assume that sooner or later someone will stumble across it," said Earl. "It's not the kind of mistake that fits the profile of a hired killer."

"Maybe Fern was not being completely honest with where she really found it," said Dalrymple. "Perhaps she was snooping around on private property."

Patty whirled around to face the D.A. in the back seat. "Are you saying Fern deliberately lied to us? She wouldn't do that."

"Not lie exactly. Just not telling us the whole truth. She was vague about the location. Like some phantom cove. I couldn't figure out where she was talking about," Dalrymple said.

"I couldn't get a visual on the cove in that stretch of beach either, but

Fern's not the type to enter someone's property without a warrant," said Earl. "She's pretty much by the book."

"We really don't know what she's doing in this new job, though, do we?" Dalrymple persisted.

"Nope," said Earl.

"Nope," said Patty.

"I also thought it was strange, although I was greatly relieved, that she and Jay didn't push me more on warrants," he smiled.

"You're not off the hook yet, David," said Patty. "This raft turning up might be just the evidence we need to take this investigation to the next level. I think they're waiting until we learn if we can identify the gunman, and/or we get lucky with the ship's registration."

"Agreed," said the sheriff. "Those results will either send us down a whole new rabbit hole or confirm that we were on the right path all along. With Ray Peng and Zhang Chen."

"Well, I guess we just wait and see," said Dalrymple from the back seat.

"I'd go to Ray Peng's house tonight if you give me permission," said the sheriff.

"Look, Earl, we've been over and over this. You don't have strong enough probable cause to pester that young man any further."

"That young man has a cache of ghost guns, may I remind you," said Patty. "One of those guns may be the one that shot Matt. We need to talk to him again. And we need access to his records. Even for you, you're being stubborn on this one, David."

"Let's wait and see what we get off the raft, and maybe I'll reconsider. Is that a deal?"

"For now, I guess," said Patty reluctantly. "You're the D.A. We're just a couple of cops trying to catch the guy who shot our friend."

"And I'm just trying to do the job I was elected to do," Dalrymple said.

They rode the rest of the way in silence.

• • •

In the end it was Joe Phelps who broke the case wide open on Thursday morning, one week after the first attempt on Matt's life. The DEA's forensic lab found a fingerprints match in their extensive database to the ones Dr. Ryder took off the raft.

The prints belonged to a man, Michael Christopher Winston, who was arrested nineteen years ago at Hartsfield Airport in Atlanta for carrying a concealed handgun without a permit. He was twenty-seven years old at the time of his arrest.

His mug shot showed a white male, blonde hair, blue eyes, average build. His home address at the time of his arrest was in Los Angeles, the Laurel Canyon area. Phelps noted that was a ritzy real estate area for a twenty-seven-year-old. A former marine, he was also a graduate of UCLA.

So, not Chinese, good old American born and bred, thought Phelps. A former marine possibly gone bad—he hated these stories. Before he called Fern with the ID, he checked the TSA database for ports of exit out of the U.S. Nothing. So, Michael Winston had either escaped via other means of transportation—bus, train, car, ship—or he used a fake passport, or he was still in the country...possibly still in Oregon.

Part of him had hoped he would be able to tell Fern that her husband's shooter had fled to another country. But if he didn't get on an airplane, and he got off the Chinese ship as the raft indicated, the odds went up that he was still in the U.S. Not a certainty, by any means, but more likely. That meant they had a chance to find him.

Phelps dialed Fern's number. At 7:00 a.m. in Port Stirling, she and Jay were eating breakfast in Fern's kitchen and planning their day. She took Joe's call in Matt's office. Fern liked working in there because it was a luxurious space, but also because she could feel his presence.

"We've got a name," Phelps started the conversation.

"Hot damn!" said Fern.

He brought her up to speed on what he'd learned.

"That would make him forty-six today, right? We don't know how he got off the OHSU hill," Fern said, "but at least now the Portland police can check his name and photo at PDX, the Greyhound terminal, the train station, and rental car agencies."

"I've already checked TSA for PDX, and he didn't fly out, at least, not under his real name. But Portland should hurry and check the other places. Tell them to get that done immediately. I think he's likely got a car and is now out of Portland. I'm not sure he'd risk public transportation, especially with a bullet in his leg." Phelps thought for a minute. "Maybe he's crossed into Canada or Mexico by car or is planning to. I'll check the likeliest border crossings. And I'll have my people research his life."

"Is it alright with you if I ask Sylvia to do that as well? She's good at this background thing. Has sources all over the place."

"Sure," Phelps said. "It never hurts to have staff coming at it from different angles. I also want someone on the scene in Portland to talk to both the cop who was wounded and to Matt again, now that we have a description of this guy."

"That will be me, Joe. I'm headed back to Portland tomorrow. Matt's doing better and I need to be with him. Plus, I did what I had to do here, spying on Zhang Chen's property. We're trying to light a fire under our district attorney for warrants to search both Ray Peng's place and Chen's, but our hands are tied until that happens."

"Not enough probable cause?" asked Phelps.

"Correct," Fern answered. "Our major crime team disagrees with him, but he's not budging so far. Patty Perkins and Sheriff Earl are keeping a close eye on Peng in Twisty River, and so far, there's nothing suspicious with him. Patty saw him at a restaurant Sunday night, and she told us he was friendly and with his wife and kids."

"Just a regular guy who beats up his wife and has a scary gun collection, huh?"

"Yeah. Patty and her husband go to that restaurant almost every Sunday, and she thought it was quite the coincidence that Peng showed up this week. Almost like he was trying to look normal, knowing she'd be there," said Fern.

"Interesting. It looks like Zhang Chen is doing the same thing. Just a normal holiday with his family."

"Patty would love to talk to Peng's wife, but she has to wait for Dalrymple." She paused. "This is for your ears only, Joe. Jay is here, and we decided that he and Ed Sonders would do a stakeout of Chen's beach to see if anyone comes back for the raft. Bernice is bringing it back to Port Stirling this morning, and we're going to photograph and document it, and then I'm going to sneak it back to where I found it."

"Be careful, Fern."

"No worries. I'm scared of this guy and won't leave anything to chance. Now that I know where I'm going, there's a safer way to get there than the way I went on Monday. I'll be quick and quiet."

"Where will Ed and Jay be?"

"There's a good hiding place on a treed ridge just north of the sand dunes where I found the raft. They'll be able to hide easily and will get binocs on the raft. It's tough access, but they can do it and they're chomping at the bit to do something active. We're not telling anyone else what they're doing—not even our crime team."

"OK, I copy that. I'm sending Winston's mug shot to Sylvia now with all the info I have on him. It's also going to all the state police on the west coast, and to the Portland police. Be sure you take a photo with you to the hospital to show Matt and the cop. How's she doing, by the way? Taking a bullet even with a vest is no picnic."

"It was rough on Gabby, but she's doing better. I talked to her last night, and she's back on her feet, but not back at work yet. Honestly, I think she's got more emotional damage than physical. What she witnessed was not pretty."

"Take her some flowers or something from us, would you?" Phelps said.

"Rudy in our police department is cooking her a big dish of lasagna for me to take to her," Fern said. She laughed. "He's the best cook we've got and wanted to show his appreciation to Gabby for saving Matt's life. We're covered."

"That's perfect. Thanks, Fern. Call me after you've shown the photo to her and Matt. Anything you need?"

"The only thing I need is to see my husband."

• • •

Fern recapped Joe's information for Jay, adding, "I hope it's OK that I volunteered Sylvia to help research our shooter."

"Usurping my authority," Jay joked. "That I don't really have."

"Bill Abbott named you acting chief," Fern reminded him. "And everybody is comfortable with that. Especially me."

"I'm so afraid of screwing up." He rubbed his chin. "The freakin' stakes are so high."

"That's natural. This is the first time you've been in charge, and, honestly, it's a little bit soon for you. But you have completely nailed this investigation so far. You've done everything right, Jay, and your instincts are spot on. You've assigned tasks to the team, and we're all following your lead. Including the State Department." She laughed. "Who else in Oregon can say that?"

"Since we're being honest," Jay said, "I have to tell you that I'm coming around on your leaving us and taking this job with Phelps. It makes sense to me now. First the Anselmo and now this Chinese ship. We can't handle this international stuff with our little department."

"My new boss is a sharp cookie," Fern said. "He knew way back before he installed Clay Sherwin in Chinook County that we were smack in the middle of a potential trouble spot. I give him a lot of credit, which is why I thought I could help. I told you we'd still be working together, didn't I?" Her eyes crinkled.

"You did. I just didn't think it would be trying to catch whoever shot Matt."

· · ·

Detective Patty Perkins looked at herself in the mirror and laughed out loud. "What do you think?" she asked Ted and turned to look at her husband.

"I think you look like a hick farmer," smiled Ted. "It's the blue and red neckerchief that cinches it for me."

Patty was dressed in denim overalls, an old blue shirt, the aforementioned neck scarf, and a small straw hat.

"Will he recognize me?"

"Not sure I recognize you, and I'm married to you. I think you're good to go," Ted said.

"I don't look like myself, do I? I need to be careful," she said. "Two reasons. Ray Peng could be dangerous, and David Dalrymple could do me even more harm if he thinks I'm breaching Peng's rights."

"Are you? Breaching Peng's rights?"

"Not yet, but technically today might take me close to the edge," Patty told her husband. "This guy is hiding something, and it's making me crazy."

"So, you're going to follow him in my pickup if he leaves his house. In your farmer's disguise."

"Correctamundo."

"What if I need to go somewhere?"

"You said you were going to be home all day reading your new organic vegetable gardening book."

"I am," Ted said. "Going to build a fire and sit my butt in that chair." He pointed to his favorite beat-up dark green armchair nestled up to the brick fireplace. "But what if I have an emergency?"

"Take my squad car," Patty said, more irritably than she meant. "The keys are hanging on the hook by the garage door."

"I can't drive around in a police car!" he protested.

"True. But you said emergency," she reasoned. "If you have an emergency, take my car. Otherwise, I'll be home before you know it."

"Will you have backup?" Ted asked. "What if you get into some trouble? What if Peng sees you?"

She took his hand and looked him in the eye. "I do far more dangerous things than this on a regular basis. I'll be fine. I just want to see where he goes if he goes anywhere. And if it turns to shit, I'll call my sergeant. Got it?"

He rubbed her cheek. "I don't want you to end up like Matt," he said tenderly.

"I won't. I promise. Now go pour me a thermos of your delicious coffee while I find my old hick farmer boots."

. . .

Patty pulled off the road just past Ray Peng's driveway in another narrow driveway. This one was a small dirt road that took off uphill through some trees. Awkwardly, she backed the big pickup in so she was facing downhill and could eyeball any cars coming or going into Peng's drive. She took out today's newspaper, took a sip from her thermos, and began the wait.

At 10:30 a.m. Peng eased his tricked out yellow Mustang onto the road and took off downhill toward town. He was alone.

Patty waited until the Mustang had rounded the first corner, and then she started up Ted's pickup in pursuit. She loved tailing a suspect. *If you shot Matt Horning, I'm going to nail you*, she said to Peng's car. Another car had pulled onto the road and was now between her and Peng—perfect.

She followed him as he entered Twisty River's town limits, and then took a right turn on the old highway toward Buck Bay. He didn't make any stops in town. Patty slowed at the right turn and let another car coming from her left go in front of her. Once past the high school, as Peng sped up on the highway, Patty, too, picked up her speed. He was now two cars in front of her, but she could see the Mustang clearly from the pickup's high perch.

After following him north for about fifteen miles, Peng turned left onto McAdams Road, which she knew would take him along the Twisty River briefly and then over the hill to Highway 101. Some people thought McAdams Road was a shortcut to Port Stirling, but Patty always felt it seemed longer than the old road which usually flooded in the winter. Maybe because of all the sharp turns up and down the hill.

Is Peng going to Port Stirling? Usually, people from Twisty River only took this road if they were going south on 101. And it would get tricky for her following him now because this road had less traffic. *I'll have to mind my p's and q's.*

She slowed down and hung back while they were on the stretch along the river. There were a few curves, but she'd be able to see far enough ahead if he took off up the hill.

Which he did. Patty paused at the right turn stop sign off McAdams Road to give Peng a head start up the hill and around a corner or two. There was no one behind her; no other cars that she could see. And this being a

Thursday morning in December, there would probably not be much traffic on this road until 5:00 p.m. when people went home from work.

She counted to thirty, and then made the turn. While she drove, she called Jay.

"Hi, Patty," he answered. "What's up with you?"

"I'm following Ray Peng up Raccoon Hill Road. He's headed toward 101, and I'm hanging back now because there isn't any other traffic and I'm afraid he might spot me. I'm in Ted's pickup, so pretty inconspicuous, but still. Are you in a position where you could drive north on 101 and sit where you could see if he pulls onto the highway? My gut feeling is that he's headed to your town."

"Yeah, I'm at city hall. I'll leave right now."

"He's in a yellow Mustang."

"Oh, I remember his car. I'll find him. Check with you soon."

Patty visualized gangly, earnest Jay Finley grabbing his jacket off the coatrack and jogging to city hall's parking lot. *That young man is going to make his boss proud*, she thought. She would remember to tell Matt how in the face of horrific fear and crushing grief, Jay had held it together. He had turned into a leader in a matter of days…simply because he had to. It was in him all along. She suspected that Matt knew this about his budding detective, perhaps as early as the Emily Bushnell case.

As she got closer to the top of the hill, the morning fog and sprinkles dissipated, and she saw blue sky overhead. The road straightened out, and she did not see Peng's car. *Shit! I lost him. He either turned off, or he's almost to the highway.*

She punched Jay's number again. "I lost him. Where are you?"

"On 101 almost to the turnoff to Raccoon Hill," Jay said. "I haven't met his car yet, so he's either still ahead of you, or he turned north to Buck Bay."

"OK, good. Keep going until you get to Raccoon Hill. I'm going to double back and see if he turned on Cherry Drive—it's the only road I've passed since I lost him."

"Will do. And, Patty, if he doesn't get to the highway in the next five minutes or so, I'll come down to Cherry Drive. You might need backup."

"I might."

TWENTY-THREE

Ray Peng pulled up in front of the non-descript building at the end of Cherry Drive. The road actually ended about two hundred yards before the building, turning into a dirt rut, and the large building was concealed behind a substantial stand of fir trees. If you didn't know the warehouse-looking building was there, you'd never find it.

Ray was happy to see several vehicles in the clearing behind the building. It meant guys were working and the production line was operational again after the Thanksgiving holiday. He entered the door code, and strolled through into the enormous, open room. The production manager, Wong Li, came up to greet him.

"Everything OK today?" Ray asked his manager.

"You bet," Wong answered and rubbed his belly. "Plenty of turkey and dressing—it's a nice holiday." He grinned.

"I know, right?" laughed Ray. "Football and food –what's not to love? Are we going to make Mr. Chen's quota by the end of the year?"

"I think so," Wong said. "Most of our crew doesn't care about Christmas, so we shouldn't drop off much at the end of December. I calculated this morning that we should meet it on December 26, so we've got a few days leeway."

"Good to know, and thanks, man. If it starts getting close and you need to offer a little financial incentive to the guys, do it and I'll cover the extra bonus."

Wong looked across the room. "We've got about twelve guys on the job now, so that would cost you." He rubbed his chin.

"Doesn't matter," Ray assured him. "It's important we do not disappoint Mr. Chen."

"Got it. I assume that means the sales channels are holding up?"

"Yep. More than we can handle, honestly," Ray said. "This is a goldmine, and we need to keep going. You and I are going to be able to retire at a young age, my friend."

Wong slapped his old friend on the back and said, "You're da man. Should I be thinking about recruiting mo…"

Both men turned suddenly and looked at the open door a few feet behind them which had made a squeaky noise.

"Mind if we come in, gentlemen?" said Detective Patty Perkins, drawing her pistol.

"That's not really a question," said Jay at her side, gun also in his hand. "Since, you know, we're already in."

Ray Peng examined the two cops' faces, turned to Wong, and said, "You get back to work, I'll handle this."

"Just a minute," Patty said to Wong. "Your name is?"

Wong looked at Ray, who nodded. "Wong Li," he answered.

"Do you live in Port Stirling?" she asked.

"No. Buck Bay," Wong said. Patty thought he looked uncomfortable.

"I think that's enough questions," Ray Peng said. "May we see your search warrant?"

"Not necessary," said Patty. "We're just checking business permits today and stumbled across your obvious business." She made a show of looking around the giant room.

"You usually point your guns at businessmen?" Ray said with more than a touch of sarcasm.

"It looks to me like you guys are plenty cozy with guns," Jay said.

"This is a reputable manufacturing operation," Ray said defiantly.

"Perfectly legal." He looked at Patty. "Did you fucking follow me here this morning? Was that you in that pickup?"

"Not that I need to answer any questions from you, Mr. Peng, but no. I was on my way to a farm on the other side of the highway, and I noticed your car—it's visible, being bright yellow and all—turning in here and I just wondered where this road went. I'd never been on it before this morning." She smiled sweetly at him.

"Are you on duty?" Ray asked. He looked her up and down, checking out her ridiculous outfit.

"I am now." Another smile. "What, exactly, are you manufacturing here? Looks like guns to us. Right, Detective Finley?"

"Right, Detective Perkins," Jay said.

"As I said," Ray began, "this is a legal operation. You have no grounds to even be here. We've checked the law and there is nothing that prohibits our business."

"Not unless any of you," Jay waved his hand around, "are convicted felons. Are you? Because if you or any of your crew are, I should remind you that you're not allowed to possess firearms."

"And if we should happen to see any illegal drugs or contraband while we look around for your business permit," added Patty, "that makes this wonderful enterprise also a no-no. We often find that guns and drugs go together."

"None of my men have broken the law," said Wong. He actually stuck out his chin.

"No felons, no drugs," said Ray. "Now, get out."

"You're losing your sense of humor, Mr. Peng," noted Jay. "We would like to see your business permit before we leave. You do have one, amiright?"

"Yes. Issued by Chinook County," Peng said.

"It's supposed to be posted," said Jay. "Please point it out to us."

"I don't know exactly where it is," Peng stalled. "Do you know, Wong?" looking at his colleague.

"I don't remember where we put it, but I know we have it somewhere," said Wong, wrinkling his brow.

"Well, then I'm afraid you're going to have to send your workers home for the day, and both of you will need to come to the police station while we confirm your operating permit."

Patty added, "We'll also need a list of your employees so we can check for any felony convictions. We will wait here while you get your records and look for your biz permit." Patty holstered her gun but let her hand rest on the butt. Jay did the same.

"We don't keep our records here," said Peng.

"Where do you keep them?" Jay asked.

"At a secure location."

"Which is where?" Jay again.

"Listen," said Peng. "You can't do this. We're a legit business. I'm not giving you a list of our employees and we aren't going to the station with you." He rubbed a hand on his pant leg.

Patty and Jay looked at each other. Patty nodded.

"I'm sorry you feel that way," said Jay. "Ray Peng and Wong Li, I'm arresting you as persons of responsibility for the fraudulent activity of operating a business without a license. We could fine you an amount equal to a percentage of your gross revenue, but I'm gonna make a wild guess you don't have access to that information either. So, we're gonna consider your activity here an extreme situation, and place you under arrest until we can sort out your license to operate, and the status of your employees where your product is concerned."

"You will be very sorry about this," said Peng.

"We're the police and we're shutting you down," said Patty, ignoring Peng's comment. She turned to the production line where most of the gang was frozen watching the confrontation. Speaking loudly, she said, "You should all leave now. Go home while we investigate. You will all be notified by Mr. Li when it's OK to return to work."

Wong Li said something quickly in Chinese, and all the workers headed for the exit.

Jay read them their rights, and Peng said, "Yeah, yeah, yeah. Let's get this over with." Patty and Jay marched the two of them out the door.

"You might want to lock your car, Ray," Patty said as they approached

Jay's squad car and showed them the back seat. "It's a tempting target for thieves."

• • •

Bernice rang the doorbell of Matt and Fern's house.

"Well, this is weird," said the Chinook County Medical Examiner when Fern opened her front door. "I can't get used to you not being with the Port Stirling police department." She was carrying a large shopping bag.

"I know," smiled Fern, ushering her friend into the house. "Some days it doesn't feel any different, and then on days like today I understand my new role has more pressure and a bit more weight."

"I've never returned evidence to a personal residence before," Dr. Ryder said uneasily. "I hope to hell you know what you're doing, Fern. And I've never seen you dressed head-to-toe in black before, so I'm going to assume that means you're about to do something scary." Bernice, always nicely dressed when out of the morgue, was wearing a beautiful camel hair coat over wine-colored wool pants and a wine sweater.

"Yes, black for this afternoon's work. You, on the other hand, look gorgeous. That coat!" said Fern.

"I bought it to celebrate the opening of the Native cultural center, figuring we'd be outside. I'm wearing it today in case our favorite district attorney arrests me for the destruction of possible evidence. I'd like to look good for the perp walk."

"He'll never know. Besides, it will be me who goes down if this is ever discovered."

"True that. You'll be careful, right?"

"I got it out of its hiding place and to you, didn't I? Today will be a piece of cake compared to "borrowing" it," Fern said confidently. "Is it in the bag?" She pointed at the bag Bernice was still gripping tightly.

Bernice nodded, and Fern took the bag from her. "Oh, good, you folded it up nice and small. I can just barely fit it under my down vest." She smiled to show Bernice that all was well.

Unconvinced, Bernice said, "Does anyone else know you're doing this?"

"Yes, but I can't say anything more," Fern said, serious now. "My back — and a whole lot more — will be watched this afternoon. You have to trust that we know what we're doing. Today and every day, Bernice. Your life will be easier if you let me do my job and know that I'll be safe and successful."

"I hear you, but I also know that your cute husband was almost killed right there," she pointed to the deck that was visible from the living room where they stood. "And Matt is very good at his job. My point being that these guys are obviously determined, and I have a feeling they won't care if it's a man or a woman in their way. A cop is a cop."

"But I'm not a cop. I'm a Public Affairs Liaison," Fern said in her best fake politician voice.

"And I'm Beyoncé." Bernice turned to leave, saying sternly, "Keep me posted."

. . .

As it turned out, Bernice didn't have a thing to worry about. Fern parked her car in the same spot, took the wooden, sandy stairs down to the beach, and set off jogging south on the firmly packed sand close to the waves breaking ashore. It was nasty weather, raining as if the skies meant it, but it provided good cover for the jogger, who pulled her black hood tightly around her face and hair.

Although she couldn't see them — which was a good thing — she knew Jay and Ed were in position on the wooded bluff above her as she neared the sand dunes on Chen's property. Their plan had been delayed about ninety minutes while Jay dealt with an unexpected turn of events that he told Fern he'd explain later. He was animated, and Fern was curious, but she needed to stay focused on the task at hand. She waited at her house until she'd received a "thumbs up" text from Jay.

Coolly, she turned inland from the ocean as she arrived at the location and scanned the beach in both directions. There was no one within sight. *Can't say I blame them*, she thought, shaking rain off her hood to improve her vision as she looked for the exact spot. She found the rock behind the dune where the raft had been tucked, moved quickly to it while unzipping her vest. She pulled it out, jiggled it loose from its folds, and tucked the raft behind the rock, just as she'd found it.

Fern didn't know if Ed or Jay would have their binocs on her as she jogged north, but she gave a subtle "thumbs up" gesture with her right hand as soon as she cleared Chen's space.

Jay caught the thumb, but Zhang Chen could only see the back of the jogger clad in all black. Still, he was sure he knew who it was that just replaced Michael Winston's raft in its original hiding place. He climbed down from the loft of his barn where he'd been watching all day and went to the house to get rid of his parents.

TWENTY-FOUR

Fern took a long, hot shower, and dressed in warm, comfy clothes while she packed a bag for tomorrow morning's trip back to Portland. Downstairs, she turned on the gas fireplace, pushed the button that closed the heavy velvet window drapes (she didn't even know for sure that they worked, since they'd never closed them before the shooting), and headed to the kitchen to make some dinner as she waited for Jay. It was starting to get dark, and she figured he and Ed would call it a day soon.

A glass of wine would be nice, she thought as she defrosted some chicken thighs and washed a head of escarole. Pouring a nice Sancerre, she found some Gochujang sauce and honey in the pantry. She would cook the chicken on the cooktop, and then swirl the sauce and the honey in the rendered chicken fat to pour over the torn escarole leaves.

Her phone pinged. A text from Jay: "On my way." Fern turned down the chicken and waited.

• • •

"You are not going to believe this," Jay exclaimed, bounding into Fern's house, dripping water and mud all over the floor.

"Welcome home, honey," she deadpanned.

He eyed the glass of wine in her hand and said, "I'd kill for a beer."

"You won't have to. I'll get you one if you take off your shoes and coat before you step on my beautiful carpet."

He looked down at the pool of water on the floor. "Uh, sorry." He took off his shoes and found that even his socks were soaked through, so yanked them off, too. He headed down the hall to "his room" and exchanged his wet clothes for nice dry sweats and a clean pair of socks.

"Better?" she inquired as he came into the kitchen. She handed him a beer.

"What smells so good?" Jay said, peering over the island at the cooktop.

"I'm making chicken thighs and escarole," Fern said. "Had a feeling you might be hungry after an afternoon crouching in the trees, and we could both use some protein and veggies."

"Oh, and there's so much more to my day," he grinned. "You did great, by the way."

"Easy peasy. Did you see any sign of Zhang Chen? Anybody else go to the raft site?"

"No, not while we were there. Ed thought he might have caught a glimpse of him up near his barn, but we didn't have a good angle at that — we were focused on the sand dune and your rock. We're going back tomorrow and will re-position ourselves so we can see up toward his house and barn, too. We just wanted to make sure that you were safe today on your errand."

"No problems at all for me. I didn't see another human until I got back to my car in the parking lot, and that was an elderly couple with a California license plate. They were huddled in their car enjoying the rainy view. What happened this morning and where were you?"

He lifted his beer and clinked it against her wine glass. "Here's to Detective Patty Perkins, one of the finest cops I know."

"I agree, but why now?" asked Fern.

"Because she followed Ray Peng this morning in disguise in Ted's truck. He led her straight to a major ghost gun manufacturing plant in the boonies off Raccoon Hill Road."

"Are you kidding me?!?"

Jay grinned. "I am not." He gave her a recap of the morning's activities.

"How long has this been going on?" Fern asked.

"Ray Peng wouldn't say anything, but Wong Li, the plant manager, said he'd been hired last July. He indicated the building had been constructed shortly after the earthquake."

"I thought the BLM owned that land on Cherry Drive. There never used to be any structures on it. I remember because I planted trees around there when I was in junior high."

"Brace yourself," Jay said, looking smug. "A big chunk of land at the end of Cherry Drive is now owned by an LLC."

Fern's eyebrows shot up. "How did we not know that?"

"The transaction was done shortly after the earthquake. If I recall, we were a little busy then. And, as long as they've been quiet, there was no reason we would know. When's the last time you were on Cherry Drive?" Jay asked.

"Seventh grade, I guess. I go over Raccoon Hill Road to Twisty River all the time, but I've never gone down that road. Figured there was nothing there but trees."

"Right. Same as all of us. Patty told me she hadn't been there since a brush cleanup party twenty years ago."

"Do we know if it's Zhang Chen behind the LLC?" she asked.

"Patty's tracing it now with Earl's help. The name of the corporation on the county record is TowerWest LLC, and it's not one we've associated with Chen so far. She told me she'd know who's behind it by tomorrow morning."

"If it's him, he seems to be buying up property in Chinook County. How does he know about all these remote places? His house? Ray Peng's property? And now, maybe Raccoon Hill Road? How does a guy like him know about this rural stuff?"

"Maybe he has a local connection."

"He must," Fern agreed. "Because as far as we know, this is the first time he's been here in person."

"All I know is that if Patty can tie this corporation to him, we've got grounds to bring him in for questioning. At the least, whoever built this building didn't apply for a planning permit, and there were never any inspections done — I checked."

"So, everything completely under the table?" Fern asked.

Jay nodded. "And it looked to Patty and me that it was running off the grid—solar, wind, batteries. I've got a crew going out there tomorrow to figure it all out. Whoever owns it didn't want anyone in authority to know."

"And we wouldn't know if Patty hadn't taken matters into her own hands to follow Ray Peng. I love that woman. Is she in any danger?"

"Possibly. There's a lot of chatter these days about "rogue cops", and both Earl and Dalrymple say we have to pay attention to it."

Fern thought. "Then it depends on how much Peng whines and to whom he whines. Are you holding him overnight?"

"Yes. I let Wong Li go because he told us that Ray Peng is in charge and hired everyone initially. Peng's the boss, and until we discover if he built the structure illegally, I'm keeping him safe in our jail."

"Does he have a lawyer yet?" Fern asked.

"Of course," Jay grimaced. "Some hotshot from Buck Bay. I don't know him, but Patty has dealt with him before. Says he's a real pain in the ass."

"Is it alright with you if I share this info with Joe Phelps?"

"I was going to suggest that actually," said Jay. "You and he need to be in this loop with us. There's just too much Chinese action for my comfort level. It's clear to me that we're dealing with more than a local guy who doesn't like your husband because he cut in front of him in the liquor store."

"Matt would never cut in front of someone," Fern smiled. "I think you're right. This is starting to feel big. I'm going up to Portland tomorrow, and I'll call Joe on the way and get a read on what he's thinking. Are you having a crime team meeting?"

"Uh-huh, I've scheduled it for 9:00 a.m. Can you stick around until 10:00 or so and join us?"

"Yeah, we've got a lot of pieces maybe starting to come together," Fern said. "I'll be a quiet observer while you guys hash it out."

"Does that mean you won't strike our district attorney?" he smirked.

"That was bad, wasn't it? I just hate that man. Please don't tell anyone I said that."

"He's doing his job, Fern, but your secret's safe with me. Is the chicken ready?"

• • •

Zhang Chen also took a long, hot shower after spending most of his day in the barn watching his beach for intruders. He'd been rewarded for his effort. *Matt Horning's new bride. Oh, yes, I keep up with your sleepy little village.* He had no idea how she'd found the hidden raft in the first place — and it was sloppy of him to assume his property would be safe from searches — but that was definitely her returning it. During the Anselmo operation he'd studied photos of her that Octavio had provided, and he'd continued to track all the principals in local law enforcement. *Too bad our gunman didn't get her at the same time as her husband. Apparently, I have to do everything myself.*

He dried off and dressed in a new sweater and pants his parents had bought him for his last birthday. They'd long ago given up trying to buy the perfect present for their son who had everything, and just bought him what they liked. Since he was driving his parents to the Buck Bay airport for their trip home to San Francisco, he thought it wouldn't kill him to wear his mother's favorite sweater.

Enjoying both the Oregon coast and his company, they hadn't wanted to return home yet, but Zhang insisted. He told them he had some technology work to finish this week, and he needed total concentration. Both parents were baffled by their son's business and didn't want anything to do with it. It was a built-in excuse for him anytime he didn't want them around. Like now.

When he pulled the Honda out onto the highway heading north, Zhang casually checked all his mirrors to see if he was being followed. What happened to Ray Peng this morning was inexcusable. *How could he not recognize Detective Perkins after her big role in the Anselmo's aftermath? Everybody in Chinook County knew Patty Perkins.* Now that the authorities had discovered the ghost gun manufacturing operation, they would double their efforts. He'd anticipated this day might come and was prepared to deal with the fallout, but it didn't absolve Ray of his amateurish move.

Zhang's father, who'd emigrated from China when he was thirty years old and prided himself on his difficult early life, squirmed in the passenger seat. "Why you buy this uncomfortable car?"

Zhang laughed. "You like my California limo, huh?"

"Better than this mousetrap."

"I have spoiled you, father."

"We will miss being spoiled by you, Zhang," said his mother from the back seat. "And I will miss Oregon and your beautiful home here. It's my favorite."

"You can come back anytime you want," Zhang said. "I like it here, too, but I don't think my business will allow me to be here much longer. You, however, can come back whenever you like. Did I give you the garage code? That's the way to enter."

"Yes, I wrote it down this morning," she said. "We may return as soon as we get through the busy holidays at the restaurant."

"Why do you work so hard?" Zhang asked his parents. "I know you are young yet, but you could retire."

His parents both laughed. "Big secret," said his father. "We really don't work hard at all; we make sure our employees do."

"And we like going to the restaurant because that's when we see all of our friends," added his mother. "It's very social for us. Especially between now and right after Chinese New Year in February. Lots of parties and big groups. But after that, we'd like to return to Port Stirling, OK?"

"Yes, OK," said Zhang. "You can be my caretakers." *What a great cover for my Oregon business*, he thought.

. . .

Rudy finished baking his lasagna and set it on the kitchen counter to cool. He lived just south of Port Stirling on the east side of the highway in a small apartment complex. Rudy's apartment was on the ground floor and faced the hills to the east that separated the coastal Port Stirling from the Twisty River valley.

As the afternoon wore on, the weather deteriorated, and looking out his kitchen window now, Rudy's usual view of the hills was obliterated by the steely rain whipping against the window. While the lasagna cooled, he thought it might be good to drive south the three miles to Zhang Chen's road and watch for a while until the daylight faded.

Rudy had done this every spare minute since he, Patty, and Earl had paid a visit to Chen last Friday. He'd found a mostly concealed turnout on 101 immediately south of Chen's road that allowed him to see any car coming out of his drive. So far it had been a waste of time, but he was determined to keep trying.

Like his previous visits, Rudy didn't know exactly what he was looking for, but he'd had a strong, visceral reaction to Chen. His boss, Matt, had always told him to follow his gut, and his gut was telling him to watch Chen's neck of the woods. Jay had OK'd his highway watch but told him to be 'subtle'. So, he took his own car, an older, beat-up Jetta, instead of the squad car. Rudy was saving to buy a snazzy new car more befitting a stud like himself, but he still had a few months to go.

He'd been parked about thirty minutes, running his windshield wipers occasionally to clear up his field of vision, when a black Honda pulled out of Chen's road and headed north toward Port Stirling. Visibility was poor, but Rudy thought it was Chen driving. He waited for a couple of cars to pass him, and then shoved off behind them heading the same direction.

Hanging back, Rudy followed Chen's car all the way to Buck Bay. *Airport. Is he making a run for it? Didn't the sheriff tell him to stay in Chinook County?*

Chen pulled over to the curb in a space marked 'Charter Departures'. Rudy drove past him, parking his car at the curb several cars in front of Chen's. In his rear-view mirror, he saw Chen with his mother and presumably his father exit the car. Chen and his father hauled four suitcases out of the trunk and placed them on the curb. A few seconds later, a uniformed attendant came out of a gate, bowed, and then shook hands with Chen, and loaded the luggage onto a rolling cart. He motioned for the parents to follow him, and they did so after hugging their son.

Chen watched them walk to the waiting jet, waved as they boarded, and then got back in his car and drove off.

Rudy followed him through Buck Bay until it was clear Chen was headed back to Port Stirling. Then he dropped back, not wanting to push his luck. He called Jay on the way back to his apartment and told him he'd be at Fern's soon with the lasagna to take to Portland.

"So, he dumped the old folks, huh?" said Jay when Rudy recapped his activity. "But he's staying on. Wonder why?"

"Do you want me to keep watching his road?" Rudy asked.

"Yes. And I'm starting to not care much if he knows we're following him. The shooter's getaway raft was found on his property, after all. We need a come-to-Jesus meeting with the crime team tomorrow morning."

"He's in this, Jay. Patty said it best—he's evil. I don't get why a guy with a bazillion dollars doesn't go buy a new Porsche to go with his plane and ship and play with all his toys, but he's in this somehow. I feel it."

"You sound like our boss," Jay said. "And we don't know that he owns that ship."

"Go with the gut, man," said Rudy.

"Proceed, but don't tell anyone what you're doing," Jay instructed. "Patty and I might take some heat for shutting down the ghost gun operation this morning, and we don't need all our cops in trouble. You stay squeaky clean. Hear me? If you get into a situation, call only me for backup."

"Roger that. See you in a few with the pasta."

TWENTY-FIVE

The county crime team met the next morning at 9:00 a.m.

"Welcome everyone," said Jay, standing by his whiteboard. "Thanks for coming. I want to start today by laying out the known facts." He had—like he'd seen Matt do several times—tacked up photos of people involved in their investigation so far and written what they knew about each of them below their photo and name.

Jay pointed to the photo of Michael Christopher Winston. "This is our shooter, people. Bernice took his prints off the raft that Fern found, and Joe Phelps at the State Department has identified them as belonging to this guy. This photo was taken when he was twenty-seven, and we now believe him to be forty-six."

"We don't know for sure that the raft came from the ship that you and Ed saw yet, do we?" asked the sheriff.

"No, but it's a high likelihood," answered Jay. "I remember seeing a flash of something the same color as the raft, and both crafts have Chinese lettering."

"Circumstantial," said the district attorney. "How are you going to prove that the owner of these fingerprints was on that ship, or is even in the area?"

"We don't believe he is still in the area," said Fern. "The Portland police have this photo and the details we know about him and are showing it around at OHSU. They think it's likely the same shooter, and they also think he's not still in Oregon. They think he got away."

"Where is the raft now?" asked Dalrymple. "Can we trace it further?"

"I still have it," Bernice lied. She spoke hurriedly. "I'm not finished with it yet."

Jay quickly turned back to Winston's photo. "Both Phelps' office and Sylvia are working on researching this guy. Whether we believe the raft came off the ship or not, the known fact is that he was in it at one time, probably recently, and I'd like to know why and more about him. We know with certainty that Winston was arrested carrying a concealed gun at one point in his life, however many years ago it was." He looked over at Sylvia. "Sylvia already discovered that he doesn't live in Oregon…there's no record of him anywhere in the state, now or in the past."

"That's right," Sylvia said. "We just got this information yesterday afternoon, and I've only had time to rule out Oregon residency. He was arrested in Atlanta when this photo was taken, so I'm starting on Georgia now." She patted her hair and consulted her notes. "Mr. Phelps is working on discovering which flight he may have arrived on, thereby giving us another location, although Joe said because of the many years, that's probably a long shot. He's checking with the IRS and other government entities that may have a current address for him. I should know more by this afternoon."

"At the very least," Jay continued, "Winston is a person of interest for us because he's a stranger to our town, and because of his previous gun-related arrest."

"I'm going up to see Matt today when we're finished here," Fern added, "and I'll see if he or Gabriela, the wounded cop, connects with this photo in any way."

"How is he doing?" Patty asked.

Fern smiled. "Itching to come home."

"That's great news," Ed said, beaming broadly. "Will you bring him back with you?"

"Don't know yet," Fern said cautiously. "It's up to the docs. Believe me, after everything they've done, I'm doing whatever they tell me to do."

"Smart woman," said Dalrymple. "Please keep us informed and don't hesitate if there is anything we can do to help you, Fern."

She stared at him. "You can get us search warrants for Zhang Chen and Ray Peng. That would help me."

"Maybe it would or maybe it would make all of our lives more difficult," Dalrymple said. He looked down at his notebook.

"The next news may make your decision easier, David," said Jay. He placed an index finger on Ray Peng's photo on his board and said, "I arrested Ray Peng yesterday for operating a business without a permit."

Ed laughed. "Wondered when you were going to get around to that little nugget."

"You've heard?" asked Jay.

"We've all heard," said Dalrymple. "His attorney is screaming at anyone who will listen. You need to fine Peng and turn him loose, Jay."

Jay shook his head. "Don't think so. Because the business deals with the manufacture of guns, we need to take our time and make sure that the owner and all the employees don't have any felony arrest records. We're in the process of checking that now. And it's going slow." Jay paused. "Real slow."

Sheriff Earl Johnson smiled to himself and shifted in his chair but didn't say a word.

"His attorney will rip you a new one if you hold him much longer," Dalrymple said.

"I'm prepared for that eventuality," said Jay. It sounded exactly like something Matt would have said. "We don't even know who owns the building or the land. It's a Chinese LLC and we're trying to track down the principals involved. Also slow going."

"Are you going to share with us how you discovered this business?" asked Dalrymple. "And where is it?"

"I'll take that one," said Patty. She was back in her full cop uniform this morning, attempting to look like an officer of the law who would never, ever bend the rules. "Yesterday was my day off, and I was driving over to a farm north of Port Stirling to pick up some fertilizer for Ted. I happened to notice Ray Peng's bright yellow mustang in front of me on Raccoon Hill Road, and I saw him turn on Cherry Drive. I thought to myself, "you haven't been down that road for decades, wonder where he's going?" She had rehearsed this little speech this morning on the drive to Port Stirling and repeated it word-for-word.

"So, you followed him?" asked the sheriff.

"I did," Patty said. "Out of curiosity. And when I discovered there were several vehicles there and obviously a bunch of people, I got a little nervous and called Jay for backup. I figured he was the closest to the location."

"Imagine our surprise when we walked in the open door and saw about a dozen men assembling all varieties of guns," said Jay.

"Was Peng in charge?" asked Ed. "Could you tell?"

Jay nodded. "Clearly. We also arrested Wong Li, who appears to be the shop manager. But he and all the men deferred to Peng. I let Li go last night but made it clear that they are shut down until we run some checks."

Earl banged his hand on the table, which he seemed to be doing more and more of these days. "This is my worst nightmare," the sheriff said. "If I were retired, I'd be saying 'get off my lawn', but instead I have to deal with ghost guns in my neighborhood. Why can't people just get a decent job and earn a decent living?"

"You sound like an old curmudgeon," teased Ed. "Actually, you sound a lot like me. Our unemployment rate is at a record low, and businesses are having trouble hiring qualified workers. Why do these guys have to go do shit work like this? Excuse my language." Ed stole a look at Sylvia, expecting her usual reprimand.

Instead, she said, "I agree with you, Ed, it is shit work. Making these guns you all can't track, and who knows for what dreadful reasons."

"Well, it's fairly obvious," grumped the sheriff. "There's more money to be had in guns than in flipping burgers. But it's deeply troubling. Do we know how long the operation has been running?"

"We know the land was acquired right after the earthquake," said Jay. "Our guess is that the building was constructed shortly after that."

"How could they have built it then?" asked Ed. "None of us could get any supplies in the earthquake's aftermath. It took me eight months to rebuild my little patio."

"Yeah, I wondered about that, too," said Jay. "Maybe the ship we saw on Thanksgiving brought in materials from wherever."

"So maybe all this ties together somehow?" mused Earl. "I had a bad feeling about Ray Peng when we first arrested him." He shook his head remorsefully. "I never should have let him go. Maybe Matt wouldn't have been shot."

Patty reached over to the sheriff and patted his arm. "You had no choice, Earl, and it wouldn't have changed a thing. Bad guys are gonna do bad things."

"What kind of guns are they manufacturing?" asked Buck Bay chief Dan McCoy. McCoy had been in the cop biz for almost twenty years, and he knew a lot about guns.

"Handguns, rifles, you name it," said Jay. "3-D printers along with a standard factory operation. I'd say it's a big business."

"Do we know where and how they sell them?" asked McCoy.

"Nope. Ray Peng is refusing to answer any of our questions," Jay said.

"And he won't," said Dalrymple. "On his attorney's advice, no doubt."

"Fine," said Patty, addressing the D.A. "The longer he refuses to help Jay understand if this 'business' is legally operating, the longer it stays shut down. Which is fine by me."

"You guys are really putting the county at risk, you know," said Dalrymple. "Look, I don't like this ghost gun stuff anymore than any of you cops do, and I agree with you that the law has some loopholes in it, but you can't follow everybody you don't like, you can't stake out their homes, and you can't arrest them on flimsy charges. Please, I'm just trying to protect all of us."

"Well, I don't like sending one of my best friends off in a LifeFlight helicopter because I couldn't repair an artery in his neck," said Bernice, her voice icily cold. She stared at Dalrymple. "A neck that was probably ripped apart by one of these damnable ghost guns that you say you don't like. I'm not a lawyer and I'm not a cop, but I'm here today to tell you folks that you have to do whatever you can to stop this deadly scourge. And if someone gets their tiny little feelings hurt, tough shit."

There was a quaver in her voice and her eyes reddened, but she kept talking. "Matt should be dead. Who's next, do you suppose?" Bernice asked. "Fern? Earl? Jay? What if it's open season on every law enforcement officer in Chinook County? Am I supposed to sew them back up as best I can, and hope OHSU can save their lives? Do something, dammit!"

The room was quiet.

"She's right," Fern said finally. "We have to consider people's rights under the law, of course, but we're derelict in our duties if we don't pursue every possible lead. Even those that might put us in a shady area, David."

"I thought your new job was Public Affairs," Dalrymple said. "This sounds like you're still in law enforcement to some degree."

"My husband was nearly killed," Fern glared at him. "Would you have me stand idly by?"

"Let's move on," Jay said quickly, still standing at his board. "We're not totally focused on Ray Peng and Zhang Chen; we've also been looking into people in Matt's past that may have a beef with him. Patty, did you talk to the Carmichaels?"

"I did." Patty flipped back through her notebook. "You will recall," she said to the table, "that Dianne and Nick Carmichael and their parents weren't particularly pleased at the outcome of our Tyee Kouse investigation."

Sheriff Earl snorted. "I noticed. They didn't donate to my re-election campaign this year."

"I talked to Nick earlier this week," Patty said. "He spent Thanksgiving at Mason and Marilyn Carmichael's — his parents — home in Palm Desert, California. He seemed genuinely upset to hear about Matt's shooting, and said he never wished him any harm. I checked his alibi, and he was in California. He flew from Portland to Palm Springs, and the dates jived with what Nick told me."

"Doesn't mean he couldn't have hired someone," Jay remarked.

"True," Patty said. "But if we're going full Carmichael family, Dianne or her father are more likely the hire-a-gunman types."

"Did you talk to them?" asked the D.A.

"I talked to Dianne — briefly — but dad didn't return my calls. Dianne and her husband were, and still are, in the Caribbean. When I explained to her why I was calling, she said, and I quote: 'You seem to be mistaking my family for common criminals', and then she hung up on me."

"And I'll bet her nose was stuck up in the air when she said that," laughed Earl.

Patty smiled. "Sure of it. I checked out Dianne's alibi, too, and they flew and rented a house—both legit. I'll keep trying to talk to Mason or Marilyn, and I've got their Palm Desert housekeeper's name from Nick to try as well. I believe they're in the clear, but I'll keep trying until I'm one hundred percent sure. The Carmichaels don't like us, but they're not rabid enough to kill a cop."

"I checked in on the Bushnell family," said Jay. "Matt had a role in their outcomes, you'll remember, and Fern and I thought there could be some smoldering resentment."

"Where are they now?" asked Dalrymple.

"Fred, Gary, and Susan have moved to Seattle," answered Jay. "Marjorie is now living alone in Scottsdale, and Jack remains in the Oregon State Hospital. Fred was cordial and sends his regards to all of you. He and his two kids had Thanksgiving dinner at a Seattle restaurant during the time that Matt was shot, and Sylvia confirmed that with the restaurant. Marjorie said—and I'm paraphrasing here—"Too bad your police chief didn't die. I hate Matt Horning, but if I were going to kill him, I would've done it by now."

"Pleasant woman," said Fern. "Bet there's a lot of people on her do-not-like list."

"She was home alone on Thanksgiving Day, so no alibi," Jay continued. "But the Scottsdale police did a house check for me, and they confirmed that she's home now. It feels unlikely that Marjorie flew here, boarded that ship, shot Matt, escaped, and made her way to Portland, attempted another murder, escaped again, and then flew home to Scottsdale."

"It's gotta be a pro," said Ed. "It was too carefully planned, with too many difficult details for an amateur, especially one as unhinged as Marjorie Bushnell. Is Jack doing any better?"

"They wouldn't tell me anything about his condition," Jay said. "Just confirmed that he's still there receiving treatment. Poor kid."

Another silence around the table as they all remembered that terrible, tragic day for the Bushnell family.

"Moving on," Fern said, "I had a phone call with one of the guys we arrested during the Anselmo raid, Kevin Crown. He's still in Oregon, too, a guest at the state prison. He was one of Octavio's right-hand men, and Matt got his sentence shortened because he helped us figure out some of the details."

"I remember him," Dalrymple said. "A bit player. Did he shed any light on our current case?"

"'Fraid not," said Fern, shaking her head. "He never met Zhang Chen, or whoever was Octavio's boss. Still swears he doesn't know who the head honcho was, and I believe him. Doesn't know anything about a ghost gun manufacturing facility and doubted that the two operations were connected in any way."

"Anything else from him" asked Jay.

"Said he'd go under cover for us and see what he could find out if we'd commute his remaining sentence," Fern offered.

"That's not how it works," said Ed, shaking his head. "No siree bob. That guy helped ruin the lives of a lot of young women."

"I told him you'd say that," smiled Fern.

"It's not an altogether terrible idea," said Jay. He rubbed his chin. "Would you trust him, Fern?"

"Not sure. I dismissed him like Ed did for being scum of the earth, but I did think about it last night," she admitted. "He was clearly part of the underground crooks' network. He might be able to dig out some dirt that could help us. But make no mistake, he is a scumbag."

"You're not going to get anything useful from this guy," said Dan McCoy. "Talk to Joe Phelps; he'll tell you the same thing. He just sees an opportunity and he's trying to take advantage of it."

"I agree with Dan," said Patty. "He's a low life, and I wouldn't trust him as far as I could throw him. He personally raped at least two of the girls, and I suspect there might have been more. He deserves to be where he is, and he's a clear and present danger to the community. Please don't consider this, Jay. We can investigate on our own with better results." There was a high color to Patty's face that usually came whenever the talk turned to 'her girls'.

"Where are we with the ship's owners?" asked Ed.

"Nowhere, that's where," sulked Fern. "Joe said the Chinese ambassador's staff is working on getting information on the Pearl Dragon, but the ship registry is dragging their heels. It's supposed to be public info — owners' names and so forth — but they're not forthcoming."

"That sucks," said Jay dejectedly.

"Does Joe think they'll eventually come through with anything?" asked Dalrymple. "It would be nice to at least know to whom that ship is registered, and a recent sailing itinerary."

Fern shrugged. "We don't really know. Joe told me the Coast Guard in Oregon is asking, too. The thought being that if the Hong Kong registry is being bombarded from two sides of the U.S. government, they might take it more seriously. But our ambassador says he has to be careful; there's a lot more at stake than the name of the owner of one, possibly rogue, ship."

"I get that," said Jay, "but it's frustrating. It's the best lead we've got. Otherwise, I'm back to Ray Peng and/or Zhang Chen."

"And probably getting the county sued," said Dalrymple.

The team filed out of the room. Bernice and Fern were the last two to leave.

"I owe you," Fern whispered to her.

"Yes, you do," Bernice whispered back. "I just lied to our district attorney. You'll buy me the finest dinner Chinook County has to offer, and I'll pick the restaurant."

TWENTY-SIX

After the team meeting, Fern returned to her house. She changed into a pink cashmere sweater and her favorite jeans for the drive back to Portland and OHSU. She packed her wheelie and a backpack, not knowing how long she'd be staying this time. Optimistically, she also packed a small bag with some of Matt's favorite clothes, including his well-worn Texas sweatshirt.

She held the sweatshirt close to her face, hoping to get a whiff of her husband, but it had been laundered since he'd worn it. Fern smiled, appreciating how tidy and clean Matt was. *Of course, he'd do laundry while I was in Georgia.*

There were so many things about him she loved. When she first got to know him, Fern had figured he was probably a country music fan, growing up in Texas and all. But when they first hooked up in earnest, she learned his tastes veered more to older, classic rock 'n roll. His music library, both at the house and in his car were filled with the likes of Marvin Gay, the Stones, Credence Clearwater, and Tina Turner.

As she packed, she turned on his personalized Pandora station. Even though the team meeting had been disappointing in terms of any new progress, Fern had a good feeling about today, and she danced around her bedroom as she filled their bags. By the time she'd listened to the long version of Tina's *Proud Mary*—cranked up loud—she'd finished and was ready to hit the road.

Downstairs, she paused to look out the windows, first out to sea and then to the deck. It had been thoroughly cleaned when she'd been in Portland the last time, and while she didn't ask, she knew it had been Jay who handled it, and she was grateful for his kindness and friendship. *I hope it will be as easy to wipe away Matt's injured body and any remaining bad memories of the shooting once he's safely home.*

She was worried, but not fearful, of what was ahead for her when Matt was able to come home. Would he require professional nursing, or would she be able to take care of him herself? Fern hadn't been sick at all in her life, and she knew virtually nothing about medical issues. But whatever Matt's requirements would be, she was determined to manage it. *One way or another, I will learn or do what's necessary because getting my love back to his full, wonderful self is the only thing that matters. And then, I'm going to find who did this and make them regret it for the rest of their lives.*

• • •

Today's downpour coupled with heavy winds forced her to take Matt's SUV; her little car didn't care for wet freeways and made its point by frequently hydroplaning into a skid. Traffic was heavy, especially with trucks, and it slowed her down further.

She was so excited to see Matt that she didn't mind the dreadful weather on the road this afternoon. *What do you expect? It's December in Oregon.*

Stopping briefly downtown, Fern quickly checked into The Heathman, leaving her car with the valet, and explaining that she was going right back out. She dropped her bags in the room, had a quick pee, applied some cheery makeup, and headed downstairs. It was a quick drive up 'Pill Hill' to the OHSU hospital, and not for the first time, she wondered how the shooter had escaped from here.

Gabby had shot him in the leg, and it couldn't have been easy to hike off this wooded hill to freedom. They knew he didn't drive off because no vehicles were reported stolen, and by the second day, a rental car was discovered in a far corner of the big parking garage. A trace on the driver's license and credit card used to rent it had both turned out to belong to a man who'd been dead for eighteen months. Essentially, a dead end.

To her delight, Matt was sitting up reading when she entered his room. She rushed to him and gave him a careful, but juicy, big kiss.

"You are a sight for sore eyes, Mrs. Horning. I love that sweater on you."

"Thought so. You bought it," she teased.

"I thought you weren't coming until tomorrow," he said, squeezing her hand.

"I couldn't stay away," Fern said. She meant it. "I did what needed to be done in Port Stirling like you told me, but they can do without me for a few days. I'm where I need to be." She squeezed back. "You look good, Matt. The difference since I last saw you is really noticeable." He had more color in his face, and his eyes looked brighter.

"I'm feeling pretty good. Turned a corner yesterday, I think."

"How so?" she asked.

"I'm not as fuzzy in my head." He grinned at her. "Does that make sense? I started reading night before last, I think it was, and I can follow and understand what I'm reading."

"That's progress, honey. Are you sleeping well?"

He chuckled. "That's all I do. I read for a while, then sleep for a while. The food here is not worth staying awake for."

"Don't complain," Fern admonished. "For the first few days all you got was liquids. Being able to eat real food is a blessing."

"It's not 'real' food," he laughed. "That's my point. I'd kill for a burger and fries!"

"And I suppose you'd like a vanilla milkshake along with that, right?"

"If you do this for me, I'll buy you anything in the world your heart desires," he said seriously.

"Deal," she laughed. "Oh, Matt, it's so good to see you getting better. I love you so much." She teared up.

He wagged his finger at her. "No. No. No more tears." His voice was strong. "I'm going to be fine, and we're going home and spending the rest of our beautiful lives together."

She brushed her tears away. "Do you realize that nine days ago you couldn't wag your finger. Couldn't lift your arms. Couldn't focus when I was in the room with you. They told me you might die," she said. "I'm crying tears of joy, and I'm fucking allowed."

He laughed. "Yeah, you're fucking allowed. Come here," he ordered. He put his book on the tray next to the bed.

She crawled onto the bed and nestled against his chest. Gently, he put his arm around her. They stayed like that for half an hour, chatting easily and hugging.

• • •

A knock on the door made them jump, and Dr. Nathalie Kumar entered Matt's room. Fern rose from the bed and hugged the doctor.

"Thank you so much, from both of us," Fern said.

"You're welcome," Dr. Kumar replied. She pointed to Matt. "But thank him, too; he did the heavy lifting. No giving up in this guy."

"Look at her," Matt said. "Would you give up if you were married to this gorgeous creature?"

"She's not my type, but I get your drift," the doctor said. "Now, I suppose the two of you have been discussing your departure from our elegant hotel."

"Can I go?" Matt asked.

"Not this minute, but soon," Dr. Kumar said. "Can you make it to the bathroom under your own steam?" She indicated the door in the room's corner. "That's one of my tests. No woman on this earth wants to take her man into the bathroom."

Without hesitation and without saying a word, Matt threw back the covers, swung his legs over the side of the bed, and stood. A little wobbly at first, but then he walked to the bathroom and opened the door.

"That's OK," said the doctor. "We don't need a demonstration. I wanted to test your will." Fern laughed.

"I want to go home, doc," Matt said. "I'm ready and I'm leaving you."

"How does tomorrow sound?" Dr. Kumar said.

"Today sounds better," Matt said.

She shook her head. "I need to do a couple more tests now, and then you need one more night of good sleep. But I think by tomorrow afternoon, you'll be ready." She turned to Fern. "Are you ready?"

Fern looked at Matt. "Ready and willing. Till death do us part."

"Don't push your luck, Fern," said Dr. Kumar. "I'll see you both tomorrow."

• • •

Fern drove off the hill and went to Higgins Restaurant, just up SW Broadway from The Heathman. Last time she was in town, she'd had the best burger here, and she knew Matt would love it. Grass-fed beef with blue cheese on a fresh-baked bun. Delish.

She waited at the bar while they cooked it. There'd been a little kerfuffle about the vanilla milkshake. "We don't really do milkshakes," the waiter had told her.

"Can you do this one?" Fern persisted. "It's for a special man who's been in the hospital. I happen to love him, and I want him to be happy." She smiled brightly at him.

The waiter smiled back at her and said, "In that case, let me see what we can do."

• • •

Higgins aced it, and Matt was a happy man. He wolfed down burger, fries, and shake, wiped his mouth with a hospital napkin and set it down on his tray.

"Do you know what life is about?" he asked Fern, sitting in his bedside chair.

"No, Mr. Horning," she replied. "Do tell me." She crossed her legs and sat back in her chair.

"It's about the simple things. A perfectly cooked burger, for instance."

"And love," she said.

"Love's not simple," Matt disagreed. "It's complicated, and hard, and it took me decades to find it."

"You're right," she said. "Me too. Let's just sit here a while and enjoy it." Dr. Kumar had been in earlier to take some of Matt's blood and to test his reflexes. She'd whispered to Fern to not stay too late, as she wanted Matt to go to sleep early, and he would fight it as long as Fern was there. Fern figured he'd drop off after his heavy dinner, so she was deliberately winding him down.

But he didn't take the bait. "What do you want for your reward for bringing me the best dinner I've had in weeks?" he said.

Fern gazed out the window at the dark, rainy evening. "What I want is for you and me to go back to Maui, but that can't happen right now."

"Raincheck?"

"Yes. In the meantime, I want you to be honest with me about how you're feeling." She paused. "I may not be great at this nurse stuff, and I need you to tell me the truth about what you need. It won't do either of us any good if you play Superman and don't level with me about your health."

"Understood," he said. "But I don't want to be a burden to you. I wouldn't leave here if I didn't feel I could handle it. We'll be fine. If you don't fuss over me, I won't hide anything. Deal?"

"Deal," she answered. "But right now, I need to get out of here. Dr. Kumar wants you to sleep, and, honestly, I'm worn out from my nasty drive up here this afternoon. You may have noticed that it can be stormy in Oregon." She rose from her chair and took his hand in hers. "I'm going back to the hotel now, and take a long, hot bath. I'll see you in the morning, cowboy." She smiled and kissed him.

Matt grabbed on tight to her hand, looked deep into her eyes, and said seriously, "Thank you, Fern. For being my wife, for taking care of everything, and, especially, for the burger."

She laughed loudly and waved goodbye to him from his door.

• • •

The next morning, Fern opened the black-out curtains in her hotel room and peeked out. After raining intermittently all night, it had finally stopped, and fluffy white clouds took turns wandering in front of the sun in the mostly blue sky. It was 7:30 a.m. and it was an important day — Matt was coming home.

Dr. Kumar had called her last night to let Fern know that his blood-work looked good, and that they would have him ready to leave about noon. She ordered room service and made some phone calls while she waited, calling her boss in Washington, D.C. first.

"Guess what today is?" Fern said when Phelps picked up.

"Matt's going home from the hospital?" he guessed.

"Yes! How did you know?"

"Because you sound happy for the first time in two weeks. I'm thrilled for both of you, Fern."

"Thanks, it's a great day. But I'm still working." She filled him in on the ghost gun manufacturing facility and explained Jay's strategy for keeping Ray Peng in jail while they continued their research into the background of all the employees.

"I hope you get lucky and find some felonies there," said Joe, agreeing with her and Jay that was certainly a possibility with this crew. "Jay is perfectly within his rights to hold the head guy in this situation, no matter what your D.A. says. This business of his is not like running a McDonald's, and if you can keep that operation shut down for now, it's best to do so."

"David says Peng's lawyer is squawking up a storm," Fern said. "I don't know how long Jay can hold out, but I'll tell you one thing; he's tougher than he looks. Jay has stepped up big-time in Matt's absence."

"Any peeps out of Zhang Chen?"

"Rudy followed him to Buck Bay night before last, and he took his parents to the airport and put them on a private plane."

"He didn't leave with them?" Joe asked.

"Nope. Seems like he's got a reason to stick around, don't you think? And maybe wanted his parents out of the way."

"Sounds like it. Did you get the raft back in place?"

"I did. Piece of cake. Ed and Jay covered for me, and it went smoothly. Not a soul in sight. Dr. Ryder — Bernice — had to lie for me this morning in the team meeting when someone asked where the raft was now. She told the group that she still has it."

"You trust her?" Phelps asked.

"Completely. Bernice is a rock, and she understands the stakes as much as anyone. Plus, she's one of Matt's and my best friends. She's very upset at this whole situation."

"How many people know about your real job now?"

"Jay and Ed are the only ones who know for sure. But both Patty and Bernice are sharp as tacks, and they've figured out there's more than I'm saying. But they know better than to say a word, and they won't confront me either because they respect and trust me to know what I'm doing."

"As do I, Fern," Joe said. "Just be careful about casting the net too wide. The more you can keep the details of your employment to yourself, the safer you'll be."

"I'm gonna disagree with you a little on that, Joe," she said firmly. "If Clay Sherwin had asked Matt or Ed for help, he might still be alive. This team has my back, and they're savvy. Cumulatively, they've seen more crime than you think. Granted, it's not been on the international scale we seem to be dealing with these days, but as Patty likes to say, 'crooks are crooks' the world over."

"I hear you," Joe said. "My point is that if the word gets out, more widespread around town, the greater the chances are that bad guys who might be paying attention will hear something. If that happens, your personal risk goes up, and I don't want that to happen."

"I'm doing a public relations gig next week," she told him. "A delegation from our sister city in Japan is coming to visit the new Native American cultural center. It's a good opportunity for me to be visible as the State Department's new liaison for the west coast."

"Perfect."

"Yeah. They've experienced a deadly earthquake and tsunami, too, and they want to present Port Stirling with some sort of memorial. I'll keep you posted. Also wanted to ask you if you've heard anything from the Chinese ambassador about our ship?"

"No," Joe said, sounding perturbed. "But he's calling me later today, and I hope like hell he has an update for us. He'll get the job done—he always does, but he does things in his own way and timeframe. I've learned to trust his process, but it doesn't make waiting any easier."

"We need to know who owns that ship, Joe."

"I know. I'll call you later. Go get your husband, OK?"

"That's an order I welcome. Thanks, Joe. Talk soon."

• • •

The hospital goodbyes were bittersweet. The third-floor staff, along with Matt's doctors, gathered as Fern rounded up his belongings, and a nurse took hold of his wheelchair to escort him to the main door.

He knew the situation called for some sort of speech, and he wanted to say something, but he was choked up. Dr. Kumar stepped in and said, "We understand, Chief Horning, and we feel the same about you. Please continue to heal at your excellent pace and be our best success story. Will you do that for us?"

"I will," Matt croaked, and then gathered himself. "I understand how much this place has sacrificed on my behalf, and I will never be able to repay you for the loss you've suffered. But Fern and I are so grateful, and we want y'all to know that we plan to make a donation that will be earmarked specifically for the third floor. We hope you'll spend it however you see fit to help save more lives like you saved mine." He turned to the nurse behind him and said, "Now get me out of here."

Laughter, tears, and applause accompanied them to the elevator.

• • •

Fern brought the car around as the nurse waited with Matt at the hospital entrance. He turned his face up to the sun and took several deep breaths of the cold, fresh air. He nearly leapt out of the wheelchair when Fern pulled up.

They settled him in the passenger seat for now, with his promise that when he needed to lie down in the back he would say so.

"I'm so glad you brought my car," he said to Fern as she drove slowly away from the building.

"What? You don't like my bug?"

"I love your car," he smirked. "Just not to ride four hours in." He looked around as they cleared the hospital. "Wonder how my gunman got away? This is a tough site."

"Exactly my thoughts," she said. "The Portland police closed this hill down quickly, and the dogs picked up his scent almost immediately and found a bloody sheet behind us in those woods. But that was it. Plus, he was wounded. It's a mystery."

She drove under the skybridge that connected OHSU to the tram. Matt looked out the window to his right at the terminal. "Maybe he took the tram down the hill," he said with a chuckle.

They looked at each other. Both sets of eyes widened.

TWENTY-SEVEN

Fern and Matt arrived home on Saturday evening. He hated to admit it to Fern, but he was tired from the long car ride and didn't argue with her when she insisted that he go straight to bed. He even held on to the stair rail which he'd never previously touched.

He went first to his bedroom windows and looked out to the sea. Fern quickly closed the heavy draperies and steered him away from the window.

"Remember what I said about fussing over me?" he said to her.

"There's a difference between fussing and common sense," she shot back. "We don't know where your gunman is, do we? He could be standing on our deck for all you know. I am your guard and will be on duty every minute until he's apprehended, and your life will be smoother if you don't argue with your guard."

"Yes, ma'am," he said, frowning slightly. He dropped his clothes on the bench at the foot of their bed, and gratefully climbed between the fresh bamboo sheets.

"I'm going to make us some scrambled eggs and toast," Fern said. "Be right back." She switched on Matt's nightstand lamp, kissed the top of his head, and went to the kitchen.

Closing all the downstairs blinds and drapes, Fern did a quick look around through all the windows. The moon was just rising over the Pacific, and the surf was calm, lapping at the shore gently below the house. All was quiet, and the terror that had happened here seemed far, far away.

Her kitchen was a welcome sight. Room service was nice on occasion, but she loved being in her sparkling clean, modern kitchen. Fern was still getting used to owning this beautiful house, and she rubbed her hand over the smooth island counter. For some crazy reason, that old, tired cliché popped into her head: 'Today is the first day of the rest of your life'. And, for the first time, she fully understood its meaning.

While she waited for the eggs to cook, Fern made a quick call to Jay to let him know that she'd brought Matt home. He was overjoyed.

"Can I come over?" he said.

She laughed. "Not tonight. I'm feeding him now, and I think he'll go right to sleep. He's tired from the trip. But do come over tomorrow morning. He asked me a million questions about the investigation on the way home, and he's eager to talk to you."

"Sounds good. I'll be there at 8:00 a.m," he said eagerly. "Is that too early?"

"That's good. Can you call Ed and Sylvia for me and let them know he's home?"

"Will do. See you tomorrow."

• • •

Matt slept like a baby. Fern, not so much. She heard every little sound the house made and was vigilant about their safety. Mostly, it was her imagination in overdrive. She managed a few hours at some point after 3:00 a.m, the last time she looked at her clock.

Matt woke up a few minutes after six feeling better than he had since before the 'event', as he liked to refer to his shooting. Fern was sound asleep, and he slipped quietly out of bed. He managed to wash his face and dress in his favorite Texas sweatshirt and sweatpants that Fern had placed on top of the closet island last night. *That woman knows me*, he thought. Socks and shoes seemed like too much trouble, so he crept down the stairs barefoot into the living room.

It was important to him to go outside on the deck. He needed to know if he could remember anything about what happened on Thanksgiving Day. Knowing that Fern was right about his gunman still on the loose, he paused and scanned the beach in both directions, and checked his property on that side of the house before he opened the glass door to the deck.

Nobody in sight. He stepped gingerly onto the cold, damp wood. It felt good, invigorating, and he sucked in the fresh, salty sea air like an alcoholic drinking the first drink of the day. It was that moment he loved, just before daybreak as the sky begins to lighten.

He moved to the deck's rail, grabbed it with vigor, and stared at the mighty ocean for a few minutes, watching the waves hit the beach with increasing fury as the tide came in. Then he turned and took a seat at the table he remembered sitting at with Jay and Ed. He didn't know which chair he'd been sitting in, or even if he was remembering 'that' day or one of the many others the three pals had shared a beer at that table.

A ship. There had been a ship close in. Closer than he'd ever seen one before. *I saw it twice. The night before I got shot, too.* It seemed so unlikely that someone could shoot him from a ship in the ocean, but that's what Ed and Jay said had happened. There had been no one on the beach below his house, Fern told him.

So, simple really; find out who owns that ship, and we find out who shot me. Or, probably, who hired someone to shoot me. It was a professional hitman, of that Matt was sure. Someone with the skill to deliver a bullet into him from that far away, and someone with the balls to carry out the attack at the hospital. Both shootings took someone with ice in their veins.

Fern and Jay had spent time talking to people in his past who hated him, for whatever reason. A logical progression, but Matt felt his case centered more on who wanted, needed him out of their way. *Enough to hire a pro to kill me.* The Bushnell case was a one-off; it could happen anywhere and had nothing to do with Matt's arrival in Port Stirling. Same with the Phineas Stuart case.

But the Anselmo raid was different. It happened in Port Stirling because someone picked this place deliberately. And they made it personal for him because of Fern. *But I made it personal for the bad guys, too, with the outcome.* Maybe whoever planned the Anselmo operation had even bigger plans for the area; plans they hadn't abandoned even when it went sideways. Plans that he and Fern had squelched, at least temporarily.

Was it tied to the ghost guns? Drugs, human trafficking, untraceable guns, hired hitmen — in Matt's mind the four crimes went together like pie and ice cream. Maybe they thought if they could take out the local police chief, law enforcement in the area would get distracted, and leave the coast clear for their illegal business activities. These were not local-type crimes. They took greater sophistication and bigger resources than the local crooks possessed. *I need to read the files. There must be some clues there somewhere.*

He turned back toward the ocean, and his heart lifted. *Roger!* There was his favorite seal, bobbing just offshore, and grinning wildly at Matt. He returned the grin and gave the seal a salute.

"Did you miss me, buddy?" said Matt out loud.

Roger bounced up and down vigorously, clearly responding in the positive. "Where the hell have you been?" the seal said.

"Hospital. I got shot."

"I know. It was the ship," Roger said.

"How do you know that?"

"I know. Trust me," said the seal.

"I do trust you," said Matt.

"Who are you talking to?" Fern asked, coming up behind him and hugging him around his waist.

"Roger." He pointed.

"And is he talking back?" she asked.

"Of course," said Matt with a smile. "He always answers me."

"Might I suggest that Roger is your alter ego?" Fern said.

"He is an intimate and trusted friend, so, yeah, whatever. He does always see things clearly."

"At the same moment in time you do. Hmm."

"Roger counseled me when you broke my heart. Told me I was to blame."

"Smart seal," Fern said. "Let's go in and find you some shoes. We're having company this morning."

. . .

The reunion with Jay was emotion packed. Now that he was home, Matt was getting a handle on his mental state and kept his cool, but Jay let loose. He grabbed Matt in a bear hug and sobbed into his good shoulder, carefully avoiding his wound on the other side. Fern stood by, beaming.

Breaking loose finally, Matt said, "It's my understanding that you saved my life, Detective Finley. Thank you." He was smiling but his voice took on a serious tone.

Jay wiped his cheeks with the backs of his hands. "It was really Ed. I fell apart. Just like now."

"That's not the way I heard it," Matt said. "You worked together to keep me from bleeding out and got the ambulance here fast. All while checking the surroundings and doing exactly like I've taught you. I'm proud, Jay. And I'm grateful. Shake my hand."

Jay took Matt's offered hand. "Welcome home, dude. A week ago, we weren't sure this day would come. Only your bride was sure you'd be back."

"I married a smart woman," Matt said. He smiled and put his arm around her.

The three cops moved into the living room and took seats around the fireplace, which Fern had switched on when she got up. It was a chilly morning, but the atmosphere in the room was warm and happy.

"I have questions," Matt started. "I haven't read your reports yet, but I will today."

"Shouldn't you be resting or something?" Jay asked.

Fern snorted. "Good luck with that."

"My doc wouldn't have let me come home if I weren't able to start work again," Matt said defiantly. "We've got a shooter to catch…and maybe a whole lot more. I'll be smart and rest when I need to, but I feel too good to lie in bed and stare at the ceiling."

Jay rubbed his hands together. "OK then. Let's go."

"The ship seems to be our key lead," Matt said, "that, and the raft that Fern found on Chen's property. Fern, you need to keep hounding Joe to pressure the ambassador to get an owner's name for us." He looked at Jay.

"And you need to keep squeezing our local Coast Guard contact. I'm sure the west coast admiral or whatever his position is would be able to get through to this Hong Kong registry. Once we have a name and hopefully some contact info, we can track it and investigate further."

"That's what we've been trying to do," lamented Jay. "But we are stalled out. The Chinese are reluctant to release personal information, and they are as slow as I am about releasing Ray Peng from jail."

Matt winked at Jay. "Nice work on that front, by the way. You're doing exactly what I would've done; keep him locked up for now. Have you uncovered any disqualifying arrests on any of his employees?"

"Not so far, and we're about two-thirds of the way through. Really hoping we get lucky today or tomorrow. Earl's department is researching online gun sales sites and trying to track them back to Peng's operation."

"Who's behind it, do you think?" asked Matt.

"Don't know," said Jay. "We have our suspicions, but no evidence so far. Sylvia is convinced that Peng doesn't have the resources to mount a facility and business like this one, though."

"Agreed," said Fern. "Ray's got a sugar-daddy, for sure."

Matt gazed out the window. "It's Zhang Chen, sure as hell," he said in his steeliest voice. "He organized the Anselmo operation, bought his property here to use as a base, bought the ship…"

"And probably the ship your shooter was on, too," interrupted Fern.

"Probably," Matt agreed. "I don't believe it was just a random ship that my gunman worked his way on. Pretty sure that same ship was staking out our house Thanksgiving eve. Just like the Anselmo, this ship also had a purpose."

"Do you think Chen is moving on to another lucrative enterprise?" asked Jay.

"I do," said Matt. "Selling ghost guns to an eager public of bad guys. He figured if he got rid of me, he could keep the biz going indefinitely. When Ed and I visited his man Peng and saw the guns, he knew I would suspect him immediately because he realizes I never bought his story about knowing nothing about how his property was being used."

"It's what we all think," Jay said, "but we can't seem to prove it." He rubbed his hands on his thighs.

"It's like Chen is always one step ahead of us," Matt said. "Feels like he's a phantom in the room whenever we discuss him, and he knows what we're going to do next and covers his ass before we can get to him."

"Patty and Earl said he's a real creepy guy," Jay told him. "Rudy, too. He said he's 'evil'."

"That may be true, but he's also smart," Matt said. "He finagled around me a couple of times when I thought I could outsmart him. And this is one time when Dalrymple is correct; we're going to need solid evidence before we approach him, or he'll crucify the department."

"But I found the raft on his property," Fern said. "We're sure that raft came off the ship Jay and Ed saw."

"How are you sure?" Matt asked. "What's your proof?"

"The raft had Chinese markings. How many Chinese-registered ships can there be off the coast of Port Stirling in a two-day period?" She was belligerent.

"It's suspicious, alright," Matt agreed. "But I need to read Bernice's report."

Jay's phone rang. He looked down. "Portland PD."

• • •

Sure enough, the Portland detectives found blood on the tram, not inside, but on the roof and the supports, and picked up two clear sets of prints. He'd obviously ditched the gloves he'd been wearing in the hospital and during his immediate getaway. This morning, their lab came up with a match, Michael Christopher Winston.

"Bingo!" yelled Fern when Jay told them the news. "That proves the prints on my raft came from your gunman, Matt. Same guy. He was on that ship, shot you, took the raft to Zhang Chen's cove, and made his getaway, thinking you were dead."

"And when he found out I wasn't," Matt said, "he made his way to Portland, stormed the hospital and tried again." He shook his head. "And rode on the top of the tram to the bottom of the hill and disappeared into Portland."

The three sat quietly for a moment, putting the pieces together in their minds.

"You're out of the hospital five minutes, and you solve the case?" Jay said to Matt with wonder.

Fern laughed. "That's our chief, huh?"

"It's not solved until we find Mr. Winston, and, especially, find out who hired him," said Matt. "We're just beginning."

• • •

Sunday turned out to be a busy day for the cops. Shortly after the Portland police called with their fingerprints match news, Joe Phelps called Fern. The Hong Kong Ship Registry finally shared the owner of the Pearl Dragon ship with the U.S. Chinese ambassador, and he had immediately called Phelps.

"Do you have something to write with?" Joe asked Fern. "I don't want to put this in an email just yet."

"Ready," she answered.

"The ship is registered to a corporation in San Diego called TowerWest Shipping. The principal owner is Bradley Barrington, and his address is listed as 91919 Rio Grande Drive, San Diego, CA. There is no phone number in his file, according to my contact."

"Oh, my," said Fern.

"What?"

"The land the ghost gun manufacturing plant sits on is also registered to TowerWest, according to our county records, but we didn't have the rest of your info."

"Well, that's juicy," said Joe calmly.

"This is beyond great, Joe, and an important link. Thank you, and please thank our ambassador. I'll get on it today."

"Keep me in the loop, and don't share whatever you learn about this corporation and owner until we talk it through. This is delicate."

"I get it."

"Tell Matt to take it easy and do whatever you tell him to do."

"I already did," Fern laughed. "I'll be in touch."

Fern looked down at the paper in her hand and thought about next steps. Matt was taking a nap, and she decided to turn Sylvia loose with this important information.

"Hi. It's Fern. Sorry to bother you on Sunday."

"You're not bothering me, dear," said Sylvia. "I'm sitting here reading in front of the fireplace like a little old lady. Let's chat."

Fern smiled into her phone. "Don't think that description fits you," she said. "But if I'm reading you correctly, you wouldn't mind a new work project?"

"Lay it on me."

"This is for your ears only. I'm the only one who knows this so far, and I can't reach Jay currently." Fern deliberately did not mention Matt; she wanted Sylvia to be surprised tomorrow morning at their meeting.

"I am nothing if not discreet," Sylvia said. "Sounds juicy."

"The Chinese ambassador came through for Joe Phelps and got us the name of Matt's ship owner from the Hong Kong ship registry, and I want you to poke around and see if you can turn up anything."

"Terrific news! Is it a Chinese company?"

"No, it's a corporation headquartered in San Diego and sounds American." She gave Sylvia the details that Joe had given her. "I know I'm overstepping my bounds without talking to Jay first..."

"None of that matters, Fern. We're all a team. Jay would say the same thing and you know it. We all want it to feel like you didn't leave us. Especially with Matt's problem."

"He's doing better. You'll see soon. And I didn't really leave you. I'll be just down the hall from you, a thirty second stroll."

"I'm counting on that," Sylvia said crisply. "And if Bradley Barrington is a real person, I'll find him."

• • •

During normal times, Fern loved Sunday afternoons, but today she felt at loose ends. Jay had called a crime team meeting for 8:00 a.m. tomorrow and they were planning to surprise the team with an appearance by Matt. They had this fresh information to share and could refocus their efforts to find evidence. Jay and Ed were back at their stakeout position on Chen's property, and the sheriff's deputies were busy with the ghost guns sales research. Sylvia wanted to go into the office and start work on the ship's owner, and it was better to leave her alone.

She knew Matt would sleep for a couple of hours at least, so maybe this was a good time to be a wife. *I should go grocery shopping and do some laundry. And I will call both sets of parents and tell them the good news. If Matt's still asleep at 4:30 p.m. I'll wake him as he requested; he wants to watch the Sunday night football game, Cowboys are on.*

Tomorrow morning, we start fresh.

TWENTY-EIGHT

Matt didn't want any fuss made over his return to work, but Jay and Fern overruled him, just this once.

"Your friends have been upset for almost two weeks now," Jay informed him early Monday. "You need to let them celebrate that you're alive. You need to let me celebrate, for Christ's sake! I'm going to get donuts. Let me start the meeting at eight o'clock sharp, and then you and Fern come in, OK?"

"I guess," Matt grumbled. "But that's it, and then we're getting down to work."

"Fine," said Jay. "I'll see you both at about ten after eight. Do you remember where the meeting room is?" Sarcasm dripping.

"Yes, smart ass, I think I can find my own conference room."

• • •

"I brought donuts," Jay said to the assembled team, and plopped two big boxes down in the middle of the large mahogany table. The war room, as Matt called it, looked brighter than usual to Jay this morning. The walls were still cream, the carpet still navy with cream specks, and the photos of the Port Stirling lighthouse — the old one before the tsunami leveled it — and beach scenes still hung on the walls. But it all looked more vivid and hopeful to him this Monday compared to last week. Probably because last Monday he thought his boss and friend was going to die.

"What's the occasion?" asked Buck Bay Chief Dan McCoy. "And hand me a maple-covered one, please." He grabbed a napkin from the pile and reached out to Jay.

"I just felt like celebrating this morning," Jay said. "We got some new evidence yesterday, and it's going to make all of you happy when I give you a debrief."

"Oh?" said Patty. She grabbed a donut, too.

"The Portland Police Bureau finally figured out how Matt's shooter got off that hill and escaped," Jay said. "He climbed up the supports of the tram, pulled himself on top of it, and waited for its first trip of the day, probably at 5:30 a.m.—a couple of hours after he shot the guards and tried to kill Matt. And it is a he."

"We know that how?" Dalrymple asked.

"Because Portland pulled two sets of prints off the tram and got a match," Jay grinned. "And guess what?" He could hardly contain himself.

"Don't tell me they match the prints I got off the raft?" Bernice said, leaning forward.

"They do," Jay said. "Port Stirling shooter and OHSU shooter, one and the same—Michael Christopher Winston."

Bernice raised her arms in a victory salute.

"So, that's our guy," said Ed disgustedly. "That reptile."

"Yep," confirmed Jay. "And it's all hands on deck to find him."

"Pass the donuts," said Earl. "This is worth celebrating." The sheriff took two, one in each hand.

Jay heard the door open behind him. Without turning to look, he said, "So is this."

Matt walked in. Sylvia, sitting on Jay's right, was the first to reach him. She dropped her clipboard and notebook and jumped out of her chair.

"It's about damn time," she yelled. She started to hug him and then pulled back. "Is it OK to touch you?"

Matt smiled and said, "I'm going with handshakes for a while, if you don't mind. Still a little tender in spots."

Bernice cried openly. "C'mon, Dr. Ryder, you're not the bawling type," Matt said in an attempt to lighten her up.

"I know," she choked out, but kept right on crying.

"Women. What are you going to do?" Ed said, standing for a handshake. But his eyes and nose were suspiciously red, too, and his voice shook as he talked. "I thought you were dead, man."

"I would have been if you and Jay hadn't reacted so quick," Matt said. "Thank you. I owe you one."

"Bring better beer next time we go fishing," Ed said and sat back down.

"You look thin," said Patty. She handed him a donut.

"You'd be thin, too, if you'd been eating hospital food."

Patty looked at the donut in her other hand, "Maybe I should try that. Nothing else seems to interfere with my appetite."

"I don't recommend it," Matt said. He took a second donut and passed the box to Fern, standing at his side.

"Welcome back, Matt," said the district attorney. "We're all so happy to see you on your feet."

Dan McCoy chimed in, too. "You know, you've set a bad example for your fellow police chiefs," he kidded. "We're not supposed to get shot."

"Don't sit on your deck with your back to the ocean," Matt said, not smiling. "That's the example, I guess." He pulled out a chair for Fern, and then took the empty one next to her.

Jay jumped up from the chair at the head of the table and said, "No, this is your chair. Just keeping it warm."

Matt shook his head. "Nope. You're doin' fine. When you're in a hospital bed bleeding, it dawns on you that what chair you sit in at a meeting may not be the most important thing in life."

Jay looked dubious but stayed where he was.

"Have you told them about the Portland cops' news?" Matt asked.

"Just did," Jay said.

"So, we're going to work without hearing all about your visit to the hospital?" Patty asked Matt. "Can you at least tell us how you're feeling first?"

"Fern will tell you that I had one of the best surgeons in the country. Thank you, Bernice, for shipping me off to her. But she's also one of the toughest, smartest docs I've run into. If she didn't think I was ready to come home, trust me, I'd still be in that bed at OHSU. I feel good. Maybe not as strong as normal, but I'm better every day."

"And, what he's not telling you," Jay interrupted, "is that he solved the gunman's identity five minutes after he left the hospital." He shook his head, still not believing the offhand remark Matt made to Fern led to the discovery by the Portland police. Jay shared the story with the team.

Matt shrugged and raised his hands, palms up. "What can I say? I've still got it." Everybody laughed.

"Could you recognize the gunman from the photo we got from Joe Phelps?" asked Ed. He could tell his buddy wanted to change the conversation to the task at hand.

Matt gave him a grateful look. "No, I only saw his eyes," said Matt. "And I was about half asleep when he entered my room. They were very blue though, and if we could put him in a lineup with a balaclava ski mask, I might be able to ID his eyes."

"Did he say anything to you?" asked Patty.

"Not a sound. Very professional."

"So, you think we're dealing with a pro?" asked Earl.

Matt nodded. "I do. He was precise in his movements, and clearly planned every detail of both shootings. And both jobs were complicated. Not the work of an impulsive amateur."

"What's the plan for finding him?" Dalrymple asked.

Jay looked down the table at Matt. Matt nodded. Jay said, "We've asked Sylvia to continue researching Michael Winston. All we have so far is the one prior arrest in Atlanta, and we know he's not from Oregon. The Portland PB has no leads for what happened to him when he got off the tram in southwest Portland — he disappeared. They are showing his photo around to all the hotels, restaurants, and pharmacies — he was wounded in the OHSU attack — but the captain told me they'll have to get lucky to find someone who recognizes him. Ed, we need your help on this."

"We'll put out an APB and share it with all of our neighboring states," Ed said. "And I'll personally check our databank for any other priors."

"My bet is he got out of Portland somehow," said Matt. "This is a cold-blooded killer, and that type is always going to have more than one back-up plan. He may have been on Plan B or C after Gabby got off a shot, but he clearly had a plan. You don't just think "Gee, I'll climb up on top of the tram and see what happens". He escaped, and he knew how to get out of Portland. Ed, I would like to see your guys concentrate on Washington and California."

"Agreed," said the sheriff. "I wouldn't be surprised if he's made it to the Canada or Mexico border by now either. Don't think he would've made for Idaho or Nevada, much easier to lose yourself in California or the Seattle area."

"My boss alerted Homeland Security when they first identified him from Bernice's forensics," Fern added. "We didn't know who he was then, but Phelps was suspicious enough of the raft with Chinese markings to take that step. No one with his name and ID has crossed either international border, not last week anyway."

"He wouldn't use his real name to cross a border," Matt said. "This guy has fake IDs. We need to find a connection between him and someone local. Who hired him? If Sylvia's right — and she always is — Winston has no connection to Oregon. How did he end up in my hospital room determined to kill me? Who owns that ship and who put him on it?"

"Which leads me to the next part of my debrief," said Jay. "Does anyone around this table recognize the name Bradley Barrington? Or the company TowerWest Shipping?" He paused and looked around the room.

"That's the name of the LLC who owns the land on Cherry Drive where the ghost gun manufacturing facility is operating," said Patty. "Who is Bradley Barrington? Earl and I are still trying to trace the corporation."

"We have a trend here, Patty," said Fern. She recapped what Joe Phelps had learned about their ship, and told the team that the State Department was looking into both the company and the listed owner.

"We need to pull out all the resources we have to learn more about this company," Matt said. "What we know for sure now is that my hospital shooter was also in a raft that came off the Pacific in Port Stirling. Odds are he was on that ship. I'd like to talk to Mr. Barrington if he exists. Jay, can you talk to the San Diego PD and request that they do a visit to

TowerWest's physical address on the ship registry form? We should confirm that the address exists and that the company is authentic."

"Do we want San Diego to confront the company?" Jay asked. "What should I tell them to do?"

"Not at this point," Matt said. "I'd rather keep this new info under our hat for a day or two until we see what Phelps comes up with. It's dicey because of the international ship registry, and I want to give Joe some wiggle room with China until we know for sure who exactly owns that ship."

"OK, moving on," said Jay. "Do you guys have anything new to share?"

"We've been checking the gun sales online," said the sheriff. "A couple of my deputies are posing as buyers to see if our local manufacturer pops up. One of them got a hit yesterday that looks like it could be our company, and he's following up today. I'll know more this afternoon."

"It's not illegal to buy a gun off the internet, may I remind you," the D.A. told Earl. "And you need to be careful using any trickery."

"I wasn't born yesterday, David," snapped Earl. "We know all that and we're following the rules."

"What are you doing about Ray Peng?" Dalrymple asked Jay. "Is he out yet?"

"Nope," said Jay. "Still looking at his employees."

Dalrymple gave him a cold look. "When, precisely, do you expect to finish that research?"

"Probably by late today," Jay said. It came out sounding vague.

"Please make sure you do," the D.A. said, and jotted a note in his notebook. The implication was that he was tracking Jay. "I'm going to avoid Peng's attorney today, but I can't hold him off much longer. I don't think you want a human rights violation on your first week as acting director of the police department."

"Technically, it's my second week," Jay deadpanned. "I'm in charge until the chief has a chance to read all of our reports from last week."

"And I'm gonna need a nap this afternoon," Matt said. He smiled at Jay.

Patty reported that she'd been keeping a quiet eye on the Peng residence. "From a distance, David," she said, holding up her hand, palm toward him, "before you snap at me like you did at Earl. There's nothing going on there.

Mrs. Peng taking her children to school every morning and picking them up each afternoon. All normal. Ray's attorney did visit yesterday morning, but he didn't stay long. I'm dying to have a chat with her, but I'm a law-abiding officer of the law, so I'm restraining myself."

"Same here," said Ed. He raised a finger in the air. "Law-abiding officer of the law. Just keeping my eyes and ears open for anything suspicious in and around Port Stirling. Nothing new to add after a quiet weekend, I'm afraid." He didn't happen to mention that he and Jay had been back to their stakeout of Zhang Chen's house.

"The only other thing I've got in the news department," said Jay, "is that our officer Rudy followed Zhang Chen to the Buck Bay airport Friday night. His parents left on a private plane, but Chen drove back to his house here. I thought he was probably here just for the Thanksgiving holiday week, but it looks like he's staying with us for a while."

"We saw that plane," said Dan McCoy. "One of my officers is a pilot and flying enthusiast, and he saw it land Friday afternoon. Said it was "slick"."

"Rudy said the same thing," said Jay. "Must be nice."

"Great," said Dalrymple. "Now we're back to harassing Mr. Chen." He shook his head. "You cops are going to get me fired, for sure."

"No one harassed him, David," Jay said. "Rudy happened to see him drive through town, and just wanted to see where he was going. He's driving a black Honda, by the way. Very low-key."

"How did he know it was Chen?" asked Dalrymple.

Jay swallowed hard. "He may have seen him pull out of his driveway. And he was with Patty and Earl when they went to talk to him on the day after Thanksgiving. So, he would know him."

"Did Chen spot Rudy?" asked McCoy.

"No, we don't think so," said Jay.

McCoy rolled his eyes. "I was with you the night of the Anselmo raid, Jay, remember? You couldn't put that on Zhang Chen, and I don't think you can put Matt's shooting on him either. You'd better be careful."

"He is a person of interest," Jay said. "The raft was found near his property."

"And," said Fern, "forgive me if I don't hold Mr. Chen in high esteem ever since I was locked in his barn for two days against my will." She gave Buck Bay's chief of police a look he won't forget for some time.

"But that's my point, Fern," argued McCoy. "There wasn't a shred of evidence that tied him to the Anselmo."

"Well, there is evidence that ties him to Matt's shooting," Fern said, her voice rising to go along with her red cheeks. "That raft was manned by the guy who tried to kill my husband. That raft was found near Zhang Chen. In my book, he's two-for-two. Maybe he has you fooled, Dan, but he's not fooling me, and we're going to prove it this time." She sat back in her chair.

Dan McCoy ran his hand through his short, but thick brown hair. "I just think there's a chance we're all so hung up on Zhang Chen that we might be overlooking other possibilities here," said McCoy. "We need to keep an open mind. Matt, you say that all the time, right?"

"Dan's right," said Matt. "We need to follow the evidence, not our feelings. I've got my own thoughts about Chen, but we need to pay attention to the basics: motive, means, and opportunity. And to pursue those ends, we need warrants for both Chen and Ray Peng, David. We know the shooter and we know he was on that raft that was found near Chen's property. We need to look around. If you can't see your way through the weeds on this now, I will go directly to Judge Hedges."

The two men locked eyes. "OK," said Dalrymple. "I'll request the warrants to search their premises, but you can't examine their electronic devices without a second warrant request. You have to show me evidence that justifies that invasion of privacy before I'll go any further."

"We'll take it," said Matt. "Thank you."

"What do I get in return?" asked the D.A. He looked to the head of the table, at Jay.

"As soon as we're finished searching his house, I'll let Ray Peng out of jail," said Jay. "Are you happy now?"

Dalrymple smiled.

"Gentlemen," Fern said, "I'd like to take my husband home now. That's enough excitement for one day. As soon as I hear anything further about the Pearl Dragon's ownership from Joe Phelps, I will let you all know."

"Wait," said Matt. He reached out and grabbed Fern's arm as she started to get up from her chair. "What did you say?"

"I said it's time to go home, honey."

Everyone laughed.

"No, I meant the other part," Matt said, staring at her. "The part about the Pearl Dragon."

Fern looked puzzled. "That's the name of the ship you were shot from. Bernice translated the Chinese name from the raft. It's in her report. Jay saw the same markings on the side of the ship as it took off right after you were shot. Why?"

"Pearl Dragon is the name of Zhang Chen's parents' restaurant in San Francisco," he said.

TWENTY-NINE

nteresting," said Buck Bay police chief Dan McCoy. "But Pearl Dragon is a common Chinese thing—restaurants, rivers, streets. It's everywhere in China. How is it that you possess this little nugget of info anyway?"

"I talked to Biyu Chen, Zhang's mother, after the Anselmo raid," Matt answered. "I found her at the family's restaurant. A simple Google search."

"And you remembered the name of the restaurant after a year and a half?" asked Dalrymple.

"I have a good memory."

"He does," Fern confirmed. "Especially when it's something I don't want him to remember."

Bernice, Patty, and Sylvia laughed out loud at Fern's remark. The women all got it.

"Why didn't you tell me the name of the ship?" Matt asked her.

"It didn't occur to me that it was important," Fern said. "How was I supposed to know? It's just a name."

"A name that might be an uncomfortable coincidence, or a name that points right back at Chen," the sheriff said. "We need to bring him in for questioning, Matt. Are you with me?"

"I am, Earl. And I'll bet you a steak dinner, David, that TowerWest Shipping is a shell corporation that only exists on paper, and that there is no such person as Bradley Barrington."

"I don't gamble," said Dalrymple.

"Of course you don't," Patty said to Dalrymple. She pushed her chair back and rose. "We've got work to do, ladies and gentlemen, and we need to let Matt go home and get some rest. Same time tomorrow, Jay?"

"If that works for everybody?"

Murmured agreement around the table and they dispersed. Jay and Sylvia remained seated at the table side-by-side. Once the team was gone, Jay said to her, "He almost gets his head blown off, and he's still a better detective than me."

Sylvia patted his hand. "And every minute you're around the chief, you learn something that will help you in your future. It's all good, Jay. Embrace it." She stood up. "I need to get busy. I've got two names to track down now, Michael Christopher Winston and Bradley Barrington. It's my intention to beat the feds."

She swirled out of the conference room, trailing at least two yards of purple fabric in her skirt, and hugging a lavender cardigan and her clipboard closely to her.

• • •

When they were back in the car on the way home, Fern said, "I'm going to make a quick stop at the fish market and grab some scallops. I thought I'd make some seafood linguine for our dinner tonight. How does that sound?"

"I thought you weren't supposed to buy fish on Monday?" He looked at her. "You told me that yourself."

"True. But scallops are seafood, technically not fish. There's a difference. Jason told me he was going to get some in today, and he'd save me some if I got there before 3:00 p.m."

"Last time I bought them from him, they were $38 a pound. Who's he saving them for—Jeff Bezos?" He snorted.

"Do you want them or not?"

"Yes, I want them. I'm just giving you a hard time, "Mrs.-we-have-too-much-money."

"Speaking of which, giving that donation to OHSU was one of the best moments of my life. Seriously. I think we should consider ramping up your foundation and focusing on health care. Get someone to help us figure out the need, starting with Oregon, and make it happen. Just think what would've happened to us if you didn't have health insurance or we didn't have any money. Your bills are going to be enormous. Two surgeries, LifeFlight, days in intensive care, round-the-clock skilled nursing—what do poor people do?"

"They probably don't get the care I got," he said. "I get your point, but I'm not sure we can fix the health care problems for the world."

"I'm not saying that," she argued. "But we could make a dent in the need here at home. How do you think Bernice is going to feel when she hears about our gift to OHSU? She saved your life, too, you know. If she hadn't swallowed her pride and realized that she didn't have the skill or the resources to save you, we wouldn't have gotten to Dr. Kumar. Maybe Buck Bay Hospital needs a new surgical wing, for example."

"Valid point. Let's discuss."

Fern pulled up in front of the fish shop and said, "I'll be right back. I'm locking the doors."

When she came back to the car with her scallops—and some smoked salmon that caught her eye—Matt was sound asleep. *What a terrible nurse I am*, she thought. *Too much, too soon.*

· · ·

The district attorney was true to his words; he had the search warrants for Ray Peng and Zhang Chen's residences from Judge Hedges by 4:00 p.m. He sent Peng's by courier to the sheriff, and Chen's to Jay at the Port Stirling police department. After a hastily arranged ZOOM call with the crime team, it was decided that Patty and Earl would lead the search of Peng's Twisty River house with the help of two of the sheriff's deputies. Ed and Jay would do Zhang Chen's house and property, with Rudy and Walt from the department. Dan McCoy would also lend two of his officers to the Chen search. Matt suggested an early-morning search; take them by surprise about 7:00 a.m.

Chief McCoy wanted to participate, but he had to be in court to testify on another matter on Tuesday morning, and Fern opted out for Matt,
who was still in bed from his busy day. "One day at a time," she'd told the
group. It would kill her to not be involved, but she had to consider both
her cover and her husband's health. Jay and Ed would come by the house
after and fill them in.

The district attorney ended the call with an admonition. "Please remember that you can seize electronic devices, but they are to remain out of reach
and in a safe location," Dalrymple said. "Judge Hedges was very specific
about this, especially in light of your probable cause against Chen — it's
weak. You are not allowed to turn them on. If you bring me more cause
RELATED TO MATT'S SHOOTING, then we'll talk about another
warrant to allow you access to the devices. Do you understand?"

"Yes, dad," said Ed. "Do you want me to ask Chen if he'll donate to
your campaign while we're there?"

"Funny, Lieutenant Sonders," said Dalrymple. "Try not to screw this up."

• • •

Fern and Matt had a yummy dinner and a quiet night at home. She felt
like celebrating, but Matt was not allowed any alcohol while he was still
on painkillers. He reduced the dosage as he felt better, but it still wasn't a
good idea. In support, she gave up her nightly glass of wine.

"Do you feel like watching a movie tonight?" she asked him as she
cleaned up the dinner dishes.

"Good idea. It's too early to go to bed since I had such a long nap."

"You go pick out something while I finish up here. Whatever you want
to watch is fine with me. No British murder mysteries, though; still too
early for me to hear those accents," she said lightly.

He came around the kitchen island and kissed her on the back of her
neck. "You'll never forget Penelope Stuart," he whispered, "but she'll eventually recede in your memory, and it will get easier."

"Hope so," she said. "Her face just appears from time to time, and it's
alarming."

"It comes with the territory, my love, and you can handle it. How about some Jack Reacher tonight? Maybe he'll show us a clever way to take down Zhang Chen."

She giggled. "Sounds perfect. No upper-crust English accents there."

• • •

Jay had taken himself to the Whale Rock Inn at 6:00 p.m. The only thing in his kitchen was a couple of cans of chicken noodle soup, and he was too hungry for that. He'd asked Vicky for the small booth in the corner because he wanted to think about the case and make some notes without being disturbed.

He ordered a beer and was jotting down thoughts for tomorrow's searches when his phone rang. Sylvia.

"What's up, girlfriend?" he said.

"I've been looking at Michael Winston all afternoon," Sylvia said, "and I can't find anything that tells me he's ever sold the house in Los Angeles that Joe gave us the address for."

"OK," said Jay.

"He went to college, UCLA, then he went into the Marines. When he was discharged, honorably, he returned to L.A. and bought that house. As far as I can tell, he still owns the title to it."

"So, you think he might be there?"

"It's a wild shot, but, yes, I think there's a chance. I believe it's his home. Doesn't mean he doesn't have another hideout, which is probably likely considering his profession, but he does still own that house in Laurel Canyon. I looked at it on the overhead Google map, and it's a pretty private place. Trees surrounding it, low to the ground and hidden from any neighbors' views. If he got back there, he might think he's safe."

"Have you turned up any other real estate he owns?" Joe asked.

"No, not in his real name. And he's never been arrested again since that one time at the airport, so it's possible he thinks of this place as his safe house."

"Or, he could have a penthouse in Puerta Vallarta for all we know, but this is good work, Sylvia. Let me talk to Matt. I'll call you back. Keep going, you're brilliant."

"Thanks. I'm going home now, but I will look more closely at Winston's school and Marines records tomorrow morning. I just gave them a cursory onceover after Bernice's find, but they now warrant a more thorough look."

"Sounds good."

"Be careful tomorrow," Sylvia said. "All of you, OK?"

"We will be," Jay said. "And you should stay safe, too. Lock your doors, etc. etc. We have no idea where Matt's hitman is, or what these jerks might be planning next. Check all your surroundings, especially when you're entering and leaving city hall."

"I lived through the IRA troubles in the U.K," she said. "I still check the underside of my car before I get in it."

Jay laughed. "You're good to go then."

• • •

"They know everything."

"What do you mean…everything?" Zhang Chen said into his phone.

"They know Mike Winston and Bradley Barrington and TowerWest. The Portland cops got Mike's prints off the top of the tram and the raft, so now they know the connection."

"Hong Kong must have given the U.S. the ship registration info," Chen said. "Damnation. I didn't think they would; they're usually so uptight and close-mouthed. I wonder how they discovered the name of the ship. Oh, well, doesn't matter now. You need to make sure that Winston stays hidden. They can't connect him to us, so we're good there. And as long as he doesn't talk, they can't pin it on us. I'll take care of the TowerWest problem."

"I don't see the ship being a big problem for us. It could have been just passing through. Even if they link it to you, there's all sorts of reasons why that ship could have been where it was on that day."

"Agreed," said Chen. "Mike Winston is our big problem. Why the hell wasn't he wearing gloves?"

"He wore gloves while handling the guns, but he was having trouble landing the raft on shore and took them off for a better grip. In Portland, he had to re-tie a tourniquet he'd fashioned for his leg to keep from bleeding all over the place."

"Bad luck. Do you know where he is now?" Chen asked.

"I do. He's holed up somewhere safe."

"Don't tell me," Chen said. "The less I know about Winston the better. I picked up the raft after Mrs. Horning carefully replaced it, and it's been destroyed."

"We're going to search your and Ray's places tomorrow, so be prepared. Phones and computers are safe for now, as long as we don't find anything incriminating. What will you do if they ask you about the raft?"

"I found it littering my property, it wasn't mine, so I destroyed it. Simple. And there is nothing incriminating at either house. No evidence. I have the perfect hiding place for this phone and so does Ray. We have other phones set up to give them in this event. Same with our laptops."

"I think you should leave town."

"I considered it," Chen admitted. "But it will make me look guilty, especially with this new evidence linking Winston to my raft. No, I'll stay here. Truly, unless they find him, they can't prove a thing."

"There's one more thing. Matt Horning is home from the hospital."

"And I suppose he knows about our gun operation?"

"He does."

"Just what I wanted to avoid," said Chen icily. "It's disappointing that your guy didn't finish the job."

"I'm sorry. He's never failed me before."

"Police chiefs are difficult to get rid of. You should know, right?"

"Especially this one."

THIRTY

Matt woke up before dawn, apparently still on hospital hours. He grabbed his robe and slipped into his slippers, and silently went downstairs. Since he'd been home, he hadn't had the energy to go into his home office, but he did so now.

Unbeknownst to him, at some point yesterday afternoon Fern had set up his laptop and charged it and opened his police notebook to the next blank page. His favorite pen was resting comfortably on top of the notebook. On the other side of his laptop, a glass of water and his morning medication called out to him.

I won't ever be able to fool that woman. She knows me better than I know myself. He smiled and switched on the desktop lamp, and then turned to check that his drapes were pulled closed. *Michael Winston knows I'm not dead…might he try a third time?*

But Matt woke up thinking about another name this morning—Bradley Barrington. Winston was just a hitman. Whoever owns that ship is likely the person who hired Winston and provided the means and opportunity for him to do the job. And, in spite of what he'd told Chief McCoy yesterday at the team meeting, Matt was focused on Zhang Chen. He wouldn't ignore other pathways, as he'd told the group, but he was first going to run down the Chen path as hard and fast as he could. *If I'm wrong about Chen, so be it…but I'm not.*

The first question he wrote after writing *"Bradley Barrington, TowerWest Shipping"* at the top of the page was:

· *Why would a San Diego, California, corporation register a shipping company in Hong Kong? Panama was far more common on the west coast.*

— *A Chinese or Asian connection of some sort*

— *Owner is Asian but wanted company HQ in the U.S.*

— *HKSR would keep ownership details private/confidential*

Matt thought the answer could be all three of his reasons, or some combination of them, but Bradley Barrington was not an Asian name. So, who is he?

An initial internet search brought up far too many Bradley Barringtons to even know where to begin. They needed a middle name, but according to Joe Phelps, this was all they got and all they were likely to get. So, Matt decided to work it the other way; start with Zhang Chen and work backwards.

He first tried a genealogical site and entered Zhang's parents' names. He was able to follow it back several generations. *I need coffee. I might be on to something here.*

He moved down the hallway to the kitchen in the still-quiet house. On the cabinet above the coffeemaker was a Post-it note: I bought some fresh beans for you yesterday—knock yourself out.

Am I really this predictable? But he reached for the beans, grateful for his thoughtful wife. He loaded the grinder and then wrapped his body around it to mute the sound as much as he could.

Armed with his morning drug of choice, he went back to his computer and immersed himself in Zhang Chen's family tree. After an hour or so, he was forced to give up—nothing remotely resembling Bradley Barrington.

Next, he looked for graduating students at Cal Berkeley around the time he knew Chen had been there.

"Good morning, my love," Fern said. She entered the room and came around Matt's desk to give him a kiss. "You're up early."

She was wearing a pale-yellow terry robe, which was starting to show its age, and hadn't combed her hair or washed her face yet, but to Matt she was the most beautiful woman he'd ever seen.

"Hi, darlin'. Yeah, I have to get up early since I'll probably be asleep again this afternoon." He smiled and returned her kiss. "I made coffee. My gift to you for setting up my office. That was sweet."

"I was pretty sure you'd want to do some work today. Did you take your morning pill?"

"Yes, Nurse Fern. I'm good."

"Ready for some breakfast?"

"Always," he smiled. "You cooking?"

"Yep. But don't get used to it."

"I'll milk it as long as I can. Do you want my help?"

"No, simple one today; yogurt, blueberries, and granola. How does that sound?"

"Perfect. I will keep working for a few more minutes if you don't mind," he said. "I'm looking at Zhang Chen's college classmates."

"For Bradley Barrington?" she guessed.

"Yep. Nothing so far. And no one with that name is related to Chen either."

"Do you think Barrington is a fake name? A fake person?" she asked.

"Probably. Zhang Chen is a sophisticated businessman. He would know how to hide whatever he doesn't want us to find," Matt said.

"True. But he's also arrogant and thinks he's smarter than us. Maybe not smarter than you, which is why he decided to kill you. I'll call you when breakfast is ready."

Matt returned to his laptop, going through the Berkeley records. Nothing. He wished he had a photo of Barrington, but that would not happen from the ship registry.

He turned to Chen's public company website, Redfire. First, he started through the departments and 'Contact Us' email addresses. Nothing. Then he went to the 'News' tab and started reading the press releases.

"Let's eat!" he heard from the kitchen.

Fern filled his outstretched coffee cup, and they discussed how they would pass the morning while they waited for their colleagues to perform the searches.

"I need to update Joe," Fern said, "and see what he wants me to do next."

"Jay called earlier and told me that the San Diego police checked out the physical address on the TowerWest registry and, big surprise, it doesn't exist. I'm going to keep looking for Barrington," Matt said. "He also told me that Sylvia is really focused on Michael Winston, so I can help out with our other lead."

"I haven't told you this yet, but your department has totally aced your absence. Honestly, Jay has surprised me. It's like he's channeled you or is really trying to."

"I've always felt that he has leadership potential. He was just raw when I arrived here. It takes real world experience and look what we've been through together. If there's a silver lining in me getting shot — and there's not! — it's that it gave Jay the opportunity to look inside and see what's there."

"You need to know that both he and Ed took it real hard," she said. There was sadness on Fern's face. "I couldn't help them at all since I was a total basket case, and it was heartbreaking to feel their pain."

"They're good friends," Matt said. "The best friends I've ever had, and I've had some good ones over the years. Funny how life sits you in a place so foreign to you, and it ends up being the home you never knew you were searching for."

She put her hand on his. "I tried to imagine my life without you as the helicopter took off with you unconscious. I couldn't see it, Matt. There was no life for me if you died on the way." She looked so vulnerable.

"You're strong and you would've kept going. But I would be difficult to replace." He grinned and gave her a real kiss.

"I'm not replacing you. Ever," Fern said. "As I was saying, everyone on our team has been incredible and made important individual contributions, like Patty putting her butt on the line by following Ray Peng…"

"In a direct rebuke of our district attorney's wishes," Matt interrupted.

"Yes, but even Dalrymple has come around the last couple of days," she said. "He could have remained a real horse's ass and made trouble for both

Patty and for me. I think he suspects I went on Zhang Chen's private property and took that raft, but he let it go. Bottom line is that everybody was touched and personally upset about what happened to you. You should be feeling a lot of love."

"I am, and it's nice." He took a big spoonful of the yogurt she'd placed in front of them while they were talking and swallowed. It still hurt to swallow. "But I don't want to be defined as the police chief who got shot. I want people to remember me as the guy who grabbed crime by the throat and pushed it up against the wall."

"You'll never be the victim, Matt, if that's what you're worried about."

"Right now, that's how it feels," he said. "Everyone is worried about me, fussing over me, and treating me with kid gloves. And I didn't much care for Dan McCoy's remark about making police chiefs look bad."

"Oh, c'mon, he was kidding," she said. "Just trying to lighten up the room a little."

"I'm not so sure. It came off a bit pointed to me. Like he was saying "I'd never do anything so dumb to get shot like you did."

"I think that's your meds talking, honey," she smiled.

"I don't think McCoy likes me. I think his nose got out of joint during the Anselmo case, like he thought I was taking over or something."

"Well, it was our case, especially when I stepped in it. I can't imagine why Dan would feel that you'd overstepped."

Matt shrugged. "Just a feeling."

• • •

Today was a big day for another reason as well; Matt's wound dressing could be removed, and he could take a real shower. After breakfast, Fern helped him cut off the tape.

"Hope you're not afraid of Frankenstein," Matt said. He watched her face as she removed the dressing. "Hope *I'm* not afraid of Frankenstein. I haven't seen it either."

"You know, you're not really married until you've seen your spouse's surgery scars," Fern said.

"Is that a rule?"

"I just made it up," she smiled. "But I think it should be a rule."

His neck and upper torso were purple and yellowish-green, and he would have quite the scar, but she could tell it was healing properly from his two surgeries. Matt looked over Fern's shoulder into the bathroom mirror.

"Nice," he said sarcastically. "Guess I won't be strutting around a Maui beach for a while."

"You never strutted." She tossed the dressing and tapes in the trash. "In the shower you go. Don't rub hard, but don't be afraid of soap. You need to keep the area clean. Those were the instructions I was given. And I've washed all your tee shirts and other tops—everything is clean, so wear whatever you're comfortable in." She looked him in the eye. "Will you be alright for a while? I'm going to call my boss and check-in."

"Fussing, you're fussing," he said in a sing-song voice, and waved his hand at her in a "get out of here" gesture.

• • •

Fern sat in her home office for a while and looked out the window. The surf was angry, and the sky was leaden and threatening. She was thinking about what she wanted to say to Joe Phelps. It was the classic female dilemma, but with a slight twist.

On the one hand, she wanted desperately to succeed at her new job which meant she should be focused on finding the hitman and uncovering his apparent connection to the owner of the internationally registered ship, and the "why" in why kill Matt? On the other hand, she just wanted to take care of her husband and make sure he recovered fully.

The twist, of course, was that if she was successful at her job, it would help her husband. And this waiting for the search warrant results was agonizing. Would the cops find the key to the case today? Would this nightmare be over?

Fern's phone rang. Joe.

"I was just going to call you," she said, picking up hurriedly.

"Everyone else doesn't want to bother you," Joe said. "So, I thought I would. How's he doing?"

"Please bother me," Fern said and meant it. "He's actually doing great. This is probably too much information for you, but we just removed his bandages and he's taking his first shower. The wounds from the gunshot and his surgeries looked pretty good to me…looking like they should at this stage in his recovery."

"Good news. I need you to go to work, preferably tomorrow if you feel comfortable leaving him, that is."

"You're amazing," she said, shaking her head. "I'm having that conversation with myself at this very moment. What's up?"

"Jay called me early this morning," Joe said. "It seems as if Sylvia thinks there's a chance that Michael Winston is holed up in the L.A. house he's owned for years, and one of my tech support guys thinks the same thing. The property has never changed hands since he bought it, and we can't find any other real estate that he owns."

"Why would he go to his own house?" Fern sounded dubious.

"That's what I said. But the house is very secluded in Laurel Canyon, probably with a lot of security. He doesn't know yet—we don't believe—that we've ID'd him. He thinks he got away cleanly from Portland. And it makes some sense to hide out in a private location rather than a hotel when you've got a bleeding leg."

"You want me to go to his house and see if he's there," Fern said. It wasn't a question.

"Yes."

THIRTY-ONE

After breakfast, Matt continued looking through Redfire's corporate website. More dead ends, but then he clicked on the 'Board of Directors' tab.

Fern heard his yell from the kitchen: "Are you kidding me?!?" She threw down the towel she was using and sprinted down the hall toward his office.

"What?" she asked, eyebrows raised.

"Bradley Barrington is on Redfire's board of directors," Matt said. "Look." He pointed at his laptop screen as Fern came around the corner of his desk to stand behind him. A smiling head shot of a distinguished man in his seventies in a black suit, white shirt, and gold tie filled the screen. Below the photo, the caption read: 'Bradley J. Barrington, Corporate Director'.

Matt tilted his head up to look into Fern's eyes. "Like I said, arrogant," she said.

"So, does Barrington really own the Pearl Dragon ship and the land on Cherry Drive, or is it just in his name and Chen owns it?" Matt asked rhetorically.

"Does it matter?" Fern asked. "The ties to Zhang Chen are too strong to ignore."

"It all starts and ends with him, doesn't it?" Matt said.

Fern nodded.

"You call Joe and tell him what we've found. I'm going to dig more on Barrington," Matt told her. "Even having a middle initial will help me."

She didn't tell him yet that she was going to Los Angeles tomorrow, depending on what the search warrants turned up today.

• • •

By 10:00 a.m, Matt had discovered that Bradley J. Barrington was an engineer who had invented a super-absorbent polymer that had revolutionized California's agricultural industry. He'd made millions and was now retired, tending his vineyard in Napa, and playing at making wine. There was no mention of shipping, and it appeared he lived quietly with his wife of fifty-one years, and a small circle of family and friends. He wasn't a socialite in California's elite, and he seemed to be a run-of-the-mill retired millionaire, resting on his professional laurels.

Fern came back into Matt's office. "Joe said it's obvious that Zhang Chen owns that ship and is using a board director's name and identity to camouflage the ownership."

"He thinks that Barrington may not even know that his name is on the Hong Kong ship registry as the owner?" asked Matt.

"Joe thinks it's probable," Fern answered, "or, he knows and is being properly compensated."

"He gets a generous annual stipend from Redfire," Matt said. "But so do the other directors. The amounts seem to vary, and Barrington's is the highest from what I can tell, but it may be related to years of service."

"Joe also says that we need to find a link between Chen and your shooter, Michael Winston."

"Agreed," Matt nodded. "With both the feds and Sylvia running all sorts of background checks on Winston, we'll find it." His dark eyes glowered, and his sculpted jaw was firmly set.

"Speaking of Winston," Fern started slowly.

"Yes?" Matt looked at his wife, recognized her face, and thought, *Uh-oh. Let her tell me.*

"This is for your ears only. Joe wants me to go to L.A. tomorrow morning and stakeout Michael Winston's only known address." She paused to let him react.

"I see."

"And?"

"And, I hate it," he said. "Who's going to cook my meals and wash behind my ears?"

She looked at him, speechless, her mouth open slightly. She didn't know how to reply to that.

Matt burst out laughing. "C'mere," he said and patted his knee. "Gotcha, didn't I?"

"You did," she grinned.

"I hate it," he said, "but not for those reasons. And if you're thinking of saying "no" to your boss because you're worried about me, I'm officially letting you off the hook. Got it?"

"I don't know, Matt," she said. "You're still recovering. I shouldn't be leaving you."

"You should if Joe truly believes there's a chance that Michael Winston is at his house. Someone needs to confirm it. Why doesn't he ask the LAPD to surveil?"

"I asked that, too, and he said he doesn't trust them to not go in with guns blazing if he's there and ruin our investigation. We want to interrogate him."

"If you confirm Winston is there, then what happens?" Matt asked. "And—spoiler alert—this is the place I hate this idea."

"All he wants me to do is find out if he's there," Fern said. "If he is, Joe will ask the local Alcohol, Tobacco and Firearms squad to go in and get him out safely. He doesn't want to waste their time if Winston's not there."

"Right answer," smiled Matt. "I can live with that. As I see it, you're down and back in twenty-four hours. Pretty sure I can keep myself fed and bathed for that amount of time."

"What about security for you?" Fern fretted.

"I'll invite Jay back to the guest room, if that would ease your mind," he said. "We could do with a long debrief anyway, especially once we know what, if anything, they're finding today. How's that?"

Fern laughed. "Jay would love to move back into our room. But we can't tell him where I'm going and why. We can't tell anyone."

"Settled," Matt said. "Now, let's talk about you. Did your FLETC training cover how to perform a proper surveillance? What to do and what not to do?"

"It was a main thrust in my agenda, since 'watching' is the biggest part of my job. I know what to do."

"A pro like Winston will be prepared. Might even have his surroundings wired and booby-trapped."

"I know what to look for," she said seriously. "And I know how to cover my back while I'm looking. I also understand his psychology at this point. He'll be alternately skittish and over-confident until he's sure he's in the clear on your case. If he is there, Joe wants me to figure out the best way to take him whole and communicate that to his ATF squad."

"OK, that's my girl," he said, taking her hands in his. "I knew there would be shit like this. I just didn't think it would be so soon. I'm not going to say "be careful" because that would be patronizing, right?"

Fern laughed. "You can tell me to be careful, but please know that I've learned a lot, and not just from my fed training. I've learned a lot from you, and from the mistakes I've made, especially during the Anselmo operation and on the Phineas Stuart case. I'm prepared for this next step, and I will be the most careful person on the planet."

He kissed her long and hard.

"And, I'm going to ask mom to bring some food for you guys tomorrow night. Don't tell me not to; she'll be thrilled to help."

• • •

Shortly before noon, Jay and Ed showed up at the Horning home to debrief Matt. The two cops had already met with Patty and the sheriff to compare notes on their respective searches and could give him a full report.

The search of Zhang Chen's house and property had turned up nothing of interest in Matt's case. Chen had cooperated fully, stayed out of their way, and even turned over his PC and cell phone without a fight.

Jay and Ed had personally walked the ocean front part of the property and discovered that the raft was gone.

"Which means," said Ed, "that our fingerprints evidence on Michael Winston will not be admissible in a courtroom since it was illegally obtained and now the raft has disappeared. Shame."

"We debated whether or not to ask Chen about it," added Jay, "but decided it was not in our best interests to give him anything he could possibly use against us."

"Yeah, that was the right call," agreed Matt. "Do you think he somehow knows we found it?" Matt asked.

"He might have figured it out," Ed answered, "if he went looking for it between the time Fern took it and brought it back. Or if it somehow leaked that we had it long enough to get some forensic evidence."

"Did Dan McCoy know we found the raft?" Matt asked. "Was he at those meetings?"

Jay and Ed looked at each other. Jay spoke. "I'd have to check Sylvia's notes to be one hundred percent sure, but I think so. He's been at every team meeting so far, I believe." He paused. "You can't possibly think that Dan McCoy is a rat? Can you?"

"I'm not sure what I think," replied Matt. "Probably the drugs I'm on." He smiled. "But I don't think Dan likes me much. Started with the Anselmo raid, for some reason."

"But what would he hope to gain?" asked Jay.

"Maybe he's on Zhang Chen's payroll."

"Man, I'd have trouble believing that," said Jay. "Dan's been solid in his job for years."

"Yeah, it's a stretch," added Ed. "But stranger things have happened, no?" He looked at Jay. "Do you remember how he used the word "torture" when we shared Matt's and my visit to Ray Peng? It was an odd choice of words, I thought at the time."

"Yeah, but…" Jay's sentence trailed off.

"I know, it's hard to think we might have someone working against us on the team, but I keep coming back to how Chen always seems to be one step ahead of us," said Matt. "And you have to ask yourself, how is that possible? For example, how did my shooter know I was at OHSU? Even if Ray Peng suspected I wasn't dead after your visit to him, he didn't know where I was, right?"

"No," said Ed. "He didn't even know for sure that you survived the first hit."

Jay thought for a minute. "The only people who knew you'd been transferred to Portland were Bernice's team at Buck Bay Hospital, your parents, Fern's parents, Sylvia, Walt, and Rudy here, and the county crime team."

"I'm pretty sure my parents didn't order a hit on me," said Matt. "Or the Byrnes, because I am the perfect son-in-law." He grinned. "Maybe Walt wants to be police chief instead of sergeant."

Jay snorted. "That's the last thing in the world Walt wants. He wants to retire and go fishing every day. And Bernice, Sylvia, and Rudy all love you. So that only leaves someone at the hospital or LifeFlight or…"

"Or, the county crime team," finished Matt.

"Well, if we really have a rat," said Jay, "it's obviously got to be David Dalrymple. He doesn't like anything we do, and I've never trusted him."

"Me neither," admitted Matt. "But the D.A. is slimy to my face. I always know where I stand with him. We don't like each other, but we work together because we have the same goals. Usually."

"Plus," said Ed, "can you see him risking his precious image and career to tip off Chen? That doesn't make any sense."

"It doesn't make any sense for Dan McCoy either," said Jay. "It can't be anybody on our team. I would trust my life to Patty, the sheriff, Fern, Bernice, and Sylvia — they're the only other members."

"With Chen's money, anything could make sense," said Matt. "What about Bernice's staff? The forensics guys? What do we really know about them?"

"If Bernice trusts them, I trust them," said Jay. "No one — and I mean no one on earth — could fool Bernice."

Ed laughed. "Yeah, there is that."

"Big money is important to some people," said Matt. "It can be highly motivating. And Zhang Chen has big money. As in big money. I think we should keep more of our investigation between us. Scale back on the team meetings."

"We can't drop them," Jay protested. "That would look funny."

"Not halt them altogether," Matt said. "Just stop the daily briefings and give us a couple of days to regroup. Give them the update on today's searches, and then tell them you're going to take a day or two to reevaluate your investigation."

"I could do that," Jay agreed.

"How did it go at Ray Peng's?" asked Matt.

"Earl said it was unpleasant," said Jay.

"Big surprise there," said Matt.

"They found a trap door that led to a small room under the floor, and it was filled with guns," Jay said. "Patty said it looked like Peng was starting a small army. She also said his wife stood in a corner and cried the whole time."

"Did she say anything?" Matt asked.

"Not a word, according to Patty," said Ed. "And she tried to draw her out. No dice."

"Did we get his electronics?" Matt asked.

Ed said, "Yes, both computer and cell phone. Like Chen, Ray didn't offer up much resistance on either item. Which is not like his usual MO. I find that suspicious, don't you think?"

"Suspicious, like maybe they have burner phones and PCs, and the ones we retrieved aren't their real communication devices?" Matt asked. "It crossed my mind, too, Ed."

"Also," Jay said with his hangdog look, "Earl told me he thought Ray Peng knew we were coming. They expected his usual act—histrionics, physically aggressive, you know—but they didn't get that at all. Like he'd already passed that stage and was now in acceptance."

"He didn't act out at all?" asked Matt.

"Not according to Earl," said Jay. "He told me that he wasn't friendly, but more like matter of fact. But the wife was upset. Ray tried to comfort her, but she pushed him away and kept crying."

"Did any of his guns have serial numbers?"

"Nope," said Ed. "Earl's face turned purple when he told us about the guns. All of them ghost guns and quite the arsenal."

"Is that enough probable cause for Dalrymple to give us access to the electronic devices?" Matt asked.

"Don't think so," said Ed, shaking his head. "It doesn't get us any closer to your shooting, and that's what this search was based on. We already know they're manufacturing them in Chinook County—no real new news."

"What about the missing raft?" Matt asked. "Can't we go to Judge Hedges and claim missing evidence, obstruction of justice...something like that?"

"How did we know about it in the first place?" Ed argued. "Fern went on private property and seized it. I would have done exactly the same thing, of course, and it dramatically moved our investigation forward, but the law doesn't like it."

"Yeah, but Hedges knows us, and she's been willing to give us the benefit of the doubt before," Matt debated.

"The only flaw in that argument is that David Dalrymple is afraid of Zhang Chen and what he might do," Ed said. "He'll never go for it unless you have an open and shut case."

"And we don't," said Jay. "Dammit. And, in more crappy news, I don't have a single legal leg to stand on to shut down the ghost gun manufacturing plant for another day. The only thing wrong with it is that they didn't apply for building or operating permits. All the employees check out clean. If Ray Peng pays the fines—which he did yesterday—and applies for the permit to operate a business—which he said he was planning to do right away—I can't do a thing. Hands are tied." He looked miserable. "When are you officially coming back to work?" he asked Matt.

"Soon. Just a couple of days until I can quit needing a nap every afternoon," Matt said. "Almost there. Hang in, you're doing fine."

"He's right," said Ed. "We wouldn't be doing anything different if you weren't running this thing, Jay. Let your boss fully recover."

Jay nodded.

Ed stood up to leave and said, "One more thing. My boss told me that Oregon's Attorney General is working hard on closing the ghost gun loopholes, but that she can't accomplish it overnight. Needs some help from the Oregon Legislature and probably Congress. But she's a bulldog and I'm not counting her out."

The three cops stood silent for a moment glumly looking at each other.

"So, essentially, we're at a dead end unless we find Michael Winston and get him to talk," Matt summed up.

THIRTY-TWO

Fern parked her baby-blue VW at the curb of the McDonald's in Reed-sport. Time for a pit stop. She'd decided to drive to the Eugene airport to fly to Los Angeles, rather than start her journey in Buck Bay. Her training had taught her that being unpredictable and altering her usual patterns and habits was the smartest way to stay safe in her new profession. She always flew out of Buck Bay, wanting to give their regional airport all the support she could, but on the off chance that someone was monitoring her moves, that would make tracking her easier today.

She used the restroom and then bought a coffee she didn't really want because it always felt rude to her to not buy something under the circumstances. She was in and out in five minutes, and back on the road.

The day was dreary, but her mood was light. Matt was starting to look and sound like his old self, and when she came right down to it, that was all that really mattered in her world. But she was also excited to be doing something that might help their case. The hunt for Michael Winston was a major focus for most of the west coast law enforcement agencies, and the fact that Joe trusted her to pursue the one lead on him they had was exhilarating.

Fern slept great last night. She'd taken time to plot out a plan for today and had studied the overhead photos of Winston's house that Joe had sent to her before she went to bed. She felt prepared. Once Matt had heard from

Jay and Ed that the search warrants on Ray Peng and Zhang Chen hadn't produced anything relevant to his shooting, she took off for Eugene and the afternoon flight to LAX.

The agency had supplied her with a new laptop and cell phone, both only accessible with her facial ID and fingerprint. She'd reserved a rental car, specifying a black one, and booked her flights on the new laptop. Only two people knew her target for tonight — Matt and Joe Phelps. Fern told her mother that she had a meeting in California the next day when she'd asked her to bring food to Matt and check on him. Matt had told Jay — who was happy to serve as Matt's extra security for a night — the same thing.

Everything was all set. The only question in Fern's mind was what she might do if she actually encountered the man who nearly killed Matt.

* * *

Stepping outside into the warm, dry Los Angeles early evening felt nice on Fern's skin. The rental car counter had a dual clock/thermometer that read 6:18 p.m. and 71 degrees. Night was falling on this December day, but there was a thin line of pink out to sea on the horizon west of the airport. Her rental car, a black Toyota Camry, fit the bill perfectly.

An airport shop provided her with a couple of sandwiches, some nuts, bottled water, and a banana that would see her through as long as it took tonight.

Declaring her two concealed handguns along with her carry permits had gotten her pulled out into the search lane, but eventually safely through TSA security in Eugene. Joe had given her a script for answering their questions and she'd passed through quickly. A few raised eyebrows at the tall, gorgeous redhead carrying two guns were duly noted.

She'd plugged her preferred routing into WAZE early this morning and was happy when she pulled it up now and it still showed the same: 405 north to Sunset Blvd to Laurel Canyon Blvd to Willow Glen Rd. Winston's house was on a small lane off Willow Glen, the only house on that lane. Traffic was bad leaving LAX, as expected, but Fern had all the time in the world. She was antsy to get there but composed.

She switched on the radio and pulled out of the rental car lot.

. . .

Even with the streetlights, Laurel Canyon was dark at night. She found the turn onto Willow Glen Rd, and, on purpose, first drove past Winston's lane. She wanted to see what was beyond on Willow Glen. It continued around a corner that moved away from his street.

As she drove slowly past his driveway, Fern caught a glimpse of lights through the dense trees which she knew surrounded his house. Willow Glen was a narrow road, and she was worried that her car would be conspicuous. But she got lucky; around the big corner a house directly on the road appeared to be having a small house party. There were several cars parked along the road, and she made a quick decision and pulled in behind the last one.

Quickly, she shut off the car's lights and turned off the engine. The items she needed were already stuffed into her black backpack. Fern got out of the car and locked it, placing the key carefully in a zippered pocket of her black sleeveless vest. She pulled on a black beanie, stuffed her copper hair up under it, and took off walking in the direction of Winston's house. *Nobody ever walks anywhere in L.A*, she thought, but she tried to be as inconspicuous as possible. She was only the equivalent of about two city blocks from the entrance to his private lane, and she walked at a brisk pace.

Once she got to the end of his driveway, she stepped behind a large tree that afforded her cover, both from Willow Glen Road and from his house. The immediate area around her was full of scrub brush and trees. She crouched down and held herself completely still, listening for any sound, and sniffing the air. She could hear voices and muted music; it seemed to be coming from the house party around the corner. The air was fresh and smelled predominantly of pine trees, with a hint of meat barbecuing.

Stealthily, Fern moved to another tree, this one closer to Winston's house. She repeated her crouching movement and, again, listened and sniffed. To her huge relief, she could neither see, hear, nor smell dogs. *Whew!* That was the one thing she'd worried most about.

She wore her night binoculars on a lanyard around her neck, and pulled them up now to survey the house, still quite a way in front of her with several trees blocking her view. She would have to get closer. She rose from her crouching position and moved to her left bringing her closer to the edge of Winston's driveway. With her first step, she landed on a large twig, and it snapped in half, making what to Fern was a deafening noise. She immediately froze and waited to see if the noise had attracted anyone.

But she was somewhat exposed, out in a small clearing between two tree groves, and she knew she had to move to cover. Although it seemed silly at the time, she was glad she'd rubbed eye black stick (like football players used to reduce the sun's glare) on her face to disguise her porcelain white skin. In the darkness, she was a shadowy figure moving silently.

She stopped just to the right of the driveway and was able to squeeze in among three trees in a small circle. From that enclosed vantage point, she could see the remainder of the driveway and its approach to the house. The driveway fanned out into a circular drive with a large garage off to the left. There were no cars in the driveway, and the garage doors were closed. A short stone staircase led off to the right and ended on a generous landing in front of double front doors.

The bulk of the house looked to be mostly to the right of the front door. A small lawn was enclosed by a low stone wall—maybe three feet at the most—and then surrounded by a high laurel hedge that looked like it might run on two sides of the house. Fern had seen the hedge in her aerial photos, and the plan called for her to approach the house behind the hedge and clear out a space within it where she would have an unobstructed view into at least three rooms of the house.

She checked overhead and didn't see any outdoor spotlights. From her current vantage point, she could see a light on at the left corner of the garage and a porch light at the front door. That appeared to be all the outdoor lighting, at least on this side of the house. There were definitely a few lights on inside the house, but they could, of course, be on an automatic timer to dissuade burglars.

Fern knew from looking at the aerial photos of the house that it was one story, in a gentle semi-circle around a large patio and swimming pool.

Although she couldn't tell in the photos she'd seen, common sense told her there'd be glass doors or big windows between the outdoor entertaining area and the house itself. She wanted to position herself somewhere in the hedge close to the patio for that reason, figuring she'd have a direct view into the house's primary rooms.

Holding her breath and testing every step, she crept along the back of the hedge until it turned a corner, and then took another twenty steps. That should put her near the center of the pool. Arriving at her destination, she stood silently still for a full minute. Nothing. *He's not in the pool for sure.*

She pulled out small pruners from her backpack and snipped her way through the hedge in a straight line, listening after each snip. After two minutes, she could see through the hole and to the house. She made the hole just a bit wider, and then pocketed the pruners so she could use both hands on her binocs which she trained on what looked like an open living room. As she expected, glass doors and windows ran the length of the room.

A noise came from behind her. *What was that?* Fern's adrenaline spiked but she didn't panic, instead slowly turning her head to the right in the inky blackness. *A squirrel. Give me a break.* She took a deep breath and turned back around to the hedge, raised her binocs and looked directly into the living room. It had a 1950's vibe and was furnished in that style. An orange leather sectional ending with a chaise on one end, and a matching orange leather swivel chair defined the sitting area. Sporting polished chrome legs, the seating was grouped around a white shag carpet. White drum tables and a low coffee table completed the room.

And sitting on the chaise end reading a book with a large glass of what looked to Fern like whiskey was Michael Christopher Winston. He was wearing shorts and a tee shirt, and she could see his bandaged leg elevated comfortably on a pillow. Blonde hair, right size, right age, same bone structure. She couldn't see his downturned eyes to know if they were the blue Matt described or not, but it was him. Fern had studied his photo until she could see his image when she closed her eyes.

It's you. The man who almost killed my husband, and did kill two nurses and a cop. And you sit there reading and drinking. Hope your book is good, you seem engrossed in it. I've got an open shot right at your head, you scumbag.

Get a grip. You aren't here to be a vigilante. Let law enforcement do their jobs and bring him in.

Fern put down her binocs, and inched her way back the way she'd come, tiptoeing down Winston's driveway. Once clear, she broke into a jog, jumped into her car, and followed Willow Glen Rd back down to Laurel Canyon Blvd. This time, she turned left on Hollywood Blvd before she reached Sunset, and parked in a busy area, surrounded by locals and tourists strolling on this beautiful evening. It had been less than ten minutes since she left Winston's house.

Calmly, she pressed Joe Phelps's name on her phone's frequent calls list.

"Thank God," he said instead of "Hello."

"He's there, Joe. It's him. I was less than thirty feet away and could see him clearly."

"Did he see you?"

"No. He was reading and never looked up. Plus, I was well hidden, and L.A. is surprisingly dark at night," Fern noted.

"Where you were, yes. Lots of trees. Is he alone?"

"Yes, I think so. I suppose there could've been someone in a part of the house I couldn't see, but I looked into the kitchen, primary bedroom and bath, as well as the living room where he was. And he was wearing shorts and a ratty t-shirt, barefoot—he looked alone."

"You're sure it's him?" Joe had to ask.

"One hundred percent positive," she said firmly. "Right down to his heavily bandaged leg where Gabby shot him."

"Does he have a weapon nearby?"

"I didn't see one, and I surveyed the space thoroughly. If he does, it wasn't obvious, and it wasn't on his body or anywhere in the living room."

"Great," he said and paused. "I'm a little surprised you didn't take him out."

"It crossed my mind," she admitted. "But we want justice, Joe, not revenge. Somebody paid this asshole to shoot Matt, and I want to know who that person is."

"Which is precisely why I hired you."

Fern could feel Joe's smile through the wires and miles. "What happens next?"

"We hang up, and I call my contact at ATF. They have a nifty squad for just this type of detail. Michael Winston will be in one of their cells within the hour."

THIRTY-THREE

Joe Phelps was correct. The ATF squad surrounded Winston's house and took him without much of a fight. Michael Winston tried to get away, but all exits were blocked, and he knew his ability to run on his wounded leg was limited. In the end, he went quietly, nodding in assent when they read him his rights, and not saying a single word.

Winston was booked and jailed in the ATF's Figueroa Street field office while he awaited extradition to Oregon. The Portland police bureau wanted to represent Winston's felony state, and they made plans to go to Los Angeles and pick him up for transporting to Oregon. Fern caught the last plane out of LAX to Portland, where she would brief the PPB first thing tomorrow morning on everything they knew about Michael Winston. She would do so under the guise of the victim's husband and a former Port Stirling detective, rather than in her new role.

• • •

After his wife had left the house this morning, Matt went back to bed and tried to read and rest. That was an exercise in futility.

The truth was he was feeling much better, stronger, and more 'with it mentally'. The fuzz from two surgeries was abating. He knew there were smart, capable people out there trying to solve his case, but it was starting to grate on him that he wasn't playing a more active role. Which was probably another sign that he was healing.

He got up, got dressed, and wandered downstairs. After first checking the ocean-front side of his house through the drapes and seeing no one, he went out onto the deck. Although he tried not to, he couldn't keep his eyes from gazing at the spot on the deck where his blood had been spilled.

The tang of the biting sea air hit him smack in the face and it was delicious to his spirits. Heavy, gloomy sky with a vexed Pacific Ocean angrily crashing the shore, the day didn't offer up much optimism. But Matt created his own internally—he was alive! *No complaints here.*

He surveyed the beach as far as he could see through the low clouds and mist, and there was no action. On mornings like this, Matt could almost convince himself that he was alone in the world. *But I'm not. There's someone out there who wants me dead, and until I find out who it is, I'm not safe anywhere.*

A log came in with the ferocious tide, stranding itself on the high part of the dark sand, and he watched it fight off subsequent waves for a while, twisting and moving, but ultimately staying put. A lone seagull landed on it, singing loudly, and giving credence to the log's arrival. Matt stood there for twenty minutes, just breathing in the fresh air, and it was good. Turning to go inside, something caught the corner of his eye—Roger—in the frothy surf close in, bobbing above water and then diving under it.

Matt waited patiently for him, and when the big seal resurfaced, he said out loud, "It's about time you showed up to help me recover."

Roger replied, "You don't really need me, you know."

"I know that. But sometimes it helps me to talk to you—makes things crystal clear in my brain."

"OK, what's on your mind?" Roger bobbed up and down.

"I need to do something today to move my case forward," Matt said. "Everybody else is hard at work, and I'm a useless piece of crap."

"You could try to track down Bradley Barrington on the phone and ask him if he owns a ship registered with the Hong Kong ship registry."

"I could do that from my home office, couldn't I?"

"Get to work."

Roger dived and was gone. The log took command of its new home on the beach, and Matt went inside.

. . .

He started by returning to Redfire's corporate website, but there was no contact info for the board members—no email, no phone. He knew Barrington lived somewhere in the Napa Valley, but it was a region that encompassed a big area.

Matt relied on two background check sites that the police used regularly and plugged in 'Bradley J. Barrington California'. His name, with an address, popped up within the city limits of St. Helena. With that information, he then went to a subscription website that could often provide a phone and/or email address if one had the name and street address.

Bingo. A home phone number. And, he got his wife's name, Anne, and the names of his three children.

Matt made some notes on his yellow legal pad, deciding in advance how he would take the conversation along depending on how Barrington answered his first question. Or, what kind of message he would leave if he got voicemail, the most likely outcome. He checked his watch; Wednesday 10:30 a.m. Once he was confident in his approach, he picked up his phone.

"Hello," said a man, his voice on the frail side.

"I'm calling for Bradley J. Barrington," Matt said into his phone, coming to attention. "My name is Matt Horning, and I'm the police chief of Port Stirling, Oregon, and I just need a minute of your time. Are you Bradley Barrington?"

"The one and only," he chuckled in a raspy voice. "What on God's great earth could you want with an old fart like me?"

Matt had to laugh, and he immediately liked him. "I promise to not take much of your time, sir. I'm working on a case that involved a ship that was seen off the coast of Oregon. Near my own home, actually. I have one question for you: Are you the registered owner of a ship called Pearl Dragon?"

"A ship? That goes on the ocean, you mean?"

"Yes. A mid-sized ship registered with the Hong Kong ship registry."

"No. I don't have anything to do with shipping," Barrington said. "I don't even like boats, for that matter. I've never owned anything that goes on the water. Why do you ask such a strange question?"

Matt consulted his notes on the legal pad.

"Because you are listed as the registered owner of this ship in Hong Kong." He paused to let that sink in. "Do you have any idea how that could have happened?"

There was a silence on the line, and Barrington was clearly thinking this over. Matt remained quiet and gave him time.

"No, Mr. Horning, I can't think of a reason for what you say. Perhaps one of my investments has seen fit to use my name, but that doesn't really make any sense. And surely, I would have been informed."

"I would think so," Matt agreed. "Unless whoever did this didn't want you to know they'd used your name and identity. Can you think of anyone you know who might have done that?"

"A Chinese-registered ship? It's unbelievable. I'm a California business-man with most of my work in agriculture and technology. Are you sure you have this right?"

"My information came from the United States Department of State," Matt told him. "Yes, I'm absolutely positive the information is correct."

"The State Department?!? What the living heck is going on?"

"It gets worse, Mr. Barrington. Someone on your ship tried to kill me and was almost successful."

"For God's sake, it's not my ship! I don't own a damn ship."

"No, I don't believe you do," Matt said. "So now, I need you to assist me in finding out who registered that ship in your name. Are you willing to help me?"

"Looks like I'd better help you before the State Department throws me in Guantanamo."

"That's not going to happen," Matt said. He smiled to himself. "You have my word on that. But whomever used you in this matter is in deep trouble. Here's what we're going to do."

. . .

Jay was overjoyed when Fern called him and told him where she'd been and what the outcome was. He was less happy when he heard that the Portland police were going to bring Michael Winston back to Oregon. Oh, he understood that one of their own had been killed and another one wounded, but c'mon, his best friend had been shot by this guy—he had a stake in it, too. It was important to Jay that no one mess this up. This guy had to be safely in an Oregon jail.

So, after he hung up with Fern and rationally thought it through, he called the Portland captain and told him he was going with them to L.A. He didn't ask, as he would have two weeks ago, he told him. It felt like a big step.

To his relief, the captain agreed that Jay should accompany them. "He almost got your guy," the captain had said.

"Yeah, and I was with him at the time. It was the worst moment of my life," Jay said and meant it. "I need to make sure Michael Winston is held accountable. Thanks for understanding."

"It's my pleasure. We'll process the paperwork and I'll let you know when it's on. Might be a couple of days."

"Thanks, and I look forward to meeting you," Jay said.

Truth be told, Jay was struggling. Matt's brush with death had brought his own life into focus, and he realized that there were some missing pieces. Now twenty-nine with the dreaded birthday around the corner, Jay took stock of where he was and what he wanted out of life. He loved Port Stirling, he loved his job, his family, he had good friends, and he was healthy. *Most people can't even say that*, he thought. *Most people would be happy with that.*

The problem was he had no one to share it with. Maybe it was watching Matt and Fern and their deep love for each other that sparked this empty feeling inside him. Hell, even Patty and Ted made him jealous—*those two have so much fun together!* He wanted a partner, and his own family. He wanted a house of his own instead of this apartment. Jay knew he wouldn't ever have a house like Matt's—no one else in Port Stirling did either, and he didn't care about that level of luxury—but he deserved a woman like

Fern…pretty, smart, and nice. *I need to get serious about dating, and I'm going to buy a house now. Fern will help me with both if I just ask.*

He looked at his reflection in the mirror. *I'm a catch.* He smiled.

THIRTY-FOUR

Matt called Joe Phelps after he and Bradley Barrington talked about next steps. Because of the fake registration of the Pearl Dragon, it would inevitably involve the Chinese, and he knew Joe had to be informed of what Matt had learned this morning.

"That's unfortunate," Joe said when Matt filled him in regarding his conversation with Barrington. "Unfortunate, but not surprising to me in the least. You either, I suspect."

"Nope," agreed Matt. "You and I have seen this rodeo before. We both know Zhang Chen is at the root of our problems. Barrington will confront him, Chen will deny it, but there's no denying that ship has the same name as the Chen family restaurant, or that Barrington is conveniently on Red-fire's Board of Directors, or that we found the raft from the Pearl Dragon on Chen's property. Bradley Barrington confirmed the restaurant's name, by the way. Said he eats there when he's in the city."

"What's he going to do?" Joe asked.

"He's going to challenge Chen and let him know that he knows about the ship's fraudulent registration. You're going to get a court order to wire-tap his phones, Joe. I've read Title 18, Section 2516 of the U.S. code, and we have enough probable cause that the wiretaps may provide evidence of a felony violation of federal law. That ship is falsely registered in violation of international law, for starters, which we know with certainty now, and we have good reasons to believe Chen hired Michael Winston to kill me. David Dalrymple, my district attorney, won't take that step and there's no point in me even asking him because he's a chickenshit, but you have to."

"I am philosophically opposed to wiretaps, but because of the false ship registration, I have no options here, do I? Not to mention the cold-blooded murder and attempted murder of law enforcement officers."

"Barrington is going to wait to confront Chen until I give him the green light," Matt said. "He'll do his part."

"You trust him?"

"I do. He's pissed to be embroiled in this, as he said, "in his golden years", and he's sure Zhang Chen is responsible. Chen picked the wrong guy. The last thing Barrington said to me was "Let's get this bastard.""

"God bless feisty senior citizens," Joe said wryly.

• • •

Matt spent the rest of the afternoon alternately reading in his living room and watching the ocean while he waited for Fern to get home from Portland. He'd missed the Pacific so much while he was in the hospital, and swore he'd appreciate it every day for the rest of his life. He'd turned on the gas fireplace to ward off the chill of the day and positioned himself in his favorite whiskey-colored leather chair and matching ottoman.

He'd been so worried about Fern last night while he waited for her call. He trusted her instincts, and she was the most capable woman he'd ever known, but she was up against a hired killer. Anything could have gone wrong. *And here I sat like a big bump on a log.*

But nothing did go wrong. Fern had delivered the goods, the ATF did their job brilliantly, and they had their killer.

And now they knew that Zhang Chen likely owned that ship and had hired Michael Winston to kill Matt so he wouldn't get in the way of his lucrative ghost gun operation.

So, why does it feel like we're missing a piece? What am I not seeing? He put down his book — Bill Gates on avoiding a climate disaster — and stared out to sea. Something had been nagging at him ever since he'd arrived home from the hospital.

Why here? In Port Stirling? And why is Zhang Chen so slippery, both in this case and in the Anselmo operation?

He shared his feeling with Jay last night when they ate the dinner that Mary Byrne had brought over for them — roast chicken, carrots, parsnips, and potatoes. "I want your mother-in-law," Jay said, and Mary had beamed.

But Jay thought that Matt was overreacting because he was still getting over the surgeries' hangover. "We've got your shooter, and we're close to getting Chen this time, too. Over and done. Time for a vacation." He speared a perfectly roasted carrot.

"You're probably right," Matt said. "But it seems too easy. Too neat."

"What's neat about three cops getting shot, and two nurses killed?" Jay said with raised eyebrows.

"You know what I mean. Why are we suddenly the center of Zhang Chen's evil empire? Why isn't he operating in California or Washington or Mexico or Chile? Or anywhere else but here? What makes us special?"

"We've been over that, Matt," Jay said with some frustration. "Chen picked our area because we are a remote part of the Oregon coast. There aren't big population centers with smart cops and layers of law enforcement. Our small town believes in live and let live. We mind our own business. We have a big, wide ocean for his nefarious purposes. We're a perfect fit for him if you look at it from his perspective."

"Maybe," said Matt. He still wasn't convinced. "Nefarious? Where'd you pick up that word?" Matt smiled and lightly punched his friend in the arm.

"I am becoming a man of the world. It was hanging out with all those Brits that did it."

They laughed together and finished off Mary's awesome food.

. . .

The next morning, Jay called the major crime team members and explained that they were on hiatus until Monday while he and the Portland police caught up with some paperwork and 'other bits'. He listened carefully to their individual questions; Matt's paranoia had rubbed off on him somewhat, and he wanted to make sure they weren't missing anything, especially anything close to home.

Ed said, "I only need to know one thing, Jay—how's Matt feeling?"

"He's good. I ate dinner with him last night and he ate like a horse and stayed up past 9:00 p.m. Major progress."

"Jesus, what a relief, huh? How close are we to a threesome fishing expedition?"

"I'd say not this weekend but next for sure," Jay told him. "His recovery is really gaining steam. I can see it from one day to the next now."

Buck Bay Chief Dan McCoy was a little pricklier. "Paperwork?" he said. "What kind of paperwork? What's going on?"

Jay decided to hedge his bets. "Oh, you know. We want to make sure we document everything we know about Michael Winston. Just dotting the I's and crossing the T's."

"Is there anything new with him?"

"Don't know," Jay said. "Just having my coffee now and getting caught up." It's a good thing they weren't on a face call, as Jay's face turned bright red with his lie.

"Well, please keep me in the loop, Jay. I'm around all weekend and I want to help you. My guys are uneasy, and we don't want to leave any stone unturned. Right?"

"Thanks, Dan. I'll be in touch with any news." Jay quickly ended the call.

Patty was, well, Patty. "What aren't you telling me, you young punk?" she said affectionately, while still getting her point across.

"Take the weekend off," Jay said. "Go have fun with your poor husband for a change. We'll talk on Monday."

"You dodged my question."

"I did," Jay said.

David Dalrymple asked, "So, you don't have any new information or evidence? Are you telling me we can actually have a quiet few days without police hysteria?"

Jay bristled. "Investigating the shooting of our chief of police is hardly hysteria."

"Sorry," the D.A. said. "Didn't mean that to come out so harsh. But there's nothing new on your end, correct? Nothing I need to worry about until Monday?"

"I'll tell you what I'm telling the others; do something fun this week-end and we'll reconnect on Monday." He'd be damned if he was going to give Dalrymple any morsels.

Bernice, like Ed, only wanted to know about Matt. Same with Earl, although the sheriff did tell Jay 'in confidence' that he and his deputies were still keeping a close eye on Ray Peng. "You know," Earl said, "just in case."

"I think that's wise, Earl. Thanks. Let me know if Peng gets a bug up his butt."

"Will do. Otherwise, we'll see you on Monday," said the sheriff. "Try to chill, Jay, you've been under a lot of pressure."

"I will," Jay replied. *Yeah, that's gonna happen.* He tapped his pen ner-vously on the desk as he hung up.

. . .

Fern arrived home mid-afternoon. Everything finally caught up with her: new job training, Matt's shooting, all the hospital trauma, the excitement and pure joy of his return home, and the terror of her trip to Los Angeles. She was beyond exhausted.

She set down her bag in the foyer and clung to Matt.

When they finally pulled apart, she said, "You look amazing."

"I feel good," he said. "It was great doing some meaningful work yes-terday. Not as meaningful as yours, but still." He grinned.

She shook her head. "You've probably given us the evidence that Zhang Chen is behind this mess. Putting him away I'd say ranks right up there."

Now Matt shook his head. "Taking a hired killer off the streets feels more important to me today."

"It did feel good."

"When will Portland go get him?"

"A couple of days, I think," Fern said. "They are getting all their ducks in a row, but they're in a hurry."

"Good."

"He's really creepy, Matt. He actually looks like a killer. I will never get the image of him sitting in his living room out of my mind. Like he didn't have a care in the world." She shuddered.

"I can't wait to look into his blue eyes again, and have a chat with him," Matt said. He took hold of her shoulders. "In the meantime, why don't you go upstairs and have a nap?"

She smiled. "That's exactly what I was thinking."

"I've already made a salad, and have the rest of dinner under control," he said. "I'm back. Now it's your turn to rest. We have a long road ahead of us wrapping up this case, and you need to be in tip-top form."

She gave him a brisk salute. "Yes, chief."

• • •

Two days later, Michael Christopher Winston was safely extradited to Portland, Oregon, with no issues. He still had not spoken to anyone in law enforcement, except to say six words, "I want to call my lawyer."

Jay and the Portland cops were professional and refrained from talking to Winston during the trip except to give him orders. The time would come soon enough when they could interrogate him and ask what they all wanted to know: Who hired you and why? When Jay first laid eyes on him, he stared hard at the killer, trying to see any signs in Winston's face of what could make a man do the things he'd done. Winston smiled at Jay as if he knew him, and it chilled Jay to the bone.

Winston's Los Angeles-based attorney accompanied his client to Portland, where he was booked into the Multnomah County Detention Center, a maximum-security jail in downtown Portland. The charges were first-degree murder of Officer Timothy Johnson, first-degree murder of nurses Amy Wu and Hannah Smith, the attempted murder of Officer Gabriela Ramos, and the attempted murder of Police Chief Matt Horning. Bail was denied.

Fern and Jay presented the facts of the case to the Multnomah County district attorney's office who would try it in court—Jay in person and

Fern back home on a virtual call. The lead prosecutor was happy with the police evidence that had been collected in Port Stirling, Portland, and at Winston's home. It would turn out that the fingerprints taken from the tram, and the bullet wound in his leg consistent with one that could have been caused by Gabriela's gun, put Winston at the scene of the crime at OHSU. While his prints off the missing raft in Port Stirling put him at that scene, too, the prosecutor told them that would be more difficult. "But I'm good at working in facts like this that aren't totally admissible," she'd said with a smirk.

By the time Winston's trial rolled around, the prosecutor would have a wealth of new evidence, from a Portland hotel desk clerk who picked him out of a lineup as a registered guest the night following the OHSU shootings, to Matt's identification of him by his startling blue eyes.

But the most disturbing new revelation about Michael Winston came from the Port Stirling police department's own Sylvia Hofstetter.

THIRTY-FIVE

Sylvia looked at her computer screen and blinked her eyes twice. She knew what she saw, but she was having trouble comprehending the enormity of what it meant. Her hand on the mouse trembled.

This must be a coincidence. A weird, sick coincidence. But what if it's not? I need to call Matt.

• • •

Matt's cell phone, on his nightstand, vibrated and it woke him up. He glanced at the clock, 1:30 a.m. *Now what the hell? Sylvia??*

He jumped out of bed, forgetting that he was still in recovery mode, and took his phone into the bathroom, silently closing the door while Fern was still sleeping.

"Don't bother apologizing for calling me in the middle of the night, Sylvia," he answered. "You wouldn't do this unless it was crucial."

"Thank you, chief," she said, her throat dry. "It might be crucial."

"What is it?"

"Is there any chance that you could come to my house?" He could tell her voice was shaking.

"Now, you mean?"

"Yes. Now. I need to show you something," she said. "I would come to you considering your health, but I can't really drive at night anymore—not safe."

"Give me five minutes to get dressed and fifteen to get to your house," he said without hesitation. "I'm on my way."

He dressed in the dark, and scribbled a quick note to Fern, placing it on his pillow.

Driving his car felt strange at first, but after a couple of minutes, everything felt normal to him. He turned left off Highway 101 north of town onto Sylvia's road. Hers was the only house on the street with lights on.

She opened her front door before Matt was out of his car.

He smiled when he saw her in an attempt to put her at ease. The usually unflappable Sylvia was clearly upset with a touch of hysteria about her.

"Hey, lady," he smiled. "What's going on?"

She yanked on his jacket and pulled him into her house, closing the door and locking it behind her.

He followed her to the desk in a corner of her kitchen.

"You look better than I expected," she said, really looking at him for the first time.

"Be happy you didn't see me a week ago. I'm doing what the docs tell me to do, and it's working—I feel pretty good."

She pulled up a kitchen chair next to her desk, motioned for him to sit, and turned the computer screen so he could see it better.

"This is a pdf of Michael Winston's high school freshman yearbook," she said, and pointed to a head shot of a young boy, tapping her finger on the photo. "This is Winston's photo."

It was barely discernible, but Matt recoiled as he leaned in closer for a good look at the screen. Those eyes. He would never forget those eyes.

"Yep, it's definitely him," he said to Sylvia, as lightly as he could manage. He could tell this—whatever *this* was—was hard for her.

She moved her mouse to click backward several pages, took a deep breath, and, once again, pointed to a photo of a young man.

Under the photo it read, "David Dalrymple."

Sylvia leaned back in her chair as if the exertion was too much for her. They looked at each other for a long time.

"Are you shitting me?" he finally spit out. "Dalrymple and my shooter went to high school together? How can that be?"

Sylvia sat up straight again and reached for the mouse. "Not only that, Matt, they were apparently good friends. Look at this."

She landed on a page with casual, snapshot photos of the kids. One photo showed Dalrymple and Winston with their arms around each other's shoulders, grinning at the camera at what appeared to be the end of a track race. Each had a number pinned to a singlet, and they were wearing shorts and running shoes.

She moved the mouse again. "Here's another one." The photo she pointed to showed the two on a beach somewhere, sitting in low chairs in the sand. Winston was waving at whomever took the photo, and Dalrymple was laughing, head thrown back.

"This is it, Sylvia," he said quietly. "The missing piece."

"I'm afraid it might be."

Absent-mindedly, Matt massaged the wound on his neck, where a scar was forming. Sylvia reached over and gently pulled his hand away.

"Our district attorney has been on Zhang Chen's payroll all along," he said, staring off into space. "And when Chen wanted a hitman to take me out, Dalrymple knew who to call—his childhood friend, Michael Winston. Who, as Joe Phelps has categorized, is 'a Marine gone bad'. This explains why Chen is always a step ahead of us, doesn't it?"

He looked at Sylvia and she nodded but stayed quiet and let Matt continue to talk. She knew him well enough to know that this is how he processed new information—saying it out loud.

"He sat there in our major crime team meetings over the past two years at least, probably even before I arrived in Port Stirling, and he listened," Matt said. His anger was growing; she could physically see it in him. "He took it all in, and then he told Zhang Chen everything. Everything we were doing, everything we planned, everything he knew about us as people and cops. He told him about Clay Sherwin, and where Fern likes to jog, and what evidence we'd uncovered. Everything. He told him everything."

"Including where you live, and that you boys like to hang out on your deck after work," Sylvia said. "You were a sitting duck."

"I wonder when he turned bad and how long this has been going on?" Matt asked.

"Now that I know what I know," she said, "I think this may have started even before you arrived. The sheriff used to complain that the bad guys were ahead of us. We'll have to talk to Earl, won't we? How will you handle this, chief?"

He thought for a minute. "I don't want to scare you, but we need to be careful here. And we need to prove what you and I know is the truth, and it needs to be airtight."

"Because," Sylvia said, "he is the district attorney, after all."

"Can you believe this?" he said incredulously. "I feel like such a goof ball. How did we not figure this out sooner?"

"Because he's slick and because it's illogical."

"Yeah. Why would he risk years of law school, his family, his reputation, and his decades of service to the county? Zhang Chen must have approached him and offered him buckets of cash."

"Greed and the arrogance to think you can get away with it," she said.

"Actually, now it's so obvious. Chen and Dalrymple are two of a kind—a match made in heaven," Matt said. He hesitated. "We've got a couple of options here on how to proceed."

Sylvia jumped up. "I'm going to make some coffee. I'm too scared to sleep tonight anyway, we might as well be sharp."

"Good idea," Matt said while Sylvia bustled around her kitchen. "Option one is that I call Judge Hedges right now and request a comprehensive search warrant that will get us access to his electronic devices, bank accounts, etc. and we do a surprise, simultaneous raid of his home and office tomorrow at dawn. Or, today at dawn."

"Do we trust Cynthia to not tip our hand to him?" Sylvia asked. "They've worked closely together for ages. Although, she is fond of you."

"She's rock solid in my experience. Reasonable, and on the side of law enforcement. She'll be as upset as we are, but I trust her."

"Then I like this option, and I want to go along. What's option two?"

"Option two is that we wait until I can interrogate Michael Winston and see if I can get him to admit that he and Dalrymple are working for Chen."

"Professional killer?" Sylvia raised her eyebrows. "He's not going to talk, to you or anyone else."

"If he's facing life in prison, he might. If he knows the jig is up and he might be able to take some time off his sentence if he cooperates with us."

"I still like option one," she said.

"Option three is that we bring in Zhang Chen, confront him with his fraud on the ship registration, and get him to rat out Dalrymple on hiring the shooter. Joe Phelps will bring him in for questioning anyway, and we could put the screws to him. Options two and three are safer, but slower. If we show all our cards to David and we don't get what we need to prosecute, it might go south on us."

"Matthew Horning," Sylvia said with her hands on her hips, "when have you ever played it safe? Your motto is 'Go big or go home'. We have to go after him. He hired his childhood friend to kill you. The evidence is there somewhere — phone calls, bank accounts — maybe even his wife knows. Let's go get him."

Matt leaned back in his chair, a broad grin on his face. "You're an amazing woman."

She waved him off. "I'm a decrepit old lady who just wanted to beat the feds. I'm competitive."

"The people on my staff who have saved my life and now my bacon are starting to add up," he said, now serious. "Not sure I deserve all of you."

She brought a cup of coffee to him and pulled her chair in close. "Do you remember when my grandson was acting out and I was worried about him? You gave him a job cutting your grass. Now he's a freshman at Oregon State studying ag and horticulture. You did that. The least I could do is find out who hired Winston to kill you."

He looked at her. "OK, we're going after him directly." He slapped his thigh. "It is what I want to do."

"I knew that," she said.

There was a knock on Sylvia's front door, and both she and Matt jumped.

"I'll get it," she said, standing up.

Matt put his arm on hers and said, "No you won't. I'll get it."

He moved toward the door, pausing to grab an umbrella from a rack nearby. "Who's there?" he boomed.

"It's me, your wife," came the answer.

Behind him, Sylvia laughed and laughed.

"What the heck is going on?" Fern said entering the room. She was wearing a raincoat over pajama bottoms and a sweatshirt.

Matt hugged her. "My admin assistant has just further solved our case. And you're not going to believe this one."

THIRTY-SIX

Considering the hour—4:00 a.m.—and the magnitude of Matt's request, Judge Cynthia Hedges was surprisingly accommodating.

"Something's been wrong in Chinook County for some time," she said. "I haven't been able to isolate it, but this could be it. You make a strong case. I'll grant what you need, Matt, no restrictions. All I ask is that you keep me posted, and that I learn the results of your searches before the general public."

"Oh, absolutely," Matt said. "I'm hoping to keep this quiet until we're sure we have what we need. You'll be my first call, promise."

"Take the sheriff with you," she said. "Earl hates Dalrymple."

Matt smiled into his phone, knowing it was true.

"Oh, and Matt, one more thing," she said.

"Yes?"

"You'd better be right." The judge hung up the phone.

● ● ●

Although the simultaneous search called for manpower, Matt decided to keep the search groups as small as possible to avoid word getting out. By 5:00 a.m, he had reached everyone he wanted to by phone, and they had a plan in place shortly after.

The raids would take place at 7:30 a.m. at the district attorney's home and office. Ed, Patty, Rudy, and Fern would first go to the Dalrymple house in Twisty River. If David wasn't at home, then Matt, the sheriff, Jay, and Sylvia would go to his office in the county courthouse. Fern and Rudy would keep an eye on any Dalrymple family members who were at the house to make sure David wasn't alerted to what was happening, while Ed and Patty seized the items covered in the warrant.

If he was at home, Matt, Earl, Jay, and Sylvia would conduct a thorough search of his office while Ed detained him in his house. They debated whether or not to bring him into custody until they'd had a look at his electronic devices, but Matt had decided Dalrymple was a flight risk and he wanted him in custody. That would give them forty-eight hours to charge him with whatever the evidence uncovered.

The Dalrymple home was one of the nicer ones in all of Twisty River. It was located on a small hill that overlooked both the town and the river beyond. Victorian in style, the three-story house sported a classic, but subdued paint job—medium grey with white on the wrap-around porch trim, balconies, and windows, with a punchy rust-red delineating the stories.

A gate—fancily decorated—on the driveway about halfway up the hill stood open, and Fern wondered if they'd just missed David on his way out. Ornate with stained-glass oval windows in the front door, she thought the house was lovely as she approached it.

Sure enough, Elaine Dalrymple answered the door, and informed Lieutenant Sonders of the Oregon State Police that her husband had left for work.

"We like to keep his work separate from our home. You'll find him in his office," she told Ed, and moved to close the door.

Big Ed quickly placed his size 13 shoe in the door and said, "I'm sorry, but it's not going to work like that today." He held out the warrant signed by Judge Hedges at 6:30 a.m.

Mrs. Dalrymple took the warrant Ed offered, scanned it quickly, and looked up, all color draining from her face.

"This can't be right," she said.

"I'm afraid it is," Ed said as gently as he could manage. "We have probable cause to suspect your husband of a crime or crimes, and we've been autho-rized to search the premises. Please stand aside."

Ed explained to her what would happen next, and that she was not allowed to communicate in any fashion with her husband until they'd found him. He introduced the other cops and told her that Rudy would stay by her side during the search. Ed asked her if there were any children in the house, or any other adults. Two children, ages eleven and thirteen, were upstairs asleep, and Fern headed up the central staircase to their rooms. She texted Matt from the second-floor landing:

Fern: In his office

Matt: Got it!

• • •

"If what we think is true," the sheriff said to Matt on the steps of the court-house, a building that had been Earl's second home for decades, "then you have every moral right to lead this search." He placed his hand on Matt's arm. "But I beg of you, please let me lead. I've waited for some version of this day since Dalrymple was first elected over fifteen years ago."

In spite of the gravity of the moment, Matt couldn't suppress a small smile. "You go first, Earl. Take charge. I'm tired, anyway."

The district attorney's assistant was not yet at her post. The inner door to his private office was closed. Earl placed his ear against the door, listened for a moment, and then turned to Matt, Jay, and Sylvia and made the "he's talking on the phone" motion with his hand. Then he whispered, "Ready?"

Three nods and a hearty 'thumbs up' from Sylvia. Jay shook out the tension in his upper body as Earl pushed open the door without knock-ing. Matt stared through the open door to the man seated at his desk who wanted him dead.

David Dalrymple looked up from his highly polished executive desk, placed his hand over his phone and said, "I'm on the phone, sheriff, it'll have to wait."

"Don't think so," Earl said, and in one violent sweep with his right arm, the contents of Dalrymple's desktop went flying.

Quickly saying, "I'll call you back", Dalrymple hung up, stood up force-fully and said, "What in the hell do you think you're doing?"

A brass sculpture on top of the desk had hit a tall window that over-looked the county's rose garden. The window had shattered, and a cold December-morning breeze fluttered into the room.

Sheriff Earl Johnson said, "David Dalrymple, I am detaining you on sus-picion of criminal conspiracy to commit murder, attempted murder, and solicitation of a crime. You will be held in the Chinook County jail—one floor down—for a period not to exceed forty-eight hours."

"Are you out of your fucking mind?" a red-faced Dalrymple yelled. "I'm your boss! I'm the distr…"

"I have here a search warrant issued by Judge Cynthia Hedges earlier this morning," interrupted Earl. "It allows us to search your home and office and seize any items we believe relevant to our case. Please hand me your phone, David."

"Let me see that," he bellowed and snatched the warrant out of Earl's hand.

"In case you're thinking of destroying our warrant," said Matt stepping to Earl's side, "I have a duplicate here." He held up the document, waving it.

For the first time, Dalrymple seemed to notice the other three people in the room. "What a fucking motley crew this is," he sneered. "Port Stir-ling's finest. Give me a break."

"If you calm down, this will go smoother for all of us," Matt said.

"Do not tell me to calm down, you moron," said Dalrymple. He glared at Matt. "I suppose this has something to do with you. It's always about you, isn't it?"

"No, but this time it's about me," said Matt coolly. "I believe that you hired Michael Winston to kill me, and that you are working at the direc-tion of Zhang Chen. We believe we can prove it, once we have a good look at your communications and bank accounts."

Dalrymple made a subtle move to slip his cell phone into his pants pocket. Not subtle enough, however, as Earl caught it. In a remarkably nim-ble move for the sheriff, he lunged across the desk and grabbed Dalrymple's hand, knocking the phone to the polished wood floor where it landed with a hellish clatter. Jay was on it in a heartbeat.

"Jay, please cuff the district attorney," said Earl. "Matt, the two of you please accompany Mr. Dalrymple to our fine establishment downstairs. Mrs. Hofstetter and I will begin a search of these premises, and you should rejoin us when the district attorney is comfy in his new lodgings."

Jay handed Dalrymple's phone to Sylvia and reached for the handcuffs in his back pocket.

"This is outrageous," Dalrymple said. "You cannot hold me, and you're certainly not going to put those on me." He looked at the cuffs Jay was holding.

"We can," said Matt. "Judge Hedges and I believe you are a flight risk. We can't allow that to happen while you're under suspicion of such awful crimes."

"I won't run," Dalrymple said, looking downcast. "I will fight you with every last breath of my body in court, but I won't run. Your handcuffs are unnecessary."

Matt and Jay looked at each other. "Put the cuffs away," Matt said to him. "We'll do this in dignified fashion."

With Jay on one side and Matt on the other, David Dalrymple was marched out of his office, down the hall to the elevator, and eventually into cell number twenty-three in the two hundred bed Chinook County jail.

Back in the D.A's office, Sylvia was busy scrolling through Dalrymple's cell phone. "Guess who he was just talking to?" she said to Earl.

"Who?"

She held up what appeared to be a burner phone in front of Earl's face. The top call on the 'Recent' list was made at 7:14 a.m. The call was to Zhang Chen.

The grumpy sheriff grinned his first true grin in over a year. "Imagine that."

THIRTY-SEVEN

While the Portland police interrogated Michael Winston, who still wasn't talking, the local cops took on David Dalrymple.

He was, at first, non-cooperative and continued to deny any knowledge of their suspicions. That all changed in a nano-second after Sylvia, working in close concert with Port Stirling's IT manager, Hideki Ikeda, assembled a forty-eight-page log of phone calls, texts, and email communications between David Dalrymple, Michael Winston, Ray Peng, and Zhang Chen. The first communication they could find between Chen and Dalrymple had been approximately five years ago, nearly a year prior to the Anselmo operation.

Confronted with the copious evidence of their conspiracy, and looking a bit green around the gills, Dalrymple changed his tune. "I want a deal," he said to the sheriff and Matt, who were seated across the heavy square table from him in the windowless interrogation room.

"What does that mean?" Earl said. He leaned his rotund body forward, placing his hands on the table on top of Dalrymple's file. The sheriff knew what it meant, but he wanted to hear David say it.

Dalrymple rolled his eyes. "It means, simpleton, that I will tell you what you want to know in exchange for a lesser sentence. I want a guarantee. And I want the two of you to sign it, along with Joe Phelps, so there's no wiggle room."

"My case alone involves three murders," Matt said, putting on his 'are you kidding me?' face. "And at least two more attempted murders. The Anselmo operation involved kidnapping, international drug smuggling and international human trafficking, which the feds really hate, by the way. And we expect to learn more about the ghost gun operation any minute now. It's a big ask for a reduced sentence, don't you think?"

Dalrymple shrugged. "Take it or leave it. We'll let a jury decide."

Matt and Earl exchanged looks, and Matt said, "We'll be back soon. I'll call Phelps. Sit tight."

The two cops rose from their chairs and moved to the door. The sheriff looked back at Dalrymple. "Are you comfortable?" he asked the prisoner.

"No," spat the district attorney.

"Tough cookies," said Earl. He left the room.

• • •

Matt and Earl climbed the one flight of stairs to the ground floor and made their way to Dalrymple's office.

"What do you think?" Matt asked the sheriff.

"I think getting Zhang Chen and Michael Winston put away for life is more important than seeing David Dalrymple rot in prison. He's already finished, which was all I wanted," Earl said.

"I agree," said Matt. "I want Chen, and I want to put a bullet through the heart of his takeover of Chinook County and the Oregon coast for evil purposes. Dalrymple will still get substantial jail time, and when he gets out, he'll be ruined."

"Are you going to call Phelps?"

"Yes. But he'll go along with us. He wants Zhang Chen as badly as I do, and Dalrymple is chump change for him."

Matt pressed a button on his phone and after a few seconds, without any social niceties, said, "Joe, we've got our district attorney, David Dalrymple, in a holding cell and have begun to interrogate him. He wants a deal. Your thoughts?"

"That's the outcome I've prayed for," said Joe. He paused. "Offer him ten years maximum security, and a fine equal to whatever Zhang Chen paid Winston to kill you. He can keep the millions Chen has likely paid him over the past few years. In return, he answers EVERY question we ask him. Any questions he balks at results in an extra $100K added to his fine. How does that sound?"

"Music to my ears."

Dalrymple took the deal and started talking.

• • •

It took four hours for the D.A. to give an official statement, in which he described in minute detail every interaction with Zhang Chen since the first time they'd met at Chen's request. Chen had flown David Dalrymple to San Francisco on his private plane and wined and dined him before he'd made his offer.

On the surface, it was simple: Chen wanted Dalrymple to be his eyes and ears on the ground in the Chinook County law enforcement community. Oh, and to look the other way if his operations broke any laws. At first, it was easy, and Chen was satisfied having inside information. Dalrymple took his money and watched his bank account swell.

But Clay Sherwin changed everything. When Dalrymple got a whiff that there was a possible federal agent sniffing around in Port Stirling, Zhang Chen demanded more. Did David know anyone who could be hired to 'do away' with Sherwin?

As a matter of fact, he did. He called his childhood buddy, and Michael Winston was hired. Winston killed Clay Sherwin and covered his tracks by making it look like some of Chen's Anselmo crew were the perpetrators. Dalrymple demanded a higher salary from Chen and received it. He had to open an offshore account to hide the cash. Chen didn't mind paying the district attorney because his drugs and trafficking operations were raking in millions…until the night of the Anselmo raid.

But Chen was nothing if not entrepreneurial, and pivoted quickly to the manufacturing of ghost guns, and a few other business ventures in remote southern Oregon that they would learn about in the coming days. Chen's arrogance had convinced him that he could always outsmart the locals, and he had invested heavily in Chinook County. He wasn't about to pull up stakes in Port Stirling and start over somewhere else on the west coast.

Once they'd got everything they needed on Zhang Chen and Michael Winston—Dalrymple wasn't sure how much Ray Peng was involved and couldn't provide any real evidence—Matt officially ended the interview and shut off the recorder.

"Why did you hire Michael Winston to kill me, David? You could have convinced Chen that it was unnecessary. Why did you do it?" Matt asked.

"You represent everything I hate," Dalrymple answered, as if he was bored to death. "Wealth handed to you on a platter. A wife better than mine. The adulation of the masses when it's not remotely deserved. I work harder than anyone and no one appreciates me. Only Mr. Chen appreciated me and put his money where his mouth was."

"Killing me seems like a needless risk," Matt persisted. "Especially for a man who, in my experience, is never eager to take a risk."

Dalrymple glared at him. "It was a risk I was more than happy to take, and the drama of it appealed to me." His look was pure hatred wrapped up in envy and revenge, and Matt understood.

"How much did you get for setting up my hit? What was I worth?"

Dalrymple waved him off. "It wasn't so much the money, although it's been nice. It's more the validation of my worth. Mr. Chen is an enterprising businessman who appreciates skill and finesse."

"Human trafficking? Poisonous drugs? Guns that can't be traced?" Matt's eyebrows shot up. "You call that 'enterprising'? You, a man of the law."

"Where has the law gotten me? A lifetime sentence in a podunk town. Mike and I had dreams when we were young but trying to do the right thing—me in my career and him in the Marines—killed our childhood dreams."

"So, Mike went to the dark side, and you followed along like a little puppy," Matt said dismissively.

Dalrymple slapped his desk. "It wasn't like that! Not like that at all. I recruited him. I'm the brains. I could see it coming that eventually Mr.

Chen was going to need more from me than information to carry out his master plan. I took initiative."

"Had Winston killed anyone before you hired him to off Clay Sherwin?" the sheriff asked.

Dalrymple laughed. "Oh, yes. The Marines excel at teaching young Americans how to kill. When he came back from Iraq, he was a changed man from my friend. The market for hitmen is ripe, Mike realized it immediately, and embraced his new career."

"Do you know any of his other victims you'd like to share with us?" Earl followed up.

"Mike can tell you what he wants to tell you," Dalrymple said.

"So, you do know names?" Matt said, leaning in.

He switched the recorder back on.

• • •

Joe Phelps and Fern Byrne arrested Zhang Chen at his Port Stirling home that night after Matt and the sheriff had taken David Dalrymple's complete statement. Phelps had left D.C. on a State Department jet minutes after Matt had phoned him from Dalrymple's office. Joe and Fern were backed up by officers representing the sheriff's department, the Oregon state police, and each of the county police departments, who stood at attention, uniformed and guns drawn, in a line behind the two.

Chen had answered his door wearing an immaculate red cashmere sweater, neat black jeans, and expensive black Italian loafers.

"Mrs. Horning," he'd said formally, opening the door. "To what do I owe the honor?" Then he peered behind her and nervously scanned the crowd.

"Actually, it's Ms. Byrne," Fern responded in a clipped voice.

Joe stepped forward and said, "Zhang Chen, I'm arresting you on behalf of the United States Department of State, the state of Oregon, Chinook County, and the Port Stirling police department." Joe read him his rights and motioned for the officer holding the handcuffs to step forward.

"May I inquire as to your charges?" Chen said forcefully. But his hands were shaking.

"Oh, we have a long list, Mr. Chen," said Phelps. "But I'll start with the murder of Clay Sherwin, international trafficking of humans, the murders of two OSP officers, and the attempted murder of Chief Matt Horning."

At the mention of his name, Matt stepped around Joe and approached Chen. "Eleven counts in all, I believe," Matt said, staring him in the eye. "Please turn around, Mr. Chen."

Chen smiled at Matt, shook his head in either defiance or defeat, and turned around.

THIRTY-EIGHT

The party at the ocean-front Horning home one month later became legendary. The Port Stirling police department, and everyone who had worked on any case involving Zhang Chen in the past three years, was invited.

Matt, nearly fully recovered, and Fern were in their element, and it was a raucous, joyous night. Mountains of food and gallons of booze were destroyed. Toasts were made, and stories were told. A rock band played on the deck in a tent to protect them from the elements. Matt and Bernice were the first to take to the dance floor and endured the hoots and hollers from all. The sheriff grabbed Fern and, holding her close, glided her onto the floor as well.

Jay, not wanting to be left out, looked around the living room and kitchen and spotted Amy Rose, an admin in the Buck Bay police department. "I can't let my boss beat me at dancing," he said as he approached the young brunette. "Will you join me?" He held out his hand.

"I thought you'd never ask," she laughed and fiercely took his hand. "Come on, let's dance!"

Ted and Patty sat on a sofa in the living room where they could see all the action. Ted said, "We could dance."

"We could," Patty said. "Or, we could have another glass of this stunning champagne." She held up her glass.

"I'm with you, sister," Ted said. He grabbed her glass and bounded off the sofa, heading to the bar set up at the end of the room.

Ed and Milly were trapped in a corner with several officers from Buck Bay who wanted his help on encouraging their favorite city lawyer to run for the empty district attorney for Chinook County position.

"She likes you, Ed," Chief Dan McCoy told him.

"Oh?" said Milly, looking up at her husband with raised eyebrows. "Should I be worried?"

The Buck Bay cops laughed. "No, definitely not," said McCoy. "She's gay."

"I never knew that. I always thought she was in love with me," deadpanned Ed.

"Aside from her love for you," said Milly, "would she be good at the job? It's an important position."

"As we've learned," agreed Ed. "Yes, I can see her in the role. She's tough and smart. Might be a difficult election, though, lots of rednecks that won't vote for either a female or a gay person."

"Those guys don't vote," said Milly. "They just talk."

Matt and Bernice came back inside, and he reached for a glass and tapped it with a spoon. The roar subsided.

"We have one more announcement tonight," he said. "Sylvia," he motioned to her across the room, "will you please join me?" That was city manager Bill Abbott's cue to also join Matt in front of the fireplace.

"What's going on?" Sylvia said. "I don't like surprises." She had outdone herself dressing for tonight, finding a silver lamé dress from the 60s in the back of her closet that somehow still fit her. Her date for the party, Sheldon Weinstein, approved mightily.

Bill Abbott produced a plaque from behind his back, and said, "Sylvia Hostetter, as city manager, I'm pleased to announce that in a landslide vote of your city employee colleagues, you have been chosen as "Employee of the Year."

Matt leaned in and said, "And it wasn't even close!" He bent down and kissed her on the cheek, then looked her in the eye. "Congratulations. And thank you. Thank you."

For the first time that anyone could remember, Sylvia was at a loss for words.

THIRTY-NINE

Zhang Chen's trial was quite the spectacle for the Twisty River Courthouse. Because of the preponderance of evidence collected on Chen's role in not only the attempted murder of Matt Horning, but also on his role as the mastermind of the Anselmo operation, including kidnapping and murder charges, his trial was held in Chinook County

A bevy of San Francisco attorneys filled the table on the defense side of the room. At the arraignment, they'd submitted a motion for a change of venue to Chen's home state of California based on prejudice that their client could not obtain a fair and impartial trial in Oregon, but the motion was swiftly denied.

The prosecution was led by Chinook County assistant district attorney Jeri Schrader, for obvious reasons. The Multnomah County district attorney would assist, and an attorney from the U.S. Department of State was also at the table and available to consult.

Try as they might to discredit David Dalrymple and the other key witnesses the county had produced, and the mountain of indisputable evidence, Chen's bank of lawyers were at a disadvantage from day one. Facts are facts. He did not testify in his own defense on the advice of his attorneys, and, frankly, his chilly and above-it-all demeanor did him no favors with the local jury.

The jury had been transfixed at the testimony of their long-time district attorney, David Dalrymple, who would later be sentenced to ten years in the Oregon State Penitentiary in Salem, with no possibility of an early parole.

Unanimous guilty verdicts on all of Chen's eleven counts were returned. He would not fry on the murder verdicts because of Oregon's no death penalty law, but he would die in prison if his judge and jury had their way. Arlette Sherwin, the families of the two Oregon State policemen killed in the Anselmo raid, and the families of the two OHSU nurses and Officer Timothy Johnson cheered and applauded as the foreman said 'guilty', eleven times. Officer Gabriela Ramos held the hand of Johnson's wife, and tears streamed down both their faces. Larry and Beverly Horning also cried, but their tears were tears of joy.

The media covering the trial were intrigued by one odd thing in the gallery of spectators. Mary Byrne, whose daughter had been terrorized on Zhang Chen's orders, and Detective Patricia Perkins, whose professional life had been changed forever because of him, sat on either side of the defendant's mother, Biyu Chen, comforting her. Mary and Patty felt sorry for his parents, stunned by the surprise of their son's wrongdoing. They would forever be tied to Port Stirling.

Michael Winston's trial would start next week, and all involved expected it to be even quicker than Chen's. Dalrymple, in his shocking testimony, admitted being the go-between in hiring his childhood friend Winston at Zhang Chen's direction. The price on Matt Horning's head had been a cool million dollars. Fern Byrne's role in the arrest of Michael Winston was not disclosed.

Leaving the courtroom, exhausted and spent with emotion, Matt and Fern walked down the center aisle with their arms around each other. Fern couldn't wait to get out of there and back to the sanctuary of their home, but Matt paused at the last row of chairs. A man sat stiff-backed and alone on the end of the aisle. He looked directly at Matt as the couple approached his row.

"I know you," Matt said to the man, stopping.

"Yes," replied the man.

If you enjoyed Phantom Cove and want to stay in touch,
please go to my author website at

WWW.KAYJENNINGSAUTHOR.COM

and sign up for my occasional newsletter.

• • •

Also, authors thrive on reviews;
please consider leaving one for this book and any book you've liked.
Thank you from the bottom of my heart.

ACKNOWLEDGEMENTS

It truly takes a team to produce a book, and I would like to thank mine for sticking with me. Cover designer and map illustrator Claire Brown has continued to design fabulous covers that help my books stand out in the crowded marketplace. She is efficient and, most important, delightful to work with. After three years, we might actually meet in person by the time this book is published.

Editor Peter Senftleben brings insight and perspective to the work. He notices things that never would have occurred to me, and his feedback always makes the books better. I am happy to have found him, and I value his strong role on the team.

My team of BETA readers all bring their own viewpoints to my manuscripts, and all of them contribute something unique on every book. I am grateful to them.

Hubby Steve continues to be my biggest fan and offers his unwavering support every single day. He has added a weekly takeout dinner during periods of intense writing and when Covid was raging, not an easy undertaking considering we live in the boonies. I love him to pieces.

Kay Jennings, 2022

CPSIA information can be obtained
at www.ICGtesting.com
Printed in the USA
LVHW032341200223
740023LV00005B/375

9 798985 554434